Parallel Relativity

by

Calan Hunter

About Calan Hunter

A modern day author in the style of Ian Fleming and Tom Clancy, Calan Hunter is no stranger to cyber security, military intelligence and covert operations. Now a rather eccentric recluse, Calan spends his days writing longhand on yellow pads as he finds the practice cathartic...a wonderful departure from his years at a computer's keyboard.

WWW.CALANHUNTERBOOKS.COM

PLEASE REVIEW THIS BOOK ON AMAZON.COM

IT WILL HELP ME MAKE FUTURE BOOKS BETTER
I APPRECIATE YOUR INPUT

PEACE, HEALTH AND PROSPERITY

WITH WARM THANKS TO LYNN LEACH

FOR KEEGAN AND BROGAN

Chapter One

"There has to be a better candidate," Dr. Lloyd Hawkins said addressing Drs. Seth Knowles and Trent Davis. The three scientists were trying to come to a final agreement. "With all of the scholars available, why are we picking such a flawed candidate?"

"Because he is flawed and can survive untold obstacles is the main reason we are choosing him," Davis said. The Massachusetts Institute of Technology professor had advocated for Cristopher Mointz from the beginning.

"He has been arrested for check fraud, was fired from a professorship, has filed for bankruptcy and has divorced twice, among other things," Dr. Knowles said. "I am not saying no, Trent, but, please, again try to reassure me why this Mointz is the key to saving the human race."

Davis smiled at his colleagues and sat back in his chair. Balding and 6' 3", the MIT genius weighed just over one hundred and fifty pounds and but for his incredibly high IQ, would not have intimidated anybody. Fortunately for Davis, both Hawkins and Knowles trusted his scientific prowess completely.

"Cristopher Mointz had a very difficult life growing up after suffering abuse at a cathedral camp at the age of eleven. He survived by using his charm and personal magnetism. As he entered his high school years, he managed to excel where others might have faded into social oblivion," Davis said.

A good, if not great athlete, Mointz did well in college both athletically and academically. He was always leery of males and formed deeper friendships with females. Bad knees derailed any hopes of Mointz playing professional football.

Mointz completed a PhD in History before teaching himself enough computer programming to take jobs above his skill set and experience. He joined the ROTC in college so he knows how to fire a weapon, which was a plus for the military advisers on the project. Mointz had more successes than failures until he married a woman who bankrupted his formerly successful software company with her spending habits. Mointz eventually paid back the huge debt she had amassed.

Mointz dusted himself off after that experience, met a new woman, and became a college professor and a corporate CEO. He sold software all over the world that was rather mediocre; however, people the world over, bought his sales pitch.

Mointz is an 'everyman' and has character flaws, Davis knew, but when he gave his big old smile, Davis's neighbor, Cristopher Mointz, seemed a brilliant and dynamic individual. There was no doubt in Davis's mind he had the special qualities to accomplish what was necessary to save humanity.

"I firmly believe if Mointz were not abused at eleven he would be the man in the Oval Office right now, at 49 years old, saving us from the destruction we're experiencing. You cannot teach his character," Davis said. "I also believe the demons he had to overcome on his own made him the ideal candidate."

Dr. Hawkins shrugged, "He is a charming man; I will give you that."

"Remember, we need a person who can actually win an election, not just go back in time. He is going to be a complete loner, as he has been his whole adult life. Mointz does not let anyone in and, if it were not for the drugs we used to get him to open up at my house, we might have picked a candidate with no chance of succeeding. In addition, he will be extremely motivated to fix his life with his wife, Erin, who he adores. His sons mean the world to him and he will do anything to protect them," said Davis. "Since we have the ability to make sure he has the same exact children, we can ease his transition back to 1975. His wife will also be in the womb and both his brother and sister will have been born. I know he will have at least some solace in those few things."

"You are going on a lot of gut instinct here. Thank God you have the science to back you up," Hawkins said.

"I know we do," Davis replied.

"We have to hope and pray we can get him to the very time you say, Trent. I know all the simulations and tests have come back perfectly, but if somehow we fail, all the hopes we have of stopping the nuclear firestorm will be lost. Word out of Asia today says the North Koreans have fired the last of their nuclear weapons into the already decimated Japan," Dr. Knowles reported. "I have been a liberal democrat all my life, why the hell we re-elected that buffoon, President John Reis, the most liberal President ever, is beyond my imagination. Mointz is going to have to be a political leader, a military leader, businessperson and one hell of a man to right the ship we are sailing on currently. Again, this all depends on getting him back to 1975. He will wake up one Saturday morning at the age of eight, with all his memories, assuming the embryos are successfully implanted in his mother's womb."

"I have to believe in the science and I know this will work," Davis said. "Our teams of biochemists have complete confidence it will succeed. The cloned, fertilized egg will be implanted in Mrs. Martha Mointz."

Hawkins's already white complexion was now whiter than a ghost. "I understand only you can go back because of the X854 military rocket only holding one person, but if you fail, do we have a backup plan approved by the Vice President? There are only three of us who can possibly use the machine to go back in time because of the scientific knowledge and precision required; however, I would feel better with an approved backup."

"We have been through all scenarios with the Vice President. There has to be only one authorized person to do this and only the three of us will know when this will happen. It is bad enough that the Vice President has kept the President in the dark on all of this. Vice President Ellis believes the vain son-of-a-bitch would want it to be him who went back to the other parallel," said Davis.

Vice President Valmer Ellis believed Davis right from the beginning, when Davis, a member of the President's Scientific Counsel, approached him a few months ago after the first nuclear weapons rained down on Israel. The conservative, Virginia-born Ellis immediately kept the President out of the loop when Davis approached. President Reis has sat back and done absolutely nothing heroic or statesmanlike for the country.

"If you make it…well, *when* you make it, do you really believe the nuclear military craft will cause you so much radiation damage that you will be dead in a matter of weeks?" Dr. Knowles asked.

"From the amount of radiation I will receive, there is no survival; that is for sure," Davis said. "What is the difference anyway? We will all be dead sooner rather than later because of what is happening now. The Chinese and the Russians could decide they should send their nuclear weapons our way at any time if they feel the need. With the nuclear warheads which have been detonated already, radiation poisoning will affect us for generations to come. I have to hope Mointz will stop the insanity so the human race will not perish. You both have families and my family is my work. We need to keep hoping and praying, my friends."

Hawkins had two teenage daughters and Knowles had a six-year-old son. Davis did not want to have children grow up without fathers. There was enough of it in the world because of the rogue nuclear regimes which decided to unleash a fury never before seen as they fired off a hell storm of nuclear weapons on countries which did not share their view of the world.

The Iranians fired on the Israelis, Saudis, UAE and other Sunni Muslim dominated countries. The Iranians obviously hated the Zionist Israelis and seemed to hate Sunni Muslims almost as much. The Sunni/Shia split cost half a billion lives.

Pakistan fired their nuclear arsenal at India and India returned the hostility in kind. The North Koreans started firing on South Korea and Japan as elements of Bush 43's Axis of Evil played out in real time. Thankfully, for the Western Hemisphere, the Iranians could not send their weapons farther. So far, the Western Hemisphere, Australia and the United Kingdom escaped the nuclear missiles. The situation was fluid as different intelligence agencies reported their news.

"Have you decided exactly what you want to do to help Mointz in 1966?" Hawkins asked. "I know you have to do something with your time."

Dr. Knowles somberly thought about the physical pain his friend was about to suffer. "I still cannot believe we do not have more time to perfect this technology to the point we could just send a person back and warn the world," Knowles said.

Davis shook his head. "There is no way to do it without destroying the paths which are already set in motion. A person who would take on this task might be considered a religious zealot or crackpot once they take their claims public. More likely than not, that person would be considered a whacko. We have the technology to interfere with the nuclear proliferation happening now with minimal disruption. We can change the world. We have tested this type of cloning now for ten years on lambs, dogs, pigs and chimpanzees. The science is there so the cloned embryos will also retain their memories up to the time of cloning. We can structure the brain DNA which is embedded to manipulate the timeline of the brain's development.

"I concur," Hawkins said.

"Mointz will be the one to undo time and prove its fundamental parameter of change is not at a constant rate," Davis said. "We will be able to go back to a parallel timeline moving before real time as we know it. The cross over will change and maybe we will eventually have total harmony between the two if Mointz is successful. He will prove Einstein's Theory of Relativity, but only the three of us will see its proof. At the same time, Mointz will disprove some of Einstein's other theories."

Hawkins and Knowles nodded. The theory, in fact, had already been proven. There is no such thing as time travel; however, there is a parallel universe in space which can be changed with the slower of the two parallels accessible and ready to be altered. By disproving Einstein's conclusion no object could travel faster than the speed of light, the three MIT professors could calculate to the second how fast the nuclear-propelled X854 needed to travel back down to earth to go from 2016 back to 1966.

The scientists had performed experiment after experiment, sending out five rockets into space and back down into the Atlantic Ocean. They had salvaged each vessel according to the exact time it came back to earth. The five rockets arrived in the Second Parallel in 1929, 1957, 1978, 1995, and 2013 perfectly. Researchers collected bacteria in a nuclear contamination-safe device proving the science when the vessels were taken back to the labs at MIT.

Davis was convinced Mointz would wake up on July 4th, 1975 and become the person needed to save humanity.

The council of 12 scientists who took on this top-secret Mission all agreed the age of eight was the perfect age to start making the relationships needed to develop correct life patterns. The world, the future, and everything man had known since the beginning of recorded history would weigh on the shoulders of one Cristopher Cathal Mointz.

Chapter Two

His heart was broken, as the Zac Brown Band song, *Highway Twenty Ride*, had just played in his Jeep's iPad player. The song about a father returning his son after a weekend long visitation to his mother still resonated in Cristopher Mointz's head when he dropped off his two sons at his ex-wife's house. The ink had dried on his divorce papers three years ago, but Mointz still ached to enter his home with his ex-wife, Erin and his sons, Thomas and Patrick. He lived a mile away from his boys. However, to Mointz, it might as well have been across the country.

Mointz loved his ex-wife and his children more than he could ever say, but he knew that he had messed up the relationship. He fought hard to be with his wife; however, she had tired of his indiscretions. He knew Erin still loved him and he was determined to win her back someday. Their nine and eight-year-old sons deserved two full-time parents.

After he dropped off the boys early this Sunday evening, Mointz stopped for a hasty supper at McDonald's. He was a member of the faculty at Providence College and this evening he was mandated to partake in a lecture series. Tonight was the last Sunday in April and the President wanted Americans to go back to their normal activities, even though the world was not the same place it had been a few months ago. Classes were again being conducted as families coped with the tremendous loss of life overseas.

Mointz ate his Big Mac and thought of how his children were more than likely going to be raised in a world that probably would not survive.

At six feet and two hundred pounds of mostly lean body mass, Mointz could afford a Big Mac every now and then, especially with the amount of exercise he did each day. There was nothing his stomach enjoyed more than a Big Mac, vanilla shake, and an extra-large order of French Fries. At times, a fresh apple pie accompanied his meal; however, this evening apple pie was not on the menu. He had taken the boys for an early afternoon ice cream and one more dessert would push his calorie intake way over the self-enforced limit he tried extremely hard to observe.

For every scientist who proclaimed the air and water were safe, fifteen would say the damage was now irreversible. He did not want to be far from his home in Barrington, Rhode Island tonight. He wanted to be close to his family, ignoring the unpopular President's advice. Unfortunately, for Mointz, he could not afford to lose another professorship. His job at Boston University was taken away when he threw away teacher evaluations of some disgruntled students who objected to the considerable amount of homework he assigned. Providence College was his second chance and he was not going to do anything to mess that up, no matter what happened in the world.

The parking lot at Providence College's auditorium was nearly empty when Mointz arrived. Though he was only fifteen minutes early, he could tell that almost no one was going to take President Reis's advice and go back to a normal existence. *This is a major waste of time*, Mointz thought to himself before turning around when he heard the familiar voice of Professor Deborah Valley.

"Hello, stranger," she said with her beautiful smile. Valley was an extremely attractive blond-haired, blue-eyed woman, who, at about 5' 10", had the body of a beach volleyball player. Valley was always tanned and she had the male students' and faculty members' attention.

Her heart ached for Mointz. They had been dating for about a year, even though Valley could feel he was still holding back a bit because of the love he felt for his ex-wife and their two boys. Valley had invested too much of her heart into Mointz to give up without a fight.

Mointz came over and kissed her softly on the lips. Mr. Casanova always knew how to steal the ladies' hearts. "How are you, love? Did you get my text?" Mointz asked. He was not sure if he had sent one. But, with all the

Internet and telecom message disruptions, he could get away with implying he had sent one to Ms. Valley.

"No Sweetie, I did not get anything on my BlackBerry," she said with a slight pout. "How was the weekend with the boys?"

Just the mere mention of Thomas and Patrick brought a smile to his face. "They were great. Fortunately, they are oblivious to anything that is going on in the world. However, they can sense something is not right."

Valley nodded. "The boys are very perceptive," the thirty-seven-year-old said. "So, what did the text say?"

"I was hoping you might want to come over tonight after this and drink some wine by the fire outside as we watch the tide come in."

"What a lovely idea. I would really like to spend the night doing that with you, Cristopher," she said. "Maybe we will not be here very long. I do not see a lot of people."

They walked arm in arm to the auditorium's entrance and noticed only a few students in the building. Mointz and Valley were the only professors who showed up, as the college's tenured professors could care less about attending this lecture. Only ten students actually showed up and Mointz decided to let them ask questions to address their concerns.

"Professor Mointz, do you believe we will all be safe?" Yan Han asked. Yan, of Chinese descent, had taken all of Mointz's classes and Mointz was very fond of her.

"I do, Yan. I really do believe in the resiliency of the United States of America and believe it will prevail again as it always has. Things might need to be done a different way this time, but I believe in my heart we will have some amazing successes as we get ourselves and the rest of the world back on track."

"Do you agree, Professor Valley?" A nerdy freshman asked. Mointz had seen him before a few times. Mointz did not know his name and he would make sure from now on he would do a better job of remembering students' names.

"Yes, Carlton, I do believe that Professor Mointz is 100 percent correct."

Angela Remy, another one of Mointz's students asked, "The country seems to be in a standstill and waiting instead of reacting. What do we have to do to get back in the saddle? The world has lost so many people and so many others are homeless."

"Angela, we have to, as a free people, unite with other countries and force the tyrannical governments who started this into submission to unite behind a common goal to heal the sick and become a world at peace again."

Another student, a good-looking African American young man asked, "Is this the apocalypse, Professor Mointz?"

Students were always listening to every word Mointz said in class. He captivated his students and as these ten individuals needed a semblance of reassurance, they were hoping Mointz could give them some answers.

"No, son, I do not believe this is the apocalypse. I believe the governments who formed the United Nations Security Council forgot to work together to keep rogue governments from obtaining nuclear technology. The CIA, FSB, MI6, MSS and DGSE knew this was happening and did nothing about it," Mointz stated.

Mointz continued, "This is all about governments taking a laissez-faire approach and maintaining the status quo. They waited for the next person to handle the problem. No one worried about creating jobs nor did they worry about making good sound foreign policy decisions. The United States used to make things like televisions, computers, clothes, and shoes and then stopped and sent manufacturing overseas. The jobs that went overseas to developing countries should have come with a sense of responsibility both social and economic. Oil countries in the Middle East treat women like second-class citizens and we turned our back on human rights abuses and pretended they didn't exist. These nations are no longer there as they have been obliterated and Japan suffered a nuclear holocaust for the second time in its history."

The students nodded and felt Mointz was correct in what he said. He really had them believing goodness could come to America again.

Professors Valley and Mointz continued to answer questions from the nervous students and eventually Father Sullivan, the campus resident priest, joined in. When the meeting ended, Father Sullivan commended the job that Mointz and Valley did to alleviate the students' fears.

"I feel so badly for the students," Valley told Mointz on their way back to their vehicles.

"So do I," Mointz said. "They are extremely worried that life as they know it is over."

Mointz finished walking Valley to her car and she agreed to follow him back to his house. He owned a quaint little place on the water he managed to buy with the portion of his 401K that was left after his divorce from Erin. Mointz kissed Valley quickly and got in his Jeep.

Even though it was a chilly night at the end of April, the top was off his Jeep. Mointz called Erin on his cell phone as he left Providence to return home to Barrington, Rhode Island. Traffic was incredibly heavy as people tried to go everywhere and anywhere. Gasoline was still plentiful as Venezuela and Mexico sent barrel after barrel to the United States to garner its protection. The United States had pretty much perfected its missile defense system enough to keep the Western Hemisphere clear of danger. Russia and China, so far, had been extremely friendly with the United States since the first attacks and the three nations banded together out of an instinct for survival.

Erin answered on the first ring and for a second, Mointz, worried he had called too late. Erin was notorious for going to bed by 9:30 on a work night. The insurance adjuster never liked phone calls after nine.

"Hi, Cristopher, is everything alright?" she asked when she answered her home phone.

"Yes. I just wanted to make sure you and the boys are fine and you did not need anything."

Erin had crucified Mointz in the divorce three years ago and it had taken Mointz these past three years to even begin melting the ice.

"We are fine," she told him. "Are you on your way home? Most times, in that Jeep of yours, you sound like you are in a wind tunnel."

"I am in bumper-to-bumper traffic. I might get home about two hours from now," he said. It was already twenty of eleven.

She sighed. "Sorry about that." Erin was intelligent, with the look of a movie star. The auburn-haired green-eyed woman now forty-six, had not been on a date in three years. She loved Mointz too much. "How was the lecture?"

"Only ten students showed and one other professor, besides Father Sullivan. The students we did have seemed to appreciate the conversation," said Mointz. "Were the boys alright after I dropped them off?"

"You mean because of the sugar rush? Yes, Cristopher, they had a great night. They both missed you tucking them in though. Maybe, tomorrow, you can tuck us all in," Erin said softly.

At first, Mointz thought he was hearing things. "Excuse me?" is all that came out of his normally loquacious mouth.

"I want you to tuck all of us in," Erin said confirming Mointz had not gotten some form of radiation poisoning. "The boys need their father and I need the man I love and who loves me. I know you love me, Cristopher; it is how you live your life and the things you do that ruin what should be a fairy tale life. What is the past is the past, I need to look into the future and hope there is a future. I would rather try and face all this with the man that I love, but the bimbos, the unnecessary flirtations, and the ridiculous spending on gadgets must stop or there will never be an 'us.' You have one shot at this. Prove to me you are the man that I love or don't, it will only be three hearts broken again."

Mointz started to tear up as his ex-wife's words cut like a knife. "I hope I can be all you expect of me."

Anger now entered Erin's voice. "That statement is absurd. You can be whatever you want to be. You need to stop and think of the consequences instead of just doing what every eleven-year-old boy wants to do. Cristopher, I know what happened. I know why your mind is stuck at times as the happy-go-lucky eleven-year-old who can do what he wants without fear of any consequences. However, there are consequences in the real world and you need to deal with them."

"I understand completely, sweetheart," Mointz said.

"Good," Erin said. "Why don't you let me get some sleep and tomorrow we will talk more about this and maybe we can actually spend some time doing the things we used to do."

"Certainly, Babe," Mointz said. He had not called her babe in ages and she noticed it immediately.

"That is the first time you called me Babe in three years." Erin said. "I missed you calling me Babe."

"And, I miss you. Good night, Babe," Mointz told her so he could get off the phone before he screwed anything up.

"Good night, Cristopher. Sweet dreams," she replied.

Mointz wanted to head right over there and take Erin in his arms, but he had one horned-up Deborah Valley with gorgeous breasts right on his tail. Tonight, he was going to be 'good' and he picked up the phone and politely explained he would have to cancel. Valley had not missed her exit yet and although she was disappointed, she understood his children came first. They spoke for about fifteen minutes and Mointz finally found a break in the traffic, letting him arrive home within an hour. Before the attacks, the drive would have only taken 20 minutes.

He turned left on his beach property's road to find several automobiles in his driveway that looked like undercover police vehicles. There were also vehicles in his neighbor's driveway. Dr. Trent Davis, an MIT Professor, was a good friend. Mointz's first thought was something had happened to his family, but then he figured Davis, a physicist, was probably the cause of all the commotion.

"What is going on?" Mointz asked.

"Dr. Mointz, I presume?" a man with a Homeland Security badge asked. He was wearing a dark tie and a dark suit.

Hell, Mointz thought to himself. *All these people look alike.* "I am Cristopher Mointz, is anything wrong?"

"Cristopher," said Davis, coming out of his house.

"Trent, is everything alright? What is going on around here?"

"Come inside my house. I need to ask you a big favor," the fifty-three-year-old asked.

"Whatever you need, Trent," Mointz said and then almost had a coronary attack as Vice President Valmer Ellis appeared in Davis's doorway.

"Actually, I am the one who needs the favor," the Vice President said. "You cannot even imagine how big a favor it is going to be. This might be the favor of all favors and you are just the man to ask."

Chapter Three

"No way, sir. You definitely have the wrong person here. Dr. Trent, you could not possibly have nominated me for something like this," Mointz said to the Vice President and Davis. He had always called Davis, "Dr. Trent," and Davis returned the favor by calling Mointz, "Dr. Cris." They were quite fond of one another.

"Dr. Mointz," the Vice President stated as he cleared his throat, "You have been picked out of millions of Americans. God has blessed you with the intelligence, the charm, and the ability for this mission, not just for your family, but for mine as well. I know there will be a lot of pressure on you, son; but, this could be our only chance to preserve humankind. The recent nuclear proliferation has rendered our planet almost uninhabitable. Within a year, half of the world's population will be sick because of tainted water supplies and within ten years, the cancers that will accompany the nuclear fallout will compromise the vast majority of the population," the Vice President said. Vice President Ellis received his medical degree at Johns Hopkins and knew exactly what was happening.

"You agree with all of this, Dr. Trent?"

"Unfortunately, yes," Davis said.

Mointz put his hands up to his face and said, "I have a feeling you are making a big mistake choosing me for this."

"No, we are not making a mistake. Do not dare tell me you are not the right person for this task. How many times have you poured out your heart to me telling me you would be President if you only knew then, what you know now? Please explain that one to me?" said Davis.

Mointz could only dip his head, knowing he had told Davis that very thing repeatedly.

"Who is a better speaker? A better salesman? I will tell you, no one I know," Davis said. "So you made some mistakes. Who hasn't?"

"We secretly watched you this evening at the college. What you told those students was remarkable. Up until then, I was not firmly convinced you were our guy. I know you are now," the Vice President said. "We also heard your call to your ex-wife. Good for you."

"Jesus, do you folks believe in privacy?"

"No, not during a time like this," the Vice President said. "The world is no longer what we believed it was and now we have to make a correction before there is no world left."

"You do not have to convince me," Mointz said. "Now, would you two please explain to me in greater detail what you want me to do?"

The Vice President and Davis smiled. They were both hoping Mointz would see what was needed and as Ellis stated earlier to Davis: '*He needs to immediately take the bull by the horns without much convincing or we need to find someone else.*'

"Our good friend Albert Einstein concluded no object, influence, nor disturbance of any sort can travel faster than the speed of light. Space and time are influenced by one's state of motion. The universe at its fundamental level is divided into two parallel states. However, one state is running behind the other," Davis said.

"The String Theory proves the wondrous happenings in the universe from the frantic dance of subatomic quarks, to the stately waltz of orbiting binary stars, and from the fireball of the Big Bang Theory to the majestic swirl of heavenly galaxies; the world is run on a parallel. We can get back to the slower of the two parallels and make the necessary adjustments. You, my friend, will be a second grade student in Mrs. Joint's class again and you will have all your memories restored on a Saturday morning through the magnificent process of inserting the nucleus of a somatic body cell of your DNA into an egg cell of an embryo which will have its nucleus removed and the embryo will be implanted in your mother's womb."

"Damn, Trent. What kind of Sci-fi crap do you do over there at MIT? How are my memories going to be there?"

"We can manipulate the embryo's structured double helix band to bind each pentose group you have when we take your DNA and manipulate the adenine, guanine, cytosine, and thymine and join the hydrogen bond that was paired to you when you were eight-years-old to the very second we want. We can slow down or speed up the self-replication that enables your DNA to duplicate your genes during cell division growth. All of your imperfections will be adjusted," Ellis said.

"You can give me better knees?"

"We have been working on your DNA for weeks," Davis said. "You will not be disappointed."

"Groovy, at least you have a head start. How…I cannot even fathom," Mointz said.

"People believe in you, Cristopher," Ellis said. "I know with certainty Dr. Davis is a believer."

Mointz rubbed his temples. "Who is going to believe me?"

"No one, except your wife and her parents. Not even your parents can know," Davis said. "The best psychologists in the world have told us that this is the best way to go. You love your in-laws. They love you and your personality matches well with them."

"What am I going to tell Erin?"

"The truth," Ellis said. "You will have what you need to complete your mission. You will receive your children's embryos so that you will have the same two boys.

"Thank God."

"The crafts we sent back and recovered did exactly what we needed," Davis said.

"One, in particular, sent out a new strand of bacteria which was made in the lab. The bacteria are harmless and are now found in the ocean helping to sustain the cod and haddock's food supply. We definitely know changing the slower parallel produces a carbon copy."

Mointz took in a deep breath and had to think for a moment before asking, "Only my in-laws and my wife; are you serious? God help us to love each other again!"

"You know it will happen. Both of you have been…"

"Yeah, I know. We were tested. Damn, Trent. Now I know why you got me loaded on that peach drink. I passed out after a few sips. You must have done something similar to Erin."

Davis did indeed and used a bit of suggestive hypnosis to push Erin to get her true feelings for Mointz out in the open again. "We need you to get into the training program set up for you very quickly. The craft has to be ready within two weeks."

"Two weeks. Talk about a crash course. I have one question. How quickly will things change?"

"We do not know what we will see. What we know is that three weeks after Dr. Davis goes back, we expect to see a change. If we do not, we will know that you have not completed your mission. You, my friend, need to be elected President in 2016 to change the world," Ellis said.

"I will only be forty-nine-years-old. Talk about pressure."

"You will be the same age as the last President before President Reis," Ellis said.

Mointz took another deep breath. "Will I have at least a device for knowledge of the world? I know I am a walking encyclopedia, but I will be having brain overload."

"Yes, on the device, there will be four loaded laptops with information. Under no circumstances can you let anyone but the Flahertys see what is on the laptops. History cannot be rushed, Cristopher. As much as I want to be part of all this, it could be very dangerous for me to do so," Davis said.

"I really could use you, Dr. Trent."

"The scientific community believes if I am told about your mission and then get involved, too much will change and certain scientists might never make discoveries they should have made. You are to tell me what you know in the Second Parallel when you appoint me to the President's Scientific Panel. There will be a USB drive with my research on it. Make sure I get it and we will be fine," Davis said.

"My main goal then is to become President and not revise history. Gee, sounds really simple."

"Exactly, no one in your life has dramatically changed the world, correct?" Davis asked.

"Correct."

"Then what you do will be fine. Let us hope you remember whether they threw a pass on fourth and one in the state championship game or ran the option bootleg."

"It has been on my mind for thirty years. I am the cornerback on that side of the field. I will not be caught with my head up my pooper twice."

Ellis smiled. "We are counting on it."

Ellis left after a few more minutes and Davis offered Mointz a cup of coffee while several members of the Secret Service remained outside standing guard.

"Tomorrow morning you will be brought to MIT. Everything will be squared away at the college for you and you will be able to take Erin and the boys there."

Mointz was extremely happy about it, but was worried he would not ever meet Erin. "I will be allowed to meet Erin when she turns sixteen then?"

"Yes, you will be able to enter the Flahertys lives then. You are going to re-run your life with a few changes, but this time you will be able to do it righteously and you will not make the same mistakes twice. I know in my heart you will be able to pull this off, even though the President is going to be livid when he finds out you were the one who was chosen."

"How hard has it been to keep this all under wraps?"

"We used the President's team of scientists who are extremely loyal to the Vice President. Ellis agreed to keep most of the information close to the vest until I left to do what was needed of me. Believe me, we have had to do a tip-toe act around certain people connected to the President."

"I believe you there, Trent."

"Cristopher, you have always been my choice. Drs. Knowles and Hawkins finally signed on, thankfully."

Mointz started to tear up and Davis noticed him starting to shake a bit. Davis knew he wore his emotions on his sleeve.

"What is wrong, Dr. Cris?"

"It sure as hell will be nice to see my mother and grandparents again. God, maybe I will be able to save my mother from that awful cancer. Researchers have come a long way in the last six years."

Davis smiled. "I have been authorized to give you the chemical formula of the drug that will cure your mother's cancer. I have also made a serum for you to give her secretly when she becomes ill. There is such limited room on the craft with the laptops, embryos, and the few other trinkets I need. Unfortunately, there is only one set of vials I can take with me. If the serum is destroyed or lost, take the chemical formula to a chemist and have him make it up for you discreetly. Tell them a friend had an idea and use it, but only on your mother, wink, wink. Now, go and get some sleep; you have a big day tomorrow."

"Erin is going to think I am losing my mind when I tell her what is going on with all of this."

"Do not worry about it. She thought you lost your mind when you left for greener pastures."

"You mean Cynthia."

"Bingo!"

"What the hell is wrong with you?" Erin Flaherty Mointz asked her ex-husband after he summarized what Davis had told him last night. "Cristopher, I was about to let you back into my life."

Mointz did not even bother to argue. He opened the front door and let Davis in.

"Trent, please explain to my lovely wife I have not lost my marbles."

"Everything he says is absolutely true, my dear. He found out all about this last night from the Vice President."

Erin learned every detail from Davis. She could barely believe her ears. "Why him, Trent? My God, he is brilliant, but he is far from perfect."

"You know my boy here best, Erin. Can he pull this off?"

"Of course he can. You are right. Cristopher can pull this off probably better than anyone."

"I think so, too," said Davis.

Erin looked out the front window to see a circus outside. There had to be at least five vehicles in front of her house.

"The Secret Service…I guess maybe I am finally worth something after all."

"You are worth it, Cristopher. I just hope this time the boys and I are worth it in your mind as well."

Mointz nodded holding back tears. "I am going to do this right this time. I promise you from the bottom of my heart."

They needed to pick up the boys from school before driving to the Massachusetts Institute of Technology, Mointz was about to start his preparations for the mission to the Second Parallel. Psychologists believed he needed to include his family in the preparation process to guard his psyche and better his concentration. There was going to be a ton of knowledge transferred over the next two weeks and he needed to digest all he could.

"Do you really believe I can learn what I need to in two weeks? Do you have any contingency plans?" Mointz asked as he led Erin and Davis to the waiting Cadillac Escalade. Mointz was already starting to lead. Davis could see Mointz walking with a confident bounce. Davis could not have been happier.

"Some of the scientists wanted to send multiple people back to the Second Parallel. Most of the team believed that was not a good idea. Too much could change and we could be stuck in an even worse situation with multiple people," Davis said. "Erin we trust your father to help in any way he can. He will actually be the back up to your husband. Cristopher will be completing several tasks as he goes along in his second shot at his life. Our team of scientists will know something is wrong if within three weeks, two days, eight hours and fourteen seconds nothing has changed. We hope and pray we get you everything you need to make informed decisions. You will have plenty of time to ingest all of this."

"Because you cannot keep coming back to the Second Parallel, correct?" Mointz asked.

"We have only two rockets left. You cannot fail, my friend."

Erin had been staring out the car window as the Escalade pulled into the boys' school's parking lot. As Mointz entered the school to get his two little boys, Erin said, "I believe in my heart that he will succeed. I do not know why, but all of a sudden, I feel that something inside of me is different from what was there this morning."

"Are you alright with all of this, Erin?" Davis asked.

"I am, but I am extremely nervous I will not be able to have the same children if somehow Cristopher screws up. I am sure I will not know any better. However, Cristopher will be devastated beyond belief if the boys are not the same."

"We will do our very best, but I promise you that you will have Patrick and Thomas in your life. We are a lot more advanced than you would believe. Trust me on that."

"Thank you, Trent. I do believe in your sincerity."

"The fate of the world is now in the hands of one—Cristopher Mointz. His success in the parallel world will affect everyone," said Davis.

Mointz brought a smiling Thomas and Patrick to the waiting Escalade; the boys were duly impressed by the Secret Service.

"Hey, Momma, where are we going?" Thomas asked after saying hello to Davis and the driver. "Dad said it is a surprise."

"I love surprises," Patrick added.

Erin kissed both boys. "We are all going on a field trip with Dr. Davis to his college," Erin said. "He has a bunch of cool things for you two to do."

"Awesome," said Thomas.

"Yeah, Momma, this is way cool," Patrick said.

Davis explained to the boys they would be helping him with a few experiments for a future mission to Mars. Cristopher and Erin chuckled, pleased to see their children's smiling faces as the mid-morning ride to MIT took just fifty-five minutes.

Mointz held Erin's hand as he took one deep breath after another and walked to the lab at MIT with a sudden sense of immortality. In exactly two weeks, he would be eight-years-old and it was the only thought in his head as he entered the building. He shuddered at the thought of it all.

Davis's lab held about twenty people and all eyes were on Mointz as they walked in. He felt like a movie star on the red carpet with his family in tow. The moment was further heightened as everyone applauded. The affable Mointz was dumbstruck.

Chapter Four

Davis introduced Cristopher and Erin to Drs. Hawkins and Knowles in his office as the boys were escorted to a lab to have their DNA cloned. Thomas and Patrick were told they were on a secret mission and an integral part of the team going to Mars.

"Which one of you does not think that I am the man for the job?"

"You are the ideal candidate. We both think you will be successful," Hawkins said after looking at Knowles.

"Do not bullshit a bullshitter, Dr. I bet it was you who had reservations," Cristopher said.

"Why do you say that?" the red-haired Hawkins asked.

"You answered first. It is not a big deal; I am here now."

Erin gave a shy smile to Cristopher. If anything, she knew he was brazen.

"The Vice President thinks very highly of you as a matter of fact," Knowles said.

"I still feel he should be the one doing this. He is a brilliant man," said Mointz.

"Believe me, he was asked time and time again to take the reins. However, the President's Scientific Council feels he rated way under you," Davis said. "He did not make the final cut. You did."

"The exact science may be in the how to get back to the Second Parallel, but I am sure the picking of the candidate to go back was not an exact science. Am I wrong?"

"Yes and no," Hawkins said. "We know you have the IQ and the intangibles needed to get through this. From what Dr. Davis has told us about you, you definitely have the temperament. The science involved has more to do with your people skills than anything else."

"In a crisis situation, Cristopher is calm and soothing," Erin said holding Cristopher's hand. Erin was nervous, not just for Cristopher and the boys, but for the pressure these scientists now faced.

"He also has a killer instinct," Davis said. "He hates to lose at anything. You should see him when I beat him at chess. Cristopher will pull the trigger if he needs to without a second of hesitation. He loves you, Erin, and the boys far too much not to."

Davis knew Erin and the boys would be on his mind in every decision he made. He would do what he needed to do even if it meant he would have to take a life or two. Davis hoped he could control his testosterone better, though, unlike President Clinton, who could have had a far greater legacy. Cristopher needed to concentrate on the task at hand and not on the ladies.

"I am a lot of things, but a pacifist is not one of them," said Mointz.

Hawkins nodded. "Good, let's start your training. Are you ready?"

"Ready as I will ever be," Mointz replied. "What do you have on the agenda for me today?"

"First up, we are going to give you a crash course on psychology and relationships, followed by a full physical," Knowles said. "If you would come this way, we can get you situated with Dr. Gennifer Moore."

"Sounds wonderful," Mointz said as he kissed Erin on the top of her head and followed Dr. Knowles out of the room. "You were the deciding vote in my favor, weren't you?"

Knowles just smiled as they walked. At the end of the hall, he opened the door to the office of Dr. Gennifer Moore. The government building at MIT was extremely large and the top floor was under heavy security because of the project. Office space on the top floor had always been limited. However, now it was further cramped with the extra personnel needed for the mission. When Mointz looked in at Gennifer Moore, he noticed the office was no bigger than a closet.

Knowles made the introductions and left quickly to tackle the ton of work necessary before Davis left for the parallel world.

"Please sit down, Dr. Mointz," Gennifer told him, "Nice to finally meet my new patient."

Mointz smiled at Gennifer and tried to remember he was not here to make a date. He promised himself to take all of this very seriously. The old Cristopher Mointz would have been trying to get in her pants from the first minute he walked into the office. The very well-endowed blonde-haired psychologist was wearing Channel and she smelled absolutely fantastic, he thought.

"Thank you for seeing me, Dr.," said Mointz.

"Please call me Gennifer," she replied.

"Okay then, Genny," Mointz said. "How can I help thee?"

"You are a charming one, aren't you?" Gennifer could see right off the bat why Mointz had been chosen for this and she could tell he was not that interested in what she had to say. Her part in this was to try to get Mointz to keep an open mind on how to use his brains to his advantage.

"I try, but now I need to use all of this charm for good and not evil," Mointz said.

"True, you need to use your charm and abilities now for the greater good. However, you also need to learn ways that are outside the box to get you where you need to be and you need to learn not to react always on instinct. There are ramifications for every one of your actions."

"I am ready to be taught. Please teach the professor."

"What do you know about pheromones?"

"They are positive stimuli caused by certain smells that can attract the opposite sex."

"Dr. Davis is correct; you are a very bright individual. Here at MIT we have been manufacturing them for over a decade. You will be given our formulas for pheromones and I will teach you how to use them and how you can use them for your personal advantage."

Mointz was fascinated and for the next hour he heard all about lilacs, ocean air, and what sweet cologne to wear. She also told him how certain plants and fresh flowers in his office could influence people positively. He was definitely impressed by Gennifer so far.

"Keeping people on your side with pleasurable smells—outstanding," said Mointz. "I guess garlic is now out of my diet."

"Garlic is healthy for you, Cristopher."

"I heard a rumor they are turning me into the Six Million Dollar Man and I would not need the wonderful powers of garlic."

"Be careful what you wish for, Cristopher," she said. "You still have to live a healthy lifestyle. You are not infallible."

This is some woman, Mointz thought to himself.

"What do you know about stress?"

"It leads to anxiety, depression, and psychosomatic disorders," Mointz answered, trying to remember Psychology 101.

"You will be experiencing a tremendous amount of it. There will be an initial shock when all of your memories return. You will be eight-years-old and will not be able to drive for nine years. All of your friends will be eight. Whatever you do, you cannot act like a loner and retreat."

"No sex, I guess, either, unless I find a Mrs. Robinson," Mointz said. "In all seriousness, Gennifer, I can easily act like an eight-year-old."

"That is one thing I have complete confidence in. You are going to be sexually active sooner than normal. Find someone and stick to her until you get to Erin. Remember, you do not want to have anything come back and haunt you later on in a campaign.

"I understand."

"Good," she said. "We also have to talk about what you experienced at the age eleven."

"If you mean what I plan to do to one son-of-a-bitch of a priest, I believe I have that covered."

"You must not draw attention to yourself. Deal with the incident and then move on. You have to let him continue to do what he did. We cannot change things."

"He will never hurt anyone again, bank on it. You can tell everyone you want, but if you think I am going to let him hurt another boy after I get to him, you are sadly mistaken."

Gennifer gave him a slight nod and he could see the hurt in her eyes. They say the eyes are the window to your soul and Mointz could see clearly through the window of Gennifer's.

"When did it happen to you?" Mointz asked.

She swallowed hard. "I was a senior in high school. It happened when I got off the bus, the Tuesday before Thanksgiving. He had this creepy mustache and he raped me. I would do anything to have him stopped."

"I will be there," Mointz promised. "Do not say a word to anyone, just give me the details."

"Cristopher…I cannot have you…"

"Intervene," Mointz said, interrupting her. "What do you think my mission is? You think I am going to be sent back to sit on my ass and do nothing?"

Gennifer simply shrugged.

"Now my lady, the details, if you would be so kind. You can bet your life I will be there to intervene and he will never hurt you."

Gennifer told Mointz every single detail and he burned them into his memory. There was no way he would allow anyone to hurt Gennifer.

"Do you really believe, in your heart, you can get to my house and stop this man?" Gennifer asked.

"There is a reason they picked me. I will stop him, I promise," he said and put his hand on hers. "Any other requests while I am at it?"

"You can tell me not to marry my ex-husband!"

"I will have to think about that one. I am going to have to keep myself from trying to date you when I go back."

"I wish I could give you permission, but you have a mission to accomplish," Gennifer said, deeply regretting that she had to say it, as she could easily fall for Mointz. "Let us get back to the task at hand before we get in any more trouble."

"Trouble is my middle name. Believe in me Gennifer, I will make your life a little less painful."

"I believe in you, Cristopher."

Mointz thought about the lovely Gennifer during the entire examination. Gennifer seemed to have dropped the weight of the world off her well-endowed chest after she had spent three hours with Mointz. They were to meet every day until Davis left for the Second Parallel.

Mointz felt as though he could stop things he knew about for the greater good as long as he did not change things too much. Davis had only two weeks to burn into Mointz's mind he could not prevent President Reagan's shooting or track down Jeffery Dahmer, nor could he stop Britney Spears from shaving her head.

Davis met Mointz back in his office after Gennifer finished.

"Lovely girl," Mointz said as he sat down.

"Yes, she is a great person. You will help her with that little problem that she had in high school, correct?" Davis asked.

"Were you spying on us?"

"Not at all, Cristopher, Gennifer is an absolute peach and I am very fond of her. She opened up to me before we selected her and I had a feeling that you would be able to see her pain. Moore has always been extremely emotional and becomes emotionally attached to all of her patients," Davis said. "I want you to handle it without anyone knowing."

"You know I will be there. Next time why don't you just come out and ask me to do it. For Pete's sake, Dr. Trent, we are in this together."

Davis returned Mointz's smile. "You are now using all of your people skills even though you are venturing into the unknown. The learning process you will have in the next 30 something years will make you an unbeatable presidential candidate. Become a sponge and collect all the knowledge transfers you can in the next two weeks and beyond. Everything you learn will help you in 1975."

"I will do my best. Thirty years, my God, this is going to be one hell-of-a journey. By the way, Dr. Trent, where are Erin and the boys?"

"Eating a late lunch…here, have a piece of pizza from yesterday," Davis said as he handed him a piece of yesterday's pie.

"You are lucky I am not a fussy eater," said Mointz. "What is next on the agenda, partner?"

"A history lesson…"

"I am a history professor, what would I need a history lesson for?"

"This is not just any old professor you are going to be meeting with. This one will be pretty interesting for you to hear out."

Mointz almost passed out on the floor in the private conference room when he noticed CIA Director, Lauren Gabriel, sitting in a black leather chair. Director Gabriel was the former senior senator from New York before becoming the head of the largest spook agency in the world. The only republican in the current administration, Lauren Gabriel walked with Teddy Roosevelt's big stick. At almost sixty, the six-foot blonde, nicknamed "Legs" behind her back, Gabriel looked like she could crack a walnut between her thighs. She was that tough and intimidating.

Mointz decided to forgo his normal smart-mouthed remark about meeting another beautiful woman and decided to play it straight, well, almost straight.

"Director Gabriel, I am delighted you could take the time out of your busy schedule to meet with little ole me," Mointz said, peering into the sky blue eyes of the Director of the CIA as he took her hand in his.

"It is an honor to meet the man who has been enlisted to save the world," Director Gabriel said. "Please have a seat and join me."

"My guess is that I am about to be indoctrinated into the spook community and learn things that you do not see on Fox News every night."

"Your instincts are correct, Dr. Mointz. What do you know about our foreign policy failures over the past five years?"

"To be honest, I basically watched how compromising with rogue nations is, in theory, a good idea; however, in all practicality, not something I would sign on to as President. I know budgets were slashed to our agencies and we counted on drone attacks instead of using our people on the ground. I am sure you are going to tell me we decided to stop water boarding and every other torture tactic to get the bad guys to talk. We probably knew an unleashing of nuclear weapons was inevitable while the self-centered playboy in the Oval Office believed it was a good idea to hold meetings at the United Nations instead of assassinating some of the leaders and generals from these wayward countries."

Lauren was dually impressed with the knowledge Mointz possessed and she was not one to impress easily. "I see you have an understanding of why this has been difficult for me to watch."

"Obviously, the Vice President had the confidence in you to help me. I am not sure I like the fact President Reis is out of the loop. Even though he is an abysmal leader, he is still the leader of this country."

Lauren, the person, simply nodded her head. However, the former politician and now CIA Director said, "We are not doing anything legally wrong right now. You do understand, don't you?"

"I do understand it, yes."

"Director, if the President is so out of touch the people around him cannot trust him, then obviously the country is already in a place where it will be unable to sustain prosperity for the long run. The United States used to be a manufacturing super power. It pissed that away. Tell me what this country actually makes any more besides missiles and software? I would like to buy American-made shoes and phone a call center actually in this country. You know—the simple things in life."

"You sound like you are already running for office, Dr."

The fact of the matter was Mointz always spoke as if he were a politician trying to win over a crowd with his ideas. He knew the right answers; he just needed to live his life according to those ideals. Mointz's mother had always told him to believe in the parable Jesus told of the sower in Matthew 13. Mointz needed to find the good soil so, when he heard the word and understood it, he would bear his cross and live with the good wisdom Jesus provided.

"I believe in my heart that this country needs to look in the mirror and wonder why we house 25 percent of the world's prison population. Our middle class diminished faster than our country's infrastructure, as new industry never replaced the old. We taxed companies to death and forced them to outsource overseas. The United States spent money foolishly on pork barrel projects and did not stop to hold anyone accountable if the projects had cost overruns. This country was built on Christian ideals, yet people are trying to take Christ out of Christmas. Politicians run campaigns on *Hope and Change* and before they even park their asses in the Oval Office, they worry about a second term."

Lauren had been fixated on Mointz's every word. She had hoped his passion ran deep and he was not just all talk and no action. Davis assured her he was more than just a pretty face and a fast talker. She could not understand how he was not the President now. "Do you understand how difficult life is going to be for you once you get into the public eye? There will be piranhas in the water all around you. From what I hear, you will be quite the athlete, but I am not going to divulge too much here."

"Really now?"

"Don't worry, it will all be fine," Lauren said as she handed Mointz a USB device. "These are my personal thoughts as well as several CIA and FBI files from the FBI's founding up to present day. Use me as a resource the best way you can without tipping your hand. Regardless of what anyone tells you, you cannot live your life like a choirboy. Fuck whom you need to, kill if need be, and do not pass go and collect your 200 dollars. It is a waste of time. You are going to have to be ruthless and you are going to have to be more than you ever imagined you could be. Am I right, Mr. Vice President?"

"Unfortunately, you are one hundred percent correct, Director Gabriel," Ellis said over the intercom as he watched the interview remotely from the Naval Observatory, the official residence of the Vice President. "We spent many hours together in the Senate as we were the ranking Republican and Democrat members of the Senate Intelligence Committee. The USB device that Director Gabriel has given you contains information not even Dr. Davis knows at this time. You also have both the Director's and my personal thoughts and secrets on the device. Included are some road maps to follow for your mission. Use all of the information wisely."

Mointz sank in his chair a bit. He could only imagine the type of information that he now possessed in his hand as he looked at the device.

"You will have plenty of time to study and digest the material over the next several years," Lauren said, which gave Mointz a shiver throughout his whole body.

"This is not an incredibly joyful assignment. You are basically telling me I have the green light to assassinate someone if they hinder my progress on becoming President. It sounds like a good time. However, I know I will have to do things I will not be especially proud of over the years. There have to be people I will be able to trust completely over the years, I am sure."

"The information on people on the disc can guide you in the right direction. Use those contacts. However, do not reveal your true mission," Ellis said. "You have the greatest gift and the most powerful tool in the toolbox."

Mointz was confused and asked, "What would those be?"

"You are a very likeable person and you now possess more knowledge than anyone who has ever existed because you know the future when you go back. You will know the vicissitudes of the stock market, who will be elected to office and what their skeletons are and you will know who will win every game before it is played. A special panel will guide you over the next two weeks and they will give you their ideas on the best way for you to succeed," Ellis said.

"The panel, who are they?"

Lauren handed Mointz a folder. "Dr. Davis, the Vice President, yours truly, Dr. Moore and a few other colleagues will start meeting with you tomorrow to answer any questions you might have. Sorry, but you will not be the quarterback of your beloved New England Patriots. The panel believes you need to concentrate on being an Olympic Champion in Seoul in 1988."

Mointz did not know what hit him the hardest, the mention of the panel or the possibility of a berth in the Olympic Games. "You are telling me I will be in on a panel that will tell me exactly what sport I will become famous for? Please tell me it is not going to be synchronized swimming."

Lauren smiled. "Always the comedian, huh? The panel tested…"

Mointz interrupted, "Of course they tested."

"What Director Gabriel is trying to say is that groups have been polled and you are going to get the most mileage out of winning several gold medals in

31

one Olympics. Dr. Davis knows you quit a great career in swimming to play football in college. Our scientists will make a little tweak to your DNA and with your natural athleticism, you will break all of Mark Spitz's records from Munich and go on to either law school or med school, giving you the foundation for a career in politics. You will be a media darling and a commercial juggernaut," Ellis said. "We will get into all of this tomorrow. Read what you can on the files that are marked "roadmap" on the USB device. For now, go be with your family and enjoy your evening in the suite on the first floor. Enjoy them and ingrain into your mind why you are going to need to do the things we ask. Tomorrow will be a big day."

Chapter Five

The night with Erin and the boys was magical for Mointz. Reunification with his family provided all of the motivation Mointz needed to embed in his brain that he had to make his mission a success. Reading over the roadmaps the panel provided had his head spinning.

Mointz certainly relaxed after making love to Erin last night for the first time in three years. He ate a hearty breakfast with Erin and the boys as they were scheduled for a series of genetic tests in preparation for cloning the two boys.

Mointz and Erin had held each other for hours after making love and discussed the enormous task Mointz had in front of him. They agreed becoming a family again was the right thing to do and it was wonderful for both of them. Enjoying the time they had left was extremely important to them and they looked forward to spending some alone time this evening. Mointz asked Erin to start putting together some thoughts on how they could enhance each other's lives in the Second Parallel. Erin's demeanor changed before he left, reminding Mointz she could be extremely difficult at times.

Davis greeted Mointz with a large cup of coffee, when Mointz stepped in his office. They both enjoyed Starbucks immensely.

"How was your evening?" Davis asked.

"Please tell me you did not monitor the evening," he said as he sat down in the leather chair across from Davis.

Trent Davis smiled. "No, we are not that bad yet. I can tell from your smile that you must have enjoyed your evening."

"I did very much, as a matter of fact. It is kind of a shame we are only getting back together because of the destruction of the world. Have you squared away my absence at the college? I had to tell Professor Valley I was on a panel now in Washington DC. Talk about awkward."

"Yes, I called the college and told them you have been chosen for a Presidential Panel," Davis replied. "I am glad you can change your life with Erin and I know the benefit of having your family together again is definitely worth all of this. Now, let's get over to the panel and get moving on getting you prepared to take over the world."

"You are a riot this morning."

They stood up and headed for a 500-seat amphitheater in the building. Davis told Mointz even though he would be taking a crash course in how to live his life, he was only getting suggestions from people. Mointz would have to be the one making the decisions in the end and he needed to feel comfortable with them, Davis stressed to his friend.

Mointz heard Ellis and Lauren's words still echoing in his mind as Davis spoke to him on the walk over. He knew he had to succeed in everything he did with the eyes of the world on him throughout his life if he was going to be what he needed to be.

"Dr. Trent, are there a lot of discrepancies amongst the panel in how I should proceed in the Second Parallel?"

"Patently," said Davis. "My guess is Lauren scared the bejeezus out of you in that little meeting yesterday. Remember, she is the head of a spook agency."

"Good guess, my friend. The Vice President piped in his opinions as well via teleconference. I did not realize he had been so closely aligned with Lauren when they were in the Senate. I like the fact he is a realist."

When they reached the amphitheater, Davis said, "Do what you think is right in your heart. You are the one who must succeed. Cristopher, you cannot fail."

Mointz nodded, as he had heard he could not fail repeatedly in the past two days. He followed Davis into the amphitheater where the six members of the panel sat on the stage with a seat open for Davis. Director Lauren Gabriel, Dr. Gennifer Moore, United States Senator Rebecca McGreevy, Vice President Ellis, renowned celebrity psychologist Phillip Graham, and former Secretary of State Madeleine Tanner sat around a table as Davis joined them.

"Please sit," Ellis asked politely. Mointz sat in the front row of the audience section of the amphitheater. "Thank you for joining us."

"As if I had a choice in the matter, Mr. Vice President. You made a great case for my involvement in all of this."

The Vice President introduced each member of the panel, even though Mointz knew of each one of the panel members. The panel gave Cristopher a brief overview of what they hoped he could accomplish.

Celebrity psychologist, Philip Graham asked the first question. "Cristopher, do you know where you would like to study after the 88 Olympics in Seoul when you are the toast of the town?"

"I read a lot of the roadmaps last night and I am partial to the law school idea. I would attach myself to causes which would keep me in the limelight positively. I would interact with politicians who have positive approval ratings. I believe that is the way I can gain a good solid foundation before venturing into politics myself. I hope I will be Rhode Island's native son, keeping above the corruption and pettiness of the state's local politics. There will definitely be an advantage in it for me if I can be known as someone incorruptible."

Dr. Graham nodded and smiled. "That could definitely work."

"You will have all the campaign dirt you need on candidates. Pick and choose who you run against and what platform is popular," said Lauren. "You are going to have to align yourself with friends. We know you will try to save Ronnie Mahoney, but he may not be someone you can entrust with your future."

Ronnie Mahoney had been Mointz's best friend from kindergarten up until senior year of high school, when Mahoney committed suicide. Mahoney had impregnated his girlfriend and ended his life before the second-to-last football game of the season. Mointz took the devastating loss extremely hard as he had always relied on Ronnie as his protector.

"I will try to save him, but I know he will be unstable. I am going to have to play it by ear, I guess."

"Your knee injury in college, which ended your football career put you back several years," Senator Rebecca McGreevy said. "You are going to have to take bumps in the road without the depression. I, for one, believe you will rise above it, because if you fail, we all fail. Don't be afraid to think outside the box. I have been on the Senate's Commerce Committee for the past fifteen years. You will know the economy better than anyone will and money can cure a lot of what ails you. I would strongly suggest you major in Economics and History in college. I put it all in my roadmap file that you have."

Mointz nodded. "Yes, ma'am, I read it. Brown University is the way to go for me and I can see how being an athlete will go well for me with business relationships, especially with endorsement deals. I guess the unknown lies in the pulling all of this off without a hitch. However, I agree I need to hit bumps in the road head on," said Mointz. "I read the section where Erin is going to have to go to medical school. It will not go over well with Erin. She hates fiddling with a band aid."

"It is not so bad," Ellis said. "Remember, you could always go yourself."

"The documents on the USB suggest I become the attorney and Erin the doctor. I really think that is best."

"The ROTC program in which you participated seems like it will be a real winner as well," Gennifer Moore said with a big smile which Davis and others, including Lauren, noticed.

"I agree with you, Dr. Moore," Doctor Phillip Graham pronounced. "The first Gulf War saw a barrage of yellow ribbons and Mointz will be an American Hero going into battle. It will play well on television."

"You should know," Davis said.

"The military angle will be a big key to your success," former Secretary of State Madeleine Tanner said.

Mointz's head hurt after another three hours of the panel. The panel had grilled him about his plans and given him advice until his ears hurt as much as his head. Everything made sense, at least to Mointz, and he had a feeling it was all coming together. Davis kept stressing repeatedly Mointz would be able to predict the future and be able to make his own roadmap.

The panel was to meet again on Friday, which was in three days, as the Vice President needed to get back to Washington, D.C. and deal with President Reis and his band of flunkies.

Secretary Tanner, Senator Rebecca McGreevy and Phillip Graham left duly impressed with Mointz and firmly in his corner. They looked forward to spending more time with Mointz at the end of the week.

Lauren brought Mointz into a small conference room and sat down in front of him. "Are you sure you have what it takes to get the job done?" she asked Mointz.

Mointz was now determined to pull off the mission and not entrust someone else to save his family. Without a second of hesitation, he pulled the Director of the CIA close to him and kissed her firmly on her lips as he picked up the beautiful former senator and placed her on the conference room table. After locking the door, Mointz discovered every inch of Lauren's breasts and love nest with his tongue before inserting himself into her for a steamy hot sex session which rivaled anything in his life.

"Well, do you think I can or not?" Mointz asked her as he put on his clothes after he got off the Director's naked body.

"Jesus, Mointz. What the hell were you thinking?" Lauren asked still trying to catch her breath.

"I was thinking I would do exactly what you told me I needed to do. I was not sure if you were ever going to be convinced I was the right person for the job. You know damn well I am. By the way, I always wanted to do that to you. You are pretty hot."

Lauren giggled as Mointz had turned her back into a college co-ed. "Oh, okay. I see your point. Man, you are good at that."

"Now I have to get over to my daily wrap-up meeting with Dr. Moore. I do not want to be late," Mointz said.

"That girl is enamored with you, Cristopher. Please be very careful," Lauren said as she finished dressing herself.

Mointz planted a kiss on her lips and smiled. "Jealous already Director?"

"No, Cristopher. I do not want to see you break her heart or get yours broken, for that matter."

"Holy shit, you have feelings."

"Yes, Cristopher. Just because I am the head of the CIA, does not mean I do not have real emotions," she said. "Now get out of here and try to save the world."

"Yes, ma'am."

"Olympic swimmer and lawyer...not sure how to process it. So much for fun," Mointz said to Gennifer in her office.

"You will have tons of fun," Gennifer replied. "We will get to meet earlier than we met now. I know this is overwhelming for you."

"Tell me about it. I have the Vice President and the Director of the CIA telling me I need to do whatever I can to save the planet. I am not sure how it is going to work out."

"What do you mean?"

Mointz took in a deep breath. "How do you just sleep with a person to get what you want without it bothering your conscience? Even more, how do you feel about killing someone by blowing out their brains with a slug to the back of the head, even though you know they are evil? I believe they want me to be this super-secret agent. I married young and divorced because I married one of the most selfish people on the planet. I had one hell-of-a time after that until I met Erin and had the boys. However, I never stopped being a party boy. I know what is right and wrong in my heart; I just do not know how easy it is going to be for me to ride out my conscience when I need to make life decisions which go against my heart. These decisions will be for the greater good of mankind, I know, but I certainly am not going to enjoy making them."

Gennifer put her hand on Mointz's and smiled at him. "You need to be strong, Cristopher. Do not second guess yourself or you will be bogged down with too many emotions. No one is telling you to party like a rock star and be a Tiger Woods or a Charles Barkley. Do what you have to do to achieve your goals, not what you desire to do, and you will be fine."

Mointz could feel the sexual energy from Gennifer. Right now, all he desired was to do to Gennifer what he had just done to Lauren, but this mission was not about what Mointz wanted. His very existence was now all about saving his family and the world in the Second Parallel.

He tapped her hand and said, "I understand. It will not be easy, but I understand one hundred percent."

"Good. What did you think of the Panel's advice?"

"Everyone has their own ideas I guess, but I am the one who is going to have to make it all work. I should be able to maintain some semblance of normalcy when I go back. I know I will be swimming lap after lap in pools for a while. I started swimming competitively when I was six-years-old, by then I was already on the YMCA swim team."

"Better you than me. Chlorine gives my hair split ends."

"I think I had a flat top since I was ten years old. Guys do not care about split ends all that much."

"This coming from Mr. Metrosexual himself. Better make sure the biochemists give you good hair. You do not want to be the Presidential candidate with a chrome dome."

"Hey, you are supposed to make your patients feel better about themselves."

"If you were *really* my patient, I could not do this," she said and moved across her office and kissed him. "Shhh, it was only a kiss."

Mointz did not know what to think, however he kissed her back passionately. "Well, that was a surprise."

###

"The plan seems to be working," Ellis told Davis on the phone after he boarded Air Force Two. "The man has some serious chutzpah, I see, after seducing our CIA Director."

"Does *she* know we know?" Davis asked.

"Hell, no. That is one place I am not going to go."

Davis was extremely glad. He also did not want to go down that lane with Lauren. "Cristopher is falling for Gennifer as planned. I know he does not realize it, but Gennifer is going to be a huge help to him in the Second Parallel. He will have her by his side and it should help to keep him focused. Cristopher will be able to trust her and after he saves her from her attacker, her memories will return the next day.

"I was not sure this was a good idea at first. However, the more I see them together, the better I like the idea of having her with him," Ellis said. "I am glad that we kept this to ourselves because if we were to broadcast this, we would have everyone trying to volunteer to go back and help. Mointz needs a woman in his life to count on and Gennifer will be the rock he needs. I hope she will help him keep a cool tool for once in his life. Better to be with her than with multiple partners."

"He is a good man, Valmer. I am really getting positive vibes from him as I watch how he is handling himself," Davis said.

"Agreed," Ellis said. "Mointz has certainly proven to me he is the right man for the job."

"What is so funny, Valmer?"

"I still cannot get over how he shut up Lauren. Anyone who can do that is my new hero."

Davis almost cracked up himself thinking about how brazen Mointz was. "He is one of a kind."

Chapter Six

Over the next three days, the Mointz family bonded as they spent hour upon hour with MIT scientists. The boys were having the time of their lives as their parents grew closer and closer.

Mointz and Gennifer were getting closer as well as a few of their counseling sessions had turned into some serious hours of passion. They had become each other's sounding boards and felt passion that was missing in their separate lives. He still loved Erin. However, he still felt the hurt from Erin's treatment right before they broke up; it was a deep scar which had not fully healed.

When Erin did not let Mointz see the boys for an extended period of time, he had suffered almost unbearably. Davis had heard the stories from Mointz and Davis's only fear was that Erin's attitude at times could derail Mointz's mission if she were to go back to her stubborn ways. With the brightest of the bright at his disposal, Davis knew Mointz needed a strong personality he could trust and Davis decided to bring in Gennifer. Once he had the blessing of the Vice President, he put Mointz and Gennifer together, ironically using subliminal hypnosis and pheromones on the both of them. Neither one of them had a chance to keep their hands off each other. What happened with Mointz and Lauren surprised the hell out of Davis and Ellis. Lauren and Mointz might have a few more passionate incidents in the Second Parallel if they collaborated in politics; an almost certain probability.

The day's panel session went almost exactly as the previous one and Mointz felt like he had a better grasp on things the second time around. In ten days, Davis would be going to the Second Parallel, Mointz would become eight years old again and the world would change more than anyone could predict.

All of the scientists had completed everything needed for the trip to the Second Parallel, thankfully, because on Friday evening disaster struck New York City. Several members of a terrorist cell placed dirty bombs in strategic places around the city and detonated them killing almost 500,000 people and injuring five times that number. Ellis contacted Davis and ordered him to start Operation Second Parallel immediately. He was afraid that other cells were about to unleash similar devastation across the United States.

Mointz was watching a movie with Erin and the boys when Davis knocked on the suite's door.

"What is wrong, Trent?" Mointz asked his friend who looked extremely pale as he walked into the suite. Mointz knew something was amiss immediately.

"New York City was attacked this evening in a coordinated attack. The Vice President wants me to leave this evening and we need to get you into the lab immediately to clone your embryos with your memories. We have at least two sets from the last two days. However, this set is the most important."

Erin sat stone faced as she heard the words coming from Davis. There was no turning back now for anyone.

Mointz sighed after he heard the news. "I guess it is show time. Let us make the magic happen."

The boys were still watching a movie as the adults spoke in the kitchen. They did not want the boys to hear any of this.

"When will we all disappear?" Erin asked. "I mean when will this all change?"

"You have about three weeks left before all of the First Parallel is different. Every memory that Cristopher has in the next two hours will be what he holds forever in his mind and will have when he wakes up in 1975." Davis said. "Make them count because in exactly one hour and fifty nine minutes new memories will be erased forever."

The finality of it all hit Mointz and Erin as Davis took the boys away so they could have some time to themselves. Erin took Mointz into the bedroom and made love to her husband with the most passion she ever gave him. Tears filled in her eyes as they held each other.

"You will not fail, right?" Erin asked. "Just tell me my children will be born and you will do everything no matter what you have to do to succeed."

"I will not fail, Babe. I promise you, I will not know failure."

Erin nodded and reached over to the nightstand. "Give this to me when we meet and do not read it. Do not worry, it does not mention our breakup as Trent reviewed it and gave the thumbs up. I need you to be the biggest bastard to the world, but not to yours truly. Please do not be who you were to me here, in the Second Parallel. I know you love me, but the boys need both of us."

Mointz wanted to say the feeling was mutual. However, he bit his tongue. Erin needed him right now. "I promise to do better this time, Erin."

They showered together and met the boys at the lab. Davis told Mointz that Gennifer had a few words for him before his memories were no longer.

Mointz entered Gennifer's office. Teary-eyed, Gennifer rushed over to hug him and snuggled into his arms.

"You cannot go yet, Cristopher. You just can't. "

"Genny, I have to. You know I do. Believe me; it will not be the last time we see each other."

"I know, but it will be the last time I will remember. You feel so right, now, when I am in your arms. I know you think this is some schoolgirl crush and it probably is, however, it is real to me. I do not know how you feel, Cristopher. The reality of it is, I really do not care. Selfish of me I know, but I really want to be with you."

Mointz held her tightly. He was extremely emotional right now and a bit of a basket case. He loved Erin and his family with all of his heart. However, something he could not explain pulled him to Gennifer. He wondered if it had to do with the Second Parallel. "I wish I could have had more time as well. We both feel the same in that respect," he said and kissed her passionately. "I have to go."

43

She nodded and buried her head into his chest. "I love you, Dr. Mointz."

"I love you too, Genny."

They finished saying their goodbyes and after they composed themselves, Mointz and Gennifer walked to the lab.

Mointz lay strapped to a gurney as a large needle entered his already sore left hip. Both Erin and Gennifer watched as Mointz winced in pain.

"He is a trooper; I give him that," Davis said to Erin and Gennifer as he entered the lab.

"Cristopher looks to be in excruciating pain, Trent. This is the fourth time he has had to go through this," Erin said.

Davis looked at Erin and Gennifer. "This is the last time, fortunately. I am sure he will appreciate the fact it's the last time."

Thomas and Patrick returned to the lab as Mointz finished dressing. No memory now would follow him into the Second Parallel. He walked over to his boys and hugged them hard.

"Well, that sucked," Mointz said with a smile. "Nice last memory to have."

"Sorry about that. It hurt me more than it hurt you. We are actually going to tape these last few hours starting now." He clipped a small microphone on Mointz.

"Ah ha, so I really will not miss anything significant."

Davis went into his private lab and gathered everything he needed for his trip to the Second Parallel. A camera crew followed Mointz, recording the last of his time here in the First Parallel.

The only thing left for Davis to add to the X846 were the last of Mointz's cloned embryos. Davis asked to see Mointz in his office, took the camera operator's camera, and placed it on a tripod in his office.

"What is so important that you could not put this into my memory?" Mointz asked.

"With the entire calamity of things this evening, I did not have a chance to tell you a few things. I also needed to get permission from the Vice President. You, my friend, are now the leader of the free world. Isn't that right, Mr. Vice President?" Davis said and hit the mute button on the speakerphone.

"It's the truth, Dr. Davis, President Mointz. It is an honor to speak to you." Vice President Ellis stated.

"How am I the President?"

"Because if you are not on this date we are all screwed, to put it bluntly, Mr. President," Ellis replied.

"Gotcha," Mointz said. "Any last minute advice?"

"Now that you mention it, yes," Davis said. "We want you to know after you save Gennifer Moore from her attacker, her memories will return the next day and she will be safe."

Mointz shook his head and was really miffed. "It would mean she would remember the attack in the First Parallel. That does not make a whole heck of a lot of sense to me."

"Actually, Mr. President, she will not have that memory. She was hypnotized before her DNA was extracted with a special technique the military uses. She will just remember you saving her in the Second Parallel. Gennifer will have every other memory preserved," said Ellis.

"Thank God. It would have been totally ignorant of us to do that to her," Mointz said. "Why is she having her memories restored in the first place?"

"You need someone besides yourself who has lived in the First Parallel. Erin does not need to know Gennifer lived in the First Parallel, but if you decide to tell her, that is up to you. Gennifer and you fit well together and you need her," Davis said.

"Tell me this is by chance and is not a set up."

"It is not a planned connection. Only the Vice President and I know about Gennifer," Davis said.

"We need to tell you a few things we did not need anyone else to hear," the Vice President said. "We believe you will need to right a few wrongs and, on this disc, you will get a few ideas how to do that."

"Am I even going to believe most of what you are telling me now? God, I am about to be eight years old again."

"And I am about to be dead from radiation poison, so quit your bitching and suck it up, will you?"

"Oh, good point."

"You are comfortable with everything?" Ellis asked.

"Yes, sir," Mointz said.

"No, Mr. President. You are now, the sir," Ellis said.

Chapter Seven

July 4th, 1975

Mointz's hip did not hurt, he thought to himself for the first time in a week as he was waking up. He rubbed his eyes and when he opened them, he knew Operation Second Parallel had started.

You crazy bastard, Trent, you pulled this off, Mointz thought to himself as he looked around his room at his parents' house.

Mointz stared at the white and blue sports wallpaper on the walls. He wore his favorite light blue T-shirt. His 17-year-old cousin had bought it for him at an arcade in North Carolina during a vacation at his aunt's house.

"Cristopher, breakfast is almost ready, sweetheart," his mother Martha called out from downstairs.

"Coming, Momma," he replied choking back the tears.

Cristopher went into the bathroom and looked at himself in the mirror. *Oh, my God, I am at least three inches taller than I used to be,* he thought to himself. He looked down as he was going to the bathroom and noticed his pecker was the same as before.

Mointz composed himself before he walked downstairs to see his parents. He hugged both of them as soon as he walked into the kitchen, as if he had never hugged them before.

"Would you like a couple of homemade Egg McMuffins?" his father asked.

"I am famished, Dad."

Robert Mointz laughed at his son. "Famished. Good word."

"What is with all of the lovey dovey hugs this morning?" his mother asked. "Are you alright?"

"Of course, Mother. I just missed you guys," Mointz said and sat down at the table. "What is on the agenda for today?" He remembered he always spoke older than he was.

Mointz's father laughed again. "Agenda, what agenda would an eight-year-old have?"

"Just curious what we are doing for the fourth of July. It is Grandma and Grandpa's anniversary."

"We are having a party for them, sweetie. Your grandparents are coming over for a barbeque," his mother replied. "Let me go get the baby because he probably needs a diaper change."

My brother is only one, Mointz thought. He wondered where his sister Kathy was.

"Where is Kathy?" Mointz asked.

"She is at Charlotte's, playing. You, my friend woke up late. Did you have a tough swim practice last night?" she asked, standing to pick the baby up.

Mointz shrugged and his mother smiled as she left the kitchen. He could not believe that his parents were exactly the same. They had always been like Ozzie and Harriet.

Robert gave his son two fresh homemade breakfast sandwiches and Mointz ate them with vigor. His dad almost fainted when he grabbed a cup of black coffee. Tea was always accepted in the Irish household, but not coffee so much.

"Hey fella, when does an eight-year-old drink black coffee?" his mother asked when she came back into the kitchen with baby, Sean.

Mointz was tongue tied at first; however, he rebounded quickly. "Just a quick caffeine boost before I start running. Someone at swim practice said that I need about 20 miles a week of roadwork for better endurance. I will run down Brian Avenue, take a left on Almy, and then a right on Chace Street. Then I will follow Bark Street home. I believe it is 3.1 miles."

Robert was shocked. "Who told you that?"

"I calculated it on a town map the best I could. Do you think you can see if it is accurate later, Dad?" Mointz asked even though he knew he had it on the money from all the times he had run that particular loop of road.

"Sure buddy, I am not sure you should be running all that much, though. Remember you have baseball and karate as well as swimming."

Mointz smiled. He remembered he had quit karate because of a bully named David Conley, who was older than he and better at karate. There was no way Mointz would do that now. Davis's team had given him at least three inches as well as increased muscle mass and strength. Mointz wanted to be the best martial artist he could be, as he knew he would need to be the best of the best.

Davis had told him before he harvested the final DNA that he should enjoy the first day of the Second Parallel before he went to grab the titanium-plated case with the contents Davis had brought with him from the First Parallel. Davis had also hidden three other cases in various places.

Martha came downstairs with baby Sean and Mointz laughed at his cute little brother. In the First Parallel, they barely got along and Mointz needed to change that this time around. His sister Kathy, an actress, had always been a high maintenance drama queen on stage and off. Mointz guessed he would have to put up with more of her attitude if they were ever going to see eye to eye. Kathy, no matter how successful she was, had always been jealous of Mointz's accolades. She had many accolades herself, as she was a well-known vocalist at several of New York's cabaret spots. Her voice was one of an angel, Mointz always believed, though her disposition came from the devil.

"I think it is time for my run," Mointz announced.

"Be careful," his mother said and kissed the top of her son's head.

"Do not worry, Mother. I have more than a lifetime of danger ahead of me. This is a walk in the park, believe me."

Mointz went upstairs and pulled on a pair of heavy sneakers that were all the rage in 1975. Mointz had to get used to his new body. As he got dressed, he thought that his run would indicate where he was in mind, body and spirit. After his run, he would shower and head over to Ronnie's for a reunion with his best friend.

Robert waved at his son through the window as Mointz left the driveway. Mointz could almost bet his father would drive by him in his company car, a Chevrolet Vega, at some time during his run. The elder Mointz, a sales representative for General Foods, received a new car every two years and loved to ride around in them. The family had enjoyed many "mystery rides" to different places.

The first half mile flew by for Mointz. The bad knees had been replaced with ones that moved like a well-oiled machine. He could not believe how he was not winded and thought of Davis more than likely genetically altering them back at MIT. The second mile had Mointz thinking about Erin and the boys, as well as Gennifer. It would be ten years before he would meet both Erin and Gennifer within a two-week period. Gennifer needed to be saved the Tuesday before Thanksgiving and Erin's 16th birthday was the 12th of December.

He ached for his boys and even though he could access all the videos of them, he would still worry about whether they would be born as perfect as they had been in the First Parallel. His mother had never met Patrick as she had died a few weeks before his birth. Mointz hoped the medicine brought back by Davis would save her from the cancer.

As expected, Robert drove by, smiling and waving at his son. Mointz smiled and waved back at his father, who looked fit and trim in his red Vega.

Simcock Farms, everyone's favorite dairy and ice cream parlor, had not even been built yet as Mointz passed the dairy in mile three. He still was not the slightest bit winded and started to wonder how good he was in the pool with this extra oxygen capability.

The last quarter mile was an all-out sprint that finally had the eight-year-old huffing and puffing for air. Now, he at least felt human.

"That was fast," Robert said as Mointz did several pushups in the driveway. "You practically set a new speed record." Pride beamed from his father as he said it.

"It felt pretty good, Pop, it really did," said Mointz as he finished his last set of pushups. "I am going to shower up and head over to Ronnie's house to see what he is up to."

"Go ahead, but make sure you are back in time for Grandma and Grandpa. Remember it is their anniversary."

"Do not worry, Dad. I would not miss it for all the tea in Ireland."

Ronald "Ronnie" Mahoney sat on his big wheel bike in his parent's driveway when Mointz arrived.

"Hey Buddy, what are you doing?" Ronnie asked as soon as he set his eyes on his friend.

Mointz could not believe he was with his friend again. He also could not believe how much bigger he was than Ronnie this time around.

"God, you look good," Mointz said.

Ronnie was puzzled at first by the comment. "Why, do I normally look bad?"

"No, no, of course not. What I meant was you look all chipper this morning."

"Dude, it is almost noon. Are you feeling alright?"

"I just went for a three-mile run. Maybe I am a bit loopy."

Ronnie got off the big wheel and grabbed a football from the ground and threw it at Mointz. "You ran three miles? Is that a lot?"

Mointz laughed. "Yes and no. I am trying to get in better shape for swimming."

"Ouch, stop throwing so hard," Ronnie said. "You are already a better swimmer than most 14-year-olds. What do you need to be faster for? Are you trying to beat adults, too?"

Mointz could not believe his friend. It was Ronnie who used to throw the ball too hard and hurt his fingers.

"I just want to be good at swimming, that's all."

"You are good at everything. I do not think running is going to make you any faster. However, I know what will."

"What is that?"

"Eating a popsicle."

Mointz could see the sweet innocence of his friend in his smile. It had been almost thirty years since he had seen it and he missed it. "I would love a popsicle, buddy."

They went into the house where the dashing Mrs. Mahoney handed the boys each a Creamsicle. Mointz remembered just then how beautiful she was and then quickly remembered what a bastard Mr. Mahoney was when he drank.

"Get your lazy ass out of the house with those before they drip all over the place and bring ants," Mr. Mahoney shouted. "Make me lunch, Deidre." There was no sense of the word "please" in his voice when he yelled at her from the table.

Mointz could see the heartbreak on her face and it hurt him deeply. The boys went outside with their Creamsicles. Mointz was already as tall as Ronald Mahoney and just as strong, as he discovered he had the strength he had in the First Parallel at about 18 years old.

"I have to go to the bathroom," he told Ronnie.

"You should go home then. My father is already in a bad mood."

Mointz smiled at him. "Do not worry about it. He likes me," Mointz said and walked in the house.

"What is wrong, dear?" Deidre asked, trying to shield Mointz from her husband's view. Ronald worked a ton of overtime hours at the Power Plant and with today's day off; he was well into a case of beer already.

"I think Ronnie needs you outside, Mrs. Mahoney. I have to go to the bathroom."

"Is he alright?" she asked nervously and when Mointz told her he was fine, she asked him to sneak downstairs and use the bathroom so he would not disturb Mr. Mahoney.

Mointz did not know for sure if this was a good idea or not, but he had to protect his friend. Mointz had attended Ranger School after college and he knew how to defend himself. He figured there was no time like the present to see what type of intestinal fortitude ran inside him now. Mointz grabbed a ceramic plate off the counter and walked over to Ronald in the dining room.

"What are you doing in here, Cristopher?" Ronald asked right before Mointz cracked him with the plate on top of his head and karate chopped him in the throat. Ronald went down like a ton of bricks and Mointz pounced on him like a cheetah. He grabbed the now-bleeding, 25-year-old Ronald by the shirt collar.

"If you do not start treating your wife and son with love and respect, I am going to make your life a living hell. You will also cease and desist in the consumption of alcoholic beverages. If I hear you have put your lips on one more drop, I will come back here and beat you every day until you wish you were dead. Do I make myself crystal clear?" He knew Ronald was a decent person when he was not drinking and he marveled as Ronald was cowering right now.

"Oh my Lord, what is wrong?" Deidre asked as Mointz pretended he was helping Ronald up.

"Mr. Mahoney fell and I came running in from the kitchen when I heard it."

A blubbering Ronald said, "I am so, so sorry, honey. I did not mean to be fresh. I love you and Ronnie with all my heart." He was bleeding profusely from the whack on top of the head from the plate Mointz had hit him with extremely hard.

Deidre grabbed peroxide and a bandage from the bathroom, leaving Mointz alone with Ronnie's father.

"Remember what I said," Mointz whispered to him. "You know I will be back again and again."

Real fear entered Ronald's eyes and Mointz decided he would make sure he slept over this evening to reinforce his warning to Ronald. He would also now have an easier time getting to the case Davis left him.

"Can I sleep at Ronnie's house in his tent tonight?" Mointz asked his mother once he got home. He had to explain the blood on his clothes to his mother.

"Are you sure they are feeling up to having you over given Mr. Mahoney's accident?" his mother asked. "Remember you have karate and swimming tomorrow night."

"Mrs. Mahoney said to call her if you needed to," he said and his mother gave the A OK.

Grandpa and Grandma Donnelly pulled into the driveway with their new Chevrolet Impala. Mointz's sister Kathy was there first to greet her grandparents, followed by Mointz, who sprinted out of the house and into his grandmother's arms.

"Grandpa and Grandma, how are you?" Mointz asked.

"Good, honey. Are you alright?" Grandma Rose asked her grandson. She could see the tears in his eyes.

"Yes, Grandma. I just have a problem with my allergies today."

"How are you, slugger?" his grandfather asked.

Mointz smiled, "I am good, Grandfather, as long as you play catch with me later today."

"Don't we always play catch when I come over here with your grandmother?"

Martha and Robert lit the barbeque as the party started for Rose and Leo's anniversary. Car after car arrived with family and friends of the family for the party.

Mointz gaped in awe at how everyone looked and remembered the day like it was yesterday, going back in his mind to the First Parallel. The memories were coming back to him as he scanned the yard and looked at the young faces of everyone back in 1975. He remembered it would be the last time he would see his Uncle Frankie before he succumbed to cancer shortly after July 4th, Mointz sat down with a glass of milk and his beloved chocolate syrup and wondered if he had the patience to live his life all over again. He certainly knew there would be exciting days like this one to keep the juices flowing, especially the corrective measures he had given to Ronald earlier in the day.

Two of Cristopher's uncles were arguing about whom the next president would be for almost an hour before Mointz could not take it anymore.

"Governor Jimmy Carter of Georgia is going to win; bank on it." Mointz said.

"Carter?" his Uncle Charlie said. "The peanut farmer?"

"He is going to win, guaranteed."

His other uncle just shook his head. "Son, what do you know about politics?"

"Only that the country will never forgive President Ford for pardoning Nixon."

"Oh," his Uncle Mark replied. "Got me on that one, kiddo."

"My father is really being super nice this evening. Look at all the snacks he bought us," Ronnie told Mointz as they were in the yellow and green pup tent in the Mahoney's backyard.

Mointz held a second conversation with Ronald earlier that finished driving his point across, even though Mointz almost apologized for hitting Ronald before twisting his arm and pushing him flat down on the table. Ronald groaned in excruciating pain. Mointz never knew if Ronald had hit his wife or his son, but the verbal abuse he inflicted on them when he was drinking had gone on far too long.

"Hopefully your father will stay that way, Ronnie," Mointz said.

Ronnie opened a bag of potato chips, grabbed a handful and passed the bag to Mointz. Mointz ate a few as he remembered flavored potato chips were a few years away yet.

"My dad promised to take us for Big Macs tomorrow," Ronnie said happily.

Mointz could not wait to bite into a 1975 saturated fatfilled Big Mac as the 2016 version did not taste the same. It did have a lot less calories, however.

"I need to run home in a minute," Mointz said.

"Don't go until I fall asleep. You know I hate being out here alone."

The way Ronnie said it reminded Mointz of the time he had first pitched a tent in the back yard of his house for his own boys. They made him sleep out there the whole night.

"We are in your parents' fenced in back yard. What could happen to you?"

"Can you wait until I at least fall asleep, please?"

"Sure Buddy. Now pass the licorice, please, before you eat it all."

They talked and laughed until they both fell asleep. Mointz woke suddenly from a dream of a naked Deidre Mahoney.

Mrs. Mahoney is Mrs. Robinson, Cristopher thought to himself as he slipped out of the tent. *She sure was drop-dead gorgeous.* What she ever had seen in Ronald was beyond him.

Shaking the cobwebs off, he ran to his parents' house only three houses up the street. Mointz grabbed a shovel and started to dig up the case exactly where Davis buried it three feet deep in the ground. It took him almost an hour to dig it up.

"That was an experience," he whispered to himself as he hid the titanium case up in his tree house where no one would find it. He would open the case and review its contents after swim practice tomorrow. Mointz ran back to Ronnie's and noticed Ronald watching him from his bedroom window when he slid back into the tent.

Chapter Eight

Swim practice for Cristopher went extremely well. He pushed his body to discover its limits. His abilities amazed him. He competed on the 12 to 16-year-old swim team and discovered he did not have much competition.

Martha, baby Sean and Mointz's sister Kathy met him with the car after swim practice. The Chevrolet Townsman station wagon made Mointz laugh every time he set eyes on it.

"How did practice go, sweetie?" Mrs. Mointz asked.

"Great, Momma. We have a new schedule," Mointz told her and handed her the photocopied sheet.

"So many practices for only a couple of meets, maybe you should try to join the advanced team. I just want you to have fun, dear. Remember you also have baseball and karate to fill your time. You have to decide what is best for you," she told him after pulling out of the parking lot.

"I really love all three, Mother. I hope you do not mind taking me."

"Why would I mind? You guys having fun is all that matters to your father and me. Now, who would like a slushy?"

"I would love one, Mom," Kathy said.

"So would I," Mointz added.

Martha pulled into the corner store, took baby Sean out of his car seat, and went into the store. "Whose turn is it to pick the lottery numbers?"

Mointz told her it was his. He had memorized the number for today when he looked it up on-line in the First Parallel. The extra ten thousand dollars would help the already-comfortable Mointz family even better.

Martha picked the number on the slip Mointz selected and purchased the ticket and slushies for her children.

They returned home before noon and Martha made her famous sandwich on the grill press: ham and cheese with a little mustard. Mointz skipped the chips and drank two big glasses of Ovaltine for extra vitamins. Once he finished eating, he rushed outside and scrambled up the tree house his grandfather had built for him to access the case he had hid there. The tree house was the perfect place to review the laptop's information and videos. Mointz took the case and opened it. He plugged the laptop into his treehouse's outlet and turned it on. He noticed three safety deposit box tickets in the case and the first set of vials in their small-protected nuclear powered cases. Each case had a full set of vials and a laptop.

A note had been attached to the laptop:

Dr. Cris,

I hope all is well. Once you add the password into the password-protected laptop, click on folder #47. All my notes are in there and a video describing my eleven weeks in the Second Parallel before I left for the big lab in the sky. I also placed a map where I will exhume myself later on to prove to myself I was here before. Confusing just writing it. Be well, my friend, and see you in 41 years.

Dr. Trent

Mointz typed the password into the special Apple-built computer which was to last at least forty years and clicked on folder #47. He found a QuickTime video file and clicked on it. He cringed when he noticed how sickly his friend looked on the laptop's 17-inch screen once the video started.

Hello, my friend, and welcome to the Second Parallel. I am your host, Doctor Trent Davis. For the next hour or so, you get to learn some interesting things you do not know about yourself and the future.

Davis explained the Gennifer situation first and Mointz took great delight in knowing that he would have her support.

Let us start with the good news first. It is the end of April now. Both your mother and Mrs. Moore are pregnant with child, and I know the cloned embryos implanted successfully. Please do not ask how I know. In Folder #48, you can click on the video file which says "last video." It is the taped meeting of the last meeting with me and the Vice President before I left for the Second Parallel. Watch intently what transpired. Say, it is pretty cool being eight again, eh?

Dr. Trent practically coughed up a lung after his last sentence. Mointz could tell the radiation poisoning had taken its toll on his friend.

Yes, I am a bit under the weather and my testes have practically shrunk to nothing. However, you succeeding here is the key to my and the rest of the world's survival.

Davis laughed and started to cough again.

I ran a few experiments and I have to tell you I am now more confident than ever in the science we discovered. You can and will succeed. I hope you have discovered the extra oxygen capacity in your lungs and you are three inches taller than you were before. You will easily grow to six foot six or seven. Perfect for your swimming adventures. Train hard, my friend, and as you turn fifteen, start taking the supplements I have placed for you in a few locations. I also have formulae in my folder, which you can send to chemists for the perfect vitamins. In one of the safety deposit boxes, there is at least a four-year supply. Keep following the nutrition disc from the first case.

You are eight and a half, but you should have the strength of an eighteen-year-old. You absolutely can protect yourself.

Enjoy the next nine years and study the classics. The public library will be your new best friend. I did include four iPads with massive storage with your favorite movies, books, and songs for your entertainment. Do not get caught with them.

Miraculously, your father inherited a couple hundred thousand dollars from a long lost relative. He will receive it tomorrow as a matter of fact. Learn the market and invest.

Davis took off his scaly cap; his hair was almost gone.

Now that I have your attention, listen to me. If you need me, come to me, but only if you need me. Go to the Vice President if you have to as well. Do whatever it takes to be successful.

I thought about having you save John Lennon for a while, and then I realized it would mean more Yoko and who would want that? So, let it be.

He smiled and took a few deep breaths before coughing a few times.

Do a good job, Cristopher. Make me proud and try to have a little fun in the next nine years. Please do not get discouraged. This is the time to develop your learning process. Patience is a virtue my boy. Learn my friend and learn well. I will be there for you in the end; now go and enjoy your destiny.

Mointz felt more alone than ever after the video ended. He turned on some videos of his children, finding comfort for a while at least. Lastly, he watched the video of his last meeting with Davis and Ellis, who was there via teleconference, telling him Gennifer would be part of this mission with knowledge of the First Parallel. Mointz smiled and could not wait for the next ten years to end.

"C'mon son, do a good job," Robert shouted as Mointz sparred with the fourteen-year-old David Conley, resident bully of Barrington, Rhode Island and Master Di Yang's Kung Fu Studio.

David Conley liked Mointz and the feeling was mutual, even though no one else was a big fan of Conley. Mointz liked David because he was comfortable in his own skin and did not care either way if people liked him or not.

Over the last week, Mointz had spent a considerable amount of time getting acquainted with the Second Parallel. He was more than capable of pulverizing the young Conley in this match up with his genetically-altered body.

The two boys bowed to each other and Conley smiled slightly at Mointz. The older Conley had received his black belt a year ago and Mointz had made it to green belt status. They were both the same size so it was an even match in that respect. However, Mointz had the strength and, of course, a far deeper self-defense knowledge than his belt level portrayed.

Conley came flying in at Mointz and gave him a kick to the solar plexus that bounced off Mointz like a sponge ball. Mointz wanted to make Conley work to best him and he returned Conley's initial maneuver with a sweep of Conley's legs which took Conley off of his feet. David bounced up like a cat and immediately gave Mointz a punch to the helmet that actually stunned Cristopher and had him taking a step back. David followed up by kicking Mointz in his side.

Not to be outdone, Mointz slapped Conley with an open hand on the side of his head that embarrassed Conley more than anything else, as the helmet he had on protected him. Mointz again swept out Conley's feet, knocking him on his rear end.

Cristopher could see the frustration in David's face and he allowed Conley to land two body blows. The parents and students at the Dojo watched intently as the two boys showed superior skill to anyone else in the class. Mointz and Conley continued to spar back and forth until Mointz took the proverbial dive so Conley could win the session by choking Mointz out. He let Conley win, but made sure he knew he could have easily been on the losing end as well. As they bowed to show each other respect, the two boys received a rousing round of applause from everyone.

"Good bout, Mointz," Conley acknowledged as he slapped him on the back.

"You too, Dave. It was an experience. I hope I gave you a run for your money," Mointz replied.

Conley smiled and nodded, knowing full well he had almost lost. Conley lived a few blocks from Mointz and Mointz decided to befriend him. Conley was the number one student in school as well as the Dojo in his karate class. Mointz had the feeling he would be a good asset in the future as Conley would become a successful Cardiac Surgeon and ironically a Brown University medical school graduate. Mointz would be at Brown during Conley's residency there. He could only imagine Conley would be there for him if he needed him in the future.

Chapter Nine

Over the next year, Mointz studied hard and continued to dominate in the pool, at the Dojo, and on the ball field while hanging out with Ronnie and David Conley. He also kept Ronald, on the straight and narrow. His first erection occurred during a dream of Deidre to whom he had become strangely close. Cristopher laughed his head off when it happened.

The Mointzes had a great year Mointz thought, in his first year in the Second Parallel. The two lottery wins, a mysterious inheritance from an uncle and good times all around had the family feeling grateful the rest of 1975 and into the summer of 1976.

On the Fourth of July, exactly one year after Mointz's memories had returned, the United States was celebrating its bicentennial anniversary and Mointz decided to visit Ronnie after his run. Ronald was working overtime at the plant and Deidre joined the two boys shooting baskets in the driveway. Deidre, a real estate agent, had taken the day off and loved spending time outside.

"You are a natural, Mrs. Mahoney," Mointz said, as she swished free throw after free throw.

They all were playing a game of Horse when Martha stopped by with two-year-old Seanie in the carriage to check on the boy.

"Hello Deidre, how are you today?" Martha asked.

"Trying to keep up with the young guns," she replied a little bit winded from running after the ball.

"Why don't the two of you come over and relax and have a barbeque?"

Deidre smiled, "I would not want to impose."

"We could impose," Ronnie said.

"Sure you could," Mointz added. "We do not like half the people who are going to be there anyway and the other half would love to see you."

"Cristopher!" his mother exclaimed. "What an awful thing to say about our crabby relatives."

"I am right though Mother, yes?"

"Yes, you are. Whatever am I going to do with you?" she asked. "We would love to have you two."

"Then Ronnie and I will be there."

Mointz high-fived Ronnie and laughed to himself. Another day with the beautiful Deidre and his family and friends would be a fabulous blessing.

The Mointzes's Fourth of July celebration went off without a hitch as the bicentennial fireworks displays continued through the night. Mointz soaked in the historical significance of the day as he sat outside.

Jimmy Carter was indeed the Democratic Nominee for President, much to the surprise of Mointz's uncles. Carter was just months away from becoming the 39th President of the United States. He would go on to experience failures in foreign policy that would help ensure that Mointz's hero, Ronald Reagan, would take The White House in 1980.

Tonight Mointz had one thing on his mind and one thing only; he had to complete the first task on his list the panel had set up and placed in the security road map that Mointz possessed.

Daniel Jacobson, a carpenter, had taken a van, captured a five-year-old girl named Valerie Cutler, and given her three years of hell, before killing her in the woods of Maine. Jacobson lived only three streets from Mointz. Getting to him would not be a huge problem for Mointz.

The reason this particular situation was critical to the mission at first puzzled Mointz until a blurb in Davis's roadmap journal revealed Dr. Brendan Dubois, a popular member of the Scientific Council on Climate Change, had been initially charged with young Valerie's disappearance as a result of being in the wrong place at the wrong time. The 56-year-old Dubois became blackballed in the scientific community, a situation that buried his climate control findings for years until DNA evidence, which linked the convicted pedophile Jacobson to the crime, exonerated him.

Mointz planned to take a walk with the Mointzes's new family puppy, Drew, who needed to go outside for potty training. The time was getting close to nine pm, the hour Jacobson would kidnap Valerie this evening through her bedroom window.

"I am going to take Drew for a walk. He needs to go potty," Mointz told his mother as she put Sean down for the night.

"Okay, sweetie. Be careful; it is very late."

Mointz smiled and high-tailed it out of the house as fast as he could. He arrived at Ronnie's house with the puppy in hand and rang the bell.

"Hello, Cristopher. What are you doing here at this late hour?" Deidre asked her son's friend. Mointz knew Ronald was at work this evening.

"Can Ronnie come out and go for a walk with me? I am training Drew to go outside," Mointz asked, trying to portray his angel qualities.

Deidre petted Drew, "Sure, Cristopher." Deidre called Ronnie, who was ready in a flash and out the door to join Mointz.

"I need you to do me a favor," Mointz told Ronnie.

"Sure, anything you need."

"I have to get the bat I left at the Clarks, but I am not supposed to go past Duggan Street. Can you stay here and walk Drew while I run and go get the bat?"

"No sweat. Geez."

"I will be right back," Mointz said. His watch showed eight fifty-three and he knew he had to get a move on and hustle over to the Clarks' home.

Police reports stated that as the 'Barney Miller' show started at nine pm, the Clarks had heard a vehicle peel out in front of their house, but had thought nothing of it at the time.

Mointz arrived just as Daniel Jacobson entered Valerie's room on the first floor of the ranch house to abduct her. Mointz's heart raced as he grabbed the bat he had hidden in the bushes earlier in the day and slipped into the van to wait for Jacobson.

What seemed like an eternity in reality was only two minutes, as Mointz watched Jacobson run across the yard with Valerie who had her hands, feet, and mouth all duct taped up.

"What the hell!" Jacobson exclaimed before the nine-year-old Mointz connected with his 34 ounce Louisville Slugger with the top of Jacobson's head.

"Good night, asshole," Cristopher shouted and grabbed Valerie from the now knocked-to-Queer-Street Jacobson.

"Oh my God! Oh my God!" Henry Clark screamed as he ran outside to see the carnage in his yard and watched Mointz take the tape off his little girl.

"Daddy, that man grabbed me and taped me all up," little Valerie said. "Cristopher hit him with a bat."

Her father held her tight. "Cristopher, what did you do?"

Mointz explained what had happened and the police arrived shortly. Ronnie showed up breathless with the puppy and Robert and Martha ran down the road with Kathy and Baby Sean in a carriage.

"Are you alright, son?" a frightened Robert asked his son.

"Yes, father," he replied, as his mother hugged him after they heard what had happened from the police and Mr. Clark. "I forgot my bat and we came down with the puppy to retrieve it."   He winked at Ronnie whose mother had just arrived.

"He is a genuine hero," Mr. Clark said.

"Young man, you sure are," Officer Todd stated. "That was incredibly brave, Cristopher."

"It was really nothing," he replied with a shrug.

Mointz went for his morning run, now five miles instead of the three point one he used to do. Since the Fourth of July fell on a Friday, his father was home to scramble some eggs and have them ready for his return.

"How many English muffins would you like?" Martha asked her son.

"Are they whole grain?" Mointz asked, forgetting whole wheat still had a few years to go before it hit mainstream.

"What do you mean, Cristopher?" his mother asked inquisitively.

"Just wondering what type of Triticum Aestivuum was cultivated for Mrs. Thomas' Muffins. I read it in the Encyclopedia Britannica."

Martha smiled. "You spend too much time in those books just to show up your father. We did not study a lot of science in school. I studied American Literature and your father studied Political Science."

"You are not supposed to give away our secrets, dear," her husband said, kissing her on the cheek. "Now young man, are you alright after last night?"

"Pop, as I told you last night, I am perfectly capable of processing the incident and deciphering the pros and cons on how it will affect my mental state of mind. I am truly fine and dandy." Mointz said. He loved to confuse his parents by speaking to them as if he were 50-years-old, which if you added his time in the First Parallel to his time in the Second Parallel, he was. Mointz confused even himself on that one.

"Sorry I asked," his father said with a smile and, as Mointz wanted, changed the subject. "You ready for the big game tonight?"

Mointz nodded. Tonight was the South Sectional Division All-Star Baseball game and he was the star pitcher for the 12-year-old little league team. He skipped Minor League Ball and went right to Little League this year.

The town of Barrington embraced the team as they tried to become the first Rhode Island team to represent New England in the Little League World Series.

"Dad, it really was not a big deal. You would have done the same thing if it was you."

"Probably, but not when I was nine."

Grandpa Leo came in and patted Mointz on the head. "The nine-year-old little soldier." Grandpa Leo had just retired from the Barrington Police Force last year. "I heard all of the details at the coffee shop this morning. Nice to know my family called me right away to tell me about it."

"Sorry, Dad," Martha said. "I had a real busy morning with Sean."

Her father kissed her cheek. "That is alright, honey. Your father knows it now. What I cannot figure out is how our little hero here did what he did and acted so quickly."

"It just looked wrong."

"What a young man," Grandpa Leo replied.

"I am a young princess," Kathy said, making sure she was not left out in any conversation.

Mointz had to keep from laughing too hard. He knew his sister to be always the actress. Kathy was wearing leotards and a tiara from the dance recital she had participated in last week. It was already ratty from wear and tear.

"Yes, Kathy, you sure are a princess," Grandpa Leo told her.

Kathy smiled brightly and pirouetted before she took a bow and made a grand exit from the family room.

Grandpa Leo just shook his head laughing and told his son-in-law, "She will be quite the little actress someday."

"More than likely," replied Robert.

"How did fishing go yesterday, Dad?" Martha asked.

"I caught a few plaices, nothing special."

"What is a plaices?" his daughter inquired.

"An edible marine flatfish of the North Atlantic American Waters—Pleuronectes Platessa," Mointz said, to his nonplussed parents and the surprise of his grandfather.

"A soldier and a scholar, you, my boy, could be the President someday if you wanted to. Too bad Reagan is losing the delegate count to Ford in the polls. You could have helped him out as his Vice President," said Grandpa Leo.

"It is alright Grandpa. The Gipper will beat Carter next time."

Mointz decided to walk down to the Barrington Town Beach to try to clear his head. Last night had no ill effects on him. He had saved a five-year-old from sheer disaster and it felt good. His main concern was the baseball game he was about to play. Mointz batted left-handed so his true power would not be revealed from the right side of the plate. It would look very suspicious that a nine-year-old could hit a baseball 400 feet. Even batting left-handed, Mointz could hit the ball a country mile.

There was nothing in the roadmaps about him being a dominating baseball player at an early age. In the First Parallel, he was a great baseball player, but this time around, swimming would replace baseball. The competitive juices flowed through Mointz and he wanted to play his best. He could not wait to start playing football again with two good knees and dreamed of becoming a pro player. He knew he could, but he had other priorities. An Olympic champion would have to suffice.

He had started to drop hints to his parents that the Olympics were his destiny and they started to buy into the idea by his performances in the pool over the past year.

The loneliness the panel had predicted started to get to Mointz. He missed his children and he missed the companionship of a woman. The smells of some of his pretty female teachers and of one Deidre Mahoney had his hormones racing. However, it was the boys that hurt his heart the most.

Mointz pulled out his iPad and gazed at a picture of his children through tears; he smiled and wished he could fast-forward his life to the point he had left off in the First Parallel. He chuckled, thinking about Gennifer and Erin and his soap opera love life. Mointz knew Davis and Ellis had manipulated him.

However, he understood their reasons. He knew his survival depended on trusting them as they trusted him. The nine-year-old Mointz started back home knowing he probably just needed to get laid, but who would hop in the sack with a prepubescent Mointz?

Chapter Ten

Mointz led the Barrington Mariners, the Major League Division Little League Team to the Little League World Series before losing in the finals to the Japanese team. He had another two cracks at them in consecutive years, finally winning the title in 1978 at the age of eleven and a half, with Ronnie on the team.

Baseball, swimming and karate still dominated Mointz's sports life until freshman year of high school where football replaced baseball, much to the chagrin of Coach Sullivan, the school's long-time baseball coach. Now, on the fourth of February in 1984, Cristopher Mointz turned seventeen and he fully expected a surprise party at home. The past nine years had been full of adventure and loneliness: adventure because of the little mini missions the Panel sent him on and loneliness because of his longing for the boys and adult companionship. The pool had become his sanctuary and Mointz had brilliantly followed the roadmap he received from Davis.

The young Mointz in the last nine years had scanned old newspapers from the laptops Davis had left for suspicious activities and stopped a murder or two and several muggings, saved a young woman who fell on the train tracks from an oncoming locomotive, and climbed a tree now and then to rescue a cat for a

70

panicked neighbor. His most satisfying experience had been preventing Father Richard Houle from hurting another young boy at the age of eleven.

Mointz wanted the abuse from Father Houle wiped from his memory until the day at Cathedral Camp on a warm August day when Houle attacked Mointz in a storage shed after a softball game. When Houle tried to grab the young Mointz, a noose encircled Houle's neck quicker than a Texas Cowboy. Mointz had him hanging by a beam in the shed almost as quickly. Mointz hoped the Lord could forgive his Old Testament type of justice someday, as well as the justice he had handed out to an assortment of evildoers.

Mointz pulled into Ronnie's driveway where Ronnie and Ronald were waiting. Ronald had become close to Mointz over the years and thanked him for "straightening him out." What Mointz could not straighten out was Ronald's womanizing with half of the desperate housewives in Barrington, which he knew took place right under the noses of Deidre and Ronnie. Deidre always tried to be pleasant around her husband, but Mointz knew she was lonely.

"Happy seventeenth, my boy," Ronald said.

"Look at all these people," Cristopher said noticing the cars lined up all the way down the street.

"I wanted to throw it bro," Ronnie said. "We all love you and you do so much for everyone else; it is about time someone did something for you."

"And here I believed you had a toxic influence on all of these people. You are lucky they all like me." Mointz choked back tears. His parents had thrown his seventeenth birthday party in the First Parallel. Mointz made note of the significant change.

The Mointzes and Deidre met Cristopher at the door with hugs and kisses.

"Happy Birthday, son," his father told him and moved to the side to let his grandparents in for an embrace.

"Grandma and Grandpa, what are you doing here on a Saturday night?"

"Celebrating our grandson's birthday with his family and friends," Grandma Rose replied as Seanie and Kathy hugged him. Mointz choked up.

"Look at you," Grandpa Leo said. "Six feet four and still growing like a weed with the body of Adonis." Leo was extremely proud of the boy who had now become a man in every way.

Friends and family alike greeted the popular athlete and when his current girlfriend, Deborah Howard, kissed him passionately, all of the girls in the room reeked of jealousy.

The party brought in half of Barrington and went on late into the night. The clock passed midnight before all of the stragglers left the house. Ronald left for work for the midnight-to-eight shift, as Mointz, Deidre and Ronnie sat in the kitchen and feasted on more chocolate cake.

"Ronnie and Dee, thank you so much for the wonderful night." Mointz called Deidre, "Dee," though he could not remember why or when he had started.

"You mean the world to us, Cristopher," said Deidre and then took a bite of her piece of cake and smiled. Mointz wanted to lick the little bit of frosting she left on her lip.

"Dude, watching every girl get all hot and bothered as you sucked face with Deborah Howard cracked me up. Must be nice dating a college sophomore," Ronnie said.

"I actually liked her roommate first, but I ended up with Deborah."

"Isn't her roommate a grad student?"

"Yes, but it did not last long between us. I think only a couple of dates."

Mointz dated woman older than him for the last two years and he spent most of his time wishing it was Deidre he dated. He could never shake her out of his mind.

"I love watching Deborah get jealous," Ronnie said and excused himself for a minute to pull out Mointz's present.

Deidre smiled at Cristopher and the young Mointz, full of testosterone and the charm of the 49-year-old that he was, decided he could no longer hold back his desire for her. "You were jealous, too?" he asked and before she could answer, Mointz pulled her to him and kissed her as passionately as one could kiss a beautiful 32-year-old.

"My god, you have no idea how badly I want you," she said.

"Probably only a tenth of how badly I want you."

They kissed again and Deidre whispered in his ear, "Please stay tonight Cristopher, please."

Mointz smiled as Ronnie came down the stairs and gave him his present wrapped with violet and yellow paper. The only thing running through Mointz's mind was how gonadotropicly hard Deidre had made him.

"Open it, Cristopher. The present is from all of us," said Deidre.

Mointz had hoped it would be a skimpy negligee for Deidre to wear, but that was a fantasy. He opened the present to reveal the ski jacket he had planned to purchase with his birthday money. The Mointzes were doing very well financially, but stayed grounded in Barrington's already upscale community. Mointz had "learned" investing from his father and the Mointzes had purchased a beautiful home right outside North Conway, New Hampshire, near King Pine Ski Mountain.

Mointz's parents bought him a brand new set of K2 skis for his birthday and now the Mahoneys bought the jacket to match.

"This is incredible. I will wear it proudly."

"Your parents invited us next weekend to ski with all of you," Deidre said to Mointz with a grin.

Ronnie laughed. "Your sister is all up for it."

"Please tell me you are not dating the drama queen. Heaven help us."

"Maybe."

"Are you staying tonight, Cristopher?" Deidre asked.

"If I am wanted. Ronnie and I have a game or two to play on Atari."

Mointz and Ronnie put their dishes in the sink and were ready to head downstairs into the apartment the Mahoneys had set up for Ronnie exactly like the Mointzes had done for Cristopher.

"I will go get the game," Ronnie said and ran upstairs to get it from the office Deidre had used for all of Mointz's gifts.

"Do not forget your present," Deidre told Mointz, standing on her tip toes to give him a small kiss.

"Believe me; I would not forget it for all the tea in Ireland."

###

Ronnie's sleep habits were perfect for Mointz; they allowed him to slip out and accomplish some of his missions. A truck could drive through the Mahoneys' house and Ronnie would not wake up. Tonight, Mointz was going up, not out, into the arms of Deidre "Dee" Mahoney, who he had desired since the First Parallel. Dee was waiting for him in all of her glory when Mointz arrived.

"Are you positive this is a good idea?" Mointz asked before Dee pulled him to her and they became one. Clothes flew off and Mointz buried his chest against Deidre's after they had made love the first time and he had brought his new lover to a climax she had never reached before.

Mointz and Deidre spent the next two hours discovering every inch of each other's bodies bringing the other to internal ecstasy more than once.

"Where on earth did you learn all of that?" Deidre asked.

Mointz smiled. "One such as I have acquired many talents, my lady. The gift of bringing a woman to climax is just one of them."

Deidre could barely catch her breath as Mointz entered her again for the last time. They came simultaneously and wrapped in each other's arms.

"My husband cheats on me. I have known it for a long time," she told him.

"I know. I have always known. I am very sorry."

"Don't be. You were the one who straightened him out. I watched you hit him with the plate when you were young and I heard every word you told him. You saved us from years of abuse."

Mointz shrugged and definitely felt embarrassed. "You are one of the most beautiful women on the planet, inside and out. My God, you are as sexy as a supermodel and as warm and kind a person as I will ever encounter. Screw Ronald if he does not appreciate it," Mointz said, noticing for the first time Ronald kept none of his belongings in the room. "He does not even sleep here does he?"

"Not for years. Pathetic. We cannot do this again."

"Sure we can," Mointz said. "I am no ordinary 17-year-old."

She cringed when he mentioned his age. "Explain, please."

"There is so much pressure on me to be the all-American boy, future Olympian, scholar, lawyer, and politician, people forget I am still a person. I have needs too, Dee, more than you can ever imagine and I need you."

"What are you saying, Cristopher?"

"If I tell you the most amazingly ridiculous story ever told, will you wait until the end before you comment?"

"Of course, silly, you know I will listen and believe you. You are the brightest person anyone has ever met."

"Ever wonder why I am that way? How did a nine-year-old know how to be at his friend's house to stop a child predator from kidnapping his friend's sister? How did I know to be at the beach to save another friend's brother with Down Syndrome from drowning? And, how does a 17-year-old know every erotic spot on a woman's body?"

"What are you saying, you are psychic?"

Mointz knew he could trust Deidre, and Ronnie was only months away from committing suicide in the First Parallel if he did not intervene. Deidre, a law school student and real estate agent, was incredibly bright. Mointz needed to associate with bright people. Cristopher also knew things would change as Ronnie had thrown his seventeenth birthday party instead of his parents.

"I will be right back," he told her, dressed and went downstairs to retrieve his backpack.

When he returned, he pulled out his Apple Power Book laptop.

"What is that thing?" Deidre asked.

Mointz smiled and booted up the laptop. "It is a computer from 2016—a long way from here," he said and kissed her. Mointz then went on to explain everything to Deidre during the next three hours, including the heartbreaking story of Ronnie's suicide through pictures. They held each other a good long time before breaking the embrace.

"I have always loved you, Cristopher. This is just insane."

"You believe me, yes?"

"I believe you and I love you. Please tell me you can change the world. Please tell me you were sent because you have the power," Deidre said, as she rested her head on his chest. "You received your memories back the day you hit Ronald?"

"Yes, dear. I do not know why I did it, but it felt good at the time."

"What can I do to help you in your "mission," as you say? Selfishly, being a mother, it would mean the world to me if I could help now that I know about Ronnie. Your sons are absolutely beautiful. I can only imagine how much you love them, as I know how I love Ronnie. I am at your disposal, Cristopher," Deidre told him. "Just please tell me you did not come back to seduce me and you have real feelings for me because I know I love you."

"This is all new to me Dee, believe me. I know I love you back," Mointz told her kissing her again and again.

"You have spent a lot of time thinking about all of this I am sure. I understand where you are coming from as I am sure that it is not easy being you."

"I'd better get out of here before I get all hot and bothered again and we start things we would really like to finish and we never let each other go." *Cristopher Mointz now has his Mrs. Robinson,* he thought to himself as he finished getting dressed.

"Do all swimmers shave everything?" Deidre asked staring at Mointz's body.

"Oh yeah, it is very metrosexual."

"What is metrosexual?"

"Watch 'Sex and the City' in a few years and you will learn all about it."

Mointz snuck back downstairs and, as predicted, Ronnie was still out cold. Mointz was exhausted from the party and the lovemaking, but he could not sleep; all he could think about was Deidre. He went into the kitchen and took out the ice cream cake and started to devour it when Deidre came down.

"Can I have a bite?" Deidre asked and kissed him. "Tastes good, Mr. Mointz."

"Cannot sleep, eh?"

"My head was spinning and I heard you down here. Would you like me to make you some eggs? I know they are your favorite. God, I know everything about you, or so I thought up until this morning."

Mointz kissed Deidre as she started cooking breakfast. He asked her if she felt that everything was different now.

"Well, I needed more adventure and I could definitely use another orgasm or two."

He laughed and, as he went in for another kiss, heard Ronnie walking up the stairs.

"You two are up early. Did I miss something?"

"I was hungry and your mother graciously offered to make me breakfast."

Deidre smiled as she knew that Mointz and Ronnie loved to eat her big morning meal. "Bacon and eggs coming up, Mr. President and his best friend." She and a few of the boys' friends called Mointz "the President," as they all thought he was destined for great things.

"Thank you, my lady, that would be lovely," Mointz responded.

"How goes the day?" Martha asked her son when he returned home from the Mahoneys at eight-thirty in the morning. "Are you exhausted from last night? You look like you have not slept a wink."

"I am going to take a nap and Deidre is taking Ronnie and me out later for a special birthday dinner and movie."

"She mentioned that last night. God will forgive you if you miss mass one day. Rest up; it is not every weekend that you get a Sunday off from everything."

"Where are Dad and my siblings?"

"They are out for breakfast. He told me to tell you to relax today and enjoy the day."

Mointz hugged his mother. "Thank you for everything last night. I had the time of my life."

"Sweetie, Ronnie was so cute when he came over and asked to host the party. He is the one you need to thank and you owe a big thank you to Deidre."

"Believe me, I gave her one."

Mointz went upstairs to his bedroom and hopped right into bed. He slept until almost two in the afternoon. When he had left Deidre's earlier they had planned to run around the neighborhood. They both were avid runners and she had been his running partner for the last four years as they had both joined the Barrington Runners Club. Ronnie loved his hockey and football and running was definitely not for him. Both families supported Mointz and Deidre at several races they had run and the families made outings out of each and every one of them.

Mointz and Deidre decided on a 10K run this afternoon. Deidre was dressed in a blue Gortex jogging suit and was ready to jog when Mointz showed up at her house.

"Do you really want to help?" Mointz asked Deidre as he stretched.

"You know I do," Deidre replied. She put on her gloves and they started down the driveway.

"I need a safe house to set up so I do not have to worry about being caught with the things I have from the First Parallel. People are going to start thinking I need to be in the Looney Bin. A cleaning lady cleans my third-floor bedroom and I have outgrown my tree house. It is not up to par anymore."

"What are you looking for?"

"A beach house, maybe, where I can set up shop and receive mail more easily. I have several fake IDs I can use. My laptops, my assortment of weapons, and several other possessions to help me in this mission need a home. Not many people will sell a seventeen-year-old a house, even if he has money. I figured with you as my real estate agent, we could easily work something out," Mointz said as they picked up the pace on the chilly February afternoon. The sun was bright and it kept the bone-chilling Rhode Island February wind from making their run uncomfortable. "Please make it a decent place and not one of those heinous listings you have now. All of the houses look like they are from the seventies."

"Umm, Mr. Mointz, they are from the seventies. We just left them remember?" She said breathing heavily. Her hair was in a ponytail and Mointz thought she looked amazing. Her smile as they ran had Mointz believing she looked at peace and in love with him.

"Oh, yeah, I forgot," he replied. "I will show you pictures of my style in my time. It will make me feel right at home."

"Do you have money for all of these grand ideas you have? This will not be cheap, the way you are talking."

He kept pace with Deidre, who could run like the wind. "Even if I did not, one hot stock tip or a few bets on a game or two and I will be all set. Believe me; I am well taken care of." Deidre ran at a faster pace, trying to see if she could get her new lover to beg for mercy. Mointz just smiled and slapped her on the bum, sprinting by to show Deidre he had more in him than he ever let on. He slowed down a bit and let her catch up. "Privacy is the key. Now that my parents bought me a new Bronco in New Hampshire, I can move more freely."

"Hey, how did you know? And what is up with you not even breathing heavy?"

"One, my lungs, shall I say, have some extra capacity to make sure I am a good athlete and two, Martha and Robert bought me a Bronco in the First Parallel. You guys went to New Hampshire as well and this is the weekend that Ronald moves out. Am I on to something?"

"I do not even want to know how you know all this, but you are absolutely correct on all accounts."

Mointz kissed Deidre on the cheek and went to an all-out sprint. Deidre could not keep up.

"Not fair, Mointz. Not fair at all," she cried out, giggling and smiling for the first time in eons.

Chapter Eleven

Mointz was indeed correct, as he now owned a brand new Bronco—black with tan interior. Deidre was on her way to being single again. Her impending divorce would be amicable, Mointz knew, as Ronald had a hot young 22-year-old on his arm and, of course, Deidre had him.

"This is the fifth house I have taken you through," Deidre told Mointz. They were quickly becoming inseparable, which was a challenge because of Ronnie.

"We can christen this one as well," Mointz said, nibbling on her neck as she giggled in his arms. All Deidre did now was giggle and Mointz loved every minute of it.

"So tell me, Mr. Mointz, does it serve your purpose or do we need to continue our search?"

"This is the house I purchased when I got divorced in the First Parallel from Erin. Yes, I like it. I like it a lot."

"Uh, you are incorrigible at times."

"Hey, I did not realize it would be what I really wanted and it has been an absolute blast spending time with you looking at these."

"Then remember on Valentine's Day our new little corporation purchases your future, or shall I say, former home." Deidre felt so full of puppy love for Mointz, she just laughed. They had been together for the last ten days, both of them exactly what the other needed at the moment.

They kissed and Mointz said, "Thank you for doing this for me. You have been absolutely incredible. In more ways than I can tell you."

She smiled brightly as her cheeks turned as red as the sweater she wore. "I know I am cool." Deidre looked around and started to imagine Mointz's memories here with his beloved boys. They were all he talked about. "How hard was it going back to being an eight-year-old? I cannot believe they sent you that far back."

"My best friend, Trent Davis, set it all up. He was my only true friend after Ronnie. He actually moves next door in 2013. Now, Lady Jane, how fast can you get this place up to speed so I can move in?" Mointz asked, not wanting to jump too deeply into conversation with Deidre about Ronnie.

Deidre sat down on the kitchen table and opened a folder. "Says here you can close within a week. I have an attorney friend, Linda. She can also do corporate legal work. You did say that after the 88 Olympic Games, you were going to buy this anyway."

"If I win, I guess. No one can touch me now in the pool. I lay off at times to keep it semi-competitive. I need to keep the press guessing. When I win the world championship, things will change."

"Why don't you just win the Gold Medal this year in LA?"

"Because the Soviets and all the other eastern bloc countries are going to boycott the games. It is retribution for the West boycotting the 1980 Olympics in Moscow. I do not want to compete twice in a row. The Seoul Games in 1988 heal the world. It is called 'The American Invasion of Asia.' The sponsorships after the games will allow me to easily buy this place then, if not before."

"It is settled then. We will get this place fixed up and exactly to your specifications, ASAP. You now have a home base." Deidre smiled at Mointz and held his hand on the table lovingly.

"The sooner the better, love, because I have a few things I need to accomplish."

Mointz felt at home for the first time since he had come to the Second Parallel. He wondered if Deidre had been part of the plan Davis had put together. Mointz had once told Davis how close he grew to Deidre until Ronnie died and how Deidre wasted her life away with the pills and alcohol which brought her to Wet Brain status. He had told Davis he would not let her sink to that level, no matter what, this time and he had been pretty sure Davis had believed him.

"When exactly are you supposed to meet your wife and the Gennifer girl?" she asked, with more curiosity than malice. "I know you are not here for me, but I will treasure our time together and I will appreciate you for saving Ronnie and me. Thank you for saving Ronnie." Deidre embraced Mointz in tears.

"The roadmap I was given makes sure you and Ronnie are saved. He is my best friend and you are and were the love of my life. I needed both of you when I was eighteen and neither of you were there."

"I am sorry, Cristopher. Please just make sure the roadmap, or whatever you call it, treats us well. It is all I ask." Deidre tried to speak through constant tears.

Mointz kissed the top of her head. "It does not matter one iota what happened before. All that matters are the events in this parallel. I have received the enormous task of saving the world and, by God, I am going to do it. Maybe not the way we want, but we will have a puncher's chance."

Deidre looked up at Mointz. "You are avoiding my original question about the women in your life."

"Thanksgiving next year. We have plenty of time to figure it all out by then. We will save Ronnie and we will figure us out as well. I am not losing you twice. One of the women is my children's mother and another is a team member. We are together and I love you, one day at a time, princess."

"I cannot believe you were divorced. That is hard to believe," Deidre said.

"All depends on the person that you marry; believe me. I am fortunate that I can learn from prior mistakes and I've learned that life must go on no matter what."

"His death really hurt you, didn't it?"

"I loved him and it hurt like hell," Mointz said and went on to explain Father Houle's abuse toward Ronnie and him. He also explained how he handled it.

"When did he hurt you and my Ronnie?"

"We were eleven. Believe me, please, the pain once in his eyes is now completely gone. He always felt he should have protected me and I felt the same way. It hurt him to his soul."

Deidre slipped the huaraches off her feet and pulled Mointz into the bedroom of the beach house. "Let us christen the bed. We are buying it anyway. The house comes with all the furniture. No one has ever lived here."

"Yeah, I could definitely use a little Deidre right now," he said, following her into the bedroom.

They made love and then Deidre held her lover tenderly. She felt all she could offer him was her love and compassion right now. Her heart was now his and his alone. Nothing could replace the love for her son, but Deidre was now experiencing a different kind of love, one built on a foundation of trust, passion, and understanding. She knew that Ronnie and she were the cross he bore in the First Parallel.

Mointz had to relive his life, correct the wrongs and improve the rights. Deidre could only imagine the pressure he felt to succeed. As she lay on his bare chest, she felt his heart beat; it was the heart of a champion. Mointz needed her to feel safe and she felt safe with him. Though neglected for years, Deidre had an adventurous side to her. In the last ten years of living a mundane life as a real estate agent and now law school student, Mointz's mission was exactly what the doctor had ordered for her.

"Now, what is next on your mission list?" she asked.

"Not really important," he replied.

"Cristopher," Deidre began, "if in fact I am in this, I am in this all the way."

"Fine then," Mointz stated sternly. "I have to eliminate three members of a criminal cell, who are about to reign terror on the city of Worcester, Massachusetts. They will butcher women, almost 40 that we know about, over a three-year period. I know where to find them at certain times and places. These men kill the mother of one of Davis's colleagues. This is one favor I cannot wait to do for them.

"Then I will help."

"No, not this time, love. You can help me prepare, but you cannot be caught near these three."

"They are that bad then?"

"Worse than you could ever imagine; trust me on this. I need to use all of my superpowers for this mission."

Joseph Carvalho and his twin brother Ted pulled up to their friend David's house in the suburbs of Worcester in a town called Holden. The date was Washington's Birthday Holiday and school was out for Massachusetts. The twins and David were High School Seniors and had spent the morning preparing for their weekly killing of a beautiful mother.

Over the last seven weeks, in and around Worcester, the three men, all over 18-years-old, had killed women in their homes. Before murdering them, they tortured the women in ways that should have been unimaginable.

"Are you sure this woman will be alone?" Ted asked David as they drove away in his 1974 Dodge Dart that definitely was on its last legs.

"I am sure. Her son is some hot shot college student and her husband is at a conference for the week," David replied. "I work with her at her parents supermarket. She is one sexy bitch that is dying for us to make her happy, no pun intended."

The three psychopaths were in the top of their respective classes and were not the prototypical serial killers and rapists.

"You say she is a redhead? Man, I love red-haired women," Ted said.

"There is only one way to tell if she is a real redhead or not," Joe added.

"True, very true," Ted said.

"Who remembered the condoms?" Joe asked.

Ted raised his hand. "I even remembered to get you the supersized ones."

The last time they had gone out on the prowl, they had forgotten to get condoms and had to leave their victim hogtied until they returned an hour later. They raped her as they cut out her eyes before using a blow torch on her back to carve symbols of ancient Egyptians. The three men let her live to extend the torture for the rest of her life. Tonight's plan was to do the same type of thing to Maryanne Hawkins. The plan to rape, beat, and torture the beautiful Hawkins came with an added bonus. They were to keep the hands and feet of Maryanne Hawkins as trophies.

"I hope this broad is all she is cracked up to be. I have been salivating all week, thinking about biting her nipples off," Joe said.

"Dude, trust me, she has the face of an angel," said David.

"Where does Ronnie think we are?" Mointz asked Deidre as he tried to make up time after being caught speeding in the Bronco. They approached Hawkins's house.

"I told him I had a real estate showing out here and since you had a swim meet, I would take you to New Hampshire, while your parents pick him up after his hockey game. We should be there before Ronnie and your parents get up north."

"You tricked me, you little vixen," Mointz said. "How you finagled this so I would have to take you was pure genius. You should be proud of yourself. You are getting to be as devious as me. I could have done this myself."

"Oh really, Mointz?" she asked. "What exactly were you going to say to Maryanne Hawkins? 'Hi, I am Cristopher Mointz and I have come to save you from being raped and tortured.'"

Mointz had scoped the neighborhood over the last week to discover idiosyncrasies. His made-up swim meet was his cover for the evening. Mointz and Deidre had a solid plan to take Maryanne Hawkins out of commission and out of harm's way as well as stopping the three men's reign of terror.

Mointz and Deidre parked the Bronco a few houses down and walked to Maryanne Hawkins's house. Mointz rang the bell.

The beautiful Mrs. Hawkins answered the door in her pink dress. She smiled and said, "Can I help you?"

"Yes, ma'am," Deidre replied. "I am with the real estate commission and we are here to ask you a few questions if it is a good time right now."

"Sure, please come in. I am always available to help in any way I can." Hawkins let them into her lovely home and said, "Have a seat here in the kitchen. May I get you anything before we start?"

"A glass of water would be lovely," Mointz said. As Maryanne stood up to get the water, Mointz quickly seized her shoulders and covered her mouth with a rag soaked in Sodium Pentothal. The beautiful Maryanne Hawkins slumped into Mointz's arms. He quickly carried her into her bedroom and laid her on the bed.

"You sure she will not remember any of this, love?" Deidre asked.

"I am sure darling. Dr. Trent left me plenty of this stuff. He assured me she will lose a few hours of memory and have a really bad headache. I guess it is better than the alternative."

"I trust you."

"Thank you, dear, it is not as if you have much choice right now. It is about to be show time."

Davis had indeed left Mointz with enough Sodium Pentothal to last a good long time. He had also left Mointz an eight-shooter Glock—a specialized tranquilizer gun that knocked its target out immediately. He needed both this evening.

The doorbell rang.

"They are here," Deidre said. "You ready, Mointz?"

"Yes, dear. Unfortunately, I have done this a few times."

She smiled at him nervously. Even though she was about to encounter three of the worst human beings on the planet, she felt extremely safe with Mointz.

The last time Mointz had been in a situation like this he took down Hector Esperez, a Latin American serial killer in New Mexico, when he flew there for another "swim meet" that never happened. Thankfully, his swimming had provided a great cover and alibi for him when he participated in his little adventures.

"Mrs. Hawkins, it is David here, ready to pick up that television you said I could get."

"Come in," Deidre said muffling her voice. "I am in the back of the house. Please come in."

David Mello, followed by the twins, walked into the house. The sadistic smiles on their faces immediately disappeared as they noticed Mointz pointing a Glock at them. He shot the three high school seniors; they were down instantly. Mointz hogtied the three and called out for Deidre.

"Honey, get the Bronco and bring it up to the front steps please."

Deidre was in shock and Mointz had to yell at her. She eventually snapped out of it when Mointz jumped up and kissed her, surprising the hell out of her. Once out of her panicked state, she brought the Bronco up to the steps.

Mointz dragged the three men into the back of the Bronco and had Deidre follow him in the three seniors' Dodge Dart to the abandoned mill in Holden where, ironically, the police would have found Maryanne Hawkins' body the next day after the three boys anonymously called in to the Holden Police. The events in the Second Parallel definitely would not turn out the same way for these three.

"Meet me down the road a bit, Dee," Mointz told her. He did not want her to see the coming events. She knew what he was about to do and he did not have to tell her twice.

Mointz propped up each of the boys against the Dodge Dart; they were about ready to meet their maker. He jabbed each of them with an Epi-pen to wake them up.

Mointz smiled at the three young men when they awoke and doused them with gasoline. "I wanted the three of you to see what all those women went through before you go to hell."

They panicked, struggling against their ties.

"Who are you?" David Mello shouted, choking from the gasoline fumes.

"I am Maryanne Hawkins' guardian angel. Who are you, pray tell?" Mointz asked.

"We came to pick up a television," Joe cried out.

Mointz rambled off the names of every one of their previous victims. He lit his lighter and asked, "Any other lies you want to tell me before you rot in hell?"

None of the three said a word, as fright had paralyzed each of them.

"Wise choice," Mointz said, as he dropped the lighter next to Ted's feet. He high-tailed it out of there. The fire ball shot straight up to the sky.

Mointz ran to the Bronco and hopped in. "Move out, Dee."

"Jesus that was some fire ball. Did you see the tools those men carried to torture and inflict harm on Maryanne Hawkins?"

"Welcome to my world, Deidre," Mointz told her. They left Holden and headed north trying to beat Robert, Martha and Ronnie up to the ski house.

Cristopher, it is your father. We got a late start as Ronnie's game went into overtime. Ask Deidre to take you to the store and get the essentials for breakfast tomorrow, as we probably will not get there until after one. If you guys need anything, use the Amex I gave you. Okay, Buddy, see you soon. Love ya.

Mointz smiled at Deidre when they finished hearing the voice mail message on the machine. "It is only ten. We still have plenty of time to get something to eat and maybe a little, you know, pow wow."

"Well Mr. Mointz, you definitely have a little diablo in you tonight," Deidre said and kissed him passionately. "I can wait for food."

"Me too." Mointz carried Deidre into his bedroom and slowly undressed her.

It would be hard to spend time alone this week as plenty of eyes would watch them. Mointz had grown accustomed to relations again with a woman and Deidre was all woman. He also had fallen in love.

They made love for a good long time, then showered and dressed for dinner. They decided to dine at Mario's Ristorante which was open until midnight during ski season.

The seventeen-year-old Mointz sat down with Deidre at a table at Mario's. At six feet and four inches, Mointz looked 25 and Deidre did not look a day over that. Actually, she might even look younger. They ordered a pizza and Deidre ordered a glass of Chianti as Mointz ordered a club soda with lime.

"Do you miss alcohol at a restaurant?"

"Not as much as I missed making love to a beautiful woman."

"Hell, Mointz. Do you always know what to say?"

"Of course I do. Why do you think they picked me in the first place?"

"Do you think I am awful for falling so deeply for a 17-year-old?"

"You mean a fifty-eight-year-old, don't you? I seduced you, remember? Do you think I am awful for going after a younger woman?"

"I did not stop you, Mointzie. I do not think I could have even if I wanted to."

They laughed when Cristopher winked at her. They were just enjoying the night and each other's company, not thinking about what happened earlier in the evening. Deidre told him she was more determined than ever to help him in any way she could.

"Will you become my agent after you finish law school? I figure maybe you and Ronnie could help me build my image. Ronnie told me he was thinking about a career in law. I guess it is what my future holds."

"What do I know about being an agent?"

"I hope it is something that we can do together. Ronnie told me that your divorce is going pretty amicably."

"Sure it is. Ronald can now see all the bimbos he wants, in public. Please tell me you will never hurt me like that."

Mointz swallowed a bite of pizza. He absolutely did not want to hurt her in any way. "I promise you, I will never do that to you." He was not sure if it was true, but he was sure he meant it.

They finished the pizza and stocked up for the week, it seemed, at the store. Mointz and Deidre were in love and they both knew it to be true. This was a complication Mointz definitely did not see coming at all. He knew he had to be careful with everything that he did. Mointz also knew that the mission had to come first and he did not want to ever think about having to take Deidre out of the picture if he had to. For now, he felt blessed that the Second Parallel had both Ronnie and Deidre happy and content, far from the path of the First Parallel.

Chapter Twelve

The Mointzes and Mahoneys headed to California in the summer of 1984 to the Peter Ueberroth-run Olympics, where Mointz was the hottest topic besides the Soviet-led boycott. In May, Mointz shattered three world records at the World Championship swimming trials. Everyone under the sun, especially his parents, had encouraged him to compete in the Olympics for Team USA. Mointz stated he was not prepared to enter the Olympics until he had the opportunity to break all the records Mark Spitz had set at the 1972 Munich Olympics. He told the world they would just have to wait until the Seoul Games in 1988.

Rumor had it Mointz did not want to enter a boycotted games and Mointz did nothing to stop the speculation. He told anyone who would listen he was just there to enjoy the games and that he looked forward to completing high school and playing football in the fall. The media loved him for his sincerity.

Deidre and Mointz's relationship was stronger than ever, hidden from their loved ones. In reality, Mointz convinced everyone he knew to attend the games so he could steal the spotlight and make himself more marketable for the 1988 Olympics. His parents worried that he was pressuring himself too much.

Mointz knew the powers that be in the First Parallel wanted him to get noticed but not swim in these Olympics. The United States, led by Rowdy Gaines, would do well here in LA, but the real endorsements and fame would not come until 1988. Philip Graham, the famous psychologist, was adamant Mointz strategize this way and Mointz could tell already he was dead on.

"Give them a taste and make them want more," Graham had told him in the First Parallel.

The games went off without a hitch and the country celebrated the outstanding job of Peter Ueberroth and his team at salvaging the boycotted games. One thing for sure, the world had been introduced to one Cristopher Mointz and, ready or not, Mointz would be on the world stage for a very long time to come.

When Mointz and company returned home from the Olympic Games, ESPN showed up at football camp in Barrington to watch Mointz's first practice after the Olympics. The now six-foot-six quarterback led the nation last year in high school touchdown passes.

The first game of the season had Mointz throwing for three hundred yards. As Barrington defeated last years' state champion, Mount St. Charles, 46 to 6, Mointz was almost as well known for his football as he was for his swimming.

Each and every week, the world now watched Mointz dominate the Rhode Island Scholastic League with Ronnie Mahoney, who was just as heavily recruited. The friends were seeking to defeat Portsmouth High for the first time in ten years, as last year they had lost in overtime when the Barrington place kicker missed an easy field goal.

Ronnie and Mointz sat in the stands the night before the big game listening to Athletic Director Tom Estes pump up the crowd.

"These boys have brought us to the pinnacle of the football world and we can smell the state championship. We broke the state record for offense, we broke…"

Ronnie interrupted Estes' speech and asked Mointz, "How long have you and Deidre been fucking?"

Mointz almost choked on his hot chocolate. "What are you talking about? Want to run that by me again?"

Ronnie laughed. "Dude, your face was absolutely priceless. I thought you were about to have a heart attack."

"Why would you even joke like that?" Mointz asked, as Athletic Director Estes finished his speech and started to introduce the players.

"I do not care, Cristopher. You both make each other better people. All I care about is what is going on at that awesome Beach House. Dude, you rock."

They had been friends for years, yet Mointz could not believe the words coming from his friend's mouth in the middle of a pep rally, no less.

"What are you saying, Ronnie, and why here?"

"You think I am going to ask you this when we are alone? No way. You would kill me. I like life far too much and it is much safer here."

Mointz decided he needed to open up to Ronnie, but not here. "After the rally, I will spill," Mointz said. "I did not sleep with Deidre."

Ronnie patted him on the back. "Yes, you did. I know she is hot. Do not worry, I am not judging either one of you."

"Oh, man, why did I even have to open my big mouth?" Ronnie asked, his head in his hands.

Mointz put his arm around him on one side and Deidre on the other side.

"Sorry to hit you with all of this," Mointz said, after he had told Ronnie everything.

"Why would I kill myself over a girl and put the two of you through all of this?   Am I that much of a selfish bastard?"

"Sweetie, it is not going to happen, so please stop and take a deep breath. There is no way Cristopher or I would let you do it again."

"How did you find the beach house?" Mointz asked.

"I knew the two of you were together. You only had to look at the way you acted around each other. I caught you sneaking into mom's room at the Olympics and at first I was kinda pissed. I found this place by accident, really. I was dropping off Kathy at a friend's and I noticed your cars here. I parked up the driveway and walked down, only to find the two of you naked in each other's arms. I wanted to bust up the little party and say something, but I couldn't. Believe me it has gnawed at me for over a week. What the fuck, you two? Why didn't you tell me?"

"Ronnie, please watch the expletives."

"Mom, I just found out you and Cristopher, my best friend, who I might add, is fifty-eight years old and from another universe, are fornicating and playing Bonnie and Clyde. Plus, I killed myself over knocking up Jeanne Ryan and Father Houle molesting me. "Fuck" is an appropriate word under these circumstances, Mother," he said. "We have a game in the morning; I thought it was the most important thing in the world. Now just saving the world will take Herculean effort."

"How do you think Cristopher has felt all these years?"

"Mom, I have no idea. I am drawing blanks. He has children, holy shit."

"Ronnie, the mouth please."

"Sorry, sorry Mother," he replied. "What else do the two of you have to tell me?"

"Nothing that I know of," Mointz told his friend.

"How about starting by telling me how I can help on this gig. You two cannot have all the fun."

They all laughed as it was almost midnight before they left the beach house and returned to the Mahoneys. Ronnie had asked a million questions and he was still at it when Mointz told him to cool his jets.

"Can I really help?" Ronnie asked Mointz and his mother.

"Being with me through this amazing journey helps me more than you can ever imagine. Being by my side will be the last piece of the puzzle for my success."

"Honey, Cristopher has carried the weight of the world on his shoulders because of us. He put everything aside to make sure we were saved. You will understand the magnitude of all this sooner rather than later."

"Were you supposed to tell anyone?" Ronnie asked.

Ronnie asked a valid question, Mointz thought. He did not have an answer for him at first. Mointz definitely had been told to keep it between his father in-law and Erin and no one else before the Gennifer Moore bomb dropped on his lap. He really did not know how telling Ronnie and Deidre would affect the mission in reality. There was nothing written in any of the roadmaps detailing what could happen if people in his inner circle found out. Mointz did not care at this point anyway.

"I am not sure I was supposed to tell you," Mointz responded.

"Stop the piffle talk. I bet you were supposed to keep this all to yourself. I am correct sir, aren't I?"

"Seriously, I have absolutely no idea. Too late now, there is no one I could ask if I was wrong, anyway. Any other questions?"

"How long have you and Deidre been swapping spit and other bodily fluids?" Ronnie asked with a grin. He really believed at times he was a comedian.

"Ronnie, that is between Cristopher and me."

"Mother, I am not judging either of you," Ronnie said, looking at the diary on the laptop Cristopher wrote, alongside the scanned articles from local newspapers about Ronnie's suicide.

"Believe me, it will not happen," he said. "What I really care about was how it felt to send those bastards back to hell in Holden."

Mointz could see the excitement in his friend's eyes. The now six-foot Mahoney was as strong as an ox and built like a solid piece of granite. Ronnie put in the same hours Mointz did at the gym and loved Mointz's protein shakes, all laced with Dr. Trent's team's vitamins, unbeknownst to Ronnie.

"After a while, you become numb to all of it," Mointz told Ronnie, sitting down on the couch. "Besides, I did not ask for this, they came to me." Mointz could see in Ronnie's eyes he wanted to get into the fray. The eight-year-old in the tent who wanted his friend to stay until he fell asleep was long gone.

Mointz did not go into detail about his personal life in the First Parallel, leaving the embarrassing details out of the conversation for now.

"Why were you picked? I can only imagine you had everyone eating out of the palm of your hands like you do now."

"Not really, buddy. I got lucky I guess," he told his friend. "Now we really need to get to sleep. I would like to beat those guys tomorrow."

"Yeah, I would like to win as well. I cannot wait to head north after the game," he said and realized neither his mother nor Cristopher were going. "Hey, how come you two are staying back here and not driving north after the game?"

"Work to do, Ronnie," his mother told him.

"Work, my ass, Deidre," Ronnie said.

Mointz and Ronnie played like possessed men and Barrington High won the game by a score of 48 to 0. The thrashing could have been worse; however the coach mercifully pulled Mointz and Ronnie out after the third quarter.

Martha Mointz, a former Barrington Cheerleader, was the most vocal parent in the stands, loving every minute of the win. Ten years of Portsmouth victories had the normally quiet Martha whipped up into a frenzy. She hugged her son as he held the trophy high in the air.

"You guys were phenomenal," Martha told Mointz and Ronnie. They both hugged her back. She was serious about her football and loved the boys.

"Cristopher and Ronnie, you were just splendid," Robert said with Grandpa Leo concurring.

Ronnie's father and Deidre were on at least speaking terms and they both congratulated the boys as Seanie jumped into his brother's arms and Kathy into Ronnie's.

"Now I better get into swimming shape."

"Son, you are in perfect shape," Ronald said. "You guys have one more game."

"Damn, I forgot about that one," Mointz joked and winked at Deidre and his mother.

"Rest up boys and enjoy a few days off. Practice on Monday for the state championship next Saturday at McCoy Stadium," Coach Wilson stated.

"Hey, coach. Cristopher is here all weekend. He has plenty of time to watch film," Ronnie said as he hugged Kathy.

Mointz wanted to bop him one. However, Ronnie would not be Ronnie without his sarcasm.

"I told you; I have a science fair at Brown on Saturday."

"Rest that mind, Cristopher and enjoy the fair."

"Your mother will take good care of him, Ronnie," Martha told Ronnie.

"Oh, I bet she will."

Mointz bumped his friend as he walked by heading to the locker room to shower and return home for a nice Thanksgiving dinner.

The Mointzes and Mahoneys, minus Ronald, ate Thanksgiving dinner at the Mointzes. Grandma Rose had taken over the cooking duties and by six pm dinner was served. The dinner seemed more like a celebration of a great game than Thanksgiving.

After dinner, everyone except Deidre and Mointz left for New Hampshire. The couple headed for the beach house and a little R and R.

Mointz lit a fire as soon as they arrived on the colder than usual Thanksgiving night. This weekend had been planned for months and they both wanted to lie in each other's arms this evening. Deidre snuggled in Mointz's arms on the couch and watched the fire and an old western movie on the television.

"I threw a big monkey wrench in your plans didn't I?"

"This is an unexpected and very pleasant surprise. I am glad Ronnie took it so well. I feel like an elephant has moved off my chest."

"He told me earlier he does not know what to think, but he reiterated he will not kill himself. He thinks it is funny. After a few days it will all sink in and he will understand how enormous a task you have in front of you," Deidre told him. "I love you so much, Cristopher. I know the attraction to you is not like a school girl wishing she was dating the star quarterback. I see you in the future as this intelligent wonderful man, full of life and love. I will love you all my remaining days on this earth and will forever be in your debt for saving Ronnie and me."

Mointz knew he loved her and he could not ever give her up. Soon, very soon he would have three woman in his life who loved him and he them.

"Dee, I do not know what is going on right now in my life. The funny thing is, I lived this life once already. You and I were never intimate in the First Parallel, but who knows what would have happened. The real me loves you more than I can say and not just the person who holds you in his arms now."

"I understand, believe me. I would not want to even fathom what it would be like to be you right now. How and when do we cut this all off and you break my heart?"

"We don't. We need to take it one day at a time," Mointz said. "I have come here to save the planet and if you want to bail, you can at any time."

Mointz kissed her neck and after kissing him back, she buried her head in his chest. Deidre knew the love he had for her by the way he looked at her, paid attention to her needs, and the way he made love to her.

"I will not distract you. You are too important to the world for me to hinder your progress."

"Dee, we came to each other at first out of loneliness. We were probably predestined to be with each other before I even came here. I know in my heart of hearts I want you with me and…"

"Why don't we just enjoy the alone time and figure all this out day by day?"

"I can live with that for now." Mointz pulled off her top and made love to her by the fire. They nodded off on the couch. The doorbell startled them.

"Who is it?" Deidre asked.

Mointz looked out the window and noticed the mailman at the front door. "Don't be alarmed, love; we have our friendly mailman at the door with a package."

"I will get dressed and get your package, sir," she said and ran into the bedroom to throw on sweats.

"This is a package for Connor Tisdale," the mailman said to Deidre when she opened the door.

"Connor is not here right now, I am …"

"Deidre Mahoney. Hi, I am Jon Higgins. Our sons play ball at the school together. My son, Greg is on the Junior Varsity. The boys looked good yesterday. Your son and Cristopher Mointz were incredible."

Deidre smiled brightly in her oversized Barrington High School Sweatshirt Ronnie had given her. "The boys were not going to be denied, that is for sure."

Mailman Higgins handed the package to Deidre after she told him she was a friend of Connor's and his wife's and she was house sitting for the weekend.

"Say, Deidre. I am a single dad and I was wondering if maybe you would have time for a cup of coffee sometime after work one of these days."

"Sorry, Jon. My heart is promised to another, but if things change, you will be the first to know." She was used to men asking her out. No one could figure out how Ronald had left the best-looking woman around.

Higgins shrugged and gave a small smile. He was not a bad-looking man by any means, but he was no Mointz.

Deidre brought the package inside and Mointz kissed her immediately.

"You have my heart as well, love."

"Now I am so, so confused," Deidre told him and ran out of the beach house. Cristopher ran after her quickly.

"You are going to leave me and I am going to think you are one son-of-a-bitch."

"For Pete's sake, you are not going to lose me. I fell in love with you the day you gave me that damn Creamsicle. I knew what had happened in the past and I refuse to let that happen again. I am not 17 or 58, or whatever the hell I am. I am just Cristopher Mointz…"

"Yes, Cristopher Flippin Mointz, world saver and heart breaker."

"Deidre, I love you. Stop having a meltdown. I am not going away and I am not sending you away. Come inside and be mad or aggravated. Please do not let us be caught out here."

"Do you really love me?"

"What do you think?"

"Yes, I truly believe you love me with all your heart."

"I love you more than all the tea in Ireland and as much as my children. Neither you or Ronnie will ever be without me."

The fight in Deidre subsided as Mointz urged her to go for a run. Mointz was no longer thinking of the game next Saturday or his little dust-up with Deidre. His mind was on the package that had been addressed to Connor Tisdale, his alias for Davis to send packages from the grave, usually by KPMG. Connor received the bank statements and other investment forms from Darryl DeMarco there, whoever he was.

After their run, Deidre and Mointz made up quickly and then soaked in the tub. She massaged his feet for a bit, as he had hurt his ankle yesterday and the run made the ankle sore again.

"Are we together again?" Mointz asked.

"Do I have a choice? I already lost my mind for loving you and, believe it or not, I believe you love me and will not hurt me. Maybe I should be flattered you seduced me and I was sexy enough for Super Mointz." Her giggle was magic to Mointz's ears.

"Hey, I thought we were buddies, again."

"We are buddies again. Now, what was in the package you received?"

"Great question and one I am not looking forward to answering today because whatever it is, it cannot be a good thing for my psyche."

Chapter Thirteen

"What is it, Cristopher?"   Deidre asked, as Mointz opened the package to find a computer device.

"It is a USB device from Dr. Davis."

"And that means what, to an 80's girl like me?"

"It is a high-scale floppy disc with information on it. Generally when I get these, they contain a video and some documents."

He plugged in the USB and, sure enough, an Apple QuickTime video appeared. Mointz clicked on it as Deidre snuggled up to him on the couch. They watched the screen of the Apple computer where both the Vice President and the CIA director, Lauren Gabriel, appeared to be sitting in the Oval Office.

"Oh, my God! That is an older Senator Ellis," Deidre said.

"Vice President Ellis and CIA Director, Lauren Gabriel, to be exact," Mointz told her and turned up the volume on the computer.

"Hello, Mr. President," said Vice President Ellis from the screen. "I hope you are having a grand time in the Second Parallel. My calculation will have you in your Senior Year of High School and it is safe to bet you are with the lovely Deidre Mahoney."

"How would he know that?" Deidre asked.

"Shhhh, these guys are good. I told you we were probably predestined to be together."

"Mr. President," continued Ellis, "it is time we stepped up your covert ops and even though your safety is of the utmost importance, some missions are worth the risk,"

"Mr. President," said Lauren, as a picture flashed on the computer screen of an Englishman, Adam Ferguson. "This man is the man most responsible for securing weapons of mass destruction for the Pakistanis in the mid 90's. We would like it very much if you would make sure that the SG6400 series rockets never see their way to Pakistan. Mr. President, these are the nuclear weapons which wiped out Japan. We traced them back to Adam Ferguson."

Ferguson looked to be in his mid-forties. *He looks cunning,* thought Mointz. Mointz had heard about Ferguson's ruthlessness. Lauren warned, "Do not let his bonnie good looks lull you into a false sense of security. He is one man you would not invite over to your house for tea and crumpets. In 1986, he sent the Prime Minister a jar of boric acid. It contained the Prime Minister's niece's head."

"Lovely."

"Do your best to stop him," instructed Ellis. You are now old enough to make your way across the pond and, I am sure, resourceful enough to take out this monster. This mission can only help us in the long run."

"You will not see us for a year or two," said Lauren. "And I must warn you the next two projects will not be easy ones. However, we have all the confidence in the world in you."

Her smile brought back the memories of their time together in the conference room where Mointz had explored every inch of the Jaguar Director of the Central Intelligence Agency.

"You'll find Ferguson's dossier on the disc in a folder marked 567567ets. Once you've studied these, head to Harrods's and experience a cup of Tutti Frutti ice cream. It is the best in the world. Godspeed, Mr. President."

Lauren smiled. "Good luck, sir, and thank you for your service."

"God, was it that obvious you were going to fall in love with me?" Deidre asked ignoring the fact he had just been told to take out an international terrorist.

"Do you now believe I was destined to love you?"

"Okay, maybe you have a point. So, Mr. President, how are we going to pull this off?"

"You are now taking Ronnie and me to London the third week of December and then for a ski holiday in the Swiss Alps." Mointz could almost hear his mother's voice when he told her he would be in Europe for the holidays. "Now why don't we get back in the hot tub and finish the rest of our weekend before the family comes back?"

"Yes, Mr. President, sir!"

After Monday's practice, Mointz and Ronnie showered and changed. They drove Mointz's Bronco to the beach house to spend the night together and discuss their team strategy.

"I am abstaining from sex until I am married," Ronnie exclaimed on the ride.

"That is great, considering you are dating my sister for reasons I have yet to figure out."

"I do not want to hear it from you. From what I know, you are getting plenty. Man, I liked you so much better before I knew you were fifty-eight and having sex with Deidre."

"Sorry buddy, that video has me in another world."

"Dumb ass, you are from another world! So, in all seriousness, what can I do to help?"

"We need to get this Ferguson neutralized as quickly as possible before he causes any irreversible damage."

Mointz explained to Ronnie how rogue nuclear nations brought him to the Second Parallel in the first place. Ronnie was third in his class and as bright as anyone. He understood how Mointz needed to try to slow down some of these nations while figuring how to best deal with them later down the line so maybe they would think twice about destroying the world in 2016.

"So let us get a bunch of Francs and party like rock stars and take down this evil person."

"You mean "pounds" and party-like-a-rock star days are over."

"Dude, I know they are pounds, I was just joshing. You have a hot girlfriend; you need to party a little bit." Ronnie was close to Deidre and he liked the fact she had not stopped smiling since Mointz and she became one. "You need to relax, mi amigo. All this stress is going to render you useless if you do not have some fun. Tone down some of the intensity and let people help you."

"The weight of the world is on me. I worry about you, Deidre, my children and completing these little covert ops so I even have a chance at saving the world. In three weeks after Trent Davis comes to this parallel, if there is not a change in the First Parallel, then I would be the man who failed to save the planet from demise and the world would be lost forever, wiped out never to be seen again."

"I can help you. I can handle this, no sweat."

"You used to tell me you could handle anything, right before you left me alone. You decided you could not handle it. I cannot go through it again and neither can Deidre. Comprende?"

Mointz's words hit home and Ronnie turned white. For once he was serious. "You are not going to lose me. I do not know what happened before, but whatever you did to help me along this time obviously worked. Whether it's because you took Father Houle or my father out of the equation, I am not the same man. Do you really believe I would be that selfish, again?"

"I wish you would have thought about that the last time, asshole!" Mointz said, poking Ronnie in the ribs as he parked in front of the beach house.

"If you are now done with my lecture, I have to go study for chemistry. Not all of us are college professors," Ronnie said. "I love you, you know that. I will not desert you or my mother, for that matter."

"Good. Because I would come back and kick the living shit out of you."

"You can come back for the third time?"

Mointz had no idea if he could or couldn't, but Ronnie did not need to know. "If I had to, sure I could. Please do not make me."

"Well, I plan on behaving. Say, what are your plans with the fabulous Deidre this evening?"

"Good ole Connor Tisdale has her on a secret mission this evening and I hope to see her after."

"Cool. By the way, when do you give me weapons training? You have been hunting since you were ten and now I know why you never let me hunt. I really have always wanted to."

"I will talk to Grandpa Leo after I call the travel agent and book us a trip to London and the Swiss Alps."

Deidre shook her head and smiled when Mointz handed her a list of things to do before they left for London. The Mointzes had had their passports for years and Deidre had to get one for herself and Ronnie quickly. She went to the local drug store with Ronnie for passport photos and then to the post office to fill out the rush delivery forms.

Deidre's biggest task flustered her. Mointz needed her to visit an expert in disguises and to learn the tricks of the trade, so she could turn into anyone she wanted to be, anywhere she needed to be. Lauren had recommended a top expert.

The Boston College Law student pulled into the Phillips studio in Needham, Massachusetts. The owner, Celeste Phillips, had received a call from Connor Tisdale, requesting her help in advising Deidre Mahoney on how to transform herself for the agency. Celeste welcomed Deidre into her studio and started to teach her the tricks of the trade. In almost five minutes Deidre already looked inconspicuous. She was having fun being, 'personally camouflaged' as Celeste called it and after several hours, Deidre had been transformed several times. Celeste was making a plaster facemask on Deidre's face, when a blond woman about six feet tall came into the private studio and introduced herself as Lauren.

"How are you today, Mrs. Mahoney?" Lauren asked.

"I am well," Deidre muttered through the mask before Celeste pulled it off her face. She was not positive, but Deidre could swear that the woman looked familiar.

"I did not mean to interrupt your lesson, but when I heard Celeste mention you were neighbors with Cristopher Mointz, I had to ask about him. I was a swimmer in college and I followed swimming pretty religiously before I joined the agency. I've heard good things about him."

Deidre's face lit up like a Christmas tree. "He is absolutely the real deal and is as warm and kind as anyone you will ever wish to meet. He is best friends with my son and between the two of them, they are articulate, worldly, and most of all, compassionate."

Lauren smiled inside, as she had followed Mointz since his return to this parallel. Another of the last-minute changes, Lauren received her memories back the same day Cristopher did in 1975. Lauren suffered a mild form of leukemia and Davis was able to secretly give her a T-cell transplant of her own healthy cells from 2016, which altered her DNA structure. Lauren was eighteen-years-old when her memories were returned. Ellis and Davis believed she could help Mointz from a distance as the CIA Director believed in her heart Mointz would not need her until later on. Ellis trusted Lauren and Davis more than anyone in the world, including his wife. Lauren planned to go to Mointz after he finished law school and offer him a position on her congressional staff. She could not wait to surprise him like he had surprised her in the conference room. Just thinking about the event got her wet. Lauren was extremely careful not to upset the world, as Mointz was making changes for the better.

"Did he really stop a pedophile from taking a five-year-old?" Lauren asked already knowing the answer.

"He was only nine and he knew something was out of place so he reacted. Cristopher has always been that way. A step ahead of everyone else."

When Celeste received the request from Connor Tisdale a/k/a Cristopher Mointz, to teach camouflage to Deidre Mahoney, Lauren knew immediately Deidre knew everything. The future CIA Director could also see Deidre's love for Mointz.

"He must be very popular in town," said Lauren.

"There is not a person who would say a bad word about him or my son. They are more like brothers than simply friends. Cristopher is going to smash every record in the next Olympics and become even more popular."

"What is the real reason that he did not compete in the LA Olympics?"

Deidre accepted a towel to finish wiping her face. "I spent a lot of time with his family and went to the games with them. From what I know, he has a certain swagger about him and wanted to compete against the whole world. He decided to wait for a non-boycotted Olympics to show off his talents. Cristopher also loves his football and wanted to be ready for his senior year. He owed Portsmouth High a beating, so he said he needed to get in football shape."

Davis had predicted that Mointz would bond with the lovely Deidre. Lauren could not be happier Mointz was on track.

"What are his plans for after the games?" Lauren asked.

Deidre knew from Mointz that this place was a CIA hotspot. He had instructed her to answer honestly when the CIA grilled her about him, as the CIA would know they are neighbors. Connor Tisdale was the creation of Lauren, Ellis and Davis. Tisdale was built as a man inside the agency that ran a group called, "America's Future Leaders." This group was supposedly formed to help celebrities, athletes, and future politicians understand the nuances of the spotlight. Mointz told her to be as truthful as she could and to enjoy herself.

"Cristopher wants to be a politician and a lawyer. Half the town calls him "President," as people believe he will do big things."

"He must have all the young girls going wild. I have seen his ads in magazines for all of the products he endorses," said Lauren. Deidre's shy smile confirmed Mointz and the beautiful Deidre were intimate.

"That is the understatement of the year."

"Deidre, it was a pleasure to meet you. I have to run out, but I will talk to you tomorrow. Have fun getting ready for London."

Deidre did not understand the comment and its meaning until half way home.

"Let me hear that voice again," Deidre said to Mointz, as they sat at the beach house. "Cristopher, I am positive the voice I heard tonight was Lauren

Gabriel. She seemed quite pleased with all of my answers. One would have to say she was checking up on you. She definitely was not malicious in any way."

After Mointz had played the tape a couple of times, Deidre confirmed it was Lauren at Celeste's. "She is the devil in a blue dress. You do not get to be the top spook in the country for not being crafty. Lauren can fake a lot of things," he said. "Well, there are some things that you cannot fake."

"What does that mean?"

Mointz told her how he had seduced Director Gabriel to convince her he could do anything. "I had to do anything at all costs, Dee."

"From now on, keep all the results from your conquests to yourself, thank you very much. I gave birth to Ronnie when I was fifteen, yes, but it does not mean I am a little slut. I have had sex with two men in my whole entire life. How many would you like to own up to?"

"I have only been with you, my dear."

"Stuff it, Mointzie," she said. "What are your plans for Lauren?"

"Tomorrow night, I will scare the living daylights out of her and then give her a big surprise."

"Your pants will be on this time, correct?"

"Yes, dear. My pants will be on this time." Mointz loved seeing Deidre jealous. She tried so hard not to be, but she could not help it. "Now that my concentration is blown, I cannot think about anything for the rest of the evening except my playbook. We have a championship to win."

"Liar, you could win that game in your sleep."

"Probably, but sleep is not what I had in mind. I am proud of you for picking up on this."

"Thank you, love. Helping means a lot to me."

"Well this is a big help. You are amazing in every way," said Mointz.

"Speaking of helping, did Ronnie tell you he would like to go into the military?"

"He mentioned trying to attend one of the academies. I think he would like to play ball there."

"Ronnie has his heart set on Annapolis and then joining a group called NICS.

"You mean NCIS? Very popular television show in my time in the First Parallel, Ronnie has been watching the show on my iPad. The boy is hooked."

"Do you approve of this?"

"I do actually. Let me grab my iPad and we can watch an episode after we make some serious love. I am supposed to be studying new plays, but…"

"School work comes before football. You need an anatomy lesson," Deidre said racing into the bedroom.

"Yes, ma'am. That could work."

Deidre knocked on the studio door and walked in. Celeste Phillips welcomed her. Celeste and her new protégé sat down to prepare for today's lesson. Mointz sat in his father's BMW, watching out the window anxiously for Lauren to appear. It did not take long for her to arrive on the scene. Mointz could recognize the six-foot blondes' walk anywhere, as she headed down the street towards the studio.

Mointz jumped out of the BMW and quickly closed the distance between them. The 27-year-old Gabriel was about to grab for the door when Mointz put a gun in her back.

"Hello, Director. Lovely to see you today," Mointz said as the beautiful, Lauren Gabriel turned around and smiled brightly.

"I said 'good luck getting ready for London,' didn't I?" she asked.

Mointz smiled and kissed her cheek and put the gun back in his waist.

"C'mon, Mr. President, why don't we take a walk and I will buy you a cup of coffee, as I cannot take you to a bar. You are not old enough."

"I would start with 'How were your last nine years?' However, I am going to start with, 'What the hell are you doing here?' I do not recall Lauren Gabriel being part of this."

"As they walked, Lauren explained to Mointz about her leukemia and how Davis was able to restore her T-cells in a transfusion, secretly. She went on to explain how she was a last-minute addition along with Gennifer because of serious concerns that Davis had not prepared fully and come back earlier than expected.

"I saved Hawkins's mother. She is a very charming woman."

"Yes, I know you did. Believe me; I know everything you have done and I am damn proud of you. You have done splendidly."

"Tell me you are the last surprise. It is hard enough to deal with this as it is, but the surprises, for lack of a better word, really suck. Excuse the language."

"Cristopher, my only job was to keep an eye on you and help you if you were in trouble. Obviously, you have not needed it. I can see, as predicted, you have fallen for Deidre."

"Dr. Trent's prediction, eh?"

"Yes, sir. He would be extremely glad you are together. You love her too much to let her go. This has not been easy for me either, but I do think you are blessed having her."

"What happens when I can't let her go?"

"All will be revealed in due time."

"Whatever you say, I guess. Say, are you the one who sent me all of those packages?"

"Guilty as charged. I know you completed every assignment.

"I have so far, easily. Believe me; I am not going to complain about you here. I have gotten myself into a bit of a pickle."

Lauren laughed. "You fell in love with the person you have always loved. Hell, for the last nine years I have compared every man to you. Mr. President, Deidre got you through this period. Whatever happens, happens. You can never lose focus."

"I know, I know," Mointz said. "Say, you still getting married?"

They continued to walk arm in arm. "Yes, and eventually divorced, as my future husband wanted the kid thing in the First Parallel and never the career thing. He is still going to get upset when I go into politics while he studies medicine."

Mointz led Lauren into a coffee shop and sat down with her as they grabbed a couple of cups of Java. The two of them could speak freely in the corner.

"How was your first day?" Lauren asked.

Mointz told her about sneaking out of Ronnie's tent to get the case after smashing Ronnie's father with a plate earlier in the day.

"What was your first day like, Lauren?"

"Scared I would do something or say something that would risk ruining your mission, like I almost did yesterday. I thought about being some sort of vagabond and hiding away from the world for a while, but it just seemed a wee bit over the top."

"You are still crazy, you know that?"

"I know. Cristopher, this is going to take a team effort and there was plenty of talk about bringing someone else back. However, it was nixed by Ellis."

"Who?" Mointz asked.

"Deidre," said Lauren. "Yes, you love Ronnie, but Deidre ruled your world. Your love for her made you fall apart in the First Parallel, which led you to never trusting a woman. Davis believes you need to follow your heart, no matter what the consequences."

"What is this Gennifer thing, then? How does she fit into all of this?"

For a second, Lauren looked vulnerable. Then she answered, "Gennifer is a safety net for you. Love is not an exact science. Since you became involved with Deidre you can stop Gennifer's memories from returning with a simple shot after you save her. The shot will stop her DNA from reformulating and she would go on to live a normal life. This will be entirely your call."

"When were you going to tell me that? This is all just grand."

"I wasn't unless the opportunity arose. Here is the opportunity and I am taking it. Again, one hundred percent your call."

"How much time before we need to head back?" Mointz asked. "I need to check on something."

"Any time, really. Deidre will have a lot to do tonight. Why?"

"Where is your hotel?"

She laughed and again asked why.

"Because I need to experience for myself what it is going to be like if I ever have to decide."

"Jesus, Mointz."

"We really need to get back now," Mointz told Lauren, before hopping into the shower.

"Mr. President," Lauren called out as he turned on the water. "That is the second time you stole my breath.

"You, my lady, are even sexier now than I ever could have imagined."

Lauren followed Mointz into the shower for some more explosive sex. Once they got out, she kissed him as he toweled off.

"What else did you figure out?"

"Besides I love Deidre and you are a sex kitten, not a whole hell of a lot."

"You just wanted me in bed to compare eras."

"Sure. That is it."

"Allowing Gennifer's memories does not mean you have to start where you left off. I know all about how Davis tried to manipulate you into becoming involved with her. No one wanted you to stray too far. They put in safety nets."

"What the hell am I supposed to do? Why do I love her so much?"

"Either because she is here and in the now or she is the love of your life. You need to figure it out. I am here now. What do you think?"

"You are an incredible lay, but kind of too bitchy for a guy like me to fall in love with."

"Thank you for sparing my feelings. Your goal is to save the world and have your sons. You are now in love with the lovely Deidre. Eventually you will need to make decisions, but you have some time. Here, Davis told me to give you this, once this happened. Watch it when you can."

"I cannot believe how predictable this has all become. They really knew what the hell they were talking about, huh?"

"Davis never ever wanted anyone else for this and he went to great lengths to make your life perfect. Everyone wanted to check and double check you had what you needed, henceforth me and Gennifer."

"Great, just great. This is becoming more of a headache than one could ever imagine. I am glad I have enough fire in my belly to not quit."

Mointz and Lauren left the coffee shop for the second time this evening; however, this time instead of the hotel, they headed back to Celeste Phillips' place. Deidre's face lit up as soon as she set her eyes on Mointz.

"She loves you back," Lauren whispered.

"It would be an extreme nuisance if she didn't now, wouldn't it?"

Lauren asked Celeste to excuse them for a minute as Mointz needed to properly introduce Lauren to Deidre.

"So you are the one who picked Cristopher for this. He has done an amazing job so far and I thank you for allowing him to save my son and to save me from so much pain and suffering."

"I am one of many who picked him and I agree with you, he has done beautifully. His friend Dr. Trent Davis nominated him to save the world and I am extremely pleased he has taken this mission. I also appreciate the fact you have done an amazing job helping the cause."

"Now that we've firmly established the mutual admiration society, I would like to use the little time we have here so you can fill us in on our main man, Ferguson."

Lauren sat next to the future President and Deidre and explained how Adam Ferguson had become a famous arms dealer in the Middle East at the start of the Russian/Afghan conflict in 1979, through contacts all over the world. A British Duke, he used his influence with British and American Politicians to funnel weapons to the Afghanistan resistance movement. "With those weapons, the Afghans forced the Soviets out of the country. Half of the weapons on the black market came from the conflict and ended up in the hands of the Pakistanis."

"What you are saying then is you want Cristopher to go and kill a ruthless, British terrorist? Aren't you supposed to be keeping Cristopher safe?" Deidre said "I would think his safety would be of the utmost importance to you for the mission."

"I am sure Lauren is not asking me to do anything I cannot handle."

"That is correct. I have made sure to develop all types of relationships inside the agency. We have gone over the risk and rewards of this mission and Cristopher will minimize the risk by the way he handles himself. An eliminated Adam Ferguson is definitely worth the risk and I know Mointz is far too intelligent to take unnecessary chances, right Mr. President?"

"Lauren, if he is that important then it is a no-brainer that I will absolutely take out the Duke. However, I will be very careful and make sure that it will be done with sheer precision. We need to start working together and you also need to keep accumulating contacts. Damn, I am glad to have you here. You are a going to be a Congresswoman soon and I can't wait to hold your campaign sign."

"I became a CIA agent after law school. My superiors noticed my talent and are pushing me to run for Congress. And, I have watched your little derriere for years."

"It is a cute one, I can tell you that," Deidre added.

"You two are incorrigible. Right after the game on Saturday I will get into training for England. Remember, Lauren, I am a high school student..."

"Yes, Mr. President, I am well aware of the passing record you set in the seventh game of the season at Moses Brown. I thought you were never going to get sucked in on bootlegs again."

"So you were there. Outstanding. Say, why have you not hired someone to get rid of this Ferguson?"

"Sure, Mr. President. A third-year CIA agent orders a British aristocrat killed. That will not get me into Congress; it will get me into Leavenworth.

"Touché," Mointz replied.

Chapter Fourteen

Mointz and Ronnie led Barrington High School over LaSalle in the state championship game at McCoy Stadium. The falling snow made conditions difficult for LaSalle, as Mointz and Ronnie had practically grown up on a ski mountain. The two friends relished the conditions. The celebration did not last long because of the new program Lauren wanted both Mointz and Ronnie to enter. She had arranged for them to attend the CIA's Master School at the Naval War College the day after the game. She also had a plan to keep Deidre working with Celeste Phillips. Ronnie and Mointz were excused from school on the ruse they would be attending an educational seminar in Washington DC. Mointz's parents were pleased as punch he would be among a select group of honor students. If they only knew their son was about to start receiving advanced CIA training, the hairs on the backs of their necks would be standing up.

In Newport, Lauren introduced Mointz and Ronnie to Special Agent, Derek Vaz, the head of a special unit of the CIA, which trained undercover operatives. Lauren's father played an instrumental role in getting Mointz and Ronnie into the program, as Lauren had told her father, a bigwig in the agency, both Mointz and Ronnie were interested in helping their country. She had convinced her father Mointz was under constant watch by Eastern Bloc Nations, trying to steer him clear of ever participating in the Olympic Games.

Lauren pulled Mointz aside, as she needed to speak to him alone for a few minutes. Agent Vaz brought Ronnie into the training center.

"I hope you realize you are about to get your ass kicked here for the next two weeks. These guys are the best of the best and after we come back from Europe, I want you to continue with your lessons here."

"Here's to Europe and me getting my ass kicked; do you have any good news for me? The football season was tough enough on my body and if you didn't know, I spend quite a bit of time in the pool punishing myself. I do not believe I need anyone else to do it for me, thank you very much."

"Did you watch the video I gave you?"

"Not yet, I figured I would…"

"Put it off as long as you can? Stop beating around the bush and just watch it already."

"Yeah, I am putting it off. I will watch it when I get back to my hotel room tonight, satisfied?"

"This is going to weigh heavily on you until you can decide what you are going to do. I already know the outcome."

"Have you seen the video?"

"Yes, Mr. President. I would not want to be in your shoes."

Lauren was absolutely correct, as the team led by Derek Vaz beat on Mointz and Ronnie on day one. Whatever Mointz thought he knew about self-defense and martial arts training didn't compare in the slightest to the training by Vaz and his team. They had Mointz feeling so frustrated and inferior at the end of the day, he needed to hit the heavy bag for over 20 minutes to let out his frustration.

Mointz and Ronnie ate dinner after a shower. Mointz decided he needed to go for a run afterwards to clear his mind from looking so foolish. It was exactly how the team wanted Mointz to feel, as they knew he was special and extremely gifted.

Ronnie had told Derek Vaz about his interest in being an investigator in the armed forces. Vaz offered to give him an overview and go over his options with him.

The run cleared Mointz's head. After another shower, he retired to his room at the college and opened up his Mac PowerBook. He inserted the USB device into the computer and clicked on the video file. Mointz smiled brightly when he looked at a healthy Trent Davis.

"Hello, Dr. Cris," said Trent. "I can tell you have no idea what I am doing here. Well, buddy, I have no idea at what point you are in the mission, so the confusion is mutual. What I do know is you are with the lovely and talented Deidre Mahoney and the two of you have now joined forces. If you received this video, then I assume the two of you are extremely happy together and Ronnie is well in both body and mind. Good for you, old chum. I know she is a beautiful woman from the pictures you showed me and from the ones we scanned at your house when you were not home. Stop looking so surprised. I told you we studied you a ton."

"How is Lauren? Ok? We were always intending to send her to the Second Parallel; she just did not know it. I promise you she will be the last of the First Parallel surprises. While we were testing her DNA reformulation, we noticed Lauren had leukemia at a young age. With the new T-cells, Lauren was able to have her memories. Use her, as she is a great person and friend. However, do not let her bully you."

"Now my friend, Deidre, Deidre, Deidre. She was the love of your life and I know when you told me how hard you tried to console and be there for her after Ronnie's death, I could tell a part of you died that day as well. The self-destructive behavior she started when you left for school hurt the both of you. The stories you told of how you held her for hours when you should have been at frat parties were heartbreaking to me and the rest of the team. You never recovered in the First Parallel and I am damn well sure you do not want to ever lose her again. Therefore, I have given you an option you can either accept or refuse."

"And now, 'moving forward,' as you like to say, the sci-fi crap here at MIT has come up with a form of HGH, which will allow Deidre to stop aging for twenty-two years so you can catch up and surpass her in aging. Not only can we clone an embryo, we can now start the DNA sequence over again. Without getting into a bunch of boring science, Deidre will stay at her present age of 32 until you become 39. She is quite the puma. There are plenty of cover stories we can use. Lauren is on board already and willing to help you.

The boys' embryos can be implanted in Deidre if need be just as they can be implanted in Erin."

Cristopher did not know what to think. He felt like he had been hit by another one of Vaz's sucker punches all of a sudden.

Davis continued, "Saving the world is your mission and everyone here couldn't care less about your happiness. I, on the other hand, believe we owe you more than a ticker tape parade down Pennsylvania Avenue after all this. Be with Deidre and shine, if it is what you want. Do not live a life with Erin if it is not in your heart. Good luck, Mr. President. It is always nice to have options."

Mointz's frustrations had now reached a boiling point for the day and a simple run was not going to calm him down. Yes, he loved Deidre and he loved his boys more than anything. Over the years, he had wondered why Erin was the way she was. She loved the boys, but she had made Mointz's life miserable the whole time they were married; he had always felt her mind was in another place. Deidre had said it best at one point; you would do anything for your children. He wondered if he could take Erin out of the children's lives. He had to save the world for his sons and their sons and daughters. He had no idea what he was going to do. Thankfully, he did not have to make the decision tonight.

For almost two weeks, Mointz focused all of his frustrations on Derek Vaz's team. He always learned quickly and the power he amassed from all the hours in the weight room and the pool boded well for him. He became the envy of the training team.

Ronnie and Mointz trained in explosives, self-defense, and surveillance among other things. Ronnie enjoyed the training immensely and looked forward to coming back. Mointz, on the other hand, did not enjoy the training as much, as he had too much on his mind. He planned to depart a week from Tuesday for England. With it now Friday, 12 days was enough.

Lauren picked up Mointz, as Ronnie decided to stay until Monday morning to work more with Vaz. Mointz could not wait to get back to the beach house.

"Ronnie seems to be full of piss and vinegar," Lauren said, as Mointz buckled his seatbelt in her government-issued K-car.

"A K-car? Really, Lauren?"

"Sorry, the agency fell for Lee Iacocca's sale pitch."

"I see. To respond to your comment, Ronnie is eating this up."

Lauren left the Naval War College and started up Route 24 to return to Barrington. "Did you watch the video?"

"How could I not let Erin be with her children? As much as I love Deidre, how could I allow it?"

"I knew you would say that and so did Davis. You are who you are and you should be commended for what you have accomplished so far. I could not be prouder of you. When Davis sees what you've done, he will jump for joy. There is a problem in this, however."

"What is that?"

"Can you honestly tell me you can give up Deidre? How is it fair to the woman who loves you more than you can imagine?"

"So what is the 'but?'"

Lauren stopped at a red light and looked at Mointz. "There is no 'but,' not this time."

"You are full of it Lauren, you are keeping something from me. What is it?"

"I… I…"

"Oh, will you just spit it out?"

She pulled the K-car into a grocery store parking lot and looked into the eyes of the future leader of the free world. Her face as white as the driven snow, the blonde Gabriel looked flustered. Her face matched her white ski jacket.

"Cristopher, Erin and you are totally incompatible. The panel has always known you should not be together. There was a lot of talk she should be eliminated in the Second Parallel, but Ellis and Davis nixed that idea."

"Jesus, Mary and Joseph, please help me. This is so not cool Lauren. How do they expect me to cast aside the mother of Patrick and Thomas?"

They rode practically in silence the rest of the way back to Barrington. Mointz and Lauren sat in the beach house's driveway for almost ten minutes before Mointz said, "I will not let anything happen to Erin. I am not like her and, no matter what, I am a loyal person. She might be a cold-hearted bitch at times, but she is still the mother of my children."

"The coldness relates on television. A weak first lady could derail a campaign" Lauren said.

"Ah, the real deal. Erin will not play out well in a campaign and a divorced President does not have a chance. Well, it did not hurt Reagan."

"Do you see Erin not blasting you in the news media?" Lauren said. She could see the wounded soul that was now sitting next to her. Mointz had the biggest heart in the world, as he had asked Lauren to stop to buy flowers for Deidre on the ride back. "I have no words to ease your pain over this, Cristopher. There is obviously something special between you and that pretty lady you are now with. Ellis and Davis tossed around having Deidre's memory returned as well, though her sweet innocence would probably have been lost if it was, most of the top psychologists said. Before you ask, Gennifer had said 'no,' long before you met."

Cristopher kissed Lauren and made his way out of the car as confused as he had ever been. He agreed to call her later; he had to do a lot of soul searching.

Chapter Fifteen

December 12, 1984

Mointz did not know how he felt when he walked into the beach house. He sat staring at pictures of his family until Deidre came into the house and kissed him. Her smile made him melt.

"How goes the battle, love?"

"Another day, another set of wrinkles."

"Gee, missed me, huh?"

Mointz laughed and kissed her sweetly before sitting her down in front of the computer. Mointz promised to never hide anything from her as he did not want to make the same mistakes he had made in his first two marriages.

As the video played, Deidre held Mointz's hand. She broke down in tears when Davis told Mointz about his love for Deidre and how he consoled her whenever she needed it. Deidre always wore her emotions on her sleeve.

Mointz now knew Erin had never loved him like this. He felt his emotions were now all over the place.

"I am sorry, Cristopher," Deidre said, and put her head in his lap. "I never meant to hurt you."

"Angel, how could you hurt me if you were not even aware of what was going on? This is my burden to bear, not yours."

"Mointz, you can be such a daft prick sometimes. You are the one with 58 years of earthly experience, yet you do not think. What do you mean 'your burden?' It is our burden. Cristopher, the decision about your family is yours and yours alone. All I can do is tell you I love you and I am willing to take on anything you throw at me. You saved me and my son and I will be forever grateful, but my love for you is something I have never experienced before. I would love to have your children and marry you and to be your everything," she said.

Mointz stood up, walked into the bedroom and opened the safe. One of the nuclear powered cases contained exactly what he needed. He put his thumb on the security device that secured the case to open it. There were over 80 vials in the case in storage. Mointz pulled vial D-470. As he read the directions Davis had left on his little iMini, he filled the syringe with the 80 cc's he needed for Deidre.

"Drop 'em, sexy," Mointz told her when he returned from the bedroom. "You are about to stop aging for the next 22 years."

"Cristopher," she cried out as she pulled up her skirt, "Please be sure that this is exactly what you want."

He kissed her passionately. "I have never felt more sure about anything in my life. We will figure it out as we go along. I love you as much as I love the boys; that is for sure." He cleaned the area with alcohol and administered the intramuscular shot. "You will feel like you were hit by a bus for the next 48 hours or so, but I promise you will be fine."

"I trust you, Mr. Mointz."

"There is no doubt in my mind that I love you more, love. Now, why don't you rest while I start to prepare for Adam Ferguson?"

###

Mointz tucked Deidre in. He grabbed the USB device with Ferguson's dossier on it and reached for a single-serve bottle of apple juice from the refrigerator. Knowing he had just performed more weird science made him chuckle to himself, as the USB device decoded itself before it opened.

Adam Ferguson's file read like the story of a modern day Judas. The once-golden boy of the Royal Family decided he loved money more than he loved his family and his country. With the calmness of a butterfly to the public and a sociopath in private, Ferguson was one ruthless son-of-a-bitch, Mointz thought.

Mointz's blood boiled after he had finished reading the whole dossier on Ferguson. They were very fortunate to be stopping Ferguson at the beginning of his career, before he caused too much damage. Ferguson was a member of the British Parliament and Mointz hoped with some good fortune he could stop Ferguson on his trip to England. He had seven days to get in and out of England and neutralize Adam Ferguson. Lauren had learned some valuable information earlier in the day through her CIA contacts; Ferguson would be in Parliament until the 22nd of December before leaving on holiday. At first, the Mointz family was not too thrilled about Cristopher heading over to England for Christmas. However, they relented when they learned that some of Deidre's family lived there and Mointz gave them a big guilt trip about it being the last holiday Ronnie and he would spend together.

Mointz had picked Brown University early in his senior year, while Ronnie chose the military academies. He had wanted to play football at either Annapolis or West Point. Several Division I programs hounded both of them to play football. Mointz had made it clear to recruiters he would not participate in football in college until after he had made the United States swim team for 1988. The pool had become his sanctuary, even though Ronnie continued to bust his chops, saying if he did not stop swimming, baldness would certainly set in before the 1988 games. Mointz's hair was almost as popular as his athletic ability.

Mointz added a log to the fire and checked on Deidre, now fast asleep. Mointz re-tucked her in and she smiled slightly as he did it. Deidre felt like she was living a fairy tale. The fire in the bedroom was roaring brightly as they both loved to sleep with a fire.

Mointz had cable television in the beach house and he turned on a Bruins game. At first he thought he was watching an ESPN Classic as the non-HD broadcast was a throw back. He cheated, finding out the score of the game on his Apple laptop, and changed the channel to HBO. A Clint Eastwood movie, "Any Which Way You Can' was playing and Mointz watched the simple-minded movie that took his mind off the world for an hour or two.

Deidre did feel like she had been hit by a bus when she awoke the next morning. Mointz had already used his new home gym with state-of-the-art Nautilus and cardio equipment. The setup had been exactly what Mointz needed.

The future President, with good luck on his side, had breakfast ready for Deidre when she walked into the kitchen.

"Cristopher, I cannot even think about eating. My stomach is in knots from the drug you gave me," she told him. "I still cannot fathom how cooking becomes in vogue in the early 2000's. I watched some of the cooking shows on the iThingy of yours when you were in Newport. I made a meal or two. The Food Channel is really very good.

"Babe, I made crepes just for you. Fresh, delicious crepes with whipped cream, strawberries and fresh squeezed orange juice to wash it all down. You are really going to miss out."

"Well, maybe I'll try just a few. I would hate to miss out on anything you made for me. You are such a great cook it would be a shame for you to eat by yourself."

Mointz flipped a few crepes. He set them down in front of her with the juice as promised. "Where were you supposed to travel this weekend? My parents said they had invited you to go with them to New Hampshire."

"I told them that I had a date this weekend. You know your parents never ask questions. I guess I did have a date with a big needle, thank you for that, Mr. Mointz. What in God's good name did you give me?"

"It is a type of HGH hormone that can stop the aging process for 22 to 24 years, Davis wrote in his notes in the vial description chart. The drug would be highly controversial if it was released, as you can imagine. The scientific community knows nothing of it. Congratulations, my dear, you are now a genetic marvel like me."

"Does all this genetic altering bother you?"

"Yes and no. We cannot stop the scientific process even if we wanted to. Scientists will always strive to better our lives, even if we do not want it. The curiosity factor built into a person will always look for solutions to problems, even if they are told there is no logical solution."

Deidre kissed him after she had finished all of her crepes. "It is far too early to comprehend your genius today. I think I will go back to bed and try and sleep this medical hangover off. Do you think you can keep yourself busy?"

"I know you are feeling a bit peaked, but I am able to go back to my parents today. My Washington DC trip is over."

"Maybe I will try to hit the law books today if I feel better. I still need to pass the bar."

"You need to finish up and then blend into the crowd for a while."

"Why?"

"Sweetie, you will be in the public eye for the rest of your life now that we are together."

"Oh, yeah. I forgot you have a few things to do over the next few years."

Deidre went back to bed. Cristopher jumped in her 300 series Mercedes to head for his parents' house. He was shocked to see his parents home and remembered this was the weekend Seanie would battle tonsillitis. His family had left New Hampshire to visit the pediatrician later this afternoon.

"Hey, buddy. How was the conference?" Robert asked his son when he walked in.

"Great. We just came home a little while ago.

"Why are you driving Deidre's car? Is anything wrong with the Bronco?" Martha asked. Mointz told his mother Deidre needed to borrow the Bronco with Ronnie to pick up something at the furniture store.

Martha proceeded to tell her son why they were home, explaining the tonsillitis, as Mointz had expected. "I still cannot believe you will not be here for Christmas. Who would rather go to England and ski in the Alps over my beautiful Christmas Dinner?" Martha asked her son. She was trying to be funny. However, she was still a little upset her son would not be home. What mother wouldn't be?

"Mother, we talked about this. I am going to college only 20 minutes from here. Ronnie is going away and Deidre is talking about leaving Barrington. This is our last hurrah."

Martha hugged her son. "I know, sweetie. I am still going to miss you. It is a mother's prerogative to miss her child."

"Are you going to be all set with money?" His father asked. "I know you do well keeping the credit cards under a million. Do not be afraid to use them." Robert loved that line and Mointz smiled every time Robert said it.

"I have plenty. I have so many ad campaigns going on, I cannot even count that high."

"Good man. I am proud of you." He knew his son was plenty frugal and he invested his money well. They loved to see who had the better day on Wall Street. It was a great way to bond with each other.

"Well, folks. I am off to the mall to check on the ladies of Providence College. Please do not wait up, as I will be with Ronnie."

Mointz's parents trusted their son completely. It was hard for them to enforce a curfew on him, as the superstar world champion was about to attend university soon. Ronnie and Mointz were always headed somewhere and his parents never knew what they were up to. Once Ronnie had seen the light and broken up with drama queen, Kathy, Mointz had more of a free reign. He did, however, get along with his sister much better in this parallel than the last.

"Safety first, young man," Martha pronounced to her son. She always said that line before he departed for parts unknown.

Mointz kissed his mother goodbye and hugged his father before he walked out the front door.

"Does our boy even own a pair of long pants anymore?" his father asked his wife.

"Sweetheart, when was the last time I bought him anything? Everything he wears now comes from a company trying to get him to endorse their products.

"Why don't we find him an endorsement deal that will make him wear long pants in the middle of winter," Robert said, while he scooped Seanie some ice cream to help his sore throat.

Deidre loved cannolis from Federal Hill in Providence, the Italian section of the city, so Mointz decided to stop by to surprise her. The Italian Mafia dominated Providence's 'Little Italy,' in the mid-eighties. Their ristorantes and bakeries dotted the hill.

The swimming star signed an autograph for a young swimmer, who had just come from the Providence YMCA, as he walked into Sal's Bakery. Five wannabe gangsters sat there drinking espressos. Mointz noticed them staring at him right away.

"Look mister no-pants. Who are you, a movie star signing autographs in my uncle's bakery?" one of the men asked. He could have been the widest person Mointz had ever seen.

Mointz laughed. "No, just a guy."

Another of the men did not think Mointz was very charming. He asked, "Who the hell are you then?"

"I am an athlete, alright," Mointz exclaimed, as his Irish Temper started to boil. It flared every time he felt threatened.

"You look like a fairy," Wide Guy retorted. He stood up, as Mointz tried to order cannolis from an older female behind the counter.

Mointz turned and shot him a look. "My name is Cristopher Mointz, I am a world champion swimmer. Maybe if you didn't sit here all day on a Saturday looking tough, you would know who I was." He turned back to the woman at the counter and all five of the men stood up. Mointz, at six feet, six inches tall, towered over all of them. Mointz figured if this was going to get physical, he would turn the wide guy into a pile of Jell-O on the ground first, if he needed to.

"Do you want a fist in your mouth as well as those cannolis?" Wide Guy asked. "Hey, I am talking to you." Wide Guy gave Mointz a wicked shove from behind.

"Lightning speed" would be the understatement of the year, as Mointz turned and dropped Wide Guy with a vicious chop to the throat. As Wide Guy humped over, Mointz added a spinning Kung Fu kick to the side of the head. All of the men were surprised. Without hesitation Mointz grabbed the next closest man and head-butted him in the bridge of his nose.

One of the remaining three ran out the door leaving two twenty-somethings about five foot seven and one hundred and fifty pounds each. Mointz pretended to hit one of them. He squealed like a school girl running away from a frog.

"Why don't you two idiots sit down?" Mointz again asked the woman behind the counter for his cannolis as if nothing had happened. A few seconds later, the leader of the Providence Mafia walked into the bakery.

"What the hell is going on in here?" Providence's Raymond Belvenie asked. Three rather large men stood behind him. Before anyone responded, it occurred to him who was standing in front of him. "This is Cristopher Mointz, you morons." Belvenie read the 'PROVIDENCE JOURNAL' every day and there had been plenty of press about the young superstar.

Wide Guy started to get up. "Who the hell is he? He said his name, but it did not ring a bell."

"He is Rhode Island's world champion swimmer and future Olympian. The guy is on the cover of practically every magazine in the world…how did this start?"

Mointz answered, "Mr. Belvenie, I came in here to buy some cannolis for my girlfriend and this man," he said pointing at Wide Guy, "and I had a minor disagreement on sports. I apologize if there was any inconvenience." Mointz knew exactly who Belvenie was. As Mointz would attend school here soon, he needed friends like Belvenie. Mointz extended his hand to Wide Guy, a/k/a Anthony Riggoli, and the two shook. Mointz gave Anthony a bone and he accepted it gladly. Anthony could also be a friend someday.

Belvenie grunted and looked at his nephew. "As long as you are fine with Anthony's behavior, my nephew forgets the customer is always right. It looks like this time he learned a valuable lesson," Belvenie said. Mointz had definitely impressed him in more ways than one. "I hear you will be attending Brown in the fall. Good luck. They are sure going to love having a man with your talents there."

"I look forward to it very much. Competing for the Bears will be an honor. I hope we can win a national championship in my time there."

They discussed Brown for a few more minutes before Belvenie excused himself. "Stop by any time," he invited Mointz. Mointz heard him laughing as Belvenie made it out the door with his goons following close behind.

"For what it is worth, I am glad we could bury the hatchet," Anthony told him. It was an apology without his coming directly out and saying it. He did not want to lose face with his goombas right there.

"I hope to see you guys after the holiday. You can buy me an espresso."

"Hell, why don't we grab one now? I want to hear all about this Olympic stuff." It looked like Anthony was getting a shiner from Mointz's Kung Fu kick to the head.

The six of them enjoyed espressos and pastries. After about two hours, they had all become fast friends. Mointz's self-defense skills had impressed the boys from the hill.

Mointz left with Deidre's cannolis and a few new friends. He knew he would be able to count on them if he needed help in any way.

Deidre sat on the couch reading a book on Tort Law when Mointz came home with blood all over his sweatshirt. He told Deidre what happened and she laughed at how Mointz could turn lemons into lemonade. Mointz dropped his clothes in the wash and jumped in the shower as Deidre returned the breakfast favor by cooking a roast for dinner. Mointz walked into the kitchen after his shower and was startled at Deidre's appearance.

"So, do I look like myself or what?"

"What in the world did Celeste teach you?"

Deidre sported red hair and new facial features. "Well, Mointzie, ever get it on with a redhead?"

Mointz put his arms around her and kissed her. "I love you, I love your heart, your soul and the way you love me, no matter if you were a redhead, blonde, brunette or a woman with green hair. I love you for you. However, red hair is pretty sexy on you."

"Take advantage of the many people I can be now for the next twenty-two years."

Deidre fell asleep in Mointz's arms after they ate her roast. Mointz watched a Larry Bird-led Celtics beat a Magic Johnson-led Lakers team by fifteen points in the old Boston Garden.

###

The phone in the beach house rarely rang and Mointz, as usual, let the phone's answering machine pick up.

"Mointz, it is your friend, Lauren. If you are there, pick up please."

"Hey, what can I do for you, lady?" he asked when he picked up the phone.

"Glad you picked up. Are you doing better today?"

"As a matter of fact, I am. How are you?"

"One would have to assume that you gave her the shot. I am glad that you came to your senses sooner rather than later."

"Yes, I gave her the shot. What can I do for you, Director?"

"Do you have any major plans tonight?"

"Not really. Deidre is still a little sluggish from the shot of specialized HGH. Why, what can I do for you? Tell me you do not need me for a mission."

"I could use some help. I got myself into, as you say, 'a bit of a pickle.' I could really use a friend and a person who I can trust who is in the same boat I am in."

"Come to the beach house. It is safe and we can talk here. I have plenty of room."

"Thank you," Lauren said, extremely glad it allowed her to enter into the life of Mointz. Lauren could not help herself. She really liked him more than she had liked anyone she had ever met. Mointz was trustworthy and had that special something that could make anyone smile.

Chapter Sixteen

"Damn it, Lauren, why didn't you just tell me Ferguson kills your father. I had my Father Houle. You should never have hidden the truth," Mointz said softly as Deidre slept peacefully in the next room. Deidre hoped to have all of her strength back by tomorrow.

"I am sorry, Cristopher. I know my problems are not relevant to your mission. The fate of the world is in your hands."

"Talk to me. What is your pickle?" Mointz smiled at her and she immediately felt a little more at ease until Mointz gave her a hug.

Lauren's baby blues filled with tears and she squeezed Mointz tightly. "The person who conspires with Ferguson next year to kill my father lives right here in New England, but he is untouchable."

"No one is untouchable, Lauren."

"There is no guarantee this person will give up when my father is reassigned and Ferguson is dead. He will just conspire with someone else to finish the job."

Mointz was a bit confused. "Who is this man? Please stop beating around the bush. We are in this together remember?"

"I…cannot tell you, I am sorry." Lauren was as vulnerable as she had ever been in her entire life.

"I order you to tell me."

Swallowing hard, Lauren looked into Mointz's eyes and said, "Your father-in-law, Matthew Flaherty."

Erin's father, Matthew Flaherty, had started his professional career as a Boston Police Officer. Working the night beat, he put himself through law school. The Federal Bureau of Investigation called after he had passed the bar exam in the mid-seventies. He became the agent in charge of the Boston Field Office in 1983 at the age of thirty-seven.

Cristopher almost lost Deidre's supper when he heard the news. "Tell me it is not why you wanted Deidre and I together."

"You are an asshole for implying that."

"Oh, man. Oh, man. This is not good; this is not good at all. I want to know what you know. Tell me from the beginning. Let me grab us a couple of beers and when I come back, no more secrets." He went into the kitchen and found two Millers.

Lauren accepted the beer. "I had been investigating all of my father's papers since I became the Director of the CIA. I told no one what I knew, not even Ellis or Davis. Before I came to this parallel, I had no idea Matthew Flaherty and two other members of the Bureau were in cahoots with Ferguson."

"Jesus, I met Erin when he was already retired from the Bureau. I cannot believe you are telling me he was dirty. I trust you, as even my sister is not this good of an actress, but it is hard to fathom."

Lauren took a long belt of her beer as Mointz rubbed her back. She could see how he was struggling with this information though he was not passing judgment for now. "Flaherty has major connections within the Irish Republican Army, which, by the way, is funded mostly in Boston and Chicago. Adam Ferguson sold them millions in weapons. My father made it his department's number one priority to shut down the money wing of the IRA here in the states. When your father-in-law heard my father's edict, he teamed with Ferguson to eliminate him. Their cronies took out my father and his team. I only looked into Matthew Flaherty here in this parallel because of his ties to you and this mission, as the panel had approved him as a resource for you. Cristopher, I am not a heartless bitch. My father means everything to me."

Mointz held her tightly again, trying to stop the tears. Once the tears subsided and he carried two more beers into the living room, Lauren said, "I am sorry."

"I do not understand why my father-in-law would do that," Mointz said. "He has always been an IRA sympathizer and he has never been a big fan of the crown. I never would have guessed this. However, he was always full of himself, thinking his shit didn't stink."

"Cristopher, I am sorry. I knew of your connection to Deidre and it was always Davis's intention for you to be happy. Erin and you are about as compatible as a mongoose and a snake."

"Wait. I thought we tested well."

"The two of you tested well for you to eventually become man and wife again, nothing else."

Mointz shook his head. "Erin always loved to be the belle of the ball. This is starting to make sense."

Lauren could see why Davis advocated for Mointz with such hardihood. He would not throw anyone under the bus. He was a man of conviction and, it seemed, one hell of a friend.

"Lauren, I trust you completely."

"As you say, here comes the 'but.'"

"Stop stealing my lines. When we come back from Europe, you and I will make this a priority. The IRA has lost their money connection in America."

"Aren't you an IRA sympathizer too?"

"Sure. However, I do not believe in revolution and arming terrorists to obtain independence. There are some intrepid people who fought for home rule the right way. They are the people we need to acknowledge. There is no way I will allow Matthew Flaherty to murder your father."

"I am going to Europe still?"

"Yes, Ma'am."

At that moment, Deidre walked in the room to see an emotionally drained Lauren in Mointz's arms. She saw the tears in Lauren's eyes and wondered what was wrong.

"Are you alright, Lauren?" she asked as she sat down across the room in her bathrobe.

Mointz extended his hand and pulled Deidre on the couch next to him. Mointz and Lauren explained to Deidre exactly why Lauren was upset.

"How complicated did your lives turn out to be here in this parallel?"

"I have no way to answer that yet," Mointz said.

"This is your captain speaking. The flight to London's Heathrow Airport will be approximately six hours and fifteen minutes," the Virgin Atlantic pilot said to the passengers of Flight 12 over the intercom. The passengers were all buckled up on the runway, about to take off from Boston's Logan Airport.

Lauren joined Deidre, Ronnie and Mointz in Virgin Atlantic's first class cabin on their way to meet a man named Ferguson. Ronnie, who was just coming off more training with Derek Vaz, had no idea his mother took a shot to stagnate her aging process. He loved the fact Mointz was no longer alone, being the only one who had traveled to this parallel from the first. Derek Vaz promised to take Ronnie to the Naval Academy as soon as he returned from Europe. Ronnie wanted to play ball at Navy and become a midshipman at the academy.

"Excuse me, sir," one of the beautiful first class flight attendants said to Mointz once they were airborne. The blond looked amazing to Mointz who was trying not to stare at her with Deidre next to him. "A couple of your fans would like an autograph from you. If you did not know it, a Vuarnet ad with your picture on it is on the back of our in-flight magazine."

"Sure thing, I do not mind."

The flight attendant brought two teenage girls to Mointz, who signed the magazines. Deidre playfully pinched him as the girls practically drooled all over him.

"Dude, I am going to have girls drooling all over me after I win the Heisman Trophy at Navy," Ronnie said.

"Most assuredly," Lauren voiced to Ronnie appreciating raging hormones Mointz clearly had as well. She knew from personal experience.

The red eye landed in London on Wednesday at seven in the morning and the tired foursome took a limo straight to the Holiday Inn in Mayfair for some sleep. Ronnie had told his mother they only needed three rooms, as she and Mointz were allowed to, in his words, 'cohabitate.' He did not say it with a hint of sarcasm as he could see their love for each other. Deidre was going to be thirty-three in the summer after Mointz turned eighteen in the Second Parallel in February. However, Ronnie still could not figure out his real age. He did know the two of them together made each other better people.

Mointz told Lauren and Ronnie to meet downstairs by one in the afternoon and to be ready to, as he liked to say, *"Rock and Roll."*

The bellman brought their bags to their respective rooms and as soon as Deidre and Mointz walked into theirs they jumped into bed.

"Feeling better, today?" Mointz asked.

"Yes, much better. I know you were turned on by all of the pretty flight attendants." She climbed on top of him and inserted him inside her.

Mointz was all smiles when they had finished making love. As they held each other, he said, "I am doing great, thanks to you."

"I am glad you are doing alright. I am worried about you."

"Why?"

"Besides us, there is this Ferguson thing here, the Flaherty thing at home and I am sure plenty of other 'things' down the line."

"That is a lot of 'things.' Listen, I know I love you and we will be together. Why don't we let everything else just fall into place?"

"Deal. I can live with that."

###

Adam Ferguson sat in his office in Parliament drinking a spot of Earl Grey and enjoying a piece of English pastry for dessert. He had just enjoyed a fish-and-chip plate from the pub.

The Duke of Northumberland loved to drink tea and eat pastry after lunch. He was reading the London Times when the phone on his desk rang. He took one last bite of pastry and another sip of tea before answering.

"Ferguson," he pronounced into the phone.

"Adam, William here."

"Sir William, so glad you called! To what do I owe this pleasure?"

"Our friends could use a hand with purchasing a few more of those pewter mugs from you," Sir William replied.

Ferguson owned and operated a pewter factory that made beautiful mugs for the masses and for taverns around the world. The factory also made weapons and ammunition. Mugs had been their code word for arms for years.

"Wonderful, Sir William. Shall we meet this evening and continue the conversation then? Say, six pm at Moody's Tavern?"

"That would be just splendid, see you then. Cheers."

"Cheers, Sir William," Ferguson said returning the phone to its cradle. When his secretary entered his office to tell him he had to be in the chamber for a vote on Irish self-rule, he laughed to himself. The last thing he needed was peace in Northern Ireland.

Mointz and Ronnie ordered ales, as the drinking age in England was much lower than in America where it was in the process of changing to 21. Deidre and Lauren ordered a couple of Magners cider and a couple of orders of fish and chips at Moody's Tavern.

"Ferguson's secretary said he would be in Parliament for most of the afternoon," Lauren said. She took a chip from the bowl and dipped it in mayonnaise.

"That has to be the grossest thing ever," Ronnie said. "I hate mayonnaise! Why this blessed country uses mayonnaise on everything is beyond me."

"Do not worry. Eventually they will come around," Mointz said.

"Well, I like mayonnaise," Deidre said, as she held Mointz's hand under the table.

Ronnie laughed and he ate a few chips sprinkled with vinegar. "Do we know where Ferguson goes after the session? I am dying to try out my new surveillance skills."

"Buddy, we are sitting in his hangout," Mointz told him. "When Lauren and I went to see Ferguson and asked for a tour, his secretary said he always came here after Parliament is out for the day."

"Who did you say you were?" Deidre asked.

"She recognized Cristopher right away," Lauren said. "He told her Senator Kennedy had told him to ask for a tour."

Senator Kennedy from Massachusetts was still reeling from his primary defeat by Jimmy Carter in 1980. Mointz had decided to use him as a reference when he spoke to Ferguson.

"Hopefully, the Duke of Northumberland will show up and I can be properly introduced," Mointz said. "We have to befriend him and get as much information as we can out of him, one way or another."

"Senator Kennedy is a good man, no?" Deidre asked.

Mointz and Lauren chuckled mightily. They were not big fans of the Liberal Lion.

"Depends who you ask. He is a champion for some; to others, he is the Anti-Christ."

It took about twenty minutes before a few travelers from Australia recognized Mointz. They had read the article which accompanied the Vuarnet ad in the magazine on all Virgin Atlantic flights. Mointz learned from a few of the pub's patrons that Ferguson generally appeared around five.

Almost on cue, Ferguson entered the pub at two minutes to five. The waitress who had served Mointz's party brought the Duke over.

"Lord Ferguson, this is Cristopher Mointz, the American world champion swimmer," the waitress said, introducing the two men.

"Lord Ferguson, our Senator Kennedy told me to look you up. He said you might be able to arrange a tour of Parliament for me and my family. We stopped by your office earlier and your secretary said you might eat here. This seemed like a great place for fish and chips."

From all the reports in his dossier, Mointz knew Ferguson to be extremely friendly to the public. He played the politician perfectly and invited Mointz and his family for a tour of Parliament tomorrow.

Mointz thanked him profusely. As Ferguson left, they ordered one more round of drinks.

"Nice guy, eh?" Mointz said when Ferguson sat down at his own table. "Why don't we wait to see who he is meeting with? Maybe it will be someone of importance."

"Great job getting the tour," Deidre said.

"Yeah. Not bad."

"Buddy, you are as smooth as silk. How is that?" Ronnie asked.

"He is in his element with all his years of experience as a professor," Lauren said.

They did not have to wait long to see who would be meeting Adam Ferguson as they watched Sir William Stewart walk in.

"Son-of-a-bitch, he is meeting with William Stewart," Cristopher said.

"Who is William Stewart?" Deidre asked.

"The IRA's top gun. He was a part of the British ruling party in Ireland before he turned to the dark side. He worked diligently to force the British to surrender Northern Ireland to the Republic of Ireland," Lauren said.

"What do we do?" Ronnie asked.

"Pay the bill. Tomorrow we invite Adam Ferguson to our hotel for a drink and find out what the hell they are up to."

"Thank you again for the amazing London experience, Lord Ferguson," Mointz said at the Holiday Inn in Mayfair. Lord Ferguson gladly gave Mointz and company a tour of London after the tour of Parliament. He accepted their invitation for a nightcap back at the hotel.

Lauren excused herself to visit the rest room as Ferguson told the group one story after another.

"Oh, no!" Lauren screamed out. Mointz jumped up immediately to see what had happened.

"What did you do?" he asked Lauren, who sat on her bum in the restroom.

"I slipped and twisted my ankle."

"Can you get up and put pressure on it?"

Lauren shook her head, "no." Since Ferguson and Ronnie were the same size, Lauren used them as crutches to return to her room. Mointz turned the key in the door and stepped to the side so Ferguson and Ronnie could set Lauren on the bed. As Ferguson turned around to face Mointz, Mointz met him with a karate chop to the throat.

"Tie the prick up," Lauren said.

Mointz tied him up in no time flat. He noticed Ronnie's eyes almost pop out of his head. Mointz had plenty of time to learn this was going to be the norm if he entered into this type of lifestyle.

"Go downstairs and stay with Dee," Mointz ordered. "Please hurry, as I do not want her to be left alone." He wanted to protect Dee and he also wanted Ronnie to not experience what was about to happen to Lord Ferguson.

Ronnie nodded and left quickly. Mointz was proud of how he had handled himself so far. Once Ronnie left, Mointz and Lauren proceeded with their long awaited discussion with Lord Adam Ferguson, who needed a little encouragement to open up.

"What is this all about?" Lord Ferguson asked in a low voice as Mointz's blow to the throat had injured his windpipe.

"Selling guns to the IRA, Lord Ferguson. The question is, what have you been up to?" Lauren asked a bloody Ferguson.

"None of your business, you twat!" Ferguson exclaimed before Mointz blasted him in the jaw.

"Say something crass again and see how I react. I would love to start chopping your fingers off one by one." From Ferguson's dossier, both Mointz and Lauren knew Ferguson would wilt under pressure.

"Let me be more specific, Lord Ferguson. Why did you meet Sir William Stewart last evening?" Lauren asked.

Ferguson huffed. "He wanted guns from our factory for Sinn Féin in Northern Ireland. I sell him weapons and he distributes them."

"What is the connection between the IRA, Stewart and the IRA sympathizers in Boston?" Lauren asked.

Ferguson received a backhand from Mointz that kept him talking. "The Purple Shamrock hosts a meeting in Boston every other week of people who support the cause. Sir William knows who does what to whom."

"Tell us about arm shipments to the middle east," Mointz asked.

Lauren gave him a small grin. "Years away, sir."

"Ah, shoot. Sorry. This is about the IRA and the underworld; I forgot my head for a second."

Lauren and Mointz grilled the battered Ferguson for his underworld connections for another hour before Mointz snapped his neck from behind. Lauren had used connections from both parallels to organize a disposal team made up of some serious underworld bosses. They would arrive shortly to remove Lord Ferguson from the hotel. Lauren had told them Ferguson was planning to speak to Scotland Yard about their illegal activities. Mointz and Lauren quickly escaped from the hotel and caught up to Ronnie and Deidre.

"How did it go?" Ronnie asked, when Mointz and Lauren arrived at the pub designated as their rendezvous point.

"Our friend was very enlightening before he made his way to the gates of hell," Mointz said. "We need to send our agency friends over to his factory sooner rather than later, before it turns into a pile of rubble."

"What about our friend, Sir William Stewart?" Deidre asked.

"A very astute question, my dear," Mointz said. "The agency will now watch him carefully and the agency will have a new lead source of information."

Chapter Seventeen

August 1ˢᵗ, 1985

"Honey, we do not have a lot of time," Mointz told Deidre. He kissed her quickly before putting more of his clothes in the locked closet at the beach house.

"Calm down," she said. "Are you sure they will be here soon?"

Mointz had decided to purchase the beach house from the company Deidre had created, now that he would start college soon. His nerves were shaky and his stomach in knots from hiding the fact he already lived here. Mointz would reside at a dorm at Brown supposedly, but he would never be there, he told his parents, because he was becoming too popular as a result of his ad campaigns. The now eight-time world champion gold medalist was even more popular after smashing five world records in Sydney the previous month.

The NCAA ruled he could no longer swim in college because of his endorsement deals. The new, just-passed-the-bar lawyer, Deidre, helped him with contract after contract. Ronnie took his talents to the Navy Academy to play for the Midshipmen and continued training with Derek Vaz.

Mointz's parents, at first, were not in favor of Mointz living on his own. They relented at a restaurant one night when fans swarmed Mointz. It only took a "pretty please" and a little prodding from Deidre to convince Robert and Martha to allow Mointz to live at the beach house, which, Deidre told the Mointzes, was fully furnished.

Robert and Martha were dually impressed with the house and raved at the privacy. The house next door, the one Trent Davis would purchase, was used for about two weeks out of the year in July.

"What a find," Robert told Deidre. "I was not crazy about him moving out here, but I can see how he needs his privacy now that he appears in every magazine in the world."

"Thanks, Dad, I think," Mointz said.

"This place is immaculate. The way you kept your room, when you were there, will give you the discipline to keep a neat house," Martha said. Mointz had always been a neat freak and so was Deidre, who made sure to keep the place immaculate.

"Make sure you haggle over the price, buddy," Robert said, "even though I bet Cristopher already knows what to offer."

Martha hugged Deidre. "I cannot believe the boys are all grown up and out on their own. Soon they will be married and we will have grandchildren."

Mointz winked at Deidre. A week ago, Mointz had sat with Ronnie before leaving for school and tears had flowed out of his eyes at the pride he felt about his friend doing things right this time around. Ronnie thought he was nuts and deemed him as crazy as a cuckoo clock for thinking that way.

"Cristopher needs to stick to one girl. From what Ronnie says he is all over the place on women," Robert said laughing.

Mointz's parents and Deidre took a walk on the beach. Deidre would soon start to transform herself into her own sister, a fabrication of Mointz and Lauren's imagination. Lauren was already helping start the ruse. Ronnie still had no idea Deidre would remain the same age for the next twenty-two or so years.

Robert and Martha finally left to return home and drop off Kathy at the outdoor drive-in movie theatre in Barrington where she served ice cream. She had been babysitting Seanie.

Mointz and Deidre told his parents they needed to wait for the seller's real estate agent to close the deal. After his parents left, Mointz chased Deidre into the house while she laughed and giggled. They made love and then sat in the wicker swing on the beach house's deck, waiting for Lauren to arrive.

"What are you two up to?" Lauren asked when Mointz hugged her.

"Faking out the folks that I bought this place today," Mointz told her.

"I came to tell you Sir William Stewart will be at the Purple Shamrock tomorrow night," Lauren said, as she took the other wicker swing.

"Do you plan on breaking up their little gathering?" Mointz asked. "I wish I would not stick out and could do some reconnaissance for you. However, I am pretty well known now."

"It also does not help that Scotland Yard tried to connect the dots between us and Lord Ferguson," Deidre said.

Scotland Yard had indeed interviewed Mointz, as Lauren had anticipated, after Lord Ferguson was found beaten and dead in a seedy part of Soho in London, the same day he had given Mointz a tour of Parliament.

"I have it covered, guys. There are no worries for either one of you," Lauren said. Over the last nine months Stewart had been watched closely. During that time, Lauren had dropped the "sir" or "Mr. President" when addressing Mointz and concentrated on making him feel like part of her family. Lauren and Mointz became like brother and sister. Deidre and Lauren had bonded and were quite fond of each other, as the 28-year-old Gabriel was a rising star in the agency. It definitely helped she had access to terabytes of data stored on Apple laptops everywhere, like Mointz.

"Listen you old bag, stop trying to do it all yourself," Mointz told Lauren.

"I will give you 'old bag,' young man. I am well aware of how to do my job."

"How big of a riot were you two in the First Parallel?"

"She was a pretty big witch to me," Mointz said.

Lauren gave him a half smile which Mointz knew meant trouble. "We need to put our heads together about Matthew Flaherty. Now that my father has been made Deputy Director of the CIA, he has stepped up his investigation of the IRA money connection. Flaherty is bound to become increasingly active."

Mointz had been avoiding this problem like the plague. "Give me a couple of days. I have a lot of ideas running through my mind. We have a lot to deal with soon with Gennifer coming back and me going to college for the second time."

"Jesus, Mointz, what are you worried about? Didn't you pass the first time?" Lauren asked with a laugh.

"It isn't that, I just thought I would be able to swim and now I am ineligible to enter competition."

"Oh, you big baby. Go play football, will you?" Lauren told him.

"I always wanted to date the quarterback," Deidre said.

"I am eligible for football, but I could blow out a knee and…"

"Play," Lauren said interrupting. "It will be fine and it will get some of those muscles doing something besides pumping iron all day and pushing water in the pool all night.

"I have plenty of fun," Mointz responded and kissed Deidre's neck.

"Why don't you play and let us have fun? I know you can multi-task; you are an Ivy Leaguer. You can ride into the sunset after the Olympics and play a little ball while you train. It is not like you will win the Heisman," Dee said.

"Play sweetie, please. I want you to have a little fun and stop stressing over every single thing."

"Brown plays Navy in October," Mointz said.

"Yes, I heard something like that from my son a million times. He thinks you need to stay off the field," said Deidre.

Lauren laughed. "We will be your personal cheering section in the stands."

"Maybe on Monday I will go speak to Coach Worth and after church tomorrow, I will see if I can still throw."

Lauren and Deidre high-fived and knew he was going to play. The only problem with this plan, thought Lauren, was Deidre could be wrong. Mointz could easily turn out to be a Heisman winner, even from Brown.

###

After a meeting with an extremely happy Coach Worth early on Monday, Mointz belonged to the Brown Football team. School officially started in three weeks, but football practice began on Wednesday. Mointz decided after meeting with the coaches to go out for an espresso with the boys at the bakery. He came down at least once a week to listen to the goombas talk trash to each other. It was like the real-life Sopranos, Mointz thought remembering the HBO show from the First Parallel.

Anthony smiled when Mointz walked in. "Look at the new hot-shot QB. I see an Ivy League title this year at Brown."

"How do you know that already?" Mointz asked as he sat down with his friends.

"WJAR Radio in Rhode Island here just announced you are suiting up for the Bears. Nice buddy, real nice."

"I am bored since those bastards at the NCAA will not let me swim. Oh, well. What are you guys up to?"

Rico, Mointz's former head-butt victim, answered, "We are going to Colt State Park and look for chicks. Wanna go scoop a few up with us?"

"Sounds fun, but I need to speak with Mr. Belvenie, if he has a minute."

"No sweat. He asks about you all the time. C'mon, I will bring you to him. He always tells me you are alright for a bright mick," Anthony said. "I bet you can get him for a plate of veal and pasta."

Mointz followed the hulk of a man next door into the ristorante and walked with him to the back office.

"Uncle, Cristopher would like to speak to you for a minute privately, if he may," Anthony said. Mointz could only imagine how his Uncle put up with his sister's only child.

"Only if you have the time, sir," Mointz stated.

"I always have time for you, Mr. Quarterback," Mr. Belvenie answered with a smile. The mid-fifty-year-old indicated to everyone in the room to leave. "Now, what can I do for you?"

"I have heard through the back channels from people doing security for me at a photo shoot and at clubs for promotions that the agent in charge of

Boston is allowing a certain, shall I say, Boston mobster with Providence ties, to play both sides of the proverbial fence. I might be only a college freshman, but I am worldly enough to figure out what that means and how it could hurt my friends. I hope you do not mind me interrupting your day."

The head of the Providence Mafia smiled at the young Mointz, "Thank you for the tip." It was all Belvenie said on the matter. He quickly started talking about Brown Football. Mointz knew how grateful he was just by the way he interacted with him.

Belvenie gave him his veal lunch and when Mointz tried to pay to avoid the NCAA rule of free food, Belvenie told him to let them come to him to complain as they were like "family" here. He also told Mointz, in the future, if he ever needed to speak to him, his door was always open and just come straight to him.

Coach Worth was astonished on Wednesday at how quickly Mointz picked up the offense on the first day of practice. The Providence media blanketed the practice with camera crews and reporters as they watched Mointz complete pass after pass. The school was abuzz that Mointz had decided to play football and there was a new spirit on a team which had experienced a few lean years. Mointz answered plenty of questions about the upcoming season and his quest for Olympic glory before he left to shower and head home.

Deidre was crying when he arrived at the beach house. His heart skipped a beat or two or three.

"What is wrong, sweetie pie?" Mointz asked.

"My parents decided to come to town this week from Florida."

Mointz wanted to burst out laughing, but he really enjoyed making love to Deidre and he did not want couch duty. Her parents and she were like oil and water. They had practically turned their backs on Deidre when she had become pregnant at barely 15. They had tried to hide the pregnancy and even considered making her enter a convent.

Deidre's mother, Gertrude, and father, Wilhelm, eventually decided to move to the United States from Luxemburg and Deidre moved in with Ronald. While they adored Ronnie, they still had icy relations with their daughter.

"Why are you so down in the dumps?" Mointz asked.

"They are incorrigible. Plus, they did not even bother to give us a head's up. This means no "*you*" for a week."

"Please, I will sneak upstairs. Remember, Gertie and Willie love me."

"They do love you, Mointzie."

"Wanna tell them that we are having sex and are going to be together forever?"

"They do not like you that much."

Mointz and Deidre avoided talking anymore about their future. It was a given they would spend the rest of their lives together. They would eventually have to go public with their relationship. However, Mointz and Deidre decided to wait until he finished school and Mointz's looks evened out a bit with hers. Somewhere down the line they already had a plan worked out to perfection, with Lauren's help.

The Santers, Deidre's parents, rolled into Barrington on Thursday and Dee begged Mointz to spend the night at her house. Mointz made her promise massages, sexual favors, free get-out-of-trouble passes and anything he wanted for a month before he agreed to comply with her request.

Mointz started to drive toward Deidre's house after practice when his new car phone in the Bronco rang.

"Hello," Mointz said, still getting used to the gadget he had used years ago in the First Parallel. His father had bought it for him and he really liked the fact he had one again.

"Matthew Flaherty was found floating in the Charles River. What do you know about this?" Lauren asked.

Mointz immediately knew what had happened and he felt sick over it. "I spoke to a friend on Monday and I might have let it slip what a total dickhead my father-in-law was, but I swear that is all I know. I cannot believe he is dead."

"Mointz, I never said he was dead. He has three bullets in him, but so far he is hanging on."

"How did it happen?"

"He was thrown off a boat and barely managed to survive until another boat showed up in the nick of time. This is the end of his career and I can tell you the bastard deserved what happened to him. I am sorry to say it to you." Lauren felt pangs speaking those words as it must have torn her friend apart to do what he had done.

Mointz beeped the horn at an older woman who cut him off and then ran a red light. "Lauren, you reap what you sow. You know I would probably have protected him no matter what. However, when I needed him most, he dropped me like a bad habit. I had loved Erin's parents like they were my own parents and when I got divorced; I really could have used a friend. They turned their back on me like I meant nothing to them. I loved Erin and maybe I was not perfect, but I never would have done to her what they did to me. I treated her like a queen. Now her father is going to need help…"

"And you are going to help them."

"No, Lauren, I am not going to help him. He wanted to murder your father. I have to save the planet and stay out of the life of Matthew Flaherty. My boys are my world. Besides, how can I trust him now?"

"Cristopher, he was not a very good person. Think it over."

"I will. I still have to save Erin."

"Think it over. By the way, good luck with the Santers tonight."

"Spoke with Deidre, I see."

"I called her earlier. Call me later if you need me."

Mointz spent the night entertaining the Santers as only he could. The Santers went to bed early and Mointz told Deidre he needed to go out for a while. Mointz drove to Mass General to see Matthew Flaherty. In his heart, Mointz knew he still loved Flaherty and he felt ashamed his words to Raymond Belvenie had caused Flaherty's predicament.

Mointz took the stairs to the Intensive Care Unit. One of the third shift nurses immediately recognized him. He explained to her he was a friend of the family. The world champion swimmer and cover boy easily talked her into bringing him to Flaherty's room.

"Excuse me, son, you cannot go in there," the FBI agent guarding the door told him.

"My name is Cristopher Mointz and I am a friend of the family," Mointz said, as tears rolled down his cheeks.

"You are the swimmer who wanted to wait before entering the Olympics."

Mointz nodded and wiped his eyes.

"Go in for a minute, but do not tell anyone I let you in."

Mointz thanked him and walked into the room to see Matthew Flaherty hooked up to a half dozen machines, his eyes closed.

"Dad, what did you do?" Mointz mouthed to him as he sat in the chair next to his bed. "Why would you allow a guy like Ferguson to kill Philip Gabriel?"

Mointz sat in silence holding Flaherty's hand for a few minutes. He kissed Flaherty's forehead before he left. As he walked down the hall, he spotted Celia Flaherty with her sister-in-law Debra. He wanted to hug her and reach out, but he couldn't, not yet. Celia and Mointz had been like two peas in a pod until it had all ended with Erin accusing him falsely of having an affair with a hairdresser. Broken hearted, Mointz left the hospital and cried all the way back to the Bronco.

"Sucks, doesn't it?" Lauren told him and hugged him. She had been leaning against his Bronco in the hospital's parking lot.

"What are you doing here?"

"I called Deidre and she told me where you were. I was worried about you."

Mointz opened the passenger side door and she got into the Bronco.

"What is the word on the street?" Mointz asked.

"Flaherty gave up what he knew to some real nasty people," Lauren replied.

"How did you find that out?"

"There are several inside people who reported the information to the agency. My father has kept abreast of the situation. He has a lot on his plate now because of this."

"Agencies still do not share information, do they?" Mointz asked. "How deep is Flaherty in it?"

"He is deep in it, but before you have to say anything, we will protect him from harm. I will not let him get hung out to dry."

"You do not have to do it."

"Yes, I do. I owe you a lot, Mr. President. I can only imagine how difficult a decision it was for you to speak to the mob to save my father. Deidre is one lucky girl."

"Hmmm, remember Gennifer Moore is about to jump back into our lives. I know it will go over like a fart in church when she finds out about Deidre."

She laughed. "You do have a way with words."

"I try my best to entertain the masses."

"Did you really fall for Miss Moore?" Lauren asked.

"Gennifer is a dynamite woman, but I cannot get Deidre out of my mind or heart. I am so in love with her, Lauren. I never realized it until this week. She broke my heart after Ronnie died. Now, I have to find a way to get the old Deidre to become a new Deidre."

"Mointzie," Lauren began, 'Mointzie' was Deidre's pet name for Cristopher, "tell your parents about Deidre when it is time. Do what you have to do. Deidre will be your biggest asset in life. I am already working on a way to make the transition seamless."

"Promise me you can do it."

"I will have it covered tighter than a drum. Remember, the Santers had two daughters. We can work it out from there. Now, go home. You have practice tomorrow. From what I understand, the Brown Bears are about to have a great season."

Mointz smiled. "I know. I really like being back on the field with two good knees. I just wish my personal life was in a better place.

Lauren kissed him again. "One day at a time, Mr. Mointz, one day at a time."

Chapter Eighteen

Matthew Flaherty barely survived. He retired the week before Halloween. Lauren and Mointz kept an eye out for any repercussions from Flaherty coming semi-clean with the bureau. Flaherty had decided to relocate his family to the Emerald Isle. Mointz needed to figure out what he would do with Erin eventually, but he had a couple of years.

Mointz was the toast of the football world as the Brown Bears upset the Ronnie-led Naval Academy 26 to 20 on Halloween with Ronald, Deidre, and all the Mointzes young and old in the stands in Annapolis, Maryland.

The following week, Brown smashed Harvard 38 to 0 and earned a share of the Ivy League crown for the first time in 22 years before winning it outright the next Saturday, defeating Princeton 48 to 6. Brown defeated The University of Rhode Island the week before Thanksgiving to end their season and take home the Governor's Cup.

The Mointzes invited Mointz and some teammates as well as Deidre and Lauren to dinner after the game before the Brown Bears partied at one of the college's frat houses. Mointz made Deidre attend. She had fun the whole night, watching the Bears shotgun beers and do keg stands, while trying to flirt with young ladies.

Mointz asked his parents to come over the next day after church as he had something really important to discuss. The beach house had a rip roaring fire going when they arrived.

"I do not know what to say," Robert said when he found out about Mointz's mission. "The fact you are my son does not change the fact you have to do this. I always knew you were too smart for your own good.

"How long have you known, Deidre?" Martha asked.

"Since his seventeenth birthday," she replied. "I was as shocked as the two of you are."

Martha and Robert stared at the picture collage Mointz had put on the computer screen. They cried when they looked at the beautiful Thomas and Patrick.

"Who knows about this?" Robert asked, as he held his wife.

"Lauren, Deidre, Ronnie, and now the two of you. In a couple of days a close friend of ours will have her memories restored," Mointz said.

"Your mother always told me we never took enough science in college. All these years, you were doing all of these things and you had to pretend you did not know anything. You knew our five-year-old neighbor would be kidnapped and you stopped it. My God, son, how did you pull this all off?"

"It wasn't easy, Pop. Deidre helped me buy the beach house and Lauren has been there as well. Ronnie found out after Deidre did, but from the age of eight until I told Deidre, I was on my own."

Deidre had looked pale when Mointz spoke privately with Lauren about what he should tell his parents. He hoped they would be able to handle what he was about to tell them on top of what he just did tell them.

"Mom and Dad, Deidre and I are together, together. We will marry and have the boys," Mointz said. "I know you might not understand completely, but I have to save the world and become the President of this country in 2016 and Deidre is an integral part of the mission."

"Please understand, Martha and Robert, the fate of the world rests in Cristopher's hands. You cannot change the way you are now. In fact, not even Seanie, Kathy or his grandparents can know," Deidre told them.

"Deidre is so much older than you," Martha said. "Well, is she?"

"Age is not relevant to me anymore, to be honest. Remember there was only a fifteen-year difference between us, but technically I am 59 if you add my years in both parallels and I am older than her. Lauren is really 68."

Martha smiled nervously. She could see Deidre's anxiety. "Deidre, Robert and I have always loved you and we are extremely proud you have helped our son. It makes me feel wonderful my son has found a soul mate in someone as special as you. Cristopher saving Ronnie and taking up such a huge endeavor is just so incredible to me."

"Mum, Ronnie isn't the only one I came back to save," Mointz told his mother. He explained her cancer. The news obviously hit her husband hard. "Do not worry Dad, everything will be fine. I promise."

Martha hugged Deidre and then her son. Many tears had been shed since Cristopher's return and this was no exception.

"So, Deidre," Robert pronounced, "you are my daughter-in-law then?"

"Working on it, Pop. It will be nice to stop having to sneak around to be with her."

"Tell me about how you are to become President," Martha asked.

Mointz explained all about how much progress he had made in the Second Parallel and how the world needed him to take the reins and stop the governments of the world from destroying each other.

"The family pictures I am looking at, will they all change over the years?" Martha asked.

"You will age the same. The only one who will not is Deidre, because of the medicine that she took to stop her aging for 22 years to let my age catch up to hers."

"This is surreal," Martha said and she hugged her son again. "Cristopher, the world will finally see how special someone can be."

"Only a mother would say that."

"Hogwash," Robert said. "What your mother just said is completely true. Fulfill your destiny, my son. To me, it seems like you, Deidre and Ronnie will be quite busy in the coming years. All of you know, when needed, Martha and I will be there to help."

"Thanks, Pop. Coming from you, it means a lot that you want to help and be involved with mother in all of our little missions. Be careful what you wish for," Mointz said with a smile.

Mointz waited on Folsum Avenue in his Bronco. He watched for anything out of the ordinary to happen before Gennifer Moore's school bus pulled up. Even though they were born two weeks apart, Gennifer was a year behind him in school, as she had started first grade a year after Mointz. She was a senior at her high school.

Mointz knew Genny's attacker came from behind a car and pulled Genny into the woods at the end of the street. Her yellow school bus turned the corner at the top of Folsum Avenue and slowly pulled past the Bronco. The bus stopped and the red stop sign came out from the side. He watched Genny step off the bus. Mointz slowly got out of the Bronco and waited for the scream Genny had said would come before she was hurt. The scream came, and Mointz was off like a rocket to save her.

The man with the mustache tried to drag Genny into the woods by the hair. Just then, Mointz showed up, in the nick of time as he had underestimated the speed of the attack. He pulverized the mustached man.

Gennifer, wearing her Catholic School checkered skirt, white Oxford and maroon sweater, held Mointz a few feet away from the man who attacked her. The man lay on the ground unconscious. Mointz hoped he was still alive.

"Genny, I need you to go and run home and call 911, understand?"

She nodded and ran to her house. Gennifer's father ran out to find Mointz standing over the mustached man, who was now taped up with electrical tape.

"You look familiar," the ex-veteran said to Mointz in a smoker's voice.

"I am kind of a celebrity."

"Yes, the swimming quarterback who just won Sportsman of the Year. What are you doing saving my Genny?"

Mointz did not want him to think something was out of place nor did he want to reveal how in depth he knew her.

"I took a wrong turn and was going to ask for directions when I heard a scream. I ran down the street and witnessed this man attacking your daughter."

The local police arrived and took away Gennifer's attacker. Mr. Moore invited Mointz to his house. A police detective wanted to interview Mointz and Gennifer in a little bit.

Barbara Moore sat with Gennifer at the kitchen table drinking cocoa with her daughter. Mr. Moore introduced Mointz to his wife and she immediately hugged him. The six-feet-six-inch Mointz sat down for cocoa as they all waited for the detective to arrive.

"Are you alright?" Mointz asked Gennifer, with a small smile.

She nodded and smiled shyly. "Thanks to you. I cannot believe that man..." Gennifer tried to say before she started to cry. Without any hesitation and to the shock of her parents, Mointz put his arms around her.

"I promise tomorrow will be a better day," Mointz said.

"Hello, Gennifer," Mointz said when she called him the next morning.

"How did you know it was me?" she asked.

"Probably because it is four a.m. in the morning and barely anyone has this number. You and Lauren are now members of the exclusive club."

"Mind telling me why you came to save me yesterday and what the hell I am doing in 1985 again?"

Mointz laughed. He had no idea the calm Gennifer would be this shocked and agitated. Gennifer was normally the most grounded out of all of them.

"Surprise, Genny."

"Surprise, my ass. You knew all about me coming back to this parallel," she exclaimed. "Lauren is obviously with us. Who else is here?"

"Just the three of us that I know of. Want me to pick you up for school?"

"Since I do not have a car and my parents think you are the best thing since sliced bread, it will be lovely."

Mointz picked her up around seven in Mattapoisett. They hugged immediately when he entered the house, but when Gennifer went for the kiss, Mointz pulled away shyly.

"Erin or Deidre?" Gennifer asked.

"Deidre. Come on, we can discuss it on the way to my house," he said and opened the front door for her to walk out to the Bronco.

On the way to Barrington, Mointz gave Gennifer a brief synopsis of his years in the Second Parallel. He could see she was stung a bit when he spoke about Deidre.

"Believe me; I really wanted you here, even though Deidre and I became one. I certainly did not think Erin's father was a rotten louse."

"I feel so incredibly numb right now. This is hard to take all at once."

Mointz laughed. "Try waking up taller than you ever were at eight and on the same day breaking a plate over your best friend's father's head."

Lauren's car was parked in the driveway as well as Ronnie's, who had just arrived for the Thanksgiving Day holiday.

"Home sweet home, Mr. President," Gennifer said and opened the Bronco door.

Snowflakes started to fall as they walked into the house. Gennifer and Lauren embraced. Mointz introduced Gennifer to Deidre and Ronnie and once the hugging ceased, they all sat down by the fire.

"Cristopher told me all about his accomplishments so far. I must say I am duly impressed."

"He has been more than impressive," Lauren added. "There is no one better suited for this mission than Mointzie."

Gennifer could barely believe her ears when the Director of the CIA called him Mointzie. "Did you just call him Mointzie? What happened to the crotchety Director Gabriel?"

"She is still crotchety and a nutcracker, just not to us," Mointz said.

"Deidre and Ronnie, you two look amazing. I am so glad to see the both of you, as your pictures did not do you justice. The two of you should be proud of yourselves."

"I used your pheromones. The stuff actually works," Mointz said.

Deidre slapped his knee playfully. "Do not start that again."

"So, rumor has it you are playing football, I did not think that you were supposed to," Gennifer said.

"He wasn't," Lauren answered. "Deidre and I made him play. Isn't that right?"

"No shit. Thanks guys."

"You and that potty mouth, Ronnie," Deidre frowned at him.

"Mom, sorry. But, if it was not for you and blondie; we would not be playing in that terrible bowl game in Toledo, Ohio. My friend here kicked our ass on Halloween. Who throws two 80-yard touchdown passes? We got beat by an Ivy League school," Ronnie said, feeling blue over Navy's defeat by the Brown Bears. In the First Parallel, Navy had won big.

"Touché," Deidre said.

"Gennifer, Mointz was moping around over not swimming and bored to death going to college again. We wanted him to have some fun and we wanted to go to football games," Lauren said.

Genny started to realize even though she was heartbroken, Mointz was not just here for himself. She remembered reading his psychological profile and his love for Deidre was never in question. The love she could see in both their eyes made the now 18-year-old psychologist understand Mointz better. Their therapy sessions always had seemed incomplete as Mointz had held his true feelings back. It was now obvious his heart had been more broken than hers over Ronnie's death. She understood how Ronnie's death had decimated Deidre. Cristopher was not only carefree, she could see, but he was carefree saving the whole wide world.

"I am glad you are having a little fun, at least. The panel worried about your mental stress from all of this. I am certainly proud of you."

"We are all very proud of him," Lauren said. "This has not been easy for any of us so far and it is going to get harder quickly."

"Oh, no. What does that mean exactly?" Mointz asked.

"It means that you need to enjoy your Thanksgiving meal because you are going on another mission. That goes for the rest of you, too. We have another Connor Tisdale mission."

"Nice," Ronnie said.

Deidre put her hand in Mointz's and she gave him a nervous smile. "Connor is Cristopher's alter ego."

"You really love her, don't you?" Gennifer asked Mointz as he drove her back home.

"Yeah, I really love the girl and I love you, too, for what it's worth. I am sorry to say it, under the circumstances."

"Cristopher, I owe you. You do not owe me a thing. I am sure you probably saved me from..."

Mointz interrupted, "His name is Keith Forcier and he will be taken care of in Walpole. We have a guy inside who is not a fan of rapists."

Walpole housed some of the worst of the worst. However, a rapist in its general population had no chance of surviving. Forcier was about to be split into pieces, Mointz knew from one of Raymond Belvenie's men.

"I know you and Erin never had what I see in your and Deidre's eyes. What are you going to do?"

"My new motto is 'one day at a time.' Maybe after a few months on the couch, you and I can figure it out, but I am not losing Deidre. The $64,000 question now is 'What are you going to do?' Providence College is about to obtain the best psychologist in the world."

"I have no idea yet. I just woke up, remember? Maybe I will just do these little excursions with you all."

"Emotionally, these 'little excursions,' as you say, rip my heart into pieces. I have no idea what they want me to do now. When I deal with the six-foot blonde, I normally do not ask too many questions until she has told me what I need to do. She runs for Congress in 1990 taking advantage of Bush's popularity spike in upstate New York related to the Gulf War. So far for me, it looks like all systems go for law school, probably at Georgetown."

Gennifer smiled as she understood now she would be the safety net that would get between Mointz and Erin. Lauren earlier had referenced Deidre saving Mointz from Erin. Gennifer held Mointz's hand on the ride home and felt comfortable.

"My mother is now going to drive me nuts. Babs has always driven me nuts. Now, it will be ten times worse."

"All right, I will play. Why does she drive you 'nuts'?"

"Babs is just Babs; she has one of those personalities which conflicts with mine."

"You mean two know-it-alls? What a lovely combination."

"Hey, what a shot below the belt," she said as he pulled into her driveway. "Well, this know-it-all is ready to help you in any way I can. I am so proud of you. Godspeed, Mr. Mointzie. Enjoy the holiday tomorrow."

"Don't get used to the Mointzie."

"As you say, 'it is what it is.'"

Chapter Nineteen

August 1988

The Olympics were approaching and Mointz was immersed in training for Seoul. Over the last two years, challenge after challenge had come the way of the '*New Panel*,' as they called themselves (Deidre, Ronnie, Lauren, Gennifer and Mointz's parents). Deidre and Cristopher's love continued to grow and Ronnie was now involved with someone in secret.

Tonight, Lauren and Mointz were going to go over their biggest task to date while Ronnie, Genny and Deidre enjoyed a night at the movies. Lauren had come up from DC to the beach house.

Mointz had not seen Lauren for almost a month and he was anxious to know why she was at the end of her tether. When she arrived, she hugged and kissed Mointz.

"What on earth have you been doing? You look all buffed up," she asked.

"I've been taking one of Trent's vitamin routines, but I still have to bust my ass training. Now, if you are done ogling my bod, to what do I owe the pleasure of your company?"

"Did you ever wonder why they picked you to go to the Seoul Olympics?"

The color drained from Mointz's face. "Please be kidding, please," he told her in a panic. He had worked his tail off to get this far.

The now-married Lauren, as predicted, was away from home quite often, infuriating her physician husband. As she sat down on the porch of the beach house she wore white shorts and an Izod Lacoste shirt.

"They want you to be invited to North Korea after you become a hero and befriend the President's grandson, Kim Jong-un, who is a swimming prodigy."

"That is not bad. Hell, I thought you wanted me to assassinate a leader or two while I was doing the 200 meter butterfly."

"Beer still in the same place?" Lauren asked.

"What do you want me to do, blow up a nuclear plant?"

Lauren opened the can of Coors Light. "Something like that…"

"What does 'something like that' mean?"

Lauren pulled the beer away from him. "No beer for you."

"What are you, the beer Nazi? You come here and tell me I am going to do something like that to a nuclear plant and I cannot have a beer? I do not like you."

"First off, you love me and you know it. Secondly, you're in training and no one loves a Silver Medalist. Now, let's go outside so I can soak up some vitamin D." She kissed his cheek and took him by the hand back out onto the porch.

Mointz, forever tan, sat on the deck of the beach house with Lauren, who sipped her beer. They both gazed at the surf coming in.

"Now, Ms. Gabriel." Mointz began, "why do you use your maiden name and not your married name?

"Would you use Stankovich?"

"Good point, why don't you tell me how you are going to ruin my Olympic glory and make me meet this Kim Jong-un? I should be thankful you are not sending me to fight the Russians in Afghanistan…please do not give me a face. Say to me you are not going to send me there."

"One day at a time, Mointzie."

Mointz's mind started to race as Lauren's words, while evasive, did not deny either the thoughts that troubled him. "Stop using my one-day-at-a-time line. Think up your own sayings."

"Fine, sir. Using your popularity to make future relationships is key, the panel believed; henceforth the Seoul games. Little Kim Jong-un is very impressionable now. Remember when you were young?"

"Which parallel? Okay, I follow you so far, I think."

"Pay attention, Mointzie. While you are in Korea we can use it to our advantage. The North Koreans are about to obtain Soviet nuclear technology. We are in a position with you in Korea to sabotage their nuclear facility."

"How?"

"Here comes the tricky part. Most, if not all, of the facilities and weapons depots are in the northern region. I believe we can get in and out quickly and take down the facility in the process."

"Do you really believe they will let me loose in that country?"

"No, Cristopher, not at all. I do believe we can get you in the hands of some of the agency's assets to make it happen though."

Mointz's continued military training had featured covert operations. Lauren, with her father's help, pushed the agency into backing Mointz and Ronnie.

"Is the agency behind this or are we talking about a Davis special?"

"Cristopher, we are operating on our own. Remember, I was sent here to help prepare your way. Whatever we do now can only help you in the future, when you become the leader of the free world. The 2016 election is not far away."

He knew she was right. Lauren had the experience he could only dream of and he knew she was on point. Along with each and every mission, she gave Mointz a choice, although he knew Lauren was probably in cahoots with

Davis's team. Trusting in Lauren and Davis completely for now was the right path, Mointz believed. He was no puppet and Lauren knew he could veto any mission at any time. Mointz loved making her sweat it out at times.

"Lauren, if you believe in your heart this is a good idea, I am in. I have a year left at the university and then off to law school. Maybe you will let me intern for you once you get elected to Congress. I wish we could do more to help, but we have to be careful not to change too much. It could bite us in the ass later on down the road. As my friend Anthony says, *capiche?*"

"*Capiche.*"

"Glad to hear you agree with me. How about a sip of beer?"

Lauren smiled and gave him one. "Ready to win some medals?"

"Hell, yeah!"

"This is the race which will make history," Rowdy Gains roared on the Olympic telecast. "Cristopher Mointz, with seven world records, will now attempt to break his eighth world record at these games in the 100 meter freestyle, but more importantly he is about to become the most decorated Olympian in one Olympic Games, summer or winter, ever."

Over one hundred million people all over the world were now watching the event on their televisions and with 2,500 people in the Olympic swimming venue in Seoul, Mointz, Lauren, Gennifer, Ronnie and Deidre appeared front and center on the television.

This was Mointz's best event. As he waited for the starter to fire the gun, he took in a deep breath. The gun went off. In his blue swim trunks he was off like a rocket. Mointz was a full body length ahead at the end of the first 25 meters. By his flip turn at the wall at 50 meters, Mointz was on cruise control and knew the record was his. Davis had always believed Mointz had the intensity inside of him and Mointz showed it here in Seoul. Mointz shattered his own world record and Mark Spitz's seven gold medal record in one Olympic Games in less than a minute.

"He did it!" Gains cried out. "Mointz is the man! Oh, my Lord, he did it!"

The pro-Mointz crowd erupted and Mointz raised his hand high in the air. He owned the pool and this Olympics.

"Cristopher, you are known both on the football field and in the pool for your elegance and class. You should be commended for it. I would be willing to bet though you are ecstatic over the fact, the Soviets and the other Eastern bloc nations now have to eat crow over the fact they predicted that you would not win one single event," said a pretty interviewer named Jane.

Mointz, with his infectious smile, looked right into the camera and responded to Jane's softball question perfectly. "Never underestimate America and her people. We do not want easy; all we want is possible. The Olympics here in Seoul was my possible and I made the most of it."

"Well said, as usual, and congratulations again," Jane said on camera. Once they were off-camera, Jane gave him a kiss on the cheek. "America has a new hero, my friend."

Mointz thanked her and hugged everyone in his entourage before heading off for an interview with Al Michaels for television. He knew there would be plenty of interviews in the next few days before heading to North Korea for a celebration before going home.

"Do you know how hard it was sneaking over here?" Mointz asked Deidre in her hotel room later that night.

"Come here, lover boy," Deidre told him, lying naked on the bed with open arms.

Mointz made love to Deidre like never before. She could feel the testosterone he had built up.

"Still fired up, I see, Mr. Gold Medalist," Deidre said, snuggling up with him after they had finished.

"I need a beer and a cigarette, my lady." They both chuckled and before long Deidre took him in her mouth and did not stop until she brought him to full pleasure.

"Someone else is fired up, too," Mointz said, glowing after the encounter.

Deidre giggled and Mointz passed out within minutes. The extra lung capacity helped, but without the training and eating properly, he could not have accomplished his Olympic feat. Deidre ran her fingers through his hair. She now realized he had accomplished mega-fame. It was time for her to make a change. She had stayed at Celeste's place for almost a week and picked a new look. She chose blonde hair that fell just below the shoulder and she loved the look in Mointz's eyes with each and every glance. Never in her life had she felt this happy. When she left Korea, she would return to America as Danielle Santer. In the First Parallel, Deidre had become pregnant at barely fifteen and married at seventeen. She had lost all of her teenage years as had Ronald. The bond she had now with Mointz had started out of loneliness and quickly developed into a relationship of love, trust, and adventure. Mointz was the key to saving her and Ronnie, she knew. However, tonight that was not on her mind. Tonight, Deidre had all she ever wanted in her bed and in her heart. She fell asleep with a smile on her face knowing Mointz had chosen her out of love and not out of necessity. *This might be extremely irregular,* she thought. But it felt so right to her, even with the new breasts and blonde hair she was about to have. Mointz not only had eight gold medals hanging from his chest, he now could add her heart to the collection. She was determined to help him reach his goal of saving the world.

###

"What time is it?" Mointz asked Deidre as she slipped out of the shower.

"Time for you to get out of here and get with the lady who runs the public relations for team USA. What is her name?"

"Katie something or other…oh, wait. It's Couric, Katie Couric. She is a perky one. I am supposed to get interviewed on a bunch of countries' Olympic telecasts," he said and jumped into the shower.

After he dressed, Deidre flipped him the paper that lay outside of the hotel door. "THE NEW YORK TIMES, International edition."

Mointz stared at himself on the front page in the pool with his hand in the air pointing to the sky after the race. The moment finally hit him. "They were right; this is a big deal. Look at the headline."

Mointz Gracious in Destroying the World.

"I read it, my love. Congratulations." Deidre could see the pride he felt this morning that filled his six-foot-six frame.

Mointz hugged Deidre. A knock at the door immediately broke the embrace. He peered through the peephole and said, "It's a very smiley Robert and Martha." He let them in the room.

"Unbelievable. You are just unbelievable," his father told him.

Martha kissed her son's cheek. "Every reporter wants to interview us and congratulate us. I never would have believed your grandparents would cozy up to the media."

Mointz laughed and walked his parents and Deidre to meet his entourage for breakfast before turning to his media obligations.

"He certainly pulled it off," Gennifer told Lauren and Ronnie on their way out to meet the Mointzes for breakfast.

"Glad this part is over," Lauren said with a sigh. She was exhausted from the stress of every race Mointz had competed in.

"He still has to go home and play football," said Ronnie. "There will be plenty of time to stress when Navy seeks revenge against the Brown Bears."

"Really, honey," Gennifer said to Ronnie.

"Do you have a timetable yet for when you are going to tell Mointzie about the two of you?" Lauren asked them.

Gennifer and Ronnie had been cohabitating for over four months, keeping it a secret so as to not distract Mointz. They had gone for a walk on the beach after dinner at the beach house one night and neither one could remember who initiated the kiss, but it happened and they were completely comfortable with each other. Ronnie had taken up the mantle as Mointz's partner. He had used his military training to push his abilities in both body and mind. Gennifer had fallen quickly for Ronnie. However, the soon-to-be junior at Providence College suppressed her feelings until the walk on the beach.

"We will tell him soon," Gennifer said, holding Ronnie's hand while they walked.

"He cannot bitch at us, for Pete's sake. He seduced my mother." The Navy midshipman did not know of Cristopher's relationship with Gennifer in the First Parallel and Gennifer was hell-bent to keep it that way.

Gennifer could see herself with Ronnie in the future. He had Mointz's internal fortitude, his swagger and Ronnie was what Mointz would never be, available to give his heart to her. She knew Ronnie would never hurt her. His eyes adored her, driving her to him. Mointz had those eyes for Deidre.

"Cut him some slack, Ronnie. Mointzie has done beautifully this week and the both of you have more to do," said Lauren.

Ronnie kissed Gennifer. Entering the restaurant, he answered Lauren. "Cristopher saved my life, brought me Gennifer and now is saving the planet. I will do whatever he needs me to do. He is my hero."

Lauren smiled, "I think he might have made 'superhero' status this week."

Chapter Twenty

"How long have you and Gennifer been fornicating?" Cristopher asked Ronnie on the plane to North Korea. "Yeah, payback sucks."

Ronnie, who had been drinking orange juice on the private plane that President Kim Il-sung had sent to pick them up, choked on his juice just as Mointz had done at the pep rally with hot chocolate.

"Cristopher, that is awful," Deidre said with a giggle. "So son, spill the beans."

"I cannot wait to hear this," Lauren said "We have 45 minutes until we land, plenty of time.

Ronnie finally stopped choking and gave his mother an innocent smile. He did not look immediately at his lifelong friend. "A wise man does not kiss and tell."

"There is no reason to. I had your room bugged at the Olympics. No worries," said Mointz.

"Tell me you are just shitting me. Why or how could you do that?"

"I didn't, but at least now I know the truth."

Ronnie came clean and Mointz felt confused. He knew Gennifer had been devastated over him because of Deidre. He thought she had handled it well. He never expected she would fall for Ronnie and Mointz hoped they would thrive together. Ronnie had certainly grown up quickly over the last few years.

"She is a dynamite woman, my friend. I hope you and Gennifer are happy together. God knows you both deserve it," Mointz stated, smiling at his friend.

Ronnie smiled back. "Are you happy, Cristopher? Did you get a charge out of smashing everyone? I know you are the most competitive person I have ever met and I could see the fires burning." He had learned the art of changing subjects from Mointz.

"Yeah, I had the juices flowing big time. It was a total rush, but now it is over. One more year of football at Brown and I will be called an ex-athlete."

Deidre rubbed Mointz's shoulder as he held her hand. Mointz had a feeling she knew about Ronnie and Gennifer long before they came out.

"Who are we meeting at the airport?" Gennifer asked Lauren.

"Alex Richards is meeting us at the airport. He is our ambassador to North Korea," said Lauren and put a finger over her mouth. She was afraid the plane was bugged.

Mointz opened his sport coat and wrote, "bug" on a napkin. He handed it to Gennifer.

"I hear you," Gennifer acknowledged.

The plane landed at noon. Kim Il-sung was expecting Mointz for a ceremony at the presidential palace at three in the afternoon and a formal-state dinner at eight. The president's grandson, an aspiring swimmer, begged his grandfather to allow Mointz to spend a little time with him tomorrow at the swimming training facility before Mointz left for the United States.

Alex Richards led a convoy of limousines to the airport. He had arranged for a small ceremony to greet Mointz. The Ambassador was astounded that the North Koreans had embraced Mointz because of the lavish praise Kim Il-sung had awarded him on Korean television.

"We are all proud of your accomplishments, Mr. Mointz," Ambassador Richards said.

"Thank you, sir. I hope I made the United States proud."

"You certainly did, my boy. What a pleasure it is to have you here."

Alex Richards was originally a Nixon appointee, as the ex-Congressman from Wyoming specialized in Asian relations. When the agency asked him to help on this mission, he was all too willing to help. Ambassador Richards could see the danger of arming the North Koreans with nuclear weapons. He would employ any means he could to slow down their acquisition process, and have all embassy personnel ready to help him in any way they could.

Several Marines guarded the American Embassy watchfully, Mointz noticed, as they pulled into the gated compound.

"Nothing like going into America on foreign soil," Mointz said to the other passengers as they arrived together in one limousine.

Lauren nodded as Alex Richards laughed.

"A few medals and an Ivy League education doesn't just make you America's next generation's best hope. I have read your dossier, Mr. Mointz; you are certainly not all about medals and football. I am proud to have you here."

Mointz had spent the last two years receiving advanced SEAL training with Derek Vaz. There were not many Olympians and world record holders undertaking this type of training.

Deidre entered the residence with Gennifer and Mrs. Richards, the lovely former Miss Wyoming, as Lauren, Ronnie and Cristopher prepared for the assault on the Pyongyang nuclear facility.

A Marine officer and a couple of CIA tactical experts were already grouped in the conference room when they arrived.

"Pleasure to meet you, Mr. Mointz," Adam Chace, a 30-year-old African-American CIA man told Cristopher as he extended his powerful hand. "I must congratulate you on all your Olympic glory. I thought this was a joke when I first received the mission package. Who knew you had Department of Defense intelligence credentials? What will they think of next?"

"I agree, Adam. I hardly could believe it myself." CIA man Charles Atwood added, "Mr. Mointz, it's a pleasure to meet you and nice meeting you,

Midshipman Mahoney. Midshipmen in the DOD, what will they think of next, Lauren?" Charles and Lauren trained at Langley together.

"Lauren, he is no ordinary midshipman," Colonel Walter Perry began. "We quite possibly could have the top midshipman and halfback Navy has ever produced. I am an Academy man myself, but I have to wonder, how in the hell did you lose to Mointz?"

Walter Perry had spent time with Lauren's father. When Lauren's father had approached Perry with this mission, Perry had jumped at the chance to be part of it.

"It will not happen again, sir."

Mointz rolled his eyes and the Colonel laughed.

Lauren reviewed the details of the mission with Mointz, Colonel Perry, Ronnie and the CIA men. They planned to head out tonight to clubs near the Pyongyang nuclear plant to celebrate Mointz's victories. Americans were not allowed near the plant, but with Mointz's celebrity status, they would blame the drunken gold medalist for leading them astray, if they were stopped. Atwood was the demolition expert of the group and he knew the exact location of the facility's weakest points.

Lauren started to get cold feet, leery of sending out Ronnie and Mointz. The plan could easily go astray, which would mean the North Koreans would discover the Americans with explosives in North Korea. With images of Mointz's six-foot-6-inch frame plastered all over Korea the last two weeks and with the ceremony and state dinner on North Korea's television, Lauren decided Mointz and Ronnie would join the expedition after all.

###

The three o'clock press conference was a propaganda fest as was the state dinner at the presidential palace. Mointz did the politically correct thing and smiled for the cameras, saying all the right things. The Korean President and his grandson, basked in the glory of the games as 1988 saw North and South Korea combining their Olympic teams for the games. Mointz and Lauren knew from the First Parallel it was all a big ruse. The North never intended to work with the South. Over the next 30 years, they would bully the South into shipping food to stop the North's aggression. Tonight, Operation Ping-Pong Pyong, one of Langley's tech geeks' play on words, would commence to blow the nuclear plant and weapons depot off the map.

Mointz dressed in a dark blue suit in his room at the embassy as Deidre sat on the bed, still in her black cocktail dress after the dinner. Mointz could not believe how amazing she looked. Many tongues hung out at the dinner.

"Are you and Ronnie confident this will go well tonight?"

Mointz smiled and nodded. "How many children do you want with me?"

Deidre had never heard Mointz bring up children other than Thomas and Patrick.

"I am not sure, it is up to you I guess."

He sat on the bed and held her hand. "Dee, you are not going to lose me ever. Your opinion matters more to me than anyone's. Honey, you must be as happy as me. The love in your heart for me is beyond my comprehension. Sweetie, you are amazing and your strength blows me away, but you need to tell me to F-off. We are equals in every way. So I ask again, how many children would you like to have?"

Deidre's eyes filled with tears and she took Mointz's face in her hands and said, "F-off Mointz, I want as many children after we have Thomas and Patrick as possible." She kissed him and held him. "Come back to me, Mr. President."

"Patently, my love. I love you."

Lauren knocked on the door to retrieve Mointz. A still-tearful Deidre hugged him. Lauren knocked on Ronnie's door. When he opened, she saw he was with Gennifer. Gennifer begged Ronnie to be careful. Deidre and Gennifer finally allowed Mointz and Ronnie to leave. This was not easy on either of them.

"They are going to be basket cases until we get back," Ronnie said. "Gennifer must be so glad she came."

Ronnie and Mointz met Colonel Perry in the carport. He had two black Cherokees gassed and ready. Mointz, Ronnie and the Colonel jumped in one with Atwood and Chace taking the other. Colonel Perry started the Cherokee and headed for a party that the embassy had set up with other countries for several embassies' personnel and some VIP North Koreans. There were several other parties planned.

"This is not how you expected to spend your first night after the Olympics," Colonel Perry said.

"Actually, the medals I am wearing are fake. My parents have the real ones. Lauren thought of everything and I knew this mission was a possibility."

"I have known her father for years. How did you two meet?" the Colonel asked, almost at the discotheque.

"The Naval War College in Newport hosted me when I first hit the public eye for a seminar. I had received some death threats after my first world championship. Lauren and I bonded from day one. She and I have been practically inseparable ever since."

"It was how I was recruited, sir," Ronnie said. "I attended the seminar with Mr. Mointz. The Naval Academy offered me a scholarship for football. It seemed natural for me to head to Annapolis."

"Try not to let Mointz beat us again."

"You might have mentioned that, sir," said Ronnie.

"The Midshipmen will lose again. Trust me."

Ronnie wondered if Brown would win the game this year as well. He never knew what Mointz could do to manipulate the Second Parallel. Mointz loved to keep him guessing.

Colonel Perry, a rather large African American, laughed as he pulled into the discotheque parking lot. Charles Atwood pulled his Cherokee next to theirs. Ronnie, and the CIA men were posing as Mointz's bodyguards. They surrounded him when he walked into the party. Applause erupted in the nightclub as the flashes of cameras mixed with the club's lighting blinded Mointz. However, he never missed a beat, smiling and waving at every person in the room.

"This place is packed," Ronnie whispered in Mointz's ear.

"No doubt about it. I could really use a beer, but we are going to need our wits tonight. Maybe it will not be too bad to attend this party sober," Mointz said. "Then again maybe not."

"I vote for beer," Ronnie told him before he got lost in the crowd.

For almost three hours, Mointz felt like a pinball, bouncing from one group to another. A couple of females who worked at the British Embassy practically accosted him at the private roped-off area in the club. Ronnie laughed heartily on the inside, while staying stoic on the outside as he played bodyguard.

"I feel like my cheeks are going to fall off," Mointz told Colonel Perry and Ronnie when they returned to the vehicles after the party. "I cannot remember smiling so much. Well, maybe when I lost my virginity, but that was it." He did not think before he spoke, forgetting for a second who Ronnie's mother was.

"Nice, sir," said Ronnie.

"There was a time back there when I did not think we could get you out," Colonel Perry said.

"After this little trip to the nuclear plant, I am going to have a nice cold beer," said Mointz.

"The opportunity awaits, as we still have a few more parties," Ronnie said.

There were several all-night parties planned and Mointz was going to try and hit as many as he could. The parties were their cover for the evening.

The Pyongyang facility was only 22 minutes away from the nightclub. Colonel Perry, with the agency men trailing close behind, sped to the facility.

They pulled onto an abandoned road the spy satellite had picked up on a routine scan of the facility.

Chace and Atwood changed their clothes on the fly. They passed out the weapons they would need. Mointz and Ronnie were pumped and jacked to get this mission rolling.

"We have about a mile walk to the facility's lab area," Colonel Perry said. "This should be an in-and-out mission."

Mointz hoped his assessment was correct, however nothing was ever just in and out.

"I have the explosives," Atwood said. "The agency tech weenies say if we can get the lab to blow up, this whole place will light up like a Roman candle."

"Are you boys ready?" Adam Chace asked.

Ronnie nodded and Mointz said, "This is not my first rodeo, gentlemen. I am ready to turn this place into a parking lot."

"Hooyah!" the Marine Colonel chimed in.

Each man wore night-vision goggles and held AK-47 weapons as they strolled down the dirt street to the edge of the perimeter. Agency intelligence had deemed the end of the dirt road the most assessable point into the plant with the least security.

"I cannot believe this fence does not have more guards around it," Ronnie said.

"Don't let that fool you," Colonel Perry said. "This is North Korea. Average citizens are so afraid of the government, they do not dare try to cross it. Our intel also said the fence is not alarmed. However, as soon as we get in, we'll run into guards with dogs protecting the lab. Remember, we blow the second lab entrance door, get in and set the charges before hauling ass out of here and getting back to the vehicles."

Charles Atwood cut the fence with wire cutters. The chain-link fence probably could have been ripped apart by the African American's large powerful hands. The fence cut, the five men went through it with eyes wide open. Mointz checked his watch. It was now two am. He did not have a tired bone in his body. The adrenaline rush was far too great for him to feel fatigue.

They moved double-time to approach the entrance they would blow up.

"Do you see anyone?" Atwood asked, a second too late, as bullets pinged the metal building around them.

"Jesus, where did these guys come from?" Mointz said, taking cover and firing back at the North Korean soldiers.

"Blow that door!" Colonel Perry yelled at Atwood. "We will cover you."

Alarms screamed and red lights flashed. Atwood blew the door. The team slipped into the double-plated corridor. Atwood quickly jammed the second door to keep out the shooting North Koreans.

"We need to get to the transformer and set the charges," Adam Chace cried out over the alarms.

The CIA had planted an asset inside the facility. When the team reached the secondary building, the awaiting asset locked the soldiers out. There were two escape routes back to the vehicles. The primary route out was through the air ducts above the lab. The main facility had the heaviest security. Even though the lab was connected to it, the lab's security was at a minimum during the day and non-existent at night. The team had not expected the firefight outside at all.

"This is not good," Ronnie said, as they searched the transformer room, the alarms almost deafening.

"Rig this thing and get us the hell out of here," Mointz screamed. Two soldiers came running down the hall and Mointz took both of them out instantly with a quick burst of the AK-47.

"Wow, that was close. Nice shot," Ronnie said.

"Okay, I have charges set for 20 minutes. We need to get out of here because this thing is going to blow," Atwood said.

"Dammit," Colonel Perry cried out. "We have to proceed carefully. There are a hell of a lot of soldiers outside." The Colonel was looking outside through the air-conditioning ductwork, which led to a small grate outside the building. The Colonel had a clear view of the mob.

The remaining four men each went into a separate duct. They quickly could see what the Colonel could see.

"Throw grenades," Colonel Perry yelled. "We need to get these guys to back off so we can hit the ground running."

They all pushed the grates to the ground on the outside. Simultaneously, they threw the grenades which exploded almost instantaneously. The men dropped the ten feet to the ground.

"Go, Go, Go!" Cristopher screamed and fired at soldiers running towards them.

Colonel Perry was the first to get hit with a bullet followed by Atwood and then Chace. Cristopher and Ronnie, who had practiced drill after drill with Derek Vaz, calmly turned and fired at the remaining soldiers. In a moment, all the North Koreans were down. Chace had pulled Atwood and the Colonel behind a North Korean security jeep while Mointz and Ronnie took care of business.

"The Colonel is hurt badly," Chace screamed.

Mointz ran over and scooped up the Colonel. He stopped the flow of blood from the Colonel's chest and carried him through the fence. Ronnie picked up Atwood, who was shot in the back. He ran as fast as he could back to the vehicles while Chace, shot in the thigh, did his best to keep up.

They had ten minutes to spare when they made it to the vehicles. Ronnie drove one and Mointz the other as they took off as fast as they could. Lauren had told the CIA men Mointz and Ronnie were more than ready for this and they had just proved it.

The ground shook as the plant blew about a mile in the sky. Radiation wouldn't leak, as the North Koreans were about a month away from having the facility live. Pyongyang was thrown into chaos, allowing Mointz and company to get back to the embassy without a problem. The compound gates barely made it open before Mointz gunned through. Lauren had the agency's medical unit waiting for their arrival.

"Get the Colonel and agents into surgery quickly," Mointz yelled.

Deidre and Gennifer hugged Cristopher and Ronnie as IV's were quickly given to the men on stretchers. All three were rushed into the three-room army hospital in the compound.

"When you called us on the shortwave radio, I alerted the medical crew," Lauren said, hugging Mointz.

"Lauren, be thankful I love you," said Mointz. "The Colonel does not look good."

The Ambassador joined them and escorted everyone into a conference room. Mointz and Ronnie explained how they had encountered heavy security resulting in a firefight.

"So, are you telling us the two of you carried the Colonel and Atwood on your backs for over a mile?" the Ambassador asked.

"That is correct, Ambassador," Mointz replied.

"Incredible," said the Ambassador, shaking his head as he marveled at the two young men. Deidre, Lauren and Gennifer could hardly believe their heroism.

"Sir that is not the half of it. Agent Chace told me Mointz and Ronnie took out at least 100 soldiers to save them," Lauren stated.

Deidre and Gennifer looked stunned and Lauren could only imagine the hell they had just gone through.

"Doesn't matter unless the Colonel, Atwood and Chace do all right in there."

Ambassador Richards left the room to call the Secretary of State, George Schultz who was standing by with Defense Secretary Frank Carlucci. Mointz and Ronnie grabbed a beer and went off to shower and clean up. The Ambassador's staff was preparing a breakfast buffet for them.

"F-off, Mointz," said Deidre, madder than a bull in a china shop. "I cannot believe you risked your lives on this." Deidre sat on a bench as he showered.

"We had to, love," Mointz muttered as the shower water sprayed his face.

"This was an unnecessary risk and I told Lauren as much. There is a time and place for everything," Deidre stated. "Before you say it, not one decent soul is expendable. You are changing history to save the world, I get it, but you cannot save the world if you're not breathing."

He grabbed her, pulled her into the shower and kissed her hard. "It was a mistake, a very big one. We need to count our blessings. Now, are you going to strip off these clothes and make love to me or what?"

Deidre smiled and kissed him. She was absolutely ready for him. "Do it for me."

Mointz struggled with the button on her blouse and suddenly ripped her blouse open. Mointz picked up Deidre and entered her in the shower. The sex turned Deidre on as if she had been without Mointz for weeks. It was the first time her emotions were on such a high over the danger Mointz faced. The animal magnetism oozed out of him as he made love to her.

Deidre's orgasm was the most powerful of her life. The lovemaking session supplanted the heat they felt the first time she and Mointz had become one. Mointz was now hers and she, Mointz's in every way.

"Good God Almighty. That was incredible," Deidre told him, bundling up in a bathrobe and then drying him off.

"Then I am forgiven?"

"Hell, no," she replied. "But I have to tell you, a few more sessions like that will go a long way. Oh, my God."

"I can see you liked it," he said.

They dressed and met Ronnie, Gennifer and Lauren in Ronnie's room.

"Mind telling me what the hell that was about?" Mointz roared at Lauren.

"Hello to you too, Mointzie," Lauren responded with a nervous grin. She knew he was irate and the former ice queen learned early that humor was the way to go when dealing with Mointz. The rest of the world got the nutcracker.

"Don't 'Mointzie' me, lady. Who screwed the pooch on this?" He could hardly contain his anger, but she batted her eyes to soften him. "Thank your stars you are a lovely lady. I said it before and I say it again."

"The two of you made it out, thankfully."

"Thanks to Mointz's decisive actions, Lauren. This was not a minor screw-up," said Ronnie.

"Hello, I am in the room," Deidre told them.

"So am I," Gennifer added.

"I don't like what went down either, but blaming Lauren is barking up the wrong tree. Intelligence is not always intelligent," said Mointz.

"I am trying not to kill the three of you," Deidre said and started to sob. She fell right into Mointz's arms. They rarely displayed PDA's in front of Ronnie.

"We are fine. It's our teammates I am worried about," said Mointz.

"Think positive," Lauren said.

"He was incredible, Mom. Cristopher did not hesitate; he saved us."

"Not 'me,' 'we' saved us. You were as big a part of this as anyone," Mointz said. "Now, CIA girl, what the hell happened?"

"Every satellite image and report that came in had the area soft."

"Soft? Like baby poop or a rock?" Ronnie asked.

"We thought lightly guarded, wise guy. My guess is they probably beefed up patrols because they were going live soon," Lauren said as her voice cracked. Mointz could tell she was taking it hard.

"Forget it now, Blondie," Mointz told her. "Any word from the North Korean government?"

"The Ambassador told me earlier that he had received a call that a fire had broken out at an ammunition plant. They are very concerned about your well-being," said Lauren.

I hope that the explosion took care of all the evidence," Ronnie remarked.

The Ambassador walked into the room and looked relieved. A doctor told him all three of the men were out of danger and should make full recoveries.

They were all relieved and praised the Lord.

"I have spoken also with President Kim Il-sung personally. He has apologized profusely for ruining your celebration. He still hopes you will be able to meet his grandson tomorrow. His grandson and the grandson's mother would be so disappointed if you couldn't go. She seems to have a crush on you, Mr. Mointz."

"Who doesn't?" Deidre said.

A look from Lauren put a lump in Mointz's throat. *This could not be happening,* he thought.

"I saw that look last night, Lauren," Mointz said to her after breakfast. They were alone in one of the empty offices after breakfast. Deidre and Ronnie had gone to sleep after eating so Lauren and Mointz had some time alone together.

"Remember the advice I first gave you?"

"Yes, 'kill who I need to and screw who I need to.' How is tagging the next president's mistress, Ko Yong-hui, here in North Korea relevant? I know your mind."

"Ko Yong-hui is a beautiful woman, who, wouldn't you know, will still be wiping her son's chin when he reaches his 30's. This is a great opportunity to make inroads here," Lauren said. "In all seriousness, it never stopped you before. I hate that you grew a conscience."

"Yeah, as a matter of fact, it is an effing nuisance when you are trying to save the world."

"I would advise you to keep Deidre here."

"Gee, do you think? Maybe Ko is a little vixen and you can come and have a three-way."

"Don't threaten me with a good time, Mointz."

"We almost bit the dust last night," Christopher said growing serious. He finally had hit the proverbial wall and needed sleep, but he couldn't because he had to be at a pool teaching a five-year-old boy how to swim.

"I am sorry. Truly, I am."

"Could you imagine the fallout if the new eight-time Olympic champion was killed blowing up a nuclear facility in North Korea?"

"No, I can't. The plant was leveled. It will take years for them to rebuild. If they do, we will blow it up again. You guys did well, Mointzie."

"So my reward is to try and boink the lovely thirty-five year old mistress of the future North Korean President. Maybe I have a shot. The next president is a lot older," said Mointz.

"She is beautiful and I'll bet she is sexually repressed."

Mointz did not want to agree with Lauren to her face, but Ko was definitely an alluring woman. Deidre was his life now but he knew he had to do what needed to be done. He certainly would not be revealing this task to Deidre.

"Who is driving me?" Mointz asked.

"The Ambassador's personal security team. Have a good time."

As Mointz sat in the limousine on the way to the private club near the British Consulate, he decided when he left for home later in the day, a stiff scotch and a decent sandwich would put him to sleep for the 14 hour flight home.

"All set, sir," a member of the security team said as they pulled in front of the club.

Mointz had asked for his name earlier but he had forgotten it. Remembering a name when he was tired was a rarity.

"Thank you, my friend. I always knew my lifeguard skills would be evoked to maintain world peace someday."

The guy chuckled as another team member opened the door for him. Mointz collected his bag and followed members of the security team into the club. Several North Korean security personnel stood inside. They escorted Mointz to the pool area where Ko Yong-hui was waiting patiently for the American hunk. She wore a bathrobe as did her son. Mointz could only imagine how the future president's mistress was allowed to dismiss all of the security out of the pool. Lauren had told Mointz the president of North Korea's grandson meant the world to the president. She was quite positive this event was all arranged for the little guy.

"Good morning, it is a pleasure to be with the both of you this morning."

"Thank you, Mr. Mointz. Please call me Ko," the Oxford-educated Japanese woman told him in only a slight Korean accent. "Son, please say 'thank you' to Mr. Mointz for taking time out of his busy schedule to come here."

"Thank you, Mr. Mointz," the smiling child said.

"You're welcome. Please call me Cristopher," Mointz said, returning the smile.

Ko instructed Mointz to use the locker room to get ready for her son's lesson. Mointz could tell the boy was excited. He did not have a proto-typical swimmer's body as he was short and stocky. All that mattered to Mointz was that the child had fun and that he would remember his day with him for years to come.

Kim Jong-un wanted to improve and with the beautiful Ko nearby in her bikini, Mointz stayed in the pool for over an hour instructing Kim Jong-un and flirting with Ko.

Lunch was to be served at the pool and to Ko's delight, Mointz agreed to stay. Ko's assistant, a very petite and pretty young woman, joined them.

"Why don't you enjoy the sauna before you prepare for lunch? I will join you in a minute," Ko whispered as her assistant helped her son.

Mointz smiled and patted her hand lightly before entering into the locker room. He immediately stripped, then entered the sauna in the men's locker room. While he sat in the sauna as naked as the day he was born, he had a feeling Ko might be shocked, but he also felt an inclination she would not mind at all.

Ko was indeed surprised, but Mointz noticed her eyes light up when she gazed at his naked body. She entered the sauna without the slightest hesitation at all.

"Too warm for clothes," Mointz said.

She removed her bikini top and bottom and sat down only inches from Mointz. Mointz immediately kissed her on the mouth. He gently squeezed her right nipple as their tongues met. He spread a towel on the bench and gently pushed her on her back and kissed her body, tasting a combination of sweat and her love juices.

Ko convulsed into a spasm as Mointz brought her to orgasm at least three times before entering the sexy Ko. He climaxed quickly as the temperature in the sauna started to affect both of them. Ko then led him to the whirlpool. She took him in her hands after a few minutes in the bubbles. When she propped him on the edge of the whirlpool, he immediately snapped back to attention and leaned back into the bubbles, pulling Ko on top of him. He entered her for the second time.

"We must prepare for lunch," Ko said after they both climaxed together. She clearly glowed.

Mointz kissed her passionately. Taking her advice to get ready for lunch, he showered quickly and joined Ko and her son for the Korean cuisine.

Ko did not touch her food as Mointz devoured his. Kim Jong-un, fluent in English, talked Mointz's ear off at lunch. Eventually, Ko allowed security in with a photographer for a photo shoot of them for the world media. It was the first time in years Ko showed her smile in a photo.

"Can she still walk?" Lauren asked Mointz in the briefing room before they visited with the Colonel and Atwood. Agent Chace was already up and about. Mointz insisted on seeing them today and would not depart Korea until he knew they were on their way to recovery. "I can only imagine her smile."

"I feel like a male gigolo, I really never felt like that in all my life. Deidre is my world, Lauren."

Lauren knew right there his kryptonite would be because of a woman. She did not say another word about it, not even in jest.

"Ready to visit the Colonel and Atwood?"

Mointz nodded.

Colonel Perry was weak. However, he thanked Mointz for saving his life over and over again. Mointz agreed to meet him as soon as the Colonel was well enough to travel back to the United States. Agent Atwood was sleeping peacefully when Mointz checked in on him. Mointz did not want to wake him.

Lauren walked side-by-side with Mointz until they reached Deidre, who was sitting with the Ambassador.

"Where is Ronnie?" Mointz asked.

"Gennifer and Ronnie are packed and ready to go home," she said.

They bid farewell to the Ambassador and Deidre and Christopher went to get their bags.

"Everything okay, love? Sweetie, what is wrong?" Mointz asked.

"I need to go home. In one night I almost lost my son and the man I love."

Lauren knocked on the door and Mointz invited her in. She saw Deidre's tears and immediately hugged her.

"They made it, Deidre. We can count our blessings."

"I know, but neither one of them are even remotely fazed by it. They're going to want to do it again and again. There is a war coming, yes?"

"The First Gulf War," Lauren replied. She immediately understood why Deidre was upset; Ronnie and Mointz had enjoyed the events of the previous night. Both of them believed they could fight the battle by themselves. Ronnie was just like Mointz—fearless—and was just as much of an unstoppable force.

"Honey, I am not fearless," Mointz said.

"Yes, you are," Lauren said. "The two of you are on the bench."

"Whose side are you on?"

"Hers," Lauren said.

"Great. Just great," Mointz said. "I need to go home. The two of you are a buzz kill."

Chapter Twenty-One

NOVEMBER 1988

"That suck-bag is playing defense," Ronnie said in the huddle. Navy clung to a four-point lead over Brown in Annapolis.

"What?" Navy's quarterback Terry Hanson inquired before calling the play.

"Mointz, he came onto the field," Ronnie replied.

The score was 38 to 34 with only 3:41 left to play in the fourth quarter. Navy tried to run out the clock, giving the ball to Ronnie four times in a row. Ronnie gained 31 yards on those carries. He had run for 165 yards so far on the ground.

"Forget Mointz, he is only one man, Ronnie. 142 down on one, ready, break!" Hansen said as they broke the huddle.

Ronnie could only roll his eyes, knowing his friend would find a way to stop Navy, which had driven the ball to the Brown nine-yard line. A touchdown here and the more than sixty thousand fans in the stands, including the now-one-star General Walter Perry, Deidre, Gennifer, Lauren, Robert and Martha, would know it would be all she wrote and the fat lady would start to sing.

Ronnie's father was now battling prostate cancer and was losing the battle. However, he sat at home praying for both boys, watching the game on television.

Mointz lined up right over center and smiled at Ronnie as Hansen barked out a cadence. Hansen took the snap from center. Before Hansen could hand off to Ronnie, Mointz blew right through the line and slammed Hansen to the ground for a four-yard loss. Hansen hit the turf and tasted the grass of the field.

"I am coming for you, Mahoney," Mointz roared, as the teams went back into their respective huddles.

"Didn't I tell you to watch him?" Ronnie yelled to everyone in the huddle. The ball was now on the thirteen-yard line, second and goal as the clock ran.

"Okay, okay, Ronnie. Everyone, watch Mointz," Hansen said and called a toss sweep to Ronnie. The play was designed to have the right guard pull left and for the left tackle to seal the defensive end.

Mointz again lined up over center and when the ball was snapped to Hansen, Mointz flew in an arc toward Hansen. Hansen pitched the ball to Ronnie just as Mointz reached him. Mointz turned his attention to Ronnie and crushed him for a four-yard loss.

"Nice run, meatball. Good play call."

"Eat turf, pal. Look at the scoreboard. You're still losing," Ronnie said and gave Mointz a shove, which almost drew a penalty.

Third and goal now from the seventeen. Hansen received the play from the sideline and went into a shotgun formation. Mointz moved to left defensive end and was off like a bullet when the center snapped the ball and sacked Hansen for an eleven-yard loss. The sack back to the 28-yard line had Navy bringing on the field-goal team for a 45-yard field goal.

"Thank God, this is the last time they play each other," Deidre said to Martha Mointz in the stands.

"Dear," Martha began, "these two are never really against each other. However, they'd better make this field goal because Ronnie will never live down two losses," Martha told her, laughing. She hugged Dee.

Ronnie's teammate, Peter LeCleng, kicked the field goal. The football sailed through the uprights, giving the midshipmen a seven-point lead with one minute and 47 seconds left to play. An eternity as far as Mointz was concerned.

LeCleng's kickoff went through the end zone. The ball was brought out to the 25-yard line where Mointz went to work, brilliantly completing four straight passes bringing the ball to the Navy twenty-three-yard line.

Mointz brought his team out of the huddle. With two timeouts left, Mointz ran a sprint draw, slicing his way into the end zone with seventeen seconds left to play. He swore he could hear his mother screaming from the stands.

Brown decided to go for the two-point conversion, as there was no overtime in 1988. Mointz yelled at Mahoney on the Navy sideline and Ronnie knew the game was over. His friend did not know how to fail and Mointz did not fail as he completed a pass to his wide-open tight-end sticking it to Navy again.

The Bears kicked a Squib kick after the conversion. Navy tried a Hail Mary; it was to no avail, as Brown had once again defeated Navy, this time by a score of 42 to 41.

"Do you purposely like to ruin my season?" Ronnie asked Mointz, hugging his friend. "I love you, man."

"I went to play defense because I figured we would lose if I didn't. We could not stop you all day."

"Nice, Buddy. Again you ruined an Orange Bowl berth for us. Twice in four years we get beat by an Ivy League school."

"Gennifer will make it all better."

"Good point," Ronnie said.

"Alright man, love you buddy. See you at Thanksgiving. I will call you Monday."

The two friends embraced again at midfield and they left for their respective locker rooms. Deidre, Robert, Martha and Lauren met Mointz at the entrance of the locker room tunnel as Gennifer consoled Ronnie. Mointz winked and blew a kiss at his posse before running down the tunnel ramp.

Mointz took about an hour getting ready. He had convinced Coach Worth to let him stay in DC using the excuse he had a military commitment. His reason did the trick. Worth had no intention of arguing with the Heisman candidate.

Mointz hugged a now-blonde-haired "Danielle" Santer. The green-eyed Deidre was permanently Celeste Phillips, camouflaged. Danielle Santer was Deidre's sister. Ronnie's grandparents had hidden Ronnie's birth by using Deidre's older sister's birth certificate information, covering Deidre's real age. The Santers gave birth to Danielle six years before Deidre was born in Luxembourg, making Deidre 21, not 15, at Ronnie's birth so Wilhelm and Gertrude could avoid embarrassment of a pregnant fifteen-year-old daughter, as Ronald had met Deidre in Germany when both their families were on a holiday there. Danielle had died from an infection only six days after birth and the death certificate was nowhere to be found, thanks to Lauren. Deidre easily took over her sister's identity, which identity Lauren altered making Danielle Deidre's younger rather than older sister. Martha and Robert helped create the ruse as Lauren made it all airtight. Danielle Santer had a new birth certificate, passport, license and a sexy new look.

Mointz kissed Danielle with his grandparents looking on, oblivious to the situation, even though they believed Danielle looked like Deidre. They would have had a conniption if they learned what mischief their grandson was up to.

Mointz hugged everyone before leaving with Danielle and Lauren in Lauren's Mercedes. Mointz made Danielle ride shotgun. As Lauren drove away, he had a big smile on his face.

"What are you smiling for, love?" Danielle asked.

"Ronnie is so upset, he did not even know what to say. In the First Parallel, we lost the game 52 to nothing.

"How did it change so much?" Danielle asked.

"I played better as I am healthier. We recruited better talent because of my star power and we had an ace in the hole this time."

"Which was?" Lauren asked.

"My years of reading defenses," Mointz replied. "Now, I am going to have to figure out what I can do to not be the number-one draft pick in the NFL."

"Play next year. Then in two years, when you serve in the Gulf War, at the end of the second season, you will have an injury. This is a great way to increase the Mointz legend. A hip injury will give you the opportunity to go to law school. A win-win in my book," Lauren explained.

"What do you think, Danielle?" Mointz asked.

She smiled at the fact that over the last few weeks, since they had returned from North Korea, he always asked for her opinion about everything. "Lauren and I went over the pros and cons of this and I do not see any drawback, sweetie. You are a bootlicker for asking."

"Why am I a bootlicker? I sincerely asked your opinion."

"Babe, I know you did. However, you are not going to listen to me or Lauren or your parents. The only thing you will listen to is your heart."

"Sorry," he replied.

"No need to be," Danielle said.

Mointz sat quietly as they drove to Lauren's home in Arlington, Virginia. Mointz and Danielle had agreed to help her pack as Lauren had thrown her hat in the ring to run for Congress in 1990. She was going home to upstate New York to re-establish her roots over the next two years. In the First Parallel, she was helped when her Democratic opponent got caught with an underage female in a hotel.

They had driven in silence for over 20 minutes before Lauren said, "Cristopher, stop stressing over minute details. Play ball for a bit."

"Sorry for spacing. I will play for sure. I am not fretting about football."

"Honey, what is wrong?" Danielle asked.

Mointz shook his head, "I am not comfortable with what is about to happen next month and I want to stop it, but I cannot, can I?"

"The election?" Danielle asked.

Lauren shook her head. "Cristopher is speaking about a mass genocide in Africa that is about to start during which hundreds of thousands of people will be killed. It will be years before the entire story comes out. This atrocity will equal the Holocaust. If you have a plan, Mointzie, I am all ears."

Cristopher perked up a bit, "I thought I would get pushback from you because I want to help."

Lauren, hesitated for a minute and then said, "Saving people has not hurt us so far. Besides, I work for you."

"We work together on this project. If we get involved, it has to be with a team of people we can trust."

"You want to go to Africa?" Danielle asked. "What happened to settling down?"

"Babe, this is who and what I am."

"F-OFF, Mointzie," she replied.

Danielle warmed up to Mointz as the night progressed. Lauren's husband had left her and moved into his own place near Johns Hopkins in Maryland. Lauren, for the second time in her life, moved on from her husband. It hurt much less here in the Second Parallel.

"Lauren, where do you keep all the cases Davis left for you?" Mointz asked.

"I have my laptop here, but the rest I've already brought up to New York."

"Let me borrow your laptop," Mointz said. They studied the political scene in Africa until long past midnight.

"We need to go to Sudan and have a chat with General Omar Bashir," Lauren said.

"Sure. Let's *help* the person who becomes the most corrupt leader in Africa," Mointz said.

"He doesn't get corrupt until the early 1990s and doesn't initiate the Janjaweed ("devils on horseback") until 2003," Lauren said.

"Do you have a plan?" Danielle asked. "This cannot be another North Korea. We were not prepared enough for that."

Mointz cringed when Danielle mentioned North Korea, thinking about Ko immediately. She had sent him several letters professing her love. Lauren cracked up when she read them.

"I take full responsibility for it, Danielle; believe me, it will never happen again." Lauren said.

"Good. Because I need you to figure out a way to deal with General Bashir."

"That is it, Mointzie. Time for bed," Danielle said.

"We can figure the rest out tomorrow," Lauren said. "Right now, I am exhausted from the win and your folks tailgating." Lauren hugged them both and wished them a good night. Most of her Arlington home was in boxes. The only two semi-assembled rooms were her bedroom and the guest bedroom.

Mointz led Danielle into the guest room. He immediately plopped down on the bed. "Left unchecked, General Bashir will eventually kill 400,000 people and cause 2,500,000 people to become refugees. I stopped at the Holocaust Museum when I visited DC in 2008. Babe, it was absolutely heartbreaking. There was a sign on the top floor that reads, 'Never again.' The sign touched me immediately. I have to try to do something."

Danielle cuddled up to Mointz underneath the covers, naked. He smiled as he felt her warmth. Her new look and genetically-altered eye color showed her as beautiful as ever. She was still his '*Deidre*,' just a little different on the outside. *Still sexy as hell*, he thought. Danielle had become a big work-out queen and was going to study law again, this time with Mointz.

"I love you, Mointzie, and I believe in you and this cause."

Lauren knocked on the door. "I need to speak with you guys," she said through the door.

"Come in, oh wise one," Mointz told her as Danielle lay under the covers.

Lauren entered with a somber look on her face. "There has been an explosion in Dingle, Ireland. The Flahertys were killed instantly."

"Erin?" Mointz asked.

"Afraid so, Cristopher."

Mointz felt like a sledgehammer had hit in the stomach. "What are the known details?"

"There is nothing left to their home. Their restaurant in downtown Dingle was destroyed. Word has it Matthew gave a bad shipment of arms to the O'Neil gang and the gang was not happy about it," Lauren told him.

Mointz got out of bed naked and put on sweatpants. Black and blue from the game, he sat down on the edge of the bed. Danielle and Lauren had no idea what to say when he did it; they just stared at him on the bed.

"What?" he exclaimed. "I am too sore and spend too much time in locker rooms to worry about walking to a chair to get my sweatpants. You both have seen me naked, for Pete's sake."

Mointz stormed out of the bedroom, grabbed his sweatshirt off the couch and walked out to the stoop of the house. He slammed the door on the way out.

Lauren and Danielle made tea and gave him some space outside.

"He loves you, Danielle. Cristopher loves you with all his heart. Right now he is out there blaming himself for exposing Erin's father. When he comes in, I have to tell the truth. Erin was no angel in this scheme her father ran here. Over the years, she invested monies the IRA raised and ran it through a washing machine. She knew early on of her father's activities; she was a money manager. Erin would meet these folks and help her father set them up. She passed on information through her business contacts, who had direct knowledge of the parties investigating the IRA in the United States and Ireland, starting in the mid-1990s. I looked deeply into this after the shooting of her father. Dr. Davis somehow found out about Erin being dirty. He sent her an anonymous disk so she could play nice in the sandbox with Mointz over the children anyway."

Danielle was not one to lose her temper; however, once she heard what Lauren had to say she was absolutely livid. "I have no idea how to respond, Lauren. I feel like I just threw up in my mouth. That evil bitch! Here I am feeling guilty for years over having her children. Dammit! Damn her!"

"Danielle, why do you think they pushed him to follow his heart? He only really ever loved you. He could have had you a million times after Ronnie passed away. At first, you blamed him for Ronnie's suicide. Because he loved you, he chose a different path. He refused to make love to you when you were vulnerable."

Danielle started to sob, "Why would I do that? Did he ever forgive me?"

Lauren nodded her head, 'yes.' "Danielle, you never forgave yourself and you left for Luxemburg. He tried to find you more than once, but his money was limited and he eventually gave up after letter after letter went unanswered. He blew out his knee and his football career ended. Cristopher lost Ronnie and you were gone, one relationship after another failed. Why don't we go get him and love the hell out of him for what he does for us and the world? He deserves happiness in his life."

Lauren and Danielle went out on the stoop to speak to Mointz. He sat hunched over until Lauren finished explaining the Flahertys' activities over the years. Lauren kissed him on top of the head and went back into the house. Mointz loved Lauren and she loved him. They were like brother and sister. Their relationship grew stronger every day as they supported each other. No matter what happened, they knew there was nothing they could not talk about.

"It broke her heart telling you that. And my heart broke after learning what a miserable bitch I turned out to be."

"Dee, stop,"

"F-off, Mointz. I am not going to stop. You didn't deserve any of this. You are kind, loving, sweet and romantic. And more than anything else, you love me unconditionally. I see how you protect me and Ronnie. Lauren told me Trent and she pushed for me. They let us fall in love and we became one and each other's everything."

Mointz held Danielle and cried on her shoulder. "I am sorry I did not do a better job saving you the first time. I will never let that happen again."

"I know, baby. I know. Don't just save me. Go save those people from their terrible fate. Now, I can see how you are who you are."

"I adore you, Dee; I will do whatever it takes to make you proud of me."

"Sweetie, I am already so proud of you. Come to bed and I will give you the best massage in the world and you are assured of a happy ending."

"Dee, I would love that."

Mointz received his massage and a very happy ending from Danielle before falling into a deep sleep for several hours. When he woke up, Danielle and Lauren sat at the kitchen table drinking coffee, in Brown University sweats, out of paper cups, as the movers had packed away all of Lauren's mugs to bring to upstate New York.

"Morning," Mointz said as he grabbed a paper cup and filled it with his favorite hot beverage.

Danielle and Lauren smiled at him as he sat on the table. His night with Danielle in the bedroom had brought him back off the cliff.

"Did you rest well?" Lauren asked.

"I feel pretty rested. I spent the rest of the night exfoliating my skin and then adding expensive emollient to my face. Don't I look good?"

"Actually, you do," Lauren said. "Do you guys have a bye-week next week? What are your plans?"

"Going to the homeland to get some beer and a couple of lads named O'Neil, while you two figure out Africa."

"Are you crazy?" Lauren asked.

Danielle looked at Lauren and decided to practice what she had preached to Mointz the night before, "Go get them, Mointzie."

Chapter Twenty-Two

The Brown coaches gave the Brown football team Thursday through Sunday off completely. The undefeated Bears had two games left against two tough Division I opponents: Rutgers and the number seventh ranked team in the country, Syracuse. Ronnie was playing a big game against San Diego State and was not available to go on Mointz's little crusade across the pond to Ireland. Mointz did not want to travel alone and thought about asking his friend Anthony Riggoli, but Anthony had a wedding to attend this weekend. On Lauren's suggestion, he invited a person who had his back no matter what.

"Are you sure you are up to this, Adam? Your leg healed enough?" Mointz asked Adam Chace while they boarded the Aer Lingus flight.

Agent Chace had made a great recovery as did the General and Charles Atwood.

"As long as they let black men in the country, I am good. Besides, you think I am some pencil-necked geek who cannot take a bullet?"

"Not at all," Mointz replied as they took their first class seats.

"Must be nice to be this world class superstar. Accommodations are always first-class," Adam Chace said. "I know you deserve it, so don't get your panties in a bunch."

Mointz laughed at the agent, who pulled out the sleep package the airline had placed in the seat pocket. The agent pulled the sleep visor over his eyes and fell sound asleep within five minutes of takeoff. Mointz asked Chace to back him up on a mission to take out the O'Neils who had killed a "friend's" family in Ireland.

Declan and Shamos O'Neil, the two brothers who had taken over for their father, Liam, had ordered the killing of the Flahertys, Lauren's contacts conveyed to her. Mointz knew that the O'Neils were hooligans growing up in and around their father's beloved pub. Declan, a year older than Shamos at thirty-three, ran the southwestern part of Ireland with an iron hand, as most of the country's heroin trade passed through there. Most of the money the brothers raised ended up in the IRA's coffers.

The O'Neil's viciousness kept the citizens of southwestern Ireland petrified of them and the government was powerless to do anything about their reign of terror. The O'Neils were about to face a man who was not at all afraid of them and that man was none other than Cristopher Mointz.

The Aer Lingus' flight touched down at 7:18 in the morning on Thursday in Shannon, Ireland. A friend of Lauren's father had left a black Renault in the airport parking lot for them with a trunk full of trinkets they might need.

Mointz grabbed the key out of the secret compartment in the front bumper of the car.

"Can you actually drive on the left side of the road?" Chace asked, after Mointz pulled out of the airport.

"Sure I can, and my mother was born here. It is embedded in me."

"Thank Christ, because I have no idea how to do it."

"Well rested, Adam?"

"Yeah but my ass is still asleep, I hope we stop soon because I need to refuel the body." Chace was in great shape and almost as big as Mointz.

"We will be enjoying a big Irish breakfast shortly."

Agent Chace slapped him on the shoulder. Mointz had touched Chace, Atwood, and the General not just because he had saved their lives, but because they all felt Mointz did what he did because he believed in what is right. He did not have to join the Defense Intelligence Agency, but wanted to.

As promised, Mointz brought Chace to his favorite breakfast spot he visited every time he came to the Emerald Isle in both parallels. Chace was not disappointed in the breakfast spot once he saw the meal in front of him. He sipped his tea after a bite of black pudding.

"This is more than a mission to knockoff a bunch of IRA hooligans?"

Mointz nodded and swallowed some tea. "Yes, it is more than hooligans and heroin. This is personal; however, I need to leave it at that. I am blessed to have you here and I thank you."

"Nonsense, Cristopher, I work for Lauren's father and she is family to you. I owe your Irish ass my life."

"Adam, no offense, but you don't owe me squat. I would never take advantage of a friendship."

"Why do you think I am here? Do you honestly believe I would sit this one out?"

"No, I don't, but thank you."

"Good man. Now, tell me how we are going to smoke these two morons and their buddies."

"I am going to get invited to play in this Saturday's rugby game."

"Hell, I thought you were an Ivy Leaguer. What kind of crazy idea is that?"

"Trust me, I am good at this."

"I am your backup, but I am not playing that crazy-ass game."

Mointz and Chace made it to O'Neil's Pub by noon. They had stopped at a couple of golf courses to scope out the landscape. They were both hungry for a lunch of chips and lamb stew. Cristopher could not wait to dive into it.

"You ever wear long pants?" Chace asked Mointz laughing.

"Sure, at church or when I ski," said Mointz and opened the Pub's door for Chace. The agent stopped in his tracks.

"Maybe we should come back later."

"Why, this is an upscale place?" Mointz peered in and was immediately shocked when a happy Danielle ran up to him and hugged him.

"Hello, Mointzie, I just want you to know there are many folks in here looking forward to meeting the Olympic Champion and American college football star.

"Oh, really! You do have a lot of moxie, you know that?" He glared at Lauren and gave Danielle a big hug and kiss. He introduced Danielle to Adam Chace.

"I met your sister in Korea, Danielle. The two of you look a lot alike."

"Nice to meet you, too."

Mointz kissed Danielle again. "I love the fact you are here, even though you do not listen."

"We are in this together. I promise to make it up to you later in a big way."

Lauren gave Adam Chace and Mointz each a kiss and a Murphy's, as the two ladies in cahoots introduced Mointz to their "bar-friends."

Killarney was one of the most happening towns in Ireland with beautiful golf courses, eateries, and plenty of watering holes. Irish, European and American patrons all saluted Mointz. Declan and Shamos O'Neil beamed with pride to see the Irish-American Mointz at O'Neil's.

"How was golf today?" Declan asked Mointz. The ladies had told him Mointz and one of his coaches were playing at the Killarney Country Club, while the women waited for them here at O'Neil's.

Thankfully for Mointz, he knew the course cold after spending many rounds there.

"I totally missed the green on the par three sixth and it went downhill from there. I am more of a contact sport kind of guy."

"Aye. Are you man enough to play a real game?" Shamos asked.

"Like rugby? I've played rugby since I was a small boy and played a few exhibitions with the Munster team. My mum lived here until she was 18 and a few of her cousins played all over the world," Mointz said, knowing the O'Neil's would take the bait.

"How good are you?" Declan asked.

Mointz smiled and gulped the rest of his Murphy's Stout. "Put it to you this way, Munster offered me five million pounds to play for them next year." Mointz was not lying, as Munster wanted him to join the club, offering the popular athlete the largest contract in rugby history.

Shamos and Declan could not believe their good fortune. The Saturday game was against their bitter rivals and archenemies, the O'Shaughnessys, the all-Irish family. They consisted of doctors, solicitors, clergymen and several business owners. Respect in rugby was the only thing that the O'Neils adhered to and the two families had always respected each other on and off the field.

"Would you be interested in a friendly match against our bitter rivals on Saturday?" Shamos asked.

"I am at the end of my college career and I should not take the risk of getting a twisted ankle or cracked rib. However, my life is all about risks. Sure, Shamos. Why the hell not?"

"Woo hoo!" Danielle yelled and high-fived Lauren.

"Excellent, absolutely lovely," Declan said.

The brothers excused themselves for a few minutes as they announced a short business meeting, however they pleaded with Lauren and Adam Chace to keep Mointz and Danielle at the bar a while longer. Mointz agreed to stay for a few more pints, as it was still early.

The bartender poured another round and Danielle asked, "Tired, sweetie?"

"Don't 'sweetie' me," Mointz said.

"Hey, I thought you said you were glad I was here," Danielle replied with a giggle.

"Well, maybe you can call me 'sweetie.'"

"When did you cross the pond?" Chace asked.

"We took a "company" jet and came in last night while Mointz flew to DC to get you," Lauren said. "Worked out well, don't you think? Agent Atwood decided to tag along just in case demolition is needed."

"Now I know why he does not like you very much," Chace said.

The four Americans actually enjoyed themselves until the seedy brothers returned with smiles. Mointz's skin crawled when they reappeared. All he wanted to do was snap their necks right there and then. Over the years, Mointz had learned incredible restraint.

"We have a practice tomorrow afternoon at four. Can you make it?" Declan asked as they were getting ready to leave.

"Absolutely," Mointz replied.

Declan told Mointz to meet him at the pub at 3:30. The O'Neils owned a coach bus for transport to and from games. Mointz agreed to be there and then left with Danielle, Lauren and Chace.

"Do you two have a vehicle?" Adam Chace asked.

"No. We took a taxi from the Brehon," Lauren responded.

"A crafty pair, Cristopher," Chace said.

"They certainly are," said Mointz, while getting in the car. "Did you make reservations? I could use a little rest before dinner. Some of us did not have a good night's sleep."

"Sure, old man," Lauren said. "Almost twenty-two and he needs a nap. How about you, Adam?"

"I am well rested, my dear."

"Adam slept the whole way here. That is why he is rested."

"Hey, I was shot. Forgive me."

"Home sweet home," Mointz said as he pulled in front of the Brehon Hotel. His mother loved this place and he stayed here often over the years. "By the way, who is working on our little problem?"

"Gennifer is running an analysis of the situation. She studied the psychological mindset of African dictators for her dissertation in the first," Lauren said. She used 'in the first' or 'in the second' when speaking about the parallels in front of outsiders.

"About time she uses her God-given talent," Mointz said. The four of them walked to the lobby.

Chace collected his key as Lauren and Danielle had already checked in. The four agreed to meet for dinner, which gave Mointz a chance to sleep for three hours. Lauren and Chace went to their respective rooms as Danielle and Mointz headed for room 506.

Mointz smiled, kissed Danielle and went into a deep sleep practically before his head hit the pillow.

When Mointz awoke, he quickly showered and read the note Danielle had left on her pillow. She wanted him to meet her at the hotel's bar once he was up and ready. He seemed to be always napping when he was on a mission.

Danielle and Lauren sat with Adam Chace drinking their second pint when a rested Mointz entered the bar. He could not wait to partake in a Guinness and a shot of Irish whiskey, Ireland's nectar from the gods. Mointz acquiesced to visit Mustang Sally's, the American-themed restaurant.

"Come on, Mointzie. We're going to have fun," Danielle said, holding his hand as they walked to the restaurant.

"I am in Ireland and we are going to Mustang Sally's where the world will know who I am."

"The world knows who you are everywhere you go, for Pete's sake. You're on every magazine cover in the world. Get over it," Lauren said.

The restaurant was a short walk and Mointz was mobbed as soon as word got around he was at a table. Although his burger and fries were fabulous, he barely had a chance to eat it while it was warm. He must have signed over 50 autographs and had plenty of pictures taken with fans of the Olympic champion.

"Glad you all ate while your food was hot," Mointz said.

"Your effrontery does not bother us," Lauren said.

Mointz loved to see Danielle and Lauren smile. Lauren still treated the world ruthlessly, but she was very protective when it came to Mointz, Danielle and Ronnie as well as Gennifer. They were now a family based as much on the love they felt for each other as the time they spent together out of necessity.

"Mointz, are you really good at rugby?" Chace asked. "It doesn't look like football."

"Yes, Adam. I have played forever, practically. There will not be any disappointed fans in the crowd."

"I still cannot believe you beat Navy again. I bet if you beat Rutgers and Syracuse, you win the Heisman.

Mointz laughed. "The last Heisman winner at an Ivy League school was Princeton's Dick Kazmaier in 1951, 37 years ago. I do not see it happening.

"Maybe you should," Lauren said. "ESPN has you as their favorite." She was a big sports junkie and she argued with Mointz about sports all the time.

"I am more concerned with getting this match over with. Then we can spend time worrying about the Heisman if I leave here in one piece.

"Excuse me, but you will be in one piece. This is not a repeat of Korea. My sister told me all about it. Tell him, Lauren."

"Danielle, I think he was talking about being beat up from the game."

"That I can deal with. I will nurse you back to health, baby."

The O'Neils could not believe how Mointz could dominate a scrum on the field during practice. Mointz laid some punishing hits after a rough day on the golf course where he had spent more time looking for his ball than hitting it.

"Jesus, Cristopher," Shamos shouted, after a bruising hit on a member of his crew named Paddy. Mointz knew from MI6 reports Paddy was one sadistic son-of-a-bitch. "Leave some of our guys in one piece for tomorrow. We need a full team."

Lauren, Danielle and Adam Chace watched Mointz from the stands with other family and friends in the small, but cozy, rugby stadium.

"He is a beast," Chace said after another big play by Mointz.

"Aye," a young lass replied, sitting with a young boy about four years of age. His eyes were as blue as the sky and he wore an Irish cap and a beautiful knit sweater. "Me husband plays for the O'Neils even though he thinks they are shite. My John is a dentist in town. He went to school with both of them."

Danielle introduced Lauren and Adam Chace to Kerry O'Callahan and they made small talk during the rest of practice. When Mointz came over after practice, John introduced him to Kerry and their son Kieran. Mointz headed back to the hotel where he had planned a nice night for he and Danielle.

"We cannot let John on the bus tomorrow," Lauren said on the way back in the Renault.

"I know," Mointz said. "He won't be on the bus. Don't worry; I have a plan."

He drove the twenty minutes back to the hotel going over the next day's script. Mointz needed to get a good night's sleep because, from what he had learned, the O'Shaughnessys played a rough game of rugby.

Lauren and Adam Chace spent the night downtown to let Danielle and Mointz enjoy a romantic evening. After Mointz showered and after Danielle dolled up for their "date," they walked across the street. The Italian restaurant was a favorite in Killarney.

"Pleasure to have your presence here tonight, Mr. Mointz," said Salvatore Laporte, the owner, an Italian immigrant. "We watched you in the Olympics win many medals." Laporte's accent was thick, but his smile warm and genuine.

"Thank you. Danielle and I have heard many good things about your ristorante."

Salvatore beamed as the hostess seated the couple. Mointz ordered a bottle of Chianti and an escargot appetizer, much to Danielle's delight. He had told her snails were an aphrodisiac.

"Remember when we first ate at a restaurant in New Hampshire and I had to order club soda?"

Danielle giggled. "We've come a long way, baby, since then. Remember, I asked you if you missed it?"

"I missed you for thirty years before I came back here. I love you."

Their waiter, Tomaso, brought the wine. As was customary with Mointz, he let Danielle taste the wine even though he was a wine connoisseur. She loved that he left it up to her to decide whether the wine was up to standard. Danielle gave the wine a thumbs up.

Mointz smiled and asked, "Does the reason I'm here bother you?"

"No, sweetie, I am proud of you."

"Really? How come?"

She squeezed his hand gently under the table and whispered, "These are evil people. Instead of sitting on the beach enjoying time off, you decided to right a wrong in the world, even after you found out how evil Erin was. At times, I wonder what goes through your mind as you work hard to be an athlete and save the planet. Everyone's problems became yours and you never shirk your own responsibilities. I watch Lauren, Ronnie, Gennifer and even Adam Chace look at you and marvel at the strength which is ingrained in you. It is infectious."

"It is what it is."

"Really? Is what it is? How am I here in Ireland, years younger, with blonde hair and green eyes? I am spiritually healthy as well as extremely ecstatic to be alive. Now, please do not tell me 'it is what it is.' I love that you are not just in my life, you share my life."

Mointz stood up, stepped over to her chair and kissed her softly. "Thank you for that. I love you," he said. "Isn't it great to actually go out in public and not have to look over our shoulders if I want to kiss you?"

"It certainly is!"

Danielle and Mointz's dinner, with the ambience of Tuscany, Italy, was perfect and not rushed. The conversation turned light and the food and wine as well as the peace they felt could not have been better, considering the reason they were in Ireland.

They left the restaurant arm in arm looking forward to continuing the evening back at the hotel.

"That's him," a man with a club said. He had walked out of the shadows; a scarf covered his face as scarves hid the faces of the other hooligans.

Mointz pulled Danielle behind him. "Can I help you?"

"We want to make sure you do not play in any match tomorrow," another man said.

Mointz sized up the seven men. Not one reached Mointz's size. The men held chains and makeshift clubs. Mointz planned to shove each man's weapon where the sun didn't shine. "I will certainly be playing tomorrow, whether you like it or not."

"Not if you cannot walk," the runt of the litter cried out to him in his Irish brogue.

Mointz turned and winked at Danielle. She actually giggled as she knew this was not a fair fight. He grabbed an old-fashioned two by four from the runt and wreaked havoc on the seven like a hurricane. He took a blow here and there, but nothing you would consider menacing. In less than a minute carnage lay scattered on the ground. None of them could move fast. Mointz grabbed the arm of the first person who stood up to him and snapped his index finger as Danielle winced.

"Who sent you?" Mointz asked as the restaurant started to empty out to watch. He grabbed the man's middle finger and gave a kick to the face of another one of the hooligans who had the insane idea of trying to get up. Mointz started to twist the man's finger. The man relented.

"We work for Steve O'Malley. He has a lot of money on the O'Shaughnessys in tomorrow's match."

Mointz winked at Danielle and, while still shaken, she was able to return the wink. She thought of how great sex was going to be tonight, as Mointz's testosterone always rose to a new level when fired up.

Lauren and Adam Chace sat at the hotel's bar when Mointz and Danielle walked in.

"Why didn't you get a hold of us?" Lauren asked when Danielle finished telling them what had happened.

"Sorry, Lauren. My cell does not work yet, yours?" Mointz said.

"Cell?" Chace asked.

"Private joke. How was I to know that a bookie put money on the O'Shaughnessys and thought it best to beat me to a pulp. We were having a great night up until that point."

Mointz ordered an Irish whiskey and Danielle decided on a Beantown ginger which consisted of ginger ale, whisky and a spray of lime juice. They had been sitting down for only 10 minutes when Shamos O'Neil showed up with two of his thugs.

"I hear you met up with a few hooligans tonight," Shamos said.

"More like I had a pre-game warm-up for tomorrow."

"That is not what I understand happened. I brought two friends of mine over to make sure you have a restful evening and accompany you to the pub in the morning."

"Thank you for your concern, but definitely not necessary."

Shamos did not take "no" for an answer. Mointz eventually relented to Shamos. It really did not matter, because Mointz had planned to take Danielle to bed anyway. Shamos made his way out, leaving his two men, Michael Dunnelly and Billy O'Hara, sitting at a table several feet away.

"Always wanted bodyguards," Lauren said.

"We should never have left them," Adam Chace stated somberly. "I know we were better off being near them. So much for being your backup."

"Adam, it worked out for the best. Danielle got to watch as I practiced my self-defense prowess."

"I've said it before; I will say it again. You are a beast, my friend."

"Thanks, Adam. Hopefully the O'Shaughnessys and the O'Neils will feel the wrath of the beast."

"C'mon beast, come show me your wild side," tipsy Danielle said.

"She's popped out of her shell," Lauren whispered in Mointz's ear.

Cristopher kissed her cheek, "Thank you for showing me the light."

"Let's go, Mointzie," Danielle said, dragging him out of the bar playfully as Dunnelly and O'Hara followed right behind him.

Mointz unleashed the beast and could not have played any better on Saturday afternoon. The O'Neils obliterated the O'Shaughnessys. Shamos, as well as Declan, were over the rainbow because of Mointz's dominating performance.

The beer flowed on the field after the game and Mointz signed several autographs.

"Time to get on the bus," Declan told Mointz. "We have plenty of beer time there."

"My family does not know how to drive here and I am going to drive them back to the pub."

"I understand. See you there," Declan said and walked Mointz to the parking lot.

Danielle gave Cristopher a hug and Mointz donned his signature flip-flops as he did after every game. The cool November afternoon on the Emerald Isle felt like summer to Mointz as his body was still on overdrive from the game.

"I cannot believe you broke John's leg," Danielle said.

"We were in the scrum; I slipped. If I did not do it, he would have been on the bus. I told you the O'Neils have a rule, if you are part of the team, you go on the bus. What else could I do?"

"Nothing, I guess." Lauren and Adam drove their friend out of sight and over to where the bus rounded the corner. "How is Agent Atwood?"

"He sends his well-wishes and says you are a beast." Lauren, Adam, and Atwood picked out a perfect spot to watch the fireworks."

"Outstanding," Mointz said. "I sat on the bus on the way here listening to the cruelty the O'Neils and their lackeys hold in their hearts. I hope they all rot in hell."

He smiled as they heard the rumble of what sounded like thunder. The fireball of smoke was not really as bad as the nuclear plant in North Korea. "Hell just invited a few more into its lair," Mointz said.

"No doubt, love," Danielle said.

Chapter Twenty-Three

Draft Day, April 1989

Mointz sat with Chris Berman, another famous Brown graduate. The Heisman trophy winner waited for the Washington Redskins to make him the first selection in the draft. The Heisman had been presented to Mointz just days after a trip to Africa on a "humanitarian" mission during which he and the rest of the team, Ronnie, Adam Chace and Charles Atwood, had a "come to Jesus" meeting with General Bashir. Mointz and company saved millions of lives in the long run laying out a better path for General Bashir to follow after taking control of Sudan.

Ronnie had a chance to be drafted in the early rounds of the draft, but his military commitment and his lack of blazing speed would keep him from being a superstar. He was already a military superstar and a now-commissioned Marine Lieutenant. Through the grace of one Lauren Gabriel, he received a Newport, Rhode Island placement.

Robert, Martha, Cristopher's grandparents, Lauren, Gennifer, Danielle and Ronnie accompanied Cristopher to New York for the draft. Seanie was at a baseball tournament and Kathy was taking final exams at USC in California.

Mointz had Jack Kent Cooke's multimillion-dollar contract in hand already when his name was called by Pete Rozelle, the Commissioner of the NFL. Danielle and Lauren did see the sparkle in his eyes as he held a Redskins' jersey with the number eight on it.

"Way to go, Mointzie," Danielle yelled.

Lauren passed out Redskins' hats to everyone around them. Grandpa Leo and Grandma Rose wore big smiles when Mointz put the caps on their head.

Mointz knew he would play for two full years in the National Football League before the Gulf War and then law school. This was now Mointz's time to take a step back and have some fun.

The Ivy League graduate finished the media portion of his day and his entourage decided to go to a Broadway show. He was introduced to the audience after 'Cats' where he received a thunderous ovation.

"I am proud of you, son," Robert said at dinner after the show. "Thank God, you and Danielle decided to buy the Georgetown house, with her going to law school."

"How is your mother, Ronnie?" Grandma Rose asked. Neither of his grandparents had any idea Danielle was Deidre.

"Very well. She met a wonderful man who puts a smile on her face every day."

"Danielle, you look a lot like your older sister. Do you take after your mother or father?"

"Definitely my mother," she replied, which was absolutely true. Thank heavens she did not have her mother's personality, she thought.

"Cristopher is one lucky young man," Grandpa Leo said. "Time to make an honest woman out of her soon, Cristopher."

"Yes, he is," Danielle said.

"Ronnie is a lucky man, too. Gennifer is a dynamite chick," Mointz said drawing laughter from everyone.

Ronnie kissed Gennifer. Mointz smiled brightly at his friend. Ronnie and Gennifer were in love, carefree and determined to be part of the team that was to save the world. If he could get Lauren a mate, things would be perfect. Too bad Lauren was so prissy.

The waitress brought over a bottle of champagne and Grandpa Leo eloquently gave the toast of his life.

"Now all you have to do is win a few games," Martha told her son. She still was the biggest football fan on the planet.

"I will try, Mum," Mointz said, tapping her champagne glass with his.

Mointz did not just try; he brought the Redskins to the brink of the NFC East title with a 13 to 2 record going into Christmas Eve's Saturday game against the Cowboys. The Cowboys held the same record as the Skins and had beaten the Skins earlier in the season. A home game was perfect, as Mointz had planned a special night for after this game.

Danielle drove Mointz to the stadium, as was customary, after they ate at a small diner near the stadium.

"How many touchdown passes will break the world record again?"

"I have 49 and need one more," Mointz answered. "The yardage record, I believe, will fall with my first completed pass. Then we can celebrate a successful season tonight.

"Babe, you had an amazing season," Danielle replied. "Ronnie and Gennifer are meeting me at the family cookout before the game. Your parents and grandparents will be in the box, but they decided to skip the tailgate party. I will bring your brother and sister over to the cookout."

Mointz laughed. "Kathy is so jealous of Gennifer, I wish I could be there."

"She told me Deidre never liked her and she is so happy I am so cool," Danielle said giggling. "I cannot believe she blamed me for her breakup with Ronnie."

"My sister is one-of-a-kind," Mointz said with a smile and a shake of the head.

Danielle was waived into the player's lot and Mointz handed out a signed ball and jersey for one of the parking lot attendants to give to a nephew for Christmas.

"Go get those Cowboys," Danielle said. "I have to find Lauren."

"I will do my best, love. Any last-minute advice?"

"Try not to get all beat up. I have a surprise for you as well tonight."

Mointz left for the locker room as "the rookie with the cool temperament of a veteran," read Sports Illustrated's cover story. Lauren had called him on Wednesday, begging him to avoid Sports Illustrated's cover jinx, where athletes seemed to have bad weeks after appearing on the cover.

Thankfully for mega-Redskin-fan Lauren, Mointz avoided the jinx and broke both the regular season passing and touchdown pass record. The Redskins' win gave them the NFC East title and Cristopher Mointz, a number one in the hearts of the Redskins fans. His number eight jersey was the top-selling in the league.

Danielle and Mointz's Christmas party had a celebration of Mointz's accomplishments angle to it. The alcohol in the eggnog flowed and the carols sung in the evening went on as Danielle hosted a great feast.

"Cristopher, help me get something out of the car, please," Ronnie asked just before midnight.

"Sure, bud," he replied and walked outside with his friend.

"You ready to give Danielle her present?" Ronnie asked.

"I hope she likes it. Are you ready for your night?"

"Hell, yeah. About time we give good gifts. You always give good gifts, you are such a chick," Ronnie said. "Dude, you were awesome today, I am so proud of you."

"Buddy, you could be playing too," Mointz said.

"Back-up running back? No thanks. I do not have the speed. You know that. Maybe for college, sure, but not on this level. I will live vicariously through you. Besides, I love doing what I am doing and so does Gennifer," Ronnie told him, taking Gennifer's present out of the car. "You have to know that there was not a dry eye in the stands when tears filled your eyes after the game. I owe you my life and so does my mother."

"Stop it, will you. I just love you being in my life," said Mointz.

The two embraced and the friends walked back to the house. Ronnie and Mointz felt closer than ever, dedicated to a common cause. They had found the women who made them feel like they were not alone in this.

"My mother is now my peer, my best friend is sixty-three years old and the love of my life is what?" Ronnie asked.

"She was forty-nine in 2016 and she is almost twenty-two, so quick math, with her being back over six years with her memories, your lady, take a few months here or there, is 55."

"Nice!" he exclaimed. As Mointz and he entered the house they both high-fived.

"Do you want your surprise?" Danielle asked.

Mointz nodded and Danielle, who was sitting on the bed in the bedroom, jumped up and went into the bathroom. Mointz could not wait for her to appear as this was perfect for what was about to happen. He lit the bedroom's fireplace, and slipped into bed. His eyes almost popped out of his head when Danielle appeared in a red negligee and a Santa's cap.

"Holy smoke," Mointz cried out.

Danielle proceeded to entice and stimulate her favorite quarterback until she no longer wore anything besides her Santa hat. Mointz and Danielle made love. Once they had exhausted themselves, she lay her head on his chest, which she loved to do after they had made love so he could stroke her hair.

"I love you, Mointzie," she said.

"Enough to marry me this spring?" Mointz asked, pulling a diamond the size of a Halls cough drop out from under his pillow.

"Oh, my God!"

"Shhhh," Mointz whispered. "We have a house full of people."

Danielle grabbed the ring faster than a defensive back picks off a wobbly pass and said, "Yes, baby, I will marry you. I love you with all of my heart."

"You better."

Her smile was too wide for Mointz to even comprehend how she had fretted over the day he would ask her. "Tell me you have a plan."

"Sunset Key in Key West at sunset. We can keep it small and elegant. It will be absolutely beautiful, but not as beautiful as you."

"Oh, Mointzie, you are so smooth." Danielle was one happy lady.

"Just an FYI, Ronnie is asking Gennifer tonight to marry him."

"I knew he was. The boy was way too happy and nervous today."

"Are you happy, sweetie?" Mointz asked.

"I am so happy, Mointzie. Please tell me this will last forever."

"My word is all I can give you, as you know I do what I say. Angel, you have my word."

Danielle kissed him again and again. Before long they were making love.

The next three weeks were a blur to Mointz as the newly engaged Danielle was on cloud nine talking wedding, wedding, wedding and the Redskins made it to the Super Bowl in Los Angeles. The team arrived via Jack Kent Cooke's private jet. When Mointz walked off the plane, Lauren was waiting for him in the private hangar.

"Hey lady, what are you doing here?" Mointz asked, and then had a really bad feeling. "Hold on, Blondie," Mointz stated. She walked with him away from the team bus and the media to tell him what she needed from him. "Let me get this straight. You want me to take out an Iraqi general here at the Super Bowl and kidnap his woman. Has Philip been hitting the bottle? The two of you have finally cracked. Go loosen up and get laid, will you? Maybe you'll get your brain back to normal."

"I have plenty of sex, thank you," she said.

"Yeah, you have been humping our starting-outside linebacker. I think our blonde-haired USC golden boy is in love."

"Not funny, Mointzie. There is a real problem here. We are changing the world, remember? Iraqi General Musa Malik teamed with Adam Ferguson's ex-partner Andrew Buckley. Buckley is about to sell a few hundred surface-to-air missiles. Not to mention we think Malik is holding a defense contractor's Chief Executive Officer's niece against her will."

"How come General Malik is in the country?" Mointz questioned and then caught himself. "Jiminy Cricket, Lauren. The idiots at the CIA let him in. One can only guess he is a football fan."

"A big one. This is important, Cristopher. The missiles will destroy planes and take American lives, many of them."

"I hate you sometimes. Meet me in my hotel room later and make sure my fiancée makes it there safely, please, since you are here."

"Do you want to get fined for having a woman in your room?"

"Tell Coach Gibbs to bench me then. I could care less about a football game anymore."

"Liar, you love this stuff," Lauren said. "Remember, my dad would not ask you if he did not really need to."

"Sure, Lauren. He just wants to rain on my parade because he is a Bronco fan."

"Come walk me to the bus."

They walked arm in arm to the team bus as she rested her head on his shoulder and whispered, "Disney World will still be expecting you, so relax."

Media day was a madhouse at the Coliseum as media from practically every country in the world asked the popular quarterback questions.

"Cristopher, over the last sixteen months you have won eight gold medals, won a Heisman trophy, achieved the NFL rookie–of–the–year award and have also won an MVP award, shattering records every step of the way. Will you ever come down to earth?" Bob Costas asked.

"I am going to ride the wave as long as I can, Bob. God has blessed me with some skills and I try to use them the best way I can."

"Do you look forward to breaking the heart of every woman in America this spring, as we hear you are tying the knot?" Mary Hart asked from Entertainment Tonight.

"I am a one-woman man Mary, always have been."

CBS's Irv Cross asked, "Are you worried about the Bronco's defense?"

"I know the Broncos will send the kitchen sink at me and I have to be ready for it."

Mointz answered every question thrown at him before he finally left for practice. Coach Gibbs had them practicing long and hard. Dan Reeves had the Broncos working equally hard. The Tuesday practices were closed to the media. However, they allowed a few private citizens, including Musa Malik. How Lauren and her father had convinced the Cookes to let Musa in did not surprise Mointz. Lauren watched the practice in the stands with Danielle sitting next to her. Their presence was a miracle as well, since family was never allowed in. Mointz's teammates did not seem to mind as they loved not only his football skills, but his enduring happy-go-lucky attitude.

Lauren advised Mointz to run out of bounds and make a quick connection with Malik. Mointz did one better as he stuck out a hand to Malik when knocked out of bounds on his keister. Musa Malik helped him up and Mointz patted him on the bum playfully, as coach Gibbs screamed at the defense for hitting Mointz. Malik got a huge kick out of it. Lauren loved Mointz's ingenuity. She also loved how quick he was on his feet.

The team members were supposed to be in their rooms by nine after the team meeting the night before the big game. However Mointz, with permission, was going to sneak out as Philip Gabriel had asked for a big favor from Jack Kent Cooke. Philip needed Mointz to meet a foreign official and Cooke obliged. They had been friends for years and were very close.

"No way are you going with me," Mointz told Lauren in her hotel room. Danielle had joined him there.

"There are people in the room with him. What do you plan to do?" Lauren asked. "We planned this out, remember?"

"No, you planned this out. You said his room was un-penetrable, remember? That is why you asked me to go in. I will take out Malik and his two guards and the team takes care of the guys outside. Lauren, stay here."

"Cristopher, your safety is my responsibility."

"Not tonight. If I feel I cannot do it, we'll find another way. Tonight we follow my rules not yours. You said yourself he will not be paying close attention to me. In your words, relax, and stop worrying."

Lauren stopped complaining as she knew it was useless to argue. Mointz announced his opinions more like edicts when he felt Danielle's and Lauren's safety come into play.

"If asses were leading the parade, you would be the grand marshal," Lauren said, causing Danielle to burst out laughing.

"Still, your ass will be staying here, so I will be seeing you later."

Mointz left the hotel with Lauren still barking at him. He wanted to get this over with and focus on football. His friends and family were extremely excited to watch Mointz in the game tomorrow and he had about 100 tickets for them. Mointz hoped Ronnie's father would make it to the game, but there was no chance. He was rapidly declining from the cancer.

Mointz felt confident the team Philip Gabriel had assembled would be as good as advertised. The upscale LA hotel hosted Malik in its private penthouse.

An aide for General Malik escorted Mointz from the front desk up to the penthouse. A gorgeous Middle Eastern woman named Marianne talked his ear off on the way up and handed him her phone number, along with a room key.

The General acted like a kid in a candy store as soon as Mointz walked in. He introduced his "moon and stars," Julie Gagnon, the niece of Enron's CEO and the six elite Republican Guards in the room. Mointz knew he was screwed because the team assigned to take out Malik were monitoring the wire he was wearing. There were supposed to be outside guards and inside people, not all inside men. Mointz needed to call off the operation if this was the case except he could see Julie was shaky. No doubt the General was holding Julie against her will, no doubt at all.

"Thank you for sitting with me. Please have a cup of coffee. It is our special blend. I know I only have a few minutes," the General said.

"I have time. I would love a cup," said Mointz. "Tell me sir; I am a bit curious how you became such a big football fan."

"My cousin, the President, allowed me the good fortune of studying at Harvard and I fell in love with the game."

Harvard still breeds the best terrorists, Mointz thought to himself.

"My rival, sir," Mointz said. He could not stop staring at Julie Gagnon.

The General and Mointz spoke of the game while Mointz sipped his coffee. Mointz knew he had to do something. He could not walk away. Three of the guards had left the sitting area and were out of earshot.

"Where did you two meet?" Mointz asked.

"We met at an energy conference in Dallas. We have been together ever since," said the General.

"That is wonderful," said Mointz. "She is an extremely attractive woman, you are a lucky man." Mointz was trying to unnerve the General to see an opening. He never expected him to offer her to him.

"She is willing to pleasure you, Mr. Mointz. It would be an honor for me to share her with you tonight," the General said.

Mointz almost choked. He needed to play it cool if he had any chance of saving her. "The honor would be mine, sir."

General Musa Malik's eyes lit up. "Splendid! Julie my love, please take our superstar quarterback here and show him how a good woman takes care of a man."

The young woman's eyes fought back tears. However, she did not cry. Her hand shook as she reached out for his hand and guided him into the bedroom. She turned to face him as soon as they walked into the room. "I have never been made to do this before, please be patient with me," she was scared to death.

Mointz smiled at the petrified 23-year-old. "I am here to rescue you, not hurt you."

Julie started to sob. As soon as Mointz opened his arms, the pretty, auburn-haired woman with chestnut eyes fell into them.

"He has raped me repeatedly and he has kept me with him. Musa says he will kill my family and me if I do not stay."

Mointz held her tightly and kissed the top of her head. "I will get you out, but you are going to have to help me."

"Anything, Mr. Mointz."

"Sweetie, I am the same age as you. Please call me Cristopher," he said. "Where did the three other guards go? Are they armed?"

"Those guards walk around here armed. I believe they go into the other bedroom and play cards or backgammon. They are really cruel; they don't like me at all. There are about six men altogether in here and several outside."

Mointz went into the bathroom, groped behind a panel under the sink and grabbed the Glock the agency had planted. "Julie, you get under the covers. I will be right back."

"Please don't leave me. Please," she cried out softly.

"Trust me, I will not let them hurt you, I am going to take care of all of them," he said wondering how he was going to fulfill that promise.

"We need to get in there," Lauren said in the command center at the players' hotel.

"Lauren, he is in trouble," Danielle began, "Get him the hell out of there!"

"Agent Gabriel," one of the CIA agents said. "If we storm the place, it might be worse. Just wait."

Mointz's voice came over the receiver. "Listen to me," he said in the bathroom as Julie lay under the covers. "I know you heard what she said. Get the team ready and when I throw that mother fucker off the balcony, haul ass up here."

"Did he say he was going to throw the General off the balcony?" Danielle asked. "Lauren, do something, will you please?"

"I am trying," she exclaimed as she attempted to prepare the assault team to move in.

Danielle ran out of the room with a walkie-talkie. Lauren ran out after her.

"Dammit," Danielle screamed at the elevator, which seemed to take forever.

"Relax, Danielle. He knows what he is doing."

"Who are you trying to reassure, me or you?"

"Probably both," Lauren said when the elevator finally found their floor. They headed down to do what they could.

Mointz put the silenced Glock behind his back in his belt, covered it with his blazer and walked out onto the balcony with a big grin on his face. "Thank you for that wonderful experience."

"An honor for me, like I said, to share the wealth, as you Americans say," the General said.

Mointz pulled the silenced Glock and in sequence shot three of the Republican Guards before pushing the gun into the General's mouth. "Pulling the trigger is too good for you," Mointz said. He grabbed the General by the throat and, as promised, threw him off the balcony. The General's screams pierced right into the microphone. Mointz quickly ran into the second bedroom and shot the three men in the bedroom, who were, indeed, playing cards.

Mointz ran to the other bedroom and gave Julie his hand. When her eyes opened wide like they had just seen a ghost, Mointz spun around and fired at one of the General's men, who had been in the bathroom when he had burst into the second bedroom and killed the three men. The soldier fired at Mointz at the same time. As the Iraqi fell from the shot to his chest, Mointz cried out in pain from the bullet he received just below the hip. Mointz fired into the Iraqi two more times and fell to the ground in pain.

"Cristopher, Cristopher are you all right?" Julie screamed.

"I'm fine," he replied on the floor.

Mointz pressed on the wound for ten minutes before the Calvary finally stormed in.

"Are you all right, sir?" one of the CIA team members asked once the area was clear.

Mointz nodded. "Please get Ms. Gagnon on to safety I need to get to the hospital without my future wife finding out."

"Well, she knows." Danielle said, having heard everything on the two-way radio.

"Hi," Mointz said smiling.

Danielle immediately dropped to the floor and hugged her man. "What the hell were you thinking?"

Lauren stared at him in disbelief, "Do you ever listen to anything?"

A paramedic helped Mointz stand up and steady himself. "Get me to the hospital," said Mointz. "I have a game tomorrow."

"How can you play?" Danielle asked. She was crying, as was Lauren.

"I don't have many shots at this. I will figure it out," Mointz said as he left for the private military hospital set up for government and military personnel here at the Super Bowl. Danielle and Lauren accompanied Mointz in the private ambulance.

Three hours of shots, blood drawings and doctor visits did not give Mointz a decent answer on the seriousness of his injuries until a very familiar face came in.

"Mr. Conley, I mean, Dr. Conley, how are you?" Mointz asked. Dr. Conley, a doctor in the Naval Reserves, was the father of his childhood friend, David Conley. David was finishing up his residency back in Rhode Island.

"How is David? I have not seen him since I left Brown. I spoke to him a few times during this past season.

Dr. Conley smiled, "What are you doing getting shot the night before the Super Bowl?"

"Trying to save the world, sir."

"Is he all right, doctor?" Danielle asked.

Dr. Conley nodded and smiled. "I know your sister Deidre, Danielle. Congratulations on your engagement. My son told me last week. And to answer your question, yes, he is all right. However, the back-up quarterback had better warm up and prepare for the game."

Tears started to rain from Lauren's eyes. Danielle was too stunned to even process what she had just heard.

"No offense, Dr. Conley, but we need to figure out a way to pull this off while Lauren calls good ole' Phil so he can call Mr. Cooke to square this away with Coach Gibbs."

"I know the bullet went all the way through, but please rethink this," Dr. Conley stated.

"Sorry, sir. I will play with or without your help, but I really could use it. Do what you have to do, please," Mointz said. His face told Lauren all she needed to know. The guilt she felt for Mointz, her friend, not Mointz, the future President, broke her.

"What can you do, theoretically, to allow him to play? The bullet did not cause any damage to the hip, correct?" Lauren asked.

"The bullet went through muscle and straight out just above the groin. Nothing vital was damaged; however, he would have to be a freak of nature to play. There is no way I could stop the blood unless I stitched it temporarily and covered it with a special pad. I played football, Ms. Gabriel, and if it was anyone other than Cristopher Mointz here I would not even bother," the doctor stated. He could see in Cristopher's eyes he would not be denied. Dr. Conley was very familiar with his look.

"I will not even deny my future husband should not play, but I know my Mointzie and he is going to play no matter what, and I bet he plays well. I believe in him," said Danielle.

"Cristopher, you have a long career ahead of you. Please be positive this is what you want to do. I am concerned your long-term health could be affected if you play and infection sets in. I will consult with the team physician as soon as Lauren gives me the okay," said Dr. Conley. He left to order the mold to protect Mointz's hip.

Danielle held one of Mointz's hands and Lauren the other as Mointz tried to put on a brave front. "I am fine, really."

"Neither one of us are asking you what went down because we heard it," Danielle said. "I would've done the same, for once."

"I screwed up. I did not see the seventh guy and I let my guard down. I probably should not have tossed the prick off the building."

"Mointzie, you amaze me every day," Lauren said. "How the hell you saved that girl was not just heroic; it was mind-boggling. I cannot believe this was as difficult as it was. My father asked me to scope out the place and take out the General. You took them all out."

###

"Oh, Cristopher, how did you get stabbed?" Coach Gibbs asked his rookie quarterback when he entered the hospital room with Mr. Cooke, the team owner.

"Coach, a man jumped off the hotel's balcony near the team hotel. I crossed the street and a crazy Bronco fan came up and stabbed me," said Mointz. Tony Downs, Lauren's former subordinate at the agency, had told Coach Gibbs and Mr. Cooke a man was now in custody.

"I am fine, coach. I can play," Mointz said. "Dr. Conley is an old family friend and along with our team doctor, they say I can play."

Jack Kent Cooke made sure the team doctor did not tell anyone that Mointz had been shot and not stabbed. Mr. Cooke conferred with the doctors and verified Mointz could play.

Danielle and Lauren returned to the hotel with Coach Gibbs and Mr. Cooke after about an hour so Mointz could rest. Mointz hoped by the time he woke up he would be miraculously cured, but that didn't happen. There was no miracle at 8:00 am as Mointz could not get out of bed. He could barely move and kickoff was at 3:29 pm. The Redskins' team meeting was at 9:00 am and Mointz was getting nervous.

Dr. Conley walked into the room with Danielle and Lauren in tow. They were concerned when they saw he was crying and could barely move.

"Sweetie, I am so sorry. There is no way you should even try to move. Stay lying down I will call Coach Gibbs," said Danielle.

"I am fine, baby. I will be able to play. I have to walk it off and hope Dr. Conley has a nice drug cocktail to help me. I wish Dr. Trent were here with a magic drug to help me in this situation."

"Who is Dr. Trent?" Conley asked.

"A good friend of ours. Believe me, he is brilliant," Mointz said and smiled, thinking about his good friend.

"Maybe he can help," said Lauren.

"He's actually in France at the Pasteur Institute. Dr. Trent has developed an emergency 'pain drug' he has kept in the agency's lab. It is being flown here as we speak. It will be here in time."

"Good, because when I said it would take a freak of nature to play, I meant it. Let's hope this Dr. Trent can make Cristopher a freak of nature," Dr. Conley told Lauren. "Now, if you'll excuse me, I have to finish the protective pad for Cristopher's hip."

"Tell me Trent has a drug to cure me before kickoff."

"No, but it will allow you to play, I bet. I searched the documents Trent left me describing the medicine I had put away at the CIA. Lucky for you, he left vials of a drug to help you fight the pain of a wound and help in the recovery process. An agency plane is delivering it shortly from Langley. My dad doesn't ask questions, but he thinks the drugs Trent left are special research drugs. This drug will help, as Trent left it for you if you needed to get through a mission or if you were injured while you were running for office or in office. I can get more made up; I have the formula," Lauren said.

"I also spoke with Mr. Cooke. The team has been told you had an emergency operation because of an infection and if you are able to play it will be a miracle."

"Run and shoot, Lauren?" Mointz asked.

"Absolutely."

"What is the run and shoot?" Danielle asked.

"The early 90's offense the Houston Oilers used with no running backs. The Oilers threw the ball almost every single down. Mointz could throw to save his hip," Lauren told her.

Dr. Conley gave Mointz a morphine shot. Mointz felt better instantly. Danielle and Lauren helped him into the car and brought him to the team's hotel for the Redskins' morning meeting.

Before the meeting, Mointz met with Coach Gibbs. Together they designed the run and shoot on a blackboard. The team decided to run through the plays at noon. Lauren told Mointz she would have the drug before then.

After the meeting, the Redskins held the team breakfast and prayer service; however, Mointz skipped the events to rest up in his room with Danielle.

Mointz started to bleed a bit through the gauze and Danielle changed the dressing.

"I spoke to everyone and they wish you good luck," Danielle said. "Lauren is going out of her mind over this."

"Dee, she's always out of her mind. It is who she is."

"Lauren loves you. Not like I love you, but like brother and sister, like you and Ronnie. She worries about us and she is the best friend I ever had."

"Dee, I love you; we fit together and we have made a family, as crazy as this situation is. My brother and sister are both doing well. My parents still don't know what to think, but are ecstatic for us. Ronnie has Genny and they want a family together. Moving forward, I have to stop getting shot."

"Oh, you freshie," Danielle said. They snuggled and slept together for almost an hour before Lauren knocked on the door.

"If it is not Dr. Kevorkian…" Mointz said to her when Danielle let her in.

"Not funny, Mointzie."

"Who is Dr. Kevorkian and don't tell me it is an inside joke," Danielle told him and went to the Apple computer to look up 'Kevorkian' as Lauren drew the syringe. "Does this doctor not believe in repercussions for his actions?"

Mointz and Lauren laughed before they gave Danielle an abridged version of the great doctor of death.

"Drop 'em, Mointzie," Lauren said after drawing the syringe. She administered the shot to Mointz's right butt cheek, "Here is some acetaminophen to keep a fever from sprouting."

"That hurt like hell. So not cool, Lauren."

"Listen, you big baby, are you or aren't you the one who thinks it's a good idea to play today?" Danielle asked giggling.

"Whose team are you on?" Mointz asked.

"Lauren's. If I did not hate you so much right now, I probably would like you better."

Lauren and Mointz looked at each other and simultaneously cried out, "Yogi Berra." They both loved their Yankees and their Yogisms.

###

Mointz felt halfway decent as he warmed up minutes before game time on the sidelines. His teammates were amazed he was able to play.

"Are you alright, Cristopher?" Coach Gibbs asked as the Broncos were about to kick off.

Mointz smiled, "Never better. How are you Coach, nervous?"

"Not in the slightest," Coach Gibbs responded as he could not suppress a laugh. "You are one in a million, son. Go get 'em."

Gibbs gave his star rookie quarterback a play. The team of John Madden and Pat Summerall watched in shock with the Skins coming out in a five-receiver set and in the shotgun.

"Yellow 31, yellow 31, set, hut, hut, hike," Mointz barked out the cadence before Jeff Jacoby snapped the ball. Mointz hit Art Monk on a go pattern for the first touchdown of the game on the first play.

The Broncos had no idea how to stop the Redskins' offense. When they blitzed, Mointz threw short passes, when the vaunted Orange Crush defense sat back and didn't blitz, Mointz threw the ball deep. It was not until early in the fourth quarter that Mointz was knocked to the turf for the first time. With the game out of reach for the Broncos and the Redskins leading 42 to 7, the hit opened Mointz's wound.

"Blood is spurting from Mointz's hip!" John Madden screamed as they rushed Mointz back into the locker room.

A few minutes went by before Pat Summerall said, "We have heard reports Cristopher Mointz had an infected cyst removed yesterday and the sutures opened up. Our sources say he should have never played."

"That is amazing, Pat. He has thrown for over 400 yards and six touchdowns!"

"Mointz has just returned to the sideline. We will try to get Leslie Viscer to get a word."

Leslie grabbed Mointz on the sideline with three minutes left in the game with the score now 42 to 14.

"Cristopher, how did you manage to play after surgery yesterday?"

"Wasn't easy. We actually put in this offense around noon. I tried to play as long as I could before I had to give up. I did not want to let the team or our fans down."

"Truly mind blowing you played this well."

"Thanks, Leslie."

The final gun went off with the Redskins winning 42 to 21. Mointz held the Vince Lombardi trophy high in the air. Named after the Packers' legendary coach, the trophy was given to the Super Bowl champion. The trophy shined brightly as confetti rained down like snow on a cold winter's day. Mointz spoke a few words and teammate after teammate described the pain Mointz had played through. They all were in awe of him.

Mointz held Danielle on the field after the game. "We did it, Dee."

"No, sweetie. You did it, you were awesome."

"Thanks, baby," Mointz said before collapsing on the field.

Mointz was rushed into the locker room and was given an IV. Dr. Conley believed dehydration was to blame for the collapse.

"He needs a good night's sleep and will need to be hospitalized for a few days," Dr. Conley told Danielle and Lauren. "Eventually, he will be fine. I still cannot figure out how the hell he played."

For the second time in two nights, an ambulance took Mointz to the hospital. This time, Dr. Conley accompanied Mointz to LA's County Hospital. Lauren and Danielle followed in a limousine.

"He did it! Six touchdown passes. Woo hoo!"

"My Redskins are the best," Lauren said grinning. "Unfortunately, we have to take him back to the hospital. Disney World will have to wait."

###

Family, friends and teammates visited Mointz over the next 48 hours.

Danielle visited at around 8 am on Tuesday. Mointz watched ESPN with her. Mointz could not believe how viral his play on Sunday had gone. It was all TV talked about.

"Honey, you can't be still surprised at how much press you are getting?"

"Dee, of course I am. The world has now met Danielle Santer. I would never have believed this would be where I would end up after Super Bowl victory. What did your parents say?"

"Dad's Alzheimer's is progressing rapidly and he did not realize anything. My mother does not even watch television so when I told her I was on the tube she said, 'Very nice, dear.' Typical of my mother."

"Sorry about dad, love."

"I caught up with Ronnie and Gennifer before they left with your parents and grandparents on the private plane you reserved. Seanie is staying out here with Kathy for a few more days."

"He told me, he is almost 15 now and he cannot wait to hit the USC campus. Having a famous brother will help."

"Your parents told me he's getting recruited already," Danielle said.

"Seanie is a great tight end, Dee. Hopefully he doesn't quit this time," Mointz said. He told Danielle how Seanie was a lot more motivated this time around.

"Lauren says you are in the clear on the Iraqi mess. No one can place you at the General's hotel room. She left for Langley this morning."

"Now that you are here, it is time for me to get sprung."

"Says who?"

"It is fine, Dee I was given permission."

"Mointzie, you probably threatened half the hospital."

Chapter Twenty-Four

April 17th, 1990

"Do you, Danielle Santer, take Cristopher Mointz to be your lawfully wedded husband?" Pastor Jeff Williams asked Danielle on Sunset Key in Key West, Florida.

"I certainly do."

Mointz also pledged his love to her. As he held her hand, he said, "My life was never easy; I never wanted easy, just possible. My life became easy when you became my everything. Your beauty inside and outside is breathtaking and as I move forward in life with you by my side there is nothing we cannot accomplish. I love you with all I am."

The newly-minted married couple kissed and Mointz spun her gently in the air.

"Let me say this succinctly. I love you and I want to make it clear, as you save the world, know you already have saved me," she whispered.

What was supposed to originally be a small affair turned into a 400-person elegant bash.

Lauren and Ronnie, best man and matron of honor, converged on the happy couple and the party commenced.

Since the Super Bowl, Ronald had passed at the end of February and Danielle's mother in mid-March.

This night was a celebration of life, though, and the memory of departed loved ones was in their hearts. Danielle, Deidre, "Dee" Santer felt born again as she danced the couple's first dance with Mointz kissing and whispering "I love you's" to her. She felt peace and love in her heart even though she believed the word "peaceful" would never be associated with her until "Mointzie" left The White House.

Ronnie cut in and danced with his "aunt" and Mointz danced with Gennifer.

"Ready for this soon?" Mointz asked.

"Yeah, I cannot believe I found love with him so deeply. Who would have expected this? I bet Trent would not have."

"Probably not, but I am glad you two are happy. The two of you are great together."

"I love him, I really love him. He is funny, strong, and romantic and he doesn't try to be you. Ronnie is comfortable in his own skin. He doesn't have to be you to be happy because you made sure he became his own person. Cristopher, you raised him, if that makes sense."

"Sort of, but I am just glad the both of you are in love and form each other's support network."

The Air Supply song ended and Mointz kissed Gennifer on the cheek. Mointz may not have been a psychologist, but he could see the love Ronnie and Gennifer felt for each other. Mointz did not want the guilt of hurting either one of them when he had fallen for Danielle and he thanked God it all worked out.

Mointz and Danielle proceeded to cut the cake. They could not have been any happier. Mointz stepped up to the band and grabbed a guitar.

"Tonight, I married my best friend and I want to give her a memory she'll never forget." Mointz strummed his six string and Danielle giggled loudly.

"Lady, I am your knight in shining armor and I love you. I am what I am and I am yours." Mointz continued to sing the Lionel Richie song as he walked across the floor to Danielle. He played and sang from the heart.

"Don't make me cry," Danielle said. When he dropped to one knee, her eyes became wet.

When he finished the song, he handed the guitar to his brother Seanie and gave his new bride a hug. Mointz made Danielle cry a few more times. She made him cry a few times and they both made the guests laugh, cry and party until the sun came up. It was almost six before Mointz and Danielle made their way to their cottage on the private island. All of the guests stayed either at the Hilton on the mainland or in the cottages.

"We did it, lady," Mointz told Danielle when they came into the cottage that Kathy and Martha had decorated perfectly.

"I have a really special video to play for you," Danielle said.

"Show me, Mrs. Mointzie," Mointz said with a bottle of champagne in hand.

Danielle opened up the Apple laptop and inserted the USB device. "I am getting good at this."

"Trent!" Mointz exclaimed with a smile as his friend appeared on the seventeen-inch screen.

"Well, well, Dr. Cris. Congratulations on your wedding to the lovely Deidre, or shall I say, 'Danielle.' I knew in my heart you would choose wisely. Hello Danielle, nice to meet you. However, I will be seeing you sooner rather than later. I have a major surprise for you," Davis stated and sat smiling on the screen. "Turn around."

Mointz turned around. To his astonishment, Lauren introduced Dr. Trent Davis, a 27-year-old Davis.

"Tell me you know me," Mointz said to him.

"Cristopher, of course I know you. Don't just stand there; give me a hug and introduce me to your lovely lady over there."

Mointz complied with both requests.

"When did you get back?"

"Well, after I dug myself back up, about a month," Trent said with a smile. "Lauren made me do it before I returned my memories."

"Trent had to come back once you and Danielle decided to join forces in love and battle," Lauren said.

"I ought to ring your proverbial neck for putting me through this," Mointz said to Davis.

"Cristopher, you always loved the word 'proverbial.' Lauren has given me a full account of all of your successes. I am so proud of you. God, you actually have done even more than I expected of you and I expected a lot."

"Danielle and Lauren are my angels and Gennifer has done amazingly well. I would assume that you know she is marrying Ronnie on the fourth of July."

"I do," Davis said. "I know it all and I know that you have become quite the daredevil. North Korea, Africa, Ireland, LA and so many more, I have lost track. I do know saving Mrs. Hawkins and a five-year-old girl was as amazing as your love life has been. Man, I am proud of you."

"Proud of me? Be glad I am not kicking your ass right now for all you put me through without telling me Jack do-do, but I am glad to see you."

"Dr. Davis, Cristopher has done everything you expected and then some. I hope you appreciate how hard this is been not only for him, but for Lauren as well. They have had to improvise and the dangers they have faced at times were overwhelming," Danielle said.

"Danielle, if I did not believe in them I would not have allowed them to improvise. These two and Gennifer as well as you are four of the brightest people I know."

"Why are you back now?" Mointz asked.

"I am only here to start preparing for the next 22 years of science. Remember, I cannot change anything too dramatically, but I have high hopes I can help with several of the problems you are going to face."

"Wouldn't it have made more sense to just return with me when I came here?" Mointz asked.

"That is a negative. I had to become published on my own and get my MIT appointment. Lauren didn't even know until the day before she came to me. I kept it quiet so I could surprise you; however, when Lauren said you were getting married, I couldn't wait."

"I had the wedding video made so I could give you a gift from Trent. One would assume this is much better," Lauren said.

"Hell yeah, I am so grateful you are here. However, you could have come back sooner."

"I have reasons you will never understand. I am here now and thank God you and Danielle have found each other."

"We certainly have. Trent, I have to put in a request you need to stop the twists and turns. I am too old for this stuff."

Davis laughed. "I will try to refrain from any more, sir. Now, I have to get to my room so you can consummate your marriage and enjoy your wedding bliss. I will see you tomorrow sometime; you can buy me a drink."

Mointz and Davis embraced. Davis could see in the flash how close the team had become. He was an MD and a PhD physicist as well as a chemist. Davis believed in chemistry in the lab and in life. You mix two elements of people and you either get a poisonous gas or a beautiful crystal. Danielle Santer and Mointz, Lauren and Mointz, Gennifer and Mointz, Gennifer and Ronnie, all made beautiful crystals together because of their good chemistry.

"Mointzie, you are the man," Danielle said after they had consummated their marriage.

"Would you like to make a baby?"

Danielle sat right up in bed, "I thought you wanted the boys during the same years."

"Doesn't mean we cannot have children now. Together in love, having a baby or two would add to us, no?"

"When I think I cannot love you anymore, you do or say another incredibly sweet thing, honey; I would love to have a baby."

"And I will love trying to have a child with you."

Danielle fell asleep in his arms as it was almost 8:00 am, Cristopher finally shut his eyes and as he fell into a deep sleep he could not help but smile over how wonderful a day he had just spent, no matter what parallel he was in.

The newly married couple woke up at around 11:15. Continental breakfast had been left on the front stoop of the cottage and, as he had done every day since they arrived, Mointz grabbed the basket of fresh muffins, bagels, and fruit, taking it in to the bedroom with a pot of coffee.

"Are you hungry, Mrs. Mointz?"

"Starving, Mr. Mointz."

Mointz grabbed a cheese Danish and a cup of coffee and devoured both. "I still cannot believe we are married and, to top it off, Trent showed up here in the flesh. The only thing better would be for you to tell me you are pregnant. Are you pregnant?"

"Not that I know of, unless you have bionic sperm, but who knows anymore?"

"Okay, I think we want to go for an invigorating swim in the ocean, I hear it will make you fertile."

Danielle gladly agreed with Mointz and on a beautiful 87° morning they took a dip in the ocean water. Eventually Ronnie, Gennifer and Lauren joined them.

Key West had beautiful beaches. However, the sand was not as soft as the ones further south in the Caribbean, but no one minded today as the weather was perfect.

"Davis is back? What did he have to say for himself?" Gennifer asked.

"Same old Trent, shrugs it all off and says he is glad Danielle and I got together, still avoids why he did not come back with me at the same time. Still says he needed to wait until his MIT appointment before his memories returned. He claims he would have changed too much and would have lost too many relationships," Mointz said. "I am also not happy with the blonde matron of honor for holding out on telling us."

"He asked me to keep a lid on it until the wedding. No offense, Mr. President, but I keep all of your secrets."

"Secrets? What secrets?" Ronnie asked.

"Exactly the question I was about to ask," Mointz said.

Lauren raised an eyebrow. "Nothing I want to reveal on the record in front of your new wife at her wedding."

Danielle gave Mointz a stern look as only she could. "Spill the beans, husband."

"Dee, I have no idea what she has on her devious mind. Lauren obviously has spent too much time in the sun Wait until she asks me to stump for her on the campaign trail."

"Totally below the belt," Gennifer said.

"I am glad Trent is back. He will straighten all of you out," Mointz said grinning.

###

Davis, as pasty as ever, covered in suntan lotion and wearing a big hat, met Mointz and company on the beach, Mai Tai's in hand.

Gennifer ran up to Davis and hugged her friend. She introduced him to Ronnie and Davis smiled widely at her fiancé.

"Ronnie, I am proud of you, son. You have done an amazing job getting up to speed on all of this and helping out. I am also in awe of you as you tamed this wildcat over here," Davis said, hugging Gennifer tightly.

As Davis handed Mointz a Mai Tai, Mointz said, "Since you have crashed our party, what do you intend to do?"

"Besides watch you win another Super Bowl, my main goal is to work as hard as I can to back your troublemaking butt. Imagine my surprise when my memories returned and you were in the winning Super Bowl."

"Blame these two," Mointz said pointing at Danielle and Lauren. "They made me play."

"They must've really twisted your arm. Oh, by the way, did Lauren tell you I purchased my beach house next to yours? Cost me more than it did in 2013."

"Darn, Trent. I could have been your real estate agent and made a commission," Danielle said giggling.

Davis smiled at Mointz. "Didn't you tell me she always had the sweetest giggle? Why do you wonder how I picked up on all of this?"

Mointz smiled back. "Was it that obvious?"

"Your love for a Deidre Santer, yes it was obvious. We shared many beers together on our decks and there was never a time when we were together where Deidre was not mentioned."

Mointz realized then and there that there was never a time he did not love Dee in the First Parallel. Having her now and loving her made this all the more worthwhile. He also realized he was a fool for letting Erin bring him down.

"Why didn't you tell me about getting my children back by blackmailing the wicked witch of the west?"

"Cristopher, I have no idea what you're talking about," Davis replied. "This is a happy occasion. Let's not spoil it with such nonsense."

"Dude, Blondie already outed you."

Lauren laughed and pulled her Jimmy Buffett Margaritaville hat over her eyes. "I am innocent and I resent the implication. This girl here is so not a tattletale."

They all laughed.

"Does this mean we do not have to watch any more of your homemade videos?" Danielle asked.

"I like those videos," Ronnie said. "It is priceless watching Cristopher squirm and get all flustered."

"I like them, too," Gennifer added.

Davis wanted to laugh at how much love and respect they all showed for Mointz. The world now knew the real Cristopher Mointz.

"What time are we meeting all the guests?" Lauren asked. "This should be fun."

"One o'clock at the pool restaurant," Danielle replied. "I cannot wait for our goodbye luau, tonight. I promised Cristopher he does not have to limbo with his healing hip."

Davis laughed. "I will be Lauren's date at the luau, if that is all right, since I crashed the wedding."

"Luckily, she broke up with her linebacker friend," Mointz said.

"We never dated, Mointzie, nor did I sleep with him, you big ogre," said Lauren.

"I know, I know."

"Next year at this time, the Country will have won Desert Storm, Lauren will be in Congress and I do not see a damn thing I can do to change anything this time around. Now that we're all here, maybe we can bounce ideas off each other," said Mointz.

"Cristopher, you have a year to play some ball, spend quiet time with Danielle and tackle a mission or two, including Desert Storm," Davis said. "Things are moving nicely and you have done a brilliant job making 'Cristopher Mointz' the brand. The work you did up until this point cannot be put into words. I could not have envisioned how you took bull after bull by the horns and became a living superhero. We are able to do much more than we expected because of your successes."

"I do not like the sound of this," Danielle said.

"Nothing to fear, my dear, it is more important than ever to keep your husband as healthy as a horse."

Mointz laughed at him before Danielle told him not to say he was 'hung like a horse!' Everyone laughed at Mointz.

"Skipping the horse thing, try not to get my man here shot again," Ronnie said. "Believe me; I am not happy about that incident."

"Neither was I. A simple operation turned into a disaster. How you played with that even after you used the medicine I left will always puzzle me."

"What was that stuff anyway?" Danielle asked.

"Nothing more than a placebo," Davis replied.

"A placebo? He played in pain and it was only a placebo? Holy shit!" Ronnie said. "Dude, you are one tough son-of-a-bitch."

"Or a stupid one," Danielle added.

"Hey, Margaritaville," Mointz said to Lauren, "stick up for me will you?"

"You know you hot-dogged it," Lauren said.

"He should have never been asked," Gennifer said adamantly. "There is nothing which should put Cristopher in that situation again. We lose him, we lose the planet. I am sorry but Danielle, Lauren and I are not going to sit back and say nothing. These two are never backing down and continuing to constantly push the envelope is wrong, Trent. Giving the man a shot of placebo is ridiculous, to say the least."

Gennifer did not hold back her opinions and she also felt very protective of both Mointz and her Ronnie. She was a lot more conservative than Lauren.

"Agreed," Davis said. "Cristopher's days as a DIA operative are over. Believe me, dear, we will no longer place him near the action. Ronnie will be a leader of men in the military, not a fighting soldier."

"Adhere to the advice," Gennifer said looking at Ronnie and Mointz.

"Yes, boss. We get it," Ronnie said.

"Can we all have another Mai Tai? This is supposed to be a party," Danielle said. She called a waitress over, who carried a football and a pen.

The petite, golden-tan brunette handed the ball to Mointz and said, "My boyfriend is the biggest Redskin fan. Is there a chance you can sign this football for him?"

"Absolutely," Mointz replied. "All it will cost you is a refill for everyone." His cheese-ball smile made the waitress giggle.

"Thank you. The whole staff says you are the coolest famous person who has ever stayed here. I am not supposed to ask for autographs because of privacy; however, the manager said if I asked you it would be okay. My boyfriend will be the happiest man on the planet."

A sunbathing, still smiling Mointz said, "I am cool and people who cannot stop to sign autographs forget how they could afford to stay here in the first place. Please pass it around, and if anyone needs anything from me, please ask me."

"Cristopher, you are the best." The waitress wore a name tag, "Mary from Maryland." She smiled as she took the football from Mointz and left to order more Mai Tai's.

"Understand the power he has in his eyes and smile. Tell me how he could fail to become president," Gennifer said to Davis.

"He will be president, all right; I just need to make sure he can do what he needs to when he walks into office," Davis told Gennifer. "Cristopher, you are one talented and charming individual."

"Takes one to know one. I mean, the talented part. You have no charm."

"Yes, he does," Lauren said.

Chapter Twenty-Five

July 1990

"Did you remember the extra pickles?" Davis asked Mointz when he entered the MIT lab with a couple of submarine sandwiches from their favorite sub shop.

"Have I ever forgotten?"

"Yes, actually. Ready for training camp?"

"Probably, maybe. I am not really sure to be honest with you. Since I have been back I never know when or where things are going to happen. I am grateful to get to play a full season this year and it is a blessing. However, I really do not want this to end, if you know what I mean."

"I know, buddy. Unfortunately, there is not a lot of time to save the planet. You have to help Lauren get into office, get into law school and then run for office yourself."

"Believe me, I am not complaining."

"Regardless of what Gennifer says, you and Ronnie have to continue to run the show with Lauren. How is the new Gennifer Mahoney?"

"In love with our boy. Don't judge her too harshly. They are not the wounded souls they used to be. Take away the abuse from a mind and it flourishes."

"Amen, my friend," Davis said and took a bite of his sandwich. "The body is a temple and so is the mind. Having proper balance in life is the key."

He continued, "We cannot keep Saddam Hussein from rolling into Kuwait, not yet. You are too young to put together what you need. General Perry is a respected officer for sure, but he needs to grow as well. I met him at your wedding; the man respects you and Ronnie immensely."

"General Perry is a good man. What are you working on lately?"

"Glad you asked. In the next few months, Drs. Hawkins and Knowles start their PhD curriculum and I need to be operational. Chemistry and medicine more than physics will have my mind going. I am fortunate I have my own computer network connected to Langley. The missile defense system we have now works. I will tinker with it as a side project."

Mointz wondered what his friend was up to. "Define 'chemistry.'"

"Mr. Webster says it is the sense of the composition and reactions to matter."

"Really? I missed that in school. My guess is you, my friend, are either playing MacGyver or Q from James Bond. Care to share?"

Davis laughed and told him he was working hard at a little bit of both. He literally had just finished organizing the data he had taken from Lauren and he told Mointz there was a lot of information to process. Davis also said the surgeries he perfected in 2016 needed the equipment manufactured secretly and he still needed to do Q and A's on them.

"I hope you have my children in better storage now than in my house in my safe deposit boxes. Well, the vials at the CIA in Lauren's care are probably safe, I would assume."

"They are safe. Stop stressing over the boys. Speaking of children, how is it going for you?"

"Been a blast working on it. Supposedly Ronnie and Gennifer have started to talk about the topic as well."

"I envy you guys. It is nice to see all of you with permanent smiles. That lady of yours sure has one."

"Yes, she does. Speaking of Danielle, we're leaving tomorrow for a fundraiser for Lauren. Have you talked to Blondie since Gennifer and Ronnie's wedding last week?"

"Every day, my good lad. She wants to know what I am working on, just like your nosy self."

Davis, no matter who asked, never divulged his projects, since he had left school. Since Key West in April, Davis had spent half his time working on what he told Mointz he was working on and the other half working diligently on a way to reverse the effects of nuclear proliferation. Davis believed if some of the nations did not comply in 2016, Mointz would be forced to order a first strike, even if Davis told him it was out of the question. Davis would only advise Mointz the best he could because Davis would have to defer to the future President; Mointz would be far too entrenched as their leader by then, if he was not already.

Mointz would always listen to Davis. However, the final decision might be a tough one and Davis had faith in Mointz to make the tough one.

"Lauren and I are not nosy. You have run the show from the start," Mointz stated.

"Nonsense, Cristopher. This show was yours from the day you came back."

"If you say so, but I see me as a follower and not a leader."

"Are you serious?"

"Trent, I have been told what to do by roadmaps, videos, Lauren, her father and Danielle. I have been a soldier in this little war so far."

"Not true at all, Cristopher. People hang on your every word. Lauren *"Icebox"* Gabriel, for Pete's sake, listens to you. Be the leader in your mind. Believe in yourself. Maybe you should talk to Gennifer professionally. She comes home tomorrow. See her more regularly. I'll talk to her."

"Last time that happened, I ended up naked with her on her desk. I hope this is not a scheme because Lauren wants me to hump my way through this."

"I swear, it's not my intention. You have your lady love."

"No offense, but I do not trust you as far as I can throw you. The only reason I have not stuffed you in a barrel and thrown you into Niagara Falls is that you are right on the money so far."

"Ha! You could not throw me into the falls; you love me. Besides, I am a good time."

"I will let you get back to your sci-fi crap; Danielle is expecting me for a night out. We only have a week from today before camp opens on the 21st."

"Remember, Gennifer needs to take a more active approach with you."

"Yeah, yeah. I will talk to her and listen."

When Cristopher returned from MIT, Danielle sat with him on the double wicker swing on the beach house's deck.

"What did Trent have to say?" Danielle asked, holding her husband's hand as they watched the waves come in.

"He wants me to see Genny professionally. Trent believes I do not feel like I am running the show."

"Why would he say that?"

"I might have suggested I was a pawn in this mission. Trent is not the only one who can play games."

"Okay, I will play '*how the mind of Mointz works.*' Why would Trent believe you are not running the show?"

"Because when I step up and exert my authority, he will not dare to challenge me. He will be afraid I will tell him, 'See, I told you so.'"

"You two are having too much fun manipulating each other. The two of you might be too bright for your own good. I would bet neither one believes what the other says."

"Never thought of it that way, but whatever works. He buys the house next door and he's never home. He spends all his time trying to outthink the world. Someone has to keep him in check."

"Gee, what have you been doing since you were eight?"

"Well, you, since I was 17."

Danielle giggled and kissed him. "Mr. Mointz, you are a fresh man, but I love you."

"Dee, I love you, too, so much. It is a beautiful night. Why don't we open a bottle of wine and light the fire pit?"

"The fire sounds great. However, I need to skip the wine for the next nine months."

"Woo hoo! Who knows about this?"

"No one, for once. I wanted us to experience something by ourselves first."

"When are you due? Please tell me everything is fine."

"Yes, it is fine. We have an appointment in the morning tomorrow."

The next morning, the phone rang early --- 6:30 in the morning.

"Cristopher Mointz?" A man with a deep voice asked.

"This is he."

"Sorry to call you so early. My name is Detective Sergeant Sam Morris from the Los Angeles Police Department. Your sister Kathy is in the hospital in a coma. So far, I have been able to keep it away from the media."

Mointz was stunned. How could Kathy be in the hospital? She never had been in the First Parallel; Kathy was not in LA in the summer of 1990 he immediately remembered. She had visited Paris and now he knew why the panel did not want people to come back.

"Was she in an accident?" Mointz asked.

"Kathy was attacked outside a nightclub last night. She was brutally beaten and, if not for a couple going out into the alley to neck, she might have been raped or murdered."

Do you have any suspects?" Mointz asked.

"No, Cristopher, we don't at this time. The couple who scared the man off were pretty drunk. We have a grainy tape from a surveillance camera. I don't have a lot of hope catching this person. The whole department thinks the world of you, and this case is a priority."

"I will get the son-of-a-bitch. I am heading there now. Where can I reach you?"

"Cristopher, this is a police investigation. I can handle the search for the unknown subject. Your sister needs you."

"It was a police investigation; you have no idea who I really am. See you soon," Mointz said and hung up.

Mointz explained to Danielle what the detective had said. He called his parents to tell them Kathy had been in a small accident and he was taking an agency flight out immediately. He told his father Danielle had a doctor's appointment and she would accompany them to LA after her appointment. Danielle helped him pack a few things quickly and drove Mointz to Warwick's TF Green Airport; Davis was meeting him there.

"I'm sorry to miss the doctor's appointment, Danielle; an executive jet will be waiting for you here around 11. Thank you for helping to get my parents out there."

"Sweetie, there will be plenty of appointments. I want you to stop worrying about me and your parents. Focus on Kathy."

Davis was only 30 minutes behind Mointz, coming from Boston. Mointz, to put it best, was fuming when the plane finally took off.

"I called Lauren and she said Philip has alerted all the agents out in LA," Davis said.

"Please explain to me how my sister being in a different place could result in this event?"

Davis explained to Mointz that Kathy being in Los Angeles would change the events in this parallel. "There is no premeditation, only spontaneous action," Davis told him. Mointz sat stoically while Davis spouted off one theory after another.

Davis knew Mointz well enough to back off because he did not have solid answers for Mointz. He tried to research whatever he could on his laptop. Unfortunately, with the crime rate extremely high, there were too many suspects.

"What happened to phones on these planes? When did they come out?" Mointz inquired.

"Mid-90s, Cristopher," Davis said. "There is a satellite phone in front; go use it," Davis said. He could see the pain in his friend's eyes and his heart went out to Mointz; he was pretty fired up himself.

"I finally got through; there is at least some good news," Mointz said when he sat back down. "Kathy is conscious. The pilot said we have about an hour before we land. I also called Blondie and she is about to leave to meet us."

"She is very worried. Danielle must be going out of her mind getting your parents ready."

"Danielle is having a baby. Her first appointment was today."

"Actually it is her second; I tested her yesterday. I am so proud of you both. Do not let these events spoil her happiness or yours, for that matter. We'll find this person and then give Danielle her moment to shine."

The agency had a car waiting for them when they landed. The driver drove them right to LA County Hospital. The nurses noticed Mointz immediately when he walked to their station. A young male nurse who resembled Pee-Wee Herman escorted Mointz and Davis to Kathy's room.

Mointz nodded to the officer at the front door before he walked in alone. Davis told him he would get Detective Sergeant Sam Morris on the phone right away and for him to be with his sister.

When Mointz looked down on Kathy, he saw black and blue swollen bruises with tubes everywhere.

"How are you, sweetie?"

Kathy's eyes lit up as her big brother took her hand in his powerful mitt. "I had you as my emergency contact; I knew you would come first if I needed you."

"Kat, are you in pain?"

"I think I would be if I didn't have all this pain medicine in me," Kathy said, trying to smile at her brother. Having him there made her feel so safe.

"Kat, I hate to ask, but can you remember what happened?"

"I went outside because the club was so full of cigarette smoke I could barely breathe. A man tried to grab my pocketbook in the alley and I kicked him. I missed the sweet spot and kicked him high on the thigh."

"Don't worry sweetie, I will take care of it. All you have to worry about is getting better. Mom, Dad, and Danielle are on the way."

Kathy squeezed his hand and the fire in his belly spiked to a new level. "Cristopher, can you do me a favor?"

"Anything, anything at all, please. What can I do to help?"

"Can you catch the bastard who did this to me? I do not want him to hurt anyone else."

"I promise you I will not go home until I catch the person who did this to you. Please rest, sweetie. I need to ask you something. My friend Trent, who you met at the wedding, came here with me. Would it be all right if he examined you? He is a brilliant doctor and would like to see your charts."

"You won't leave, right?"

"I will be right here, just outside the door." Mointz opened the door and called in Davis.

Davis examined Kathy. His bedside manner put her at ease immediately. The young doctor had carte blanche at the hospital because of Mointz's influence. Little did the hospital staff know Davis was the brightest doctor on the planet. Davis nodded to Mointz to head into the corner when Kathy fell asleep.

"Kathy is lucky to be alive, believe me. Her ribs are cracked, she has a lacerated kidney and her spleen is probably going to have to be removed. When she arrived, she had a collapsed lung."

"Jesus, Lord please help her. Tell me she will be all right?"

"Eventually she will be, thank God. She covered her face and most of the blows she received were to the body."

Mointz punched the bathroom wall in the room. He wanted to hit everything in front of him.

"I am going to kill him, I swear," Mointz said as the officer outside asked him to step out of the room to meet Detective Sam Morris.

"Sam Morris, Mr. Mointz. Sorry to meet you under these circumstances. Your reputation precedes you; our police commissioner has been inundated with calls from everyone from The White House to the military. We did not realize you're in the Defense Intelligence Agency."

Morris was a Vietnam veteran about to retire from the Los Angeles Police Department. Davis had dug up information about him on his laptop. He was definitely a good detective.

Mointz shook his hand and introduced Davis, who had studied Kathy's injuries. Detective Morris could see anger in Mointz's eyes.

"There are several ways to go about this, Cristopher. Going off halfcocked is not going to do anything except get you angrier," the detective said.

"Thanks for the advice, but I am positive I can handle it."

The detective was physically fit; however the mid-50 year old looked small compared to Mointz.

"There is no way I will allow you to run wild in my city," Morris said.

Davis stepped in, "Cristopher has plenty of federal help which I am sure has been cleared with the department. This isn't the first time he has had to get involved in something in LA."

"So the rumor that a certain quarterback might have been shot after throwing an Iraqi general off a balcony might be true?"

"I have no idea what you are speaking of. I thank you for giving the copy of the videotape to the agency," Mointz said.

Morris was not about to get into a pissing match with Mointz over this investigation. The mayor would back Mointz 100% and, with a wife and three children, the detective could ill afford to resist America's hero.

"Here's my card. If you need me, please do not be afraid to call. I hope you catch the son-of-a-bitch then. Since I cannot control you, I might as well back you up." He wrote his home number on the back of the card and handed it to Mointz.

Mointz shook the detective's hand and thanked him. Once Morris left, Mointz sat in a chair at the end of Kathy's hospital bed. Davis left to grab a couple of coffees in the hospital's cafeteria. At that moment, Lauren walked in the room. Mointz immediately stood up and gave her a big hug.

"Is Kathy doing all right?" Lauren asked.

"Kathy is surprisingly in better shape than she looks. Unfortunately, Trent believes she is going to lose her spleen and she will have a long recovery ahead."

Lauren sat down with Mointz and held his hand as Kathy slept peacefully; the pain medication had taken over her body. Davis returned and told Lauren and Mointz he needed to spend some time in the lab to check Kathy's blood work.

"Looks like he took over the hospital," Lauren told Mointz, sipping on a tea Davis had brought her.

"When doesn't he take over? I am going to kill this guy who beat up my sister."

"Patently!" Lauren replied. "We have to catch him first. I called my father and the agency is working hard to get you an identity."

Lauren's father made finding Kathy's attacker a priority because he felt he owed Mointz. Lauren had dropped several hints over the years that Mointz had uncovered the scheme to kill her father via his contacts in Boston. Philip Gabriel believed the discovery must have come from one of the Belvenies and Lauren did nothing to change his mind. The soon-to-be Congresswoman had dropped everything to come to California to be with Mointz.

Danielle and Mointz's parents finally made it to the hospital and did not take Kathy's condition well. They pressed Mointz for answers on how the attack had happened and, once Mointz told them what he knew about the parallels, his parents at least believed he could not have stopped it. Danielle stayed with Mointz's parents as Mointz and Lauren decided to study the scene of the crime.

Club Sky, the famous nightclub in LA, had just started to see its employees arrive at work when Lauren and Mointz pulled up in Lauren's agency car. The front door of the club was locked and Mointz pounded on it to get someone to open up.

"Hey, don't have a cow, man," a large man the size of a linebacker said. He wore a shirt that said 'Security.' "Dude, you are Cristopher Mointz."

Mointz shoved him aside and walked into the club. Lauren rolled her eyes; they had discussed Mointz keeping his cool.

"Were you here last night?" Mointz asked.

"What is up, man?" the security guard said in his surfer dude persona.

"My sister was attacked here last night in the alley. Who was here last night, where was security and where is the alley?"

The man did not know what to say or think. However, he brought Mointz and Lauren around to employees at the club. Lauren showed the grainy picture the agency had given her of the hooded man. Davis had worked on the photo with CIA technology from 2016 at the hospital and printed it out on the printer he always took with him. He sharpened the image as well as he could.

A young college coed came up to Mointz to look at the picture. "I took a class with Kathy last year. Is she alright? She is such a sweetie."

"Kathy is pretty beat up. Please keep her in your prayers."

"I will," she replied. "That back alley has always been a problem. People generally go out there to smoke weed."

"Do you know this man?" Lauren asked.

"Some drug dealers that hang around the campus wear these sweatshirts. They approach the students who come off campus. USC is a great school, but go two blocks off campus and it's full of dealers trying to score money off college students."

The young student told them her name was Sally. She asked if they could pass along the message, 'Sally from play production class sends her love.' Sally also asked how Kathy's girlfriend, Colleen, was handling it. Mointz only said "fine," and did not ask another question inside the club.

Lauren followed Mointz out to the alley and waited for Mointz to bring up the topic of Colleen.

"Do you think Sally was implying that my sister is a lesbian?" Mointz asked.

"Maybe, maybe not," Lauren replied, even though she knew that Sally was innocently implying that very thing.

"I need to find this Colleen," Mointz said as he looked down the alley of Kathy's attack.

Mointz walked up and down the alley, basically trying to find a needle in a haystack.

"I think we should head over to the campus and see if Colleen is there. She might not know Kathy was attacked," Lauren said.

Mointz agreed with her and sat in the car with the image of Kathy's attack in the alley the previous night. They followed the signs to the private college and when Mointz rolled up to the security gate, the surprised campus police officer gave him directions to Kathy's on-campus townhouse. The officer then asked for Mointz's autograph.

"Here it is—46B," Mointz told Lauren as they pulled up in the black Lincoln. "This is her new place."

"This looks nice," Lauren said.

Mointz and Lauren walked up to the townhouse. Mointz fumbled with his sister's key chain—about 40 keys hung on it—to find the right one.

"Why my sister has all these keys is beyond me," Mointz said and finally found the right one. He opened the door and heard a voice behind him.

"Can I help you?" a female voice asked sternly. The woman immediately covered her mouth when she identified Mointz. "I'm sorry; I didn't know it was you, Cristopher. My name is Colleen, Kathy's friend. What are you doing out here? I thought you would be at camp. All she talks about are you and Seanie," Colleen said with a smile. She was a tall brunette who probably could use a few cheeseburgers as she was a bit skinny. She had a very pretty face and olive colored eyes.

Mointz felt badly immediately as Colleen looked far too peppy for bad news. "When was the last time you talked to Kathy?"

"We went out Saturday and I visited my parents yesterday and just returned. Kathy was supposed to go to Club Sky last night and meet a few friends. Is everything all right?"

"Colleen, this is my friend, Lauren. We came out here because Kathy was attacked last night and is in the hospital. I received a call early this morning."

Colleen collapsed and Mointz caught her. He sat her down on a leather chair inside the townhouse. Lauren poured her a glass of water and Colleen sipped from it.

"Can you bring me to her? We are really close," Colleen said.

"Kathy is your girlfriend, yes?"

Colleen panicked a bit, not sure what to say. "Yes, she is, Cristopher."

"I am glad she has someone."

"Really? She has been so afraid to tell you. Can I go to her?"

"Come on, honey," Lauren said.

Kathy was awake when they arrived and Colleen immediately took her hand in hers. Mointz gestured to his parents and Danielle to meet him outside the room. As they walked out of the room, Davis arrived. Mointz wanted to hear what Davis was up to before dropping the bomb about Kathy's girlfriend.

"Trent, you have news for us?" Mointz asked.

"Actually, I do. Kathy has a tear in her esophagus. They wanted to operate. However, I convinced them not to. She will heal naturally."

"Thank God, you are here, Trent," Martha told him and kissed his cheek.

"It was not easy to convince the chief surgeon, but I had a friend at Harvard Medical School verify my findings," Davis pronounced with pride.

"Maybe this isn't my place, but Kathy and Colleen here are extremely close," Mointz said.

"I know, dear. They are best friends," Martha replied.

"Mum, they are a couple She has been afraid to tell us, which is so not cool. I wish Seanie were here, not back at home at Gram's. We need to show Kathy it does not matter who she loves, only that she is in love and is loved."

"Agreed," Robert said.

"I knew it," Martha said. "I gave her space to find out who she is."

Mointz kissed his mother. "You are so 2000's, Mom."

"And, way cool," Lauren chimed in.

Danielle turned and faced Mointz. "Who are you? How do you make things better for everyone as soon as you get involved? Kathy is scared. Go in there and tell Kathy you support her and love her. After you do that, go get the person who did this."

Mointz opened the door to Kathy's room. He put his arms around Colleen and Kathy smiled. "Kat, you never have to hide anything from me or any one of us. I am always on your side and, as long as you are happy, so are we. I already told Mum and Dad. Imagine my surprise when Mum already knew."

"I'm sorry. I didn't want to tell you because I was afraid you would not understand."

In the First Parallel, Mointz had officiated two lesbian weddings and had often hung out with Kathy's gay male and female friends in the theater. He hoped it was not pressure that had kept her in the closet in the First Parallel.

"Why would I not understand? How can I look down on an angel? Colleen, welcome to the family."

The Mointzes were Irish through and through and the Irish love to hug and kiss, so Mointz kissed Colleen on the top of her head.

"Thank you for being my brother," said Kathy.

Mointz held back tears, feeling extremely emotional. Kathy and Mointz had barely spoken in the First Parallel. They loved each other; however they were different in a lot of ways. This parallel, Mointz made sure he called her every other day, wrote to her, sent cards and flowers and included her in events. He was determined to be there for Kathy.

"Kat, I am so sorry I was not here, but Lauren and I are going to get this guy. Now, I have to go back out there and track him down."

Mointz said "goodbye" and, after hugging Colleen again, he left Kathy and Colleen alone.

"He is a super guy, isn't he?" Colleen asked Kathy. "I hope he is not over his head and will be okay chasing down the SOB who attacked you. His friend, Lauren, is running for Congress. Does she know how dangerous this could be?"

Kathy smiled. "Lauren is CIA and my brother is in the Defense Intelligence Agency, remember? I am positive they can handle themselves. My brother is semi-nuts when he gets upset."

"What doesn't he do?" Colleen asked.

"The wrong thing," Kathy said with a smile, still heavily sedated. "Sometimes I think he is reincarnated."

Lauren and Cristopher bought burritos from LA's famous burrito place, Supreme Burrito, near USC, and sat in the car with Glocks in their belts.

"Ah, shit," Lauren remarked when her burrito spilled onto her jeans.

"Slob," Mointz said.

"Pound tar, Mointzie. Can you believe Danielle is pregnant?"

Mointz shook his head as he swallowed a big bite of burrito. "Danielle is pretty stoked. I know she wanted a baby and did not want to wait 15 years."

"How do you feel?" Lauren asked.

"Blessed. I feel extremely blessed she and I have made a new life."

"The smile on that mug of yours gives me all the answers I need," Lauren said. "Oh my God! There goes one of the people with the sweatshirt. He is not our guy, but he certainly is wearing the same clothes."

Lauren had barely finished her sentence by the time Mointz had the man handcuffed on the ground, his knee in the man's back. Lauren opened the car door so Mointz could throw the man—about 25-years old—in the back of the car. He was a light-skinned, black male and he recognized Mointz immediately. "What the hell do you want? Boy, you are a long way from the nation's capital," said the man. His sweatshirt sported a logo with a fist and a pinky finger pointing up.

Mointz, who was sitting in the front passenger seat, turned to look in the back seat and punched the man in the face. "Scumbag, one of your flunky friends attacked my sister last night outside of the Sky nightclub. Who is this guy in the photo?"

The sweatshirt-wearing man did not say a word and Mointz popped him again.

"Stop hitting me!" the man screamed.

"What is your name?" Lauren asked from the driver's seat.

"My name is June Bug, bitch." Mointz popped him again.

"Say something like that again and I will drag you out on the street and bang your head on the ground," Mointz said.

"Okay, okay. Truce, man," June Bug said.

"Who is the man in the picture?" Lauren tried again.

"Never seen him before."

Mointz wanted to tear into the guy, but held back. "What is up with your sweatshirt? What does it represent?"

"We are a fraternity of entrepreneurs," he said.

"Drug dealers," Lauren said.

"You think?" Mointz echoed.

"Who is the leader of this group of misfits and where can I find them?"

"No idea, amigo."

Mointz, being Mointz, had enough and pulled him out of the car and onto the ground, banging his head on the pavement as promised. A black and white police car pulled up. When one of the officers recognized Mointz, the officer nodded and the car left the scene.

"Want to start telling me the truth?" Mointz asked.

June Bug waved the white flag of surrender. "Okay, Mointz. I know who I get my stuff from; he comes around in a bronze BMW. The person in the picture—I have no idea who it is. I was given the sweatshirt from the guy in the BMW."

"African-American, Latino, White?" Mointz asked.

"He is a white dude."

Lauren tapped Mointz and nodded towards the car to bring June Bug back into the back seat of the car as they were starting to draw a crowd. Mointz followed Lauren's advice. When June Bug was settled, Lauren called an agency contact to bring June Bug to the local CIA office.

June Bug was led away, quiet as a mouse, as two men in dark suits picked him up. Mointz and Lauren waited for almost two hours before they simultaneously spotted the bronze BMW pull up to a couple of college co-eds that looked like pin-up models.

"You ever wait?" Lauren screamed at Mointz after he jumped out of the car like a rocket from a launch pad.

From experience in the First Parallel, Mointz knew a solid fist to a mid-80's BMW's front window would crack the glass easily. He shattered the window and pulled the white, twenty-something-year-old yuppie out of the car.

"What the F…" the yuppie started to scream a split second before Mointz head-butted him. The yuppie cried out in pain and Mointz pulled him up off the ground by his shirt and dragged him to the car. The yuppie, in an Izod short-sleeved polo shirt and tan shorts, shook like a leaf as blood flowed out of his nose. Mointz threw him a few tissues.

"Why did you head-butt me? Aren't you Cristopher Mointz?"

Mointz turned into the back seat again and said, "I know who I am, thank you very much. The question is, who are you and what is your connection to June Bug?"

"Who is this man?" Lauren asked, holding up a copy of the grainy picture.

Yuppie man looked at Lauren and then Mointz then back to Lauren. He was trying to decide which question to answer first.

"My name is John Carroll. I do not know who the man in the picture is, although I know June Bug."

"What do you supply him?" Mointz asked. "John, you have two choices: one, I beat the crap out of you and you tell me, or two, you tell me and all you have is a broken nose. You have one shot at this, Johnny."

"My name is John. May I ask you a question?"

"Johnny that is already asking me a question. I will let you ask me a second question."

"Why are you asking me what I give June Bug and why did you head-butt me?"

Mointz rolled his eyes. "Do you attend USC?"

He nodded.

"Then you did not major in math because you asked two questions. However, I will answer both. The guy in this photo almost beat my sister to death last night. I grabbed June Bug earlier and he said you were his supplier. Feeling where I am going with this?"

John nodded again. "I, as well as a few of my frat mates, make angel dust in the labs and sell it to June Bug and his associates. Believe me, I know who your sister is and I would tell you in a heartbeat who the man in the picture is if I knew."

"John, who is the main person you deal with?" Lauren asked.

"My fraternity mates would know better than me," he replied.

Mointz led John Carroll by the ear. Mointz and Lauren walked into the fraternity house. Mointz pushed a bloody Carroll onto the couch and both Lauren and Mointz pulled their Glocks.

"Get all of your frat mates in here right now," Mointz screamed. Four of John's frat mates were already in the living room.

In less than five minutes, a total of eleven people gathered in the frat house's living room. Mointz explained his purpose and then made everyone pile their drugs downstairs. He gave them an overview of what would happen if he brought in the feds.

Lauren then passed out the picture of the man who had beaten Kathy to see if anyone knew his identity. The last of the frat mates to look at the picture stared at it for a few seconds.

"I recognize him," the frat mate said.

"What is your name?" Lauren asked.

"Timothy Leite, ma'am."

"Tim, tell me what you know about him," Lauren asked.

"It's okay, Tim," said Mointz. "Tell us what you know, then promise to shut your mouth about our visit here. We will keep you out of jail and allow you to maintain a healthy existence. If we don't get what we need or we hear you are making and selling drugs in a lab again, it won't be your parents grounding you. Catch my drift?"

All eleven agreed with the terms as Mointz did not give them any reason to think he wasn't serious.

Tim cleared his throat. "His name is Tick Tick. They have a place about a mile from here. I met them there one night and Tick Tick was pacing back and forth, strung out."

"How many of you personally know my sister, Kathy?"

Five of them raised their hands; Kathy led most of the on-campus theater productions and performed concerts. Her piano playing and her voice were things of precious beauty.

"Kathy has more talent in her little finger than all of you put together. As she lies in a hospital bed, you fools will go and party it up tonight," Mointz stated. "I am going to clean Tick-Tock's clock.

"It is Tick Tick, Mr. Mointz," Tim said and then slumped in his seat. Mointz was the same age, if not younger, in this parallel than half these guys.

"Whatever. Just remember what I said," Mointz said. Before he left he wanted each of them to promise that he had learned a lesson.

"Cristopher," John called out. "We will make it up to her."

"Be good human beings and you will make it up to her that way. That is what she would want."

Mointz and Lauren followed the directions to the clubhouse where Tick Tick hung out.

"Tick Tock's Clock," Lauren recited. "Kind of a cliché, don't you think?" She tried to slow down the raging bull with a little humor. He cracked a small smile, so her tactic semi-worked.

Lauren wanted Mointz to call for backup, but he surprised her by saying, "When I see what we have to go up against, we'll make a decision."

"Wow, you are totally serious," Lauren said.

"Yeah, like totally, dude," Mointz responded in a California accent. It was almost 9 pm and, with an overcast sky, it was dark out. "It is pitch black; no one will see us."

When they pulled up close to the clubhouse, Lauren looked away for a second and Mointz jabbed her with one of the darts from Davis.

"Sorry sweetie. Kick my ass later," he whispered to her and kissed her cheek. Mointz took Lauren's Glock and tucked it into his belt before locking her in the car.

Mointz walked down a dirt road about 500 yards to where music blasted from the well-lit clubhouse. Two of the club members, wearing the dumb sweatshirts, were smoking weed about 100 yards away from the clubhouse. Mointz fired his Glock into both of them. Under intense interrogation at the Los Angeles CIA office, James Aldrich, a/k/a June Bug, had told members of the agency that his gang was called 'the 77's' and they distributed cocaine, heroin, and angel dust to half the USC area. June Bug had insisted no member had attacked Kathy. The LA police department had not had a lead on them yet.

Mointz glanced into the clubhouse and spotted Tick Tick through the wide open door, as it was almost 95 degrees in LA. The clubhouse was only about 800 square feet in size and five men stood in it. Mointz sprinted into the clubhouse. He surprised the men, pumping bullets into four of them, leaving Tick Tick cowering for his life.

"Cristopher Mointz! Oh, man! This is some acid flashback. There is no way this is for real," Tick Tick said.

Mointz pummeled him for a minute or two before asking, "Believe it now, asshole? The lady you beat up last night was my sister."

"She kicked me last night. I only asked for a lighter."

Mointz kicked him in the face, like he was a field goal kicker kicking the winning field goal. Tick Tick was out cold and Mointz fired two bullets into his head.

Mointz quickly left the clubhouse and used the satellite phone to call the CIA's disposal team to remove the carnage. Mointz opened up the car and carried Lauren to the back seat, driving out of the area before pulling into a gas station.

Lauren was still out cold when Mointz gave her a shot of adrenaline in the gas station's parking lot. She was not happy.

"If I were not so groggy, I would kick your ass. At least be decent and get me a drink."

"Here, I already bought you a couple of juices."

She opened one of the juice drinks and asked, "Did you get the son-of-a-bitch?"

"I got them all and called in the disposal team. The bastard tried to tell me Kathy refused to give him a light."

"Fine and dandy. Why did you knock me out?"

"Listen, you are not a soldier and I was not leading you into a situation where you would have to pull your weapon. I love you and I am blessed to be in your life. No offense, darling, but your safety is important to me."

Lauren smiled and belted him in the jaw, "I love you, too. For the record, you are still on the list of people I do not like very much, right now."

Mointz rubbed his jaw, "Nice punch."

Lauren kissed his cheek. "Yeah, I know," she said with a giggle and held his hand. "I am a bitch. What can I say?"

Davis removed Kathy's spleen using a laparoscopy procedure which surprised the surgical staff. When Kathy was brought back into her room, Mointz and Lauren had just arrived at her floor. Danielle and the Mointz family waited in the family area outside Kathy's room.

"Did you get them?" Danielle asked Mointz, hugging him immediately when he came into the waiting room.

Mointz nodded.

Danielle looked at Lauren and noticed she did not look well. "Lauren, you look pale. Are you feeling okay?"

"Your husband thought it best to drug me before taking down Kathy's attacker."

Martha and Robert begged to hear no more. They hugged Lauren and their son.

'Hear no evil and see no evil,' was their motto to live by with their son, daughter-in-law, and all of their friends.

"I am going to see her," Mointz said. "Is Colleen there with her?"

"Kathy needs to know that you took care of that terrible man. She won't feel peaceful until she hears from you that he was arrested," Martha said.

Danielle looked at Lauren and Lauren winked back at her. She would only have felt surprised if her husband had arrested anyone. He had been a man possessed when he left that hospital.

Kathy and Colleen smiled at Mointz as he walked into the room. Mointz smiled back and his sister knew right away he had not let her down.

"How are you making out, Kat?"

"A little uncomfortable. However, I hope you came here to tell me that you caught the person who put me in this God-awful place."

Mointz nodded. "I got him all right. Trust me, I got all of them," he told them and noticed the big arrangement of flowers next to the ones he had brought for Kathy. "Who sent the flowers?"

"The guys from Phi Delta Kappa. Aren't they nice?" Kathy replied.

"They are beautiful, but not as beautiful as you," Mointz told his sister. "Colleen, she is one tough chick. She is a Mointz through and through."

Colleen smiled at Mointz. "Thank you for being here, we were just talking about how great it is we do not have to hide our relationship from the family anymore."

"I promise to keep it quiet as to not embarrass you," Kathy said.

"It would embarrass me if you kept it to yourselves. Why would I want you to hide your relationship?"

Kathy winced when she tried to get comfortable. "Come on, Cristopher. You are a major celebrity. I would not want you to feel uncomfortable if my sexual orientation hurt you in any way."

"Stop the madness. What part of my personality would make you think I could give a rat's ass what people report on television or write in trash magazines? The two of you need support; I will support you every step of the way. Screw them, if people have problems with other people's business. They are the ones who have insecurities, not the two of you." Mointz kissed Kathy's cheek and told her their parents and Danielle and Lauren wanted to come in.

"Kathy, do you think that man will ever get out of jail?" Colleen asked.

"I do not think he was even arrested," said Kathy.

Colleen was instantly nervous, "He let them go?"

"Sweetie, he sent him to his eternal nap in hell. Lauren is CIA, remember? My brother didn't bring her here to arrest anyone."

"He is officially the coolest guy ever."

Kathy smiled at Colleen. "Nice to have him on our side. I should have given him a chance to make up his mind about us earlier. It was not fair to him or you."

"Cristopher doesn't seem to be indifferent to anything about you," Colleen said.

"The feeling is mutual. He is the best," Kathy said.

Chapter Twenty-Six

January 1991

Lauren and Mointz sat in a private booth at Rí Rá's, which always reserved a place for the popular Rhode Islander, while a couple of state troopers on Mointz's detail gave them a breather so they could eat without being interrupted. Mointz had told the troopers as soon as they finished eating, to let people approach them.

"How is the House Intelligence Committee treating you?" Mointz asked.

"I've just been there for a couple of weeks and most members are befuddled at the knowledge I possess about the war."

"General Schwarzkopf is the man," Mointz said. "I look forward to going to the front so I can get back home for good."

"Let's quit while we are ahead."

"Blondie, it is for two weeks. The press will eat it up. I will be fine. I have to get hurt, remember?"

"I know, I know. The only reason you are heading over there is for appearance's sake."

"Lauren, I don't want to go, but my time as an NFL quarterback needs to come to a close after the Super Bowl later this month. I have to get elected and prepare to really make a difference."

"When you go, you will take part in a ruse where your convoy gets attacked. You'll hurt your hip. We know exactly what will happen and what time it will happen. Ronnie's SEAL team will get you out. General Perry will convince President Bush to make you a hero. You will be in the hot zone for no longer than 48 hours. Nonnegotiable."

"Wow. Okay. If you say so," Mointz said.

"My, oh my, are you drunk on one beer?" Lauren inquired with a giggle. "Maybe you are high on life, either way I'll take it when you agree with me. When did this start?"

"I cannot wait to run for office. In August, I start law school as Danielle finishes. I'm about to go to school with my wife."

"Too bad little Rhody does not have a law school for a few more years."

"I know. It is also too bad Danielle had to repeat law school."

Lauren laughed. "At least you know you have a very good tutor. She already passed the bar once."

"True, very true."

January 27th, 1991

Whitney Houston stepped up to the microphone at Tampa Stadium in Tampa, Florida about to give a rousing rendition of "The Star-Spangled Banner," during the pre-game ceremonies of Super Bowl XXV between the Cristopher Mointz led Washington Redskins and the Bills of Buffalo. The game, being played during the height of the Gulf War had America in a patriotic fervor.

Mointz was only days away from heading to the Middle-east for his mission. First, Mointz needed to lead his Redskins to their second straight Super Bowl victory after another MVP season.

Danielle and Mointz spent the past football season enjoying every second of Danielle's pregnancy as well as Mointz's football accomplishments. Mointz had a better second season than his rookie season.

As Whitney Houston sang the National Anthem, Mointz could feel his heart beat a little faster. He never wanted to admit to anyone how much he loved to play football in the NFL. The Second Parallel was not only his second chance at playing football, it was his second chance at love with his beautiful Danielle. Her cheerfulness exploded each and every time Mointz told her how much he loved her and how proud of her he was.

Danielle expected Mointz to be attentive and caring to her needs. What she did not expect was Mointz's constant infectious smile he wore every single time he glanced at her. He smiled when Danielle went to the doctor. Smiled as they shopped for baby items. And smiled and smiled as he read book after book to the baby growing inside Danielle. Everything Mointz did was exactly the opposite of what she went through when she was pregnant with Ronnie. Mointz did not let her out of his sight or his loving arms through the pregnancy and Danielle loved it, absolutely loved it.

Mointz put on his helmet after Whitney Houston finished the anthem. A fly-by of F-14 fighter jets filled the stadium with a roar as the sky was illuminated by red, white, and blue fireworks. Mointz blew a kiss to Danielle and his family before warming up with Art Monk on the sideline.

"Bet you are glad you are not playing with a bad hip," Coach Gibbs said with a smile, while Mointz warmed up.

"Just think how we invented the 'Run and Shoot' offense," Mointz said.

"How could I forget? Cristopher, you set records no one but you will ever be able to break. I cannot wait to see how your career plays out, however, lets win another Lombardi trophy today.

"Mointz choked back a tear. There would be no career after today, only the memories of playing in and dominating the National Football League. Although he loved to play, Mointz could only think about Danielle, the baby, and his two precious boys as he walked to the center of the field for the coin flip.

Jim Kelly called "tails" and his tail call lost the coin toss for the Bills causing Mointz to smile from ear to ear. The Bills did not have a snowball's chance in hell of beating the undefeated Redskins, however, Mointz knew the Bills' only chance to have a lead on the score-board was to win the coin toss.

By halftime Mointz had thrown five touch-down passes to five different receivers to take a 35 to 3 lead. The second half was almost an exact duplicate of the first as Mointz threw four more touchdown passes as the Redskins completed their perfect sixteen game regular season and the play-offs with a Super Bowl win, beating the Buffalo Bills 63-10.

A seven month pregnant Danielle Mointz walked onto the field to kiss and congratulate her husband.

"Promise me you will not pass out this year."

Mointz held her sweetly, "No, I promise I have hydrated well during the game."

"Sweetheart, you were absolutely incredible today. My heart flipped every time you threw a touchdown pass."

"Ah, not bad. It isn't Rugby, but it is a game nonetheless."

Mointz was given the Lombardi Trophy by Coach Gibbs before receiving the newly named "Pete Rozelle Trophy" named after the former commissioner given to the game's 'Most Valuable Player,' which Mointz won easily for the second year in a row.

"Time to hit the shower," Mointz told Danielle after he hugged his parents, Ronnie, Gennifer, Trent and of course Lauren. "Ronnie, please keep your eye on the beautiful Momma."

"He was like a machine today," Danielle began. "Cristopher was so focused on this game he not only didn't disappoint, he reached for the stars and actually brought them home." Danielle said as her hormones raged and she started to tear up.

"Sweetie, Cristopher played the best game anyone has or will ever play. I cannot believe we had to push him to play," Lauren said.

Danielle nodded, "Lauren, he would have given up this amazing season just so he could make sure I was taken care of. Cristopher loves me with all he is and as I watched him play today, I know there is nothing he cannot accomplish."

###

"Honey, promise me this is going to be no longer than a few weeks," Danielle pleaded.

"Lauren promised me. The war is going to be over in a couple of weeks. There are only a few covert ops left. I will be home soon and my days of playing covert agent are over.

Danielle smiled and kissed her husband. "I am sorry you cannot continue to play football."

Mointz had just finished his breakfast and smiled. "Dee, it was amazing to have played. I have fulfilled a dream."

The TV screen always showed the news at the Mointzes, especially when Mointz and Ronnie were on a mission. Martha and Robert snapped to attention when they heard the special report. Today, Mointz would be in an ambush. His career would end in the National Football League so that he could concentrate on law school and a political career.

"This is ABC news with Peter Jennings," the announcer said.

A somber Jennings appeared before the nation on television. "ABC News has just learned a helicopter carrying NFL football star and Olympic champion Cristopher Mointz has been shot down in Iraq. Mointz had just led a peacekeeping mission with a team of Navy SEALs including his childhood friend and Navy all-American football player Ronnie Mahoney. Mointz and Mahoney had been pivotal in saving several medical personnel. Details are sketchy, but their helicopter was shot down and is now in the hands of coalition forces. No survivors have been found. We will continue to keep you abreast of the situation."

Martha turned the volume down, "When did they decide to make it a helicopter crash?"

"Who knows, with your son," Robert said. "I wouldn't worry about it."

No sooner had he said those words when the phone rang. They had expected it to ring off the hook as news broke of Mointz and Ronnie's accident.

"I will get it, dear," Martha told her husband.

"Hello," Martha said when she answered her phone.

"Martha, it is Danielle," Danielle said hysterically and barely audibly.

"What is the matter, dear?"

"Lauren just called. Cristopher and Ronnie's helicopter was really shot down. They are missing," she said, "although she guarantees they walked out alive. They are missing in Iraq."

Martha dropped the phone right before passing out.

"Dammit, what do you mean they were shot down?" Davis screamed at Lauren over the phone.

"I just called General Perry. A missile hit their helicopter and the helicopter went down. The SEAL Team made it to the crash site. The pilot and copilot were killed and we know Cristopher and Ronnie are on the run."

"How can we possibly know for sure?"

"Cristopher wrote the numbers "8" and "25" on the door of the helicopter. Our boys are in the midst of the last of Saddam's strongholds."

"This is a cluster fuck!" Davis said. He rarely lost his cool. The mission was secondary to finding Mointz and Ronnie. His mind was going a mile a minute.

"How are Gennifer and Danielle?" Lauren asked.

"Absolutely livid, scared, worried, among other things. Cristopher's parents and grandparents are here with Seanie. Who is leading this search?"

"General Perry has part of a SEAL Team standing by to pick them up and another part looking for them."

Lauren had all the confidence in General Perry. The media releasing the crash had really upset Lauren. Saddam Hussein was known to have a satellite dish and monitored the American news media religiously. He would stop at nothing to catch America's hero.

"Do you plan on appearing on television? The world knows your families are close. Please settle America down."

"I am about to appear on television the second I hang up with you. The camera crew is here for me to speak to Dan Rather."

"Good. Keep us informed. I would assume your father is working on this."

"As Mointz says, 'patently,'" Lauren replied.

"God, how can you be so calm? Do you know something I don't?"

"I trust in Mointz, because if I didn't I would be a damn hot mess right now. I also have to go on television in a minute and put on a strong front so Danielle and Gennifer do not worry any more than they already do. I certainly do not need you on my case."

Davis knew she was right. He took a step back. "I'm sorry, my lady. I believe in Mointz and Ronnie, too."

Lauren said "goodbye" to Davis and called her male administrative assistant, David, on the intercom to send the news crew in so she could chat via satellite with Dan Rather. Congresswoman Gabriel felt her heart beat faster and faster as the crew set up.

"Ready, Congresswoman?" The CBS evening news producer asked Lauren. She wore a pantsuit and was ready to speak to Dan Rather, whom she hated.

"Okay, Congresswoman on three, two, one…"

"Good evening Congresswoman Gabriel," Rather said. "As a close friend of the Mointz family, I can only imagine how the family is right now. We just heard from General Perry that Cristopher Mointz has been captured as well as Ronnie Mahoney and that the two were not killed in the crash. Can you shed light on the situation?" Rather asked.

"I do not believe that is true," Lauren said.

General Perry, Secretary of Defense, Cheney, CIA director, Philip Gabriel and Lauren agreed to create confusion in the media to give Mointzie and Ronnie a fighting chance.

"As a member of the House Intelligence Committee there are conflicting reports coming in minute to minute," said Lauren.

"Mointz and Lieutenant Mahoney, CBS has learned, were securing an area after news of an ambush on a military mobile hospital. They immediately flew to the area and, almost without assistance, rescued all of the Army medical personnel. While leaving the area, their helicopter was shot down. It has also been reported Mointz was injured during the firefight while he fought to save the lives of the wounded and the medical personnel in the unit."

"I cannot confirm or deny it, Dan, because I do not have all the details. What I can confirm is Mointz and Lieutenant Mahoney, from reports from members of the SEAL Team, saved many lives today as a M*A*S*H unit of National Guard soldiers were under distress. They are absolutely still alive."

"Congresswoman, my heart and the hearts of all America are with these two American heroes."

"Thank you, Dan. I believe wholeheartedly in both Mointz and Lieutenant Mahoney."

Lauren ended the interview and wanted to cry, but couldn't. Mointz was truly a hero as was Ronnie. She actually smiled for the first time since the news of their helicopter being shot down. Mointz would take on the whole country of Iraq to get home to his family.

Chapter Twenty-Seven

"Where the hell are we?" Ronnie asked.

"How the hell should I know? I am not a Navy SEAL. Correct me if I am wrong, but I am a swimming football player."

It was almost daybreak.

Mointz and Mahoney had found an abandoned farm to crash in for the night. Their helicopter was shot down unexpectedly killing the pilot and copilot. Mointz was in much tougher shape than Ronnie, as he was pretty much unscathed. The main issue now was getting out of Iraq alive.

"I feel like I've been hit by a bus," Ronnie said.

"We were shot down, buddy. I feel so badly for the families of the pilot and copilot," Mointz said. "How are our two nurses?"

"Still out cold. They are frightened, but they finally fell asleep an hour or two ago."

"We cannot leave them anywhere. There has to be a way to contact someone. Wish I had a cell phone, but I won't 'till the next Gulf War."

Ronnie shook his head. "I cannot believe we have to do this again in ten years. We should go get Saddam this time."

"If the President had the balls, he would not have to wait for his son to get him and the world would never know Monica Lewinsky's name. But I digress."

"Yeah sure, whatever you say, Mr. President. How do we get out of here with the women? I have no idea why they needed to get back to base so fast."

"They are surgical nurses; they were needed. Why do you think I agreed to take them back?"

Navy nurses Anne Kelly and Evelyn Lawler, both Navy Reservists, were in their early 30's. Mointz knew they would slow him down, but he was not going to leave them out here to fend the Iraqis off by themselves. Neither would Ronnie for that matter.

"I won't bother saying how important you are, but if we get out of this, you will be the man," Ronnie said.

Mointz and Ronnie had two M-16s and their military issued Glocks. They had enough ammo for now. Ronnie looked out the window and noticed movement outside.

"We have company," Ronnie said. "Take these night vision goggles. They were in the extra SEAL pack I grabbed."

"Dammit," Mointz exclaimed. "There are about six roving patrol soldiers outside. So much for this being a deserted place." Mointz could see pretty well with the night vision goggles; however he was underestimating the enemy outside.

"There are more than six, partner; we have to go out and get them on a sneak attack. I would say we have at least 20 of them," Ronnie said and handed Mointz a SEAL team knife. "Buddy, it is the only chance we have. They will kill us and rape our nurses."

"Wake them up and tell them to be ready, they have pistols. I will divert the patrols' attention."

"OK," Ronnie replied. He was worried about Mointz's injury, however he complied and went into the side room where the nurses slept in a makeshift bed.

Mointz snuck out the door and immediately tried to get behind the perimeter of the Iraqi Republican Guard to divert their attention away from the house. At about 100 yards away he fired into the air. All the Arabic lessons he had studied on his iPad since the age of eight paid off as he understood their leader telling them to move in to surround the house. Mointz now knew why they had lost two wars.

One by one, Mointz took out soldier after soldier with his SEAL knife or his silenced Glock. As children, Ronnie and Mointz loved to make goose calls, they did it now to make their positions known. Within minutes, not an Iraqi soldier stood, beating the oncoming sunlight by minutes.

"I don't see anyone left standing," said Ronnie, as the goose calls brought them together.

"Affirmative, that was close. We need to get far away from this place."

Ronnie had studied Arabic in college and had practiced with Mointz over the years. "I heard one of the soldiers tell another they were looking for the Olympic champion."

Mointz was stunned. "C'mon. We better collect the ladies and head out of here."

Running into the house, Mointz called out to Anne and Evelyn not to shoot.

"Ladies, collect your things. We need to be long gone from here now," Mointz said.

"Sir, what is happening?" Anne asked.

"Please, I am Cristopher. This is Ronnie. Let us forget the formalities."

"Are we any closer to figuring out where we are?" Evelyn asked, tears streaking her face.

"Besides being in Iraq, I have no idea," Mointz answered and Evelyn smiled. "Ronnie and I are pretty deadly when we have to be."

Anne, a general's daughter, could see soldiers outside, dead on the ground. "Obviously, there is carnage everywhere. I guess you are pretty destructive."

Mointz and Ronnie shouldered their packs and led the two Navy nurses, Anne and Evelyn, into the dawn to figure a way out of Iraq.

###

"This is one of the craziest things Mointz has ever done," Philip Gabriel told his daughter in the Oval Office along with Secretary of Defense Cheney, Senator Valmer Ellis of Virginia and President Bush.

"He has done things like this before?" the President asked.

Both Lauren and her father filled in the President and company on Mointz's exploits in North Korea and Los Angeles. "He was instrumental in our African mission," said Director Gabriel.

"Why would he go to save the military hospital with a SEAL Team?" Cheney asked.

"Lieutenant Mahoney is his best friend. Mointz found out his friend needed help and jumped into the fight. Mointz saved the day and, from our understanding, left in a hurry with two Navy surgical nurses who were needed at the base. One of the nurses is Air Force General Kelley's daughter, Anne," Gabriel said.

Mointz had begged General Perry to allow him to accompany Ronnie to help save the hospital unit. Perry finally relented as there was real trouble and he knew Mointz could help. Faulty intel reports reached General Perry leading him to believe it was only a small squad of Iraqi troops and not the several hundred it turned out to be.

"Lauren, how are you so close to him?" Ellis asked.

"Cristopher and I met at through the agency…" she started to say and choked up.

Philip interrupted. "The two of them are like brother and sister. She was the matron of honor in his wedding. Lauren talked me into allowing Mointz to pull off the Adam Ferguson situation."

"The British Royal?" Cheney asked. "That was Cristopher's handiwork? Ferguson was one sick bastard."

"Yes, he was," Philip replied. "Lauren and Cristopher have been like two peas in a pod ever since."

President Bush did a quick calculation. "He did it at 17?"

Lauren nodded, composing herself. "Yes, sir. He attended the agency's training program when he received threats from Eastern Bloc countries. We wanted to make sure he was safe."

Senator Ellis smiled. "Then we need to make sure he gets home safely. My Redskins need their starting quarterback healthy." Ellis could see the worry on Lauren's face.

"I hope so Senator Ellis. Cristopher is America's hero and we don't have many of them these days," said Lauren.

"Agreed," the President said. "Whatever it takes to get Mr. Mointz, Lieutenant Mahoney and the nurses back, I authorize. This is going to be a long night and I'd better call their families."

"Thank you, Mr. President," Lauren said. "I was hoping I could…"

"Leave from Andrews Air Force Base immediately?" The President said. He knew she wanted to be close to her friends.

"Hey, look! A phone," Ronnie said with a smile.

"What phone? Are you going crazy?" Mointz asked as they walked through land covered in olive trees.

"Please don't fool us, Ronnie," Evelyn said.

"No, he is right. There is a shortwave radio tower. The only problem is we will be alerting every one of our location," Mointz said, as he noticed the tower. He could see two young boys about ten-years-old kicking an old soccer ball in the distance. "I will go play nice."

"I will go with you," Anne declared. "A woman's presence would not hurt."

Mointz shook his head "no" and Ronnie knew why. "Not this time."

Anne figured it out. "Please don't hurt them."

"I am not going to hurt them. I am worried about them hurting you," Mointz replied and walked over to the boys.

"Hello," Mointz began in Arabic. "I am very lost. Can you help me?"

Mointz broke off a couple pieces of chocolate and handed them to the boys. Mointz's smile and friendly manner was genuine and easily translated into any language.

The boys devoured the chocolate. "My father and grandfather like Americans," one of the boys said in Arabic.

Mointz gave them more chocolate. "Why do you say that?"

The boys looked at each other. The second boy, who was still chewing the chocolate, asked Mointz to follow him. Mointz waved to Ronnie and the girls and followed the boys into a barn of some sort. He noticed the uniform immediately and also knew who was standing in front of him.

"Commander Harris. There are a lot of people looking for you."

"I must be bloody dreaming. Because if I wasn't, I would be going mad."

"Why is that?"

"For one, an American soldier standing in front of me, and two, the soldier is Cristopher Mointz."

John Harris had been shot down over Iraq about two weeks ago. He was presumed dead by the coalition and the media.

"What are you doing here, Mr. Mointz?"

Mointz explained how his helicopter had been shot down and he was here with Ronnie and two nurses. "Lieutenant Mahoney noticed the shortwave frequency tower could send out a message. Why haven't you used it?"

Commander Harris frowned. "The bloody thing does not work. I tried it. Maybe if we had a new receiver...but the one here is useless."

Mointz could see the frustration in his face and hear it in his voice. Several wires straggled all over the barn and the receiver looked like it had seen better days.

"I will get Lieutenant Mahoney. He is an engineer. And if you would be so kind, please bring our hosts."

Commander Harris and Mointz parted ways and agreed to meet back at the barn later. Harris was impressed with Mointz's Arabic.

Mointz and Ronnie learned that Habib, the boy's father, was no fan of President Hussein as his regime had forced the Iraqis into war. Habib used to use his shortwave radio to speak to friends in Egypt, Jordan, and Saudi Arabia as well as other Arab nations who fought against Saddam's rule.

"Can you fix it?" Mointz asked Ronnie.

"With a solder gun, maybe. This thing is total junk. You are the tech weenie. You try," Ronnie replied.

Mointz patted one of the boys on the head and asked Habib if he had some type of putty.

"I think I will give it a go," said Mointz.

Habib brought Mointz some black putty-type substance and Mointz went to work on the receiver. Mointz had the receiver completed in three hours.

"Good job," Commander Harris exclaimed. "Now what?"

Anne and Evelyn were eating honeycomb and hummus sandwiches. They smiled when Mointz winked. They felt safe amidst the three men.

"Why haven't we invaded this place and taken out Saddam yet?" Harris asked.

Ronnie frowned. "They do not want to offend the Arab coalition. We have stayed primarily near the border. The troops are never coming in, no wonder you were never…" Ronnie said.

Mointz interrupted. "I think I can call General Perry with this thing. However, if the coordinates you gave us, Commander, are correct, we are smack in the middle of the Republican Guard. I will figure something out. Once we use this radio, we're going to be chum in a shark tank."

"Better than a ball in tall grass," Ronnie said. "A ball in tall grass is lost."

Mointz set the correct frequency on the receiver with the shortwave frequency numbers the US used in the military. Within minutes, he had reached the person he wanted.

"Hello, Mr. Mointz. I will not ask where you are, but I will tell you if you get to Horn, Plantier, Greenwell, Hurst, Nipper and Williams, we are in business."

30, 29, 39, 47, 49, 9 Mointz recognized right away the old-time Red Sox players' numbers.

"Mointzie, it is me, love. How are you two?" Lauren asked.

"Good. Besides a slipped disc or two and a torn ACL, I will live. Ronnie and our two nurse friends are in good shape."

"Thank God, Mointzie.

"We lost the pilot and copilot. We were hit by a surface-to-air missile; the helicopter should not have been there, I know. We have found a missing commander alive and he is with us. Send our love to the Queen. Blondie, please make sure Captains Tandy and Rousseau's families know how sorry I am."

"We will," the General responded.

"Lauren?"

"Yes, Mointzie," she replied trying not to cry.

"Tell Danielle I love her and will be home for dinner tomorrow and tell her Ronnie sends her and Genny his heart. I love you too, Blondie."

Lauren's spirits brightened, "You bet your ass I will, Mointzie."

Lauren played the tape of her conversation with Mointz for Danielle over the phone. Relief would not be a strong enough word to describe how everyone—Danielle, Gennifer, Robert, Martha, and everyone in between up to the President—felt.

Danielle hugged everyone as Davis spoke to Lauren on the phone. Eventually, Davis handed Danielle the phone again.

"Are they really all right, honestly?" Danielle asked.

"Danielle, your husband and Ronnie are two of a kind. I cannot even imagine the hell they are going through, but they are safe," Lauren said.

"Lauren, bring them home to me, please," Danielle told Lauren.

"I will, sweetie. See you tomorrow."

Danielle and Lauren said goodbye. Davis hugged Danielle immediately. Davis insisted Danielle lie down and rest while he slipped into Mointz's office to see exactly where the other part of the SEAL Team would extract Mointz.

Davis fired up his Apple laptop and ran a search on the site Lauren had given him. He almost fell over in Mointz's favorite chair. Lauren had sent him into a ring of fire as he read an article in Time magazine.

February 27, 1991

An Iraqi elite guard unit gathered near Al Basrah in a last gasp attempt to keep the war going. This is a last stand for the Iraqis.....

Davis could not believe his eyes as he read the article which would be written the next day. Before he panicked, he dialed the emergency number Lauren had left with him to contact her.

"Congresswoman Gabriel," Lauren answered.

"The morons sent him into the base of the elite Republican Guard. I searched my Apple laptop and there is an article dated for tomorrow on how the elite Republican Guard makes a last ditch stand in Al Basrah. We missed this."

"Oh God, oh God, they already left. I don't think we can stop them."

"Do something, will you please?" Davis said.

"Let me go," Lauren shouted at him.

Ronnie guided Mointz, Commander Harris and the nurses to the rendezvous point right near the outskirts of Al Basrah. Ronnie excelled at finding his way during SEAL training once he knew his coordinates.

"Whoa, hold up," Ronnie said. "Jesus, look."

Mointz took a pair of binoculars from Ronnie and looked over a small hill.

"There is a whole battalion there. Somebody screwed the pooch," Mointz said. No sooner did Mointz speak than they heard vehicles approaching behind them. "Get down over to those rocks."

The terrain outside of Al Basrah was extremely dry and hilly likened to the American West.

"This must be the Iraqi's final stand we kept hearing about from Arab television," Ronnie said.

"What I would not give for the SEAL phone we lost in the crash."

"Mr. Mointz, you'd better think fast," Commander Harris murmured. "Look at the walking patrol." He handed the binoculars back to Mointz.

Mointz looked through the binoculars and passed them to Evelyn. Ronnie knew exactly what he was about to do. Ronnie grabbed Mointz's uniform.

"No way, Cristopher. I will go with you," Ronnie said.

"Our survey says, 'gong, thank you for playing."

"I have an idea, hotshot!" he said as F-16 fighter jets whizzed by. His smile got wider.

"Son-of-a-bitch, you knew they were coming. How?" Mointz asked.

"I could feel it," Ronnie said and took out his SEAL compass. "I hope there is a bright fly-by pilot in the air."

Ronnie started flashing the compass into the sun as he learned from Navy SEAL trainers to get the attention of a pilot. A tip of the wing of one of the Navy jets indicated they had acknowledged their position.

"Nice," Commander Harris declared.

"That a baby," Mointz said and he winked at the nurses.

"Now what?" Nurse Anne asked.

Mointz smiled at her. "We stay alive until the Calvary comes."

###

Lauren called Davis to settle him down and then sat with General Perry in the command post in Saudi Arabia.

"What is our best course of action, Walter?"

Worry lines furrowed the General's face. "We know their approximate location. A SEAL team is being brought in as well as a Ranger team. Most of the Iraqi Battalion has been destroyed by air power, but like ants out of an anthill on fire, they stay near the anthill. Thank God we have confirmation of their location because the intel around here, as Mointz would say, 'shits the proverbial bed.'"

Lauren could not help but grin at the reference. "He does love that one, doesn't he?"

"I wish I could be in his head for one day. He does whatever he wants, says what he feels. By all accounts, he rules the world according to Mointz."

"True statement," said Lauren.

"So tell me, how is the new beau?" Perry asked. He was trying to keep both of them from dwelling on Mointz.

"He is driving me crazy over this; Trent is as close to Cristopher as I am. General, you are probably the only one who knows about Trent and me, besides Danielle."

"Valid point. However, it seems no one tells Cristopher who is hooking up with whom until they have to; you like to keep him guessing."

"That's really not the case. We just sort of happened and we just recently started to get serious. Cristopher bitches to me about Trent and to Trent about me. Until this is over finally, we wanted Cristopher to be able to vent, although he goes to Ronnie and Gennifer as well. He is a talker and he always seeks opinions from people he trusts. Mointz keeps the risky things away from Danielle."

"Tell me about it. He talks about all of you to me."

"Mointz thinks highly of you, General."

He nodded. "Lauren, you are his family. Do not forget that when he says he trusts you and Trent as much as his wife. He means it and that is pretty special because unless you are from another planet, you have to be pretty dense if you cannot see his love for that lady."

"I am sort of from another planet; however, I know what you mean," Lauren said.

Mointz and Ronnie fired rapidly at the squad of Iraqi soldiers trying to climb the small hill which protected them. Ronnie noticed after the exchange was over Mointz could barely move. Mointz injected himself again in his hip with morphine.

"Hey bro, what the hell do you keep doing that for? How bad is your back, or is it the knee?" Ronnie asked.

Mointz winced. "I think my spine is crushed."

"Holy crap, are you serious? I thought you were kidding."

"I am as serious as a priest who knows crap is not holy. This isn't the Super Bowl when a placebo got me through the game," Mointz told him. "Hey, how is our water supply? We'd better grab a few of those canteens from some of these guys…"

"Gotcha," Ronnie said. His face grew white when Mointz collapsed and began convulsing.

"Cristopher, Cristopher!"

Mointz had taken too many injections of morphine and the dosage had finally caught up with him. Ronnie dragged him back up to their makeshift foxhole. Nearly an hour went by before he regained lucidity.

Ronnie could sense the SEALs would be converging on the area soon and he needed to find them. He left Commander Harris to guard Mointz and the nurses.

"Injuries can be a bloody bugger. Sorry those wankers got you," Commander Harris said.

"I am having a great holiday here in Iraq." He winked at the nurses who smiled back. They had tried to prevent him from standing up, but Mointz resisted as he did not know how safe they were.

What seemed like an eternity in actuality was only two hours before Mointz answered Ronnie's goose calls. SEAL Team 10 accompanied Ronnie. The future leader of the free world felt tremendous relief.

"Mointzie, what the hell was your goose call? It sounded like a goose in heat," Ronnie said triumphantly.

"God, I love you, man," Mointz replied. He immediately passed out again.

"Where am I?" Mointz asked Lauren, who was holding his hand.

"On your way to the States. Trent is going to perform surgery on your back and knee," Lauren said and kissed him.

"I cannot feel my legs. I am in trouble, eh?" Mointz asked nervously.

She smiled and Mointz instantly felt better. "Only from shooting up too much morphine. There are disc problems. However, you will be okay; I promise you."

"Ronnie saved us more than once, Lauren"

Where are they taking me in this flying tin can? And where are Ronnie, Anne and Evelyn and the Commander dude?"

"Ronnie is with Walter Perry and the nurses are on their way to the USS John F. Kennedy and the Commander is heading to visit the Queen."

"Kewl," He said. "I bet my football career is done no matter what. Well, that sucks."

Lauren winced a bit. "Why don't we worry about other things? The good news is that you are safe."

"No thanks to the assholes working in intelligence. What is up with them? This is the second time. How can they put us smack dab in the middle of a battalion? They even screwed up the ambush numbers at the M*A*S*H unit. They said there were 18; there were over 200. The assholes can't count."

"Shhhh, keep your voice down, Mointzie."

"Does Danielle know I am pissing myself?"

"Cristopher, that is not true. You have a catheter bag and Danielle knows you are fine. The whole world knows you are a hero. Your nurse friends and especially Commander Harris are telling every camera in front of them how you guys saved the day several times. Harris said you were the toughest son-of-a-bitch he ever met."

"Hmmmm. That is nice. Well since I am not pissing myself and I can't say 'ass hole,' I am going to sleep. Wake me up when Danielle is around" Mointz said. He reached for Lauren's hand.

Lauren kissed his cheek and smiled down at the best friend she had ever known. Ronnie had saved the day, she knew, but she also knew during the ambush everyone would have been killed if it hadn't been for Mointz. Iraqi soldiers had booby-trapped themselves to blow up the hospital. Mointz had grabbed an M-60 machine gun and mowed down the advancing troops. Legends were made from less heroic acts.

Mointz was brought to TF Green Airport and then Rhode Island Hospital. Davis was going to perform the surgery under heavy guard as the press was relentless. The surgery to save Mointz from long-term back issues was a delicate one, even for Davis. Only Davis's intervention would keep him from having back problems more severe than President Kennedy's.

Mointz had shaken off the drugs and refused any more. Mointz's excruciating pain told him the morphine injections had covered up a lot in the desert terrain of Iraq.

Danielle, Robert, Martha and Gennifer met Mointz, with Lauren at his side, and Davis in the hospital before surgery.

"Mointzie," Danielle screamed and practically jumped on top of him in the hospital bed.

Sweetheart, are you all right?" Martha asked with tears in her eyes.

"I would refer that question to my main man, Trent here, Mum. Well, Trent; how am I?"

"There are a couple of crushed discs, but I can do some magic. Also, your left ACL is toast so I will help you there as well. Officially, your football career is over. Unofficially, your football career is over. Rehab will be long and painful."

Robert held his son's good leg. "Cristopher, you are alive and you have so much left to do."

"I know, Pop. If it wasn't for Ronnie, I probably would not be here." Mointz looked at Gennifer. "Don't worry; his days of playing hero are over, too."

"The two of you have more balls than brains," Lauren said.

"Hey, I am an Ivy Leaguer."

"Exactly," Lauren replied.

"So how long have you and the good doctor here been cohabitating?" He asked moving his index finger back and forth between Lauren and Trent. "Hell, I always know what all of you are up to. So if my brain seems a little slow, it is because I am trying to figure out why you all are trying to hide things from me."

March 17th, 1991, St. Patrick's Day

"Can you please sign this?" Danielle's pediatric nurse asked before Mointz entered the delivery room.

Mointz, recuperating from Desert Storm, signed the ball and smiled. Previously he had told the young nurse to bring in anything she wanted signed. The 24-year-old Mointz in the Second Parallel looked forward to the birth of his baby girl. Though in rehab after just being released from the hospital, the NFL MVP had a smile on his face as he wheeled himself into the delivery room. His parents and siblings, as well as Lauren, Gennifer, Ronnie and Colleen, were waiting in the hospital's family room at Rhode Island Hospital with Grandma Rose and Grandpa Leo.

Danielle smiled widely in the delivery room as Davis stood ready to deliver Rose Marie Mointz.

"Hello Mointzie. The drugs Trent gave me have me feeling no pain."

"Can I get some?" Mointz asked and kissed her forehead.

"Trent, hook my man up," she said pretending to be drunk.

"Would you two stop playing and get serious?" Davis asked. "She should be yelling at you right now."

"I could never yell at him," Danielle said.

The delivery room cheered Danielle as Rose Marie emerged almost completely into the world. Mointz wore a smile the size of Texas.

"Oh, F-off Mointz," Danielle screamed, as the final push brought baby Rosie Marie, as Mointz had nicknamed her, into the world.

Chapter Twenty-Eight

September 1991 - Labor Day

"Cristopher Mointz has walked into RFK Stadium to a thunderous round of applause," Frank Gifford announced on Monday Night Football.

Danielle held him steady as Mointz walked with a cane to midfield. The crowd cheered louder and louder with every step. Mointz used the cane for impact as he could have probably played in this game if he wanted to. Davis had done a better job than even he thought he could do on Mointz's spine. Mointz was still the reigning NFL MVP.

The mainstream media had run Mointz stories non-stop since February. After his heroism in Iraq where Mointz saved a medical base, he was now more than likely the most popular person on the planet. Ronnie, soon to be a new father, also received accolades reserved for heroes.

Ronnie was now stationed at the Pentagon, while Mointz had entered Georgetown Law School in August. Tonight was Mointz's last night in the spotlight for a while, except for a few campaign events for Lauren.

Mointz flipped the coin as a Cowboy captain called 'heads' and won the coin flip. The captains of both teams hugged Mointz enthusiastically. When he left the field the crowd waved American flags. They "stood on their feet cheering," the press would write the next day, "louder than when he walked in." The applause held up the start of the game for several minutes.

"Pretty special, eh?" Danielle asked when Mointz entered the private booth Jack Kent Cooke had provided for him. The Mointz family, sat next to Davis, Lauren, Ronnie and Gennifer. Only Seanie, who had a big game today for Barrington High School back in Rhode Island where he was walking in his brother's and Ronnie's footsteps as an outstanding tight end, did not attend.

"I never would have believed I would retire at 24, but the retirement party was pretty special," Mointz replied to Danielle. "Thank the Lord, Kathy and Colleen came to watch the baby today, because I plan on tying one on tonight and getting me some lovin'. His grin was wide when he hugged his wife.

Danielle kissed him and whispered in his ear, "We have more to celebrate. I am having another little Mointzie."

"Fertile Myrtle, Woo hoo!" Mointz cried out with his biggest smile.

Lauren let go of Davis's hand and passed out beers to everyone, except to the pregnant Gennifer and Danielle.

"I really have to hand it to you two," Ronnie said. "Smiles are awesome."

"Wait until you and Gennifer hold your baby," Mointz said. "Now we have to hope Trent knocks up Lauren." Lauren's face went pasty white and Davis actually cracked a smile. Mointz loved to tease them about everything and anything.

"There is talk of a merger," Davis said, bringing the former Icebox Nutcracker to a giggling schoolgirl.

The Redskins lost to the Cowboys by the score of 38 to 0 as the Mointz-less Redskins mounted no offense without number eight. Mointz and Danielle decided to go to their favorite late-night dessert place, while everyone else went home.

"Please sit, Mr. and Mrs. Mointz," a young waitress told them. "Here is a dessert list for the night."

Olivia's Desserts and Bakery was a crown jewel in DC. Even after midnight it was three quarters full. Mointz and Danielle loved to come here with baby Rosie Marie on Sundays after church.

Danielle ordered chocolate cake with vanilla bean ice cream and Mointz ordered a piece of apple pie and an espresso.

"I can eat this now," Danielle said with a laugh.

"Honey, you are in incredible shape," Mointz said wincing.

"Sweetie, are you all right?"

"A little on the stiff side. Seriously, I need a break. I actually look forward to law school now we're in it together. While it will be a snap for you, I actually need to study since I didn't attend once already, like you. We could use the time out of the limelight and I still need to continue rehab."

Danielle reached across the table and took Mointz's hand. Iraq had taught Mointz he was not indestructible. He had set up scholarships in the names of the pilot and copilot who had perished in the crash. The scholarships were the least he could do. Their deaths weighed heavily on his mind since the accident and he made sure he stayed closely in touch with their families.

"Honey, being in the background for now is a good thing. Lauren looks forward to you getting well."

"I have a meeting with Phil tomorrow and I can only imagine what he wants. Lauren is going with me. He knows I am hurt, so I assume he doesn't want me to skydive, but assumptions are like…"

"Don't say it, I know the answer. Director Gabriel always has ulterior motives."

Stephanie, their waitress, brought their desserts and Mointz signed a jersey for her. Chocolate cake always brought smiles to Danielle. When Stephanie asked her to sign the jersey, she smiled even brighter.

Mointz paid the bill and they walked to the limousine Jack Kent Cooke had given them while Mointz went through rehabilitation. They didn't want to use the car. However, Mr. Cooke was such a great friend, his generosity was hard to refuse. The limousine driver brought them to their brownstone home in Georgetown. Mointz left him a nice tip, which had the young driver jumping for joy.

Mointz and Danielle slipped into the house. Kathy and Colleen were watching CNN, which was replaying Mointz's ceremony.

"The standing ovations gave me goose bumps all over the place," Kathy said and gave her brother a hug.

"The whole night was pretty surreal, to be honest with you," he replied.

"Did your back hurt? You look in a lot of pain," said Colleen.

"Good days and bad."

"How is our baby girl?" Danielle asked. Leaving Rosie Marie was always hard on her. When she was not in school, their baby angel ruled their lives.

Mointz had made sure Kathy had healed both physically and emotionally after the attack. He loved how she had rebounded and they had become closer than ever.

Danielle went to check on Rosie Marie and Colleen said her good night's, leaving the two siblings together.

"I bet if you were willing to risk it, you could play couldn't you?" Kathy asked.

"Probably."

"Danielle told me you played when you were stabbed. You might be the toughest person who ever lived. Why did you give up playing?"

"Kathy, when I got hurt in the middle of the desert, I discovered what really was important. I know you know it as well. Working for the government, playing football, my swimming career, and being a spokesman for products I don't even use might be personally rewarding, but my family and country come first. Yes, I could probably play. However, I won two Super Bowls and I am going to leave before I damage my body even more. Being a lawyer isn't so bad."

"Doesn't hurt to have more money than God. Could you be an announcer?"

Mointz was sure he could get a contract in a second; however, it would not be prudent. Playing in the NFL had changed the league; players were on different teams because standings had changed. He enjoyed the changes as everything was new and he now understood how the changes he made in the Second Parallel would restructure the First Parallel.

"I would love to be a broadcaster, but for me, my heart is about politics."

"Well, duh, what a no-brainer." Little sister gave him a hug and went off to bed.

Mointz checked on his daughter before retiring to the master bedroom. He was really tired.

"What did your sister have to say?" Danielle asked.

"She said I could play if I wanted to. I told her I had already accomplished what I wanted. When Kathy found out after her attack I worked for the government and you told her I had been stabbed at the Super Bowl, like I told coach, she realized I had bigger things to do," he said. "I would like to go home this weekend to see Seanie's game, if it is all right with you. We have Monday and Tuesday off."

"Yay, no school! God, I cannot believe I am almost done for the second time. I would love to go home, you know that."

"Please, school is your social hour. You skip most of your classes. Come give me some love, preggers."

Mointz adored Rose Marie. If Danielle ever wondered whether he would worry about Thomas and Patrick too much to share more of his heart, the day his Rosie Marie was born changed everything. Davis had told Danielle how great a father Mointz had been in the First Parallel. Now, watching Mointz with his daughter, Danielle felt totally blown away seeing how loving a father he really was.

Danielle kissed him passionately. "Wonderful father' does not say enough to describe you. We have almost fifteen years before our next two. I really enjoy this."

"I do, too. Now I want to enjoy you, lady." Just as he was about to hit a home run, Rose Marie let out a cry.

Danielle kissed him, giggling. "I will get Rosie Marie. Stay here, Mointzie, for my return."

Mointz sat in class taking notes. He loved being back in school. His professor, Natalie Leonard, was about 40 and a huge Redskin fan. When Mointz selected her as his faculty adviser, the married professor had invited Mointz and Danielle for dinner with her husband. The four had become fast friends.

Professor Leonard asked Mointz to stay after class for a minute, which he did. Mointz did have to meet Lauren shortly, though.

"What can I do for you, professor?" Mointz asked the-girl-next-door looking professor.

"Hank and I attended the game last night. What a magical night. I hope your test scores will be better than our offense this year."

Mointz chuckled.

"Anyway, the reason I asked you to stay after class is a very close friend of Hank's son is such a fan of yours. The poor child is struggling with his health and has been in the hospital for a couple of weeks. I was hoping you could sign a ball for him; it would do him wonders. He is at the children's hospital. His name is Brian Devens."

Mointz smiled and ripped a piece of paper from his notebook. "Write the information out and I will stop by on my way to a meeting with Congresswoman Gabriel today," Mointz said. "She won't mind." He loved to drop Lauren's name.

"Oh, my. I could not ask you to interrupt your day."

"Really, I do not see it that way."

"Say, how is Danielle doing in class? Must be tough switching off baby duty."

"Actually, we have some help. My sister and her partner are going to stay in DC because her partner is going to work for Lauren. Ronnie's wife is completing her PhD here and my mom comes for a few days during the week as it is an easy flight from Providence. Besides, we always have Lauren Gabriel, if we need her in a pinch," Cristopher said to Professor Leonard's big smile. "Now, if you will excuse me. I will go see little Brian and make him smile."

"Thank you from the bottom of my heart. This is such a wonderful thing for you to do. I heard from a little birdie you do this often," Natalie said. "Make sure you pass word to Danielle I will baby sit any time."

Mointz left to meet Lauren's agency-driven town car though Mointz really would rather drive himself.

"Hey, Lauren. Thank you for the ride."

"Nice day at school?" Lauren asked.

"Yes, dear. I hope you are not in a rush. I need to make a quick pit stop before we meet Phil."

Mointz explained the situation. He knew Lauren would not care. She was not exactly crazy about her father asking her to bring Mointz to his office.

Lauren and Mointz both met little Brian Devens who was on the upward swing with his battle with meningitis. The little guy was a fighter, Natalie told Mointz. Within the first minute, they knew it was true.

They had stopped at the Redskins fan store to buy a few things for Brian. However, the sporting goods manager gave him all he needed, once he heard the story of little Brian. Mointz signed several items as a thank you, because the manager refused to accept payment.

Mointz and Lauren not only visited Brian at DC's Children's Hospital, they also cheered up several other children. By the time they had made their way to Langley, they were three hours behind schedule. Mointz called Danielle from the lobby and told her he was three hours late. Danielle cracked up when she heard it. Mointz told her he would be home as quickly as he could.

"That was really cool, Cristopher. Thank you for sharing the experience with me," Lauren said when he hung up the phone.

"I wish I could do more of it."

"Jesus, you are an American hero."

Mointz stopped in his tracks. "What does that mean?"

"Honestly, if you had had a few breaks the first time, we would not be here. Everyone around here is better than in the first because you have a heart as big as your balls," Lauren said and hooked arms with him.

"Again, comparing something to my gonads. Why do people always do that to me?"

She giggled, "Let's go see what Papa Bear wants."

Mointz and Lauren were waved right in, as not knowing the Director's Congresswoman daughter would be a sin. However, since Mointz was with Lauren, it didn't really matter as no one even glanced at her today. Mointz was getting so many well wishes, the office staff practically ignored Lauren.

Philip greeted them warmly. Once Lauren explained their lateness, he did not mind at all, even though Philip abhorred tardiness. He always gave his daughter and Mointz a pass.

"Congratulations on last night. There was not a dry eye in the stadium," Phillip said.

"Thank you, sir. The warm reception meant a lot."

"The night was a blast, Daddy."

He smiled. "I still have not been able to figure out how the two of you became so close, but I tell you, Cristopher, my daughter has become a much happier person."

"I agree. Nice that she has a man in her life."

Director Gabriel laughed heartily. The 59-year-old George Clooney look-alike said, "Hell son, only you can quiet her down."

"Dad, that is not nice."

"Well it is true isn't it? Now let me get to why I invited you two here. Cristopher, how nimble are you?"

"Absolutely not, Dad. He is not doing anything unless it is a major national emergency," Lauren said.

Her father's eyes saddened. "This might be just that, sweetheart."

"Lauren, let's take a breath and relax and hear what your father has to say."

"I knew you would answer without caring."

"Now that the war is over, American companies have flooded the Saudi kingdom with weapons. A Saudi prince is double dipping, sending purchase orders to American companies for arms and selling them to unfriendly countries to use against the United States. The President has asked me if Cristopher could go to Saudi Arabia to figure out a way to stop the prince without upsetting the king. Certain dignitaries want Cristopher to visit the kingdom to accept an award for valor. We have not been able to get close to this prince."

"Which prince, Daddy?"

"Kareem," said Philip.

Mointz inhaled and blew out the air forcefully in disgust and frowned. "Figures, right? Sir, if I wanted to be James Bond, I would work for Sony Pictures. Do you want me to befriend this prince and off him?"

"In so many words, yes."

"What weapons are we sending to the Saudis?" Lauren asked.

"Everything besides nukes," her father replied. "We cannot stop it and the President refuses to call out Prince Kareem. The guy did stop short of Baghdad instead of getting Saddam so as not to upset the Saudis. The President has sat in my chair. He asked the agency to take care of this."

"And we have no one else to take care of this besides the two of us," Lauren said.

"I don't think the Saudis want a freshman Congresswoman running for Senator hanging around the kingdom."

"Too bad. I am going."

"Lauren, you are welcome to go," her father said.

"Nice, Director. I can see she bullies you as well."

"Patently!"

Director Philip Gabriel gave a full briefing of what needed to be done. Mointz agreed to take on the assignment. He shook hands with Lauren's dad and hugged him. Mointz and Lauren headed back to the town car. Davis had planned to meet them at Mointz's to go out to dinner, which would make the evening a whole lot more interesting.

"Events are changing more than I expected I guess," Mointz said at dinner.

Kathy practically had to throw out Danielle and Mointz before they would enjoy dinner with Lauren and Davis. Since Mointz's surgery, they rarely went out.

"Events are not changing as much as you would believe," Davis said. "Since I have joined the agency and I had my team rebuild the IBM servers to store unlimited amounts of data, we can do more cross-referencing and do deeper searches. Prince Kareem does what Phillip says for ten years, but this cooperation really hurts us down the line, especially in Bosnia. I know it seems hard to believe an Arab would help the Serbs, but Arabs love money and do not know what a bastard Milošević is. The prince is apparently a good person, just a bit money hungry."

"Shit. I really have to do this," Mointz whispered. "I have to."

"When will you leave?" Danielle asked.

"From Boston on Monday. Why don't you stay in Barrington, if you like, sweetie."

"I might. The beach house is our real home. Kathy and Colleen are going to visit your parents before they head out to LA to finish packing. Kathy's first album starts production in two weeks. She is so excited."

Mointz's sister had landed herself a record contract after several labels had recruited her. Her voice had blown studio executives away. Being the sister of Mointz might have opened the doors, but she kept them open with her talent and beauty.

"I will be home as well," Davis said. "With my lab at home, I spend more time there when Lauren is in DC." Davis smiled at Lauren and she took his hand in hers.

"Good. My baby's mama's safety and comfort is my number one priority."

"I would love to stay, but I have to campaign this weekend. However, I promised Seanie I would go to his game Friday night," said Lauren.

"And I will do the campaign event on Saturday. Albany is only a quick plane trip. I can do the rally in the afternoon and be home for dinner."

"I will go, too. Martha is taking Rosie Marie to her friends," Danielle said.

"Then I am in, sweetie," Davis said.

Mointz pretended to stick his finger down his throat. "Get a room."

Lauren laughed. Davis had actually moved in with her in DC and into Lauren's New York home, as she moved into his Barrington beach house. They found love and Davis found a soul mate in Lauren. Professing his love to Lauren came easy now to the formerly shy, First Parallel Davis.

"The omnipotent kingdom does not agree they need to follow checks and balances with the arms we give them. They feel strongly since they allowed the US to use the kingdom to fight the Iraqis, we owe them. We have to buckle down now on which weapons we allow these nations to have," said Davis.

"Lauren, is your father convinced we are heading into a terrorist period?" Danielle asked.

"Yes. He sees the long term without knowing the final answer. My father listens to me a lot more now since I nailed the Gulf War perfectly."

Besides their father/daughter connection, Lauren and Philip had a great professional relationship. Lauren had to expose the dealings of Prince Kareem as she was well aware of the Saudis activities in 2016. She did not know Prince Kareem was double dipping in this parallel, however.

"I believe we can easily help change the Prince's mind," Mointz said to Lauren. "No sense trying to fight your father on this one; the Saudis will not allow anyone to take me out."

Danielle hit him playfully. "Nice comment, Mointz."

Two boys were staring at Mointz from across the restaurant; Mointz waved the boys over to him. A blonde, curly-haired boy around ten and his five-year-old brother walked up to Mointz's table and high-fived Mointz and Lauren. The 10-year-old started to cry as the boys' parents walked over.

"What is wrong, buddy?" Mointz asked.

"You are my favorite player and now you cannot play anymore. I hate those people who hurt you. Now we stink," the 10-year-old said with tears in his eyes.

Mointz hugged him. "What is your name?"

"I am Kevin and my brother's name is Darrell."

Mointz winked at the parents. "Kevin, 'hate' is a really strong word. Even though I got hurt, I still have a family, friends and I have more important things in my life left to do."

"Like?" Kevin asked.

"Mostly, I get to meet wonderful people like you. Maybe I will coach one day or go into politics or maybe I will become a professional golfer. No matter what, I was able to play and I was also able to make a lot of people smile," Mointz told him. He proceeded to tell Kevin Enderle how he had helped several children smile at the hospital. "Life is not just about the game; it is about what you do when the game is over. As long as I can help a person smile, that is what really counts. Now, will you give me a big smile?"

Mointz handed Kevin Enderle tickets to the Redskins next game. The two boys hugged Mointz and gave him their smiles.

"That is the sweetest thing I ever heard," Kevin's mother said.

"I agree. Thank you so much," Kevin's proud father told Mointz.

The boys thanked Mointz and gave them all a parting high-five before returning to their table.

"Incredible," Davis said. "Those boys will remember this the rest of their lives."

"I agree," Lauren echoed, "When you look a person in the eye, Cristopher, you can connect to anyone's heart."

"Please, I just told them there is a lot more to life than a game. I wish someone would have told me that a long time ago."

Danielle kissed him, "I am always amazed how you underestimate your power."

"Come on, Seanie," Mointz screamed at his brother who went in motion out of Barrington's new power offense.

Barrington was leading Moses Brown 21 to 7 as Sean Mointz had caught three touchdown passes already. The 17-year-old junior was already the best young tight end in the country.

Seanie's best friend, John Cleary, the Barrington quarterback, threw a bullet to Sean down the sideline for his fourth touchdown pass of the day. The Mointzes and their friends whooped it up in the stands. Seanie pointed to his brother in the crowd and spiked the ball in tribute to him; Mointz beamed with pride.

Grandma Rose had begged to watch Rose Marie. She scooted Danielle out of the house and told Mointz that Robert and Martha were trying to get her out of the house a bit. Although Danielle appreciated it, the two hours away from a sleeping Rosie Marie tugged at her heart this Friday night. Mointz couldn't love her more and really loved the fact that she was so in tune with their daughter.

Seanie scored one more touchdown on an end around as Barrington defeated Moses Brown 35 to 7. Mointz embraced his brother at midfield after the game. He noticed for the first time in either parallel Seanie showed complete happiness after a game. He'd always had the talent, but now he had the drive as well.

Mointz grabbed the microphone and with zeal and conviction like only he could, endorsed his friend, Lauren Gabriel, for the United States Senate. A special election had been called because of Senator Luke Faulk's sudden death. Lauren's popularity had surged during the Gulf War even though she had only been in Congress for nine months. New York was "gaga" for the young Congresswoman. The open five-year term was Lauren's for the taking in the First Parallel. However, she had won by only 10,000 votes. Poll numbers had her up now 18 points. She had made a few gaffes in the First Parallel in campaigning and in the debates. Her opponent had pounced on them, especially when she predicted that the United States would return to Iraq. He also pounced on her young age. Lauren now was an ace campaigner and a more refined candidate. One Cristopher Mointz campaigning for her did not hurt her chances.

Almost 60,000 people showed up at the rally every media outlet covered. The size of the crowd was unheard of for a presidential rally, never mind a senatorial one.

Mointz's star power helped increase the numbers at the rally as well as firing up the crowd. Lauren hugged Mointz after the speech and whispered, "I hate having to speak after you."

"Suck it up, Blondie," Mointz replied.

Davis shook Mointz's hand. "Beautiful job, buddy."

"The Vice President in my administration needs to be Lauren. I could never trust anyone except her," Mointz said to an astonished Davis. "Do not look so surprised and keep what I said under your hat."

Davis nodded and smiled at Danielle.

"Finally someone gets it," Danielle said. "My husband and Lauren actually believe in what they say. The two of you will be an unbelievable combination."

"You get it as well, sweetie. I feel in my heart when you finish law school again, we can do great things together."

Danielle hugged Mointz and they enjoyed the rest of Lauren's rousing speech. The rally had started at ten and by noon it was winding down. Mointz finally had to sit, after standing for almost two hours. However, he continued to sign autograph after autograph for another hour before Danielle and Mointz were whisked off to the airport.

"Okay, this will be the last time I ask. Still positive Saudi Arabia is a good idea?" Danielle asked, after the private plane took off from Albany and headed to Providence.

"Dee, I am fine. No worries really. I am way ahead of where anyone would be at seven months. Tomorrow I will hit the gym and the pool and again on Monday morning. I promise you, I will keep getting better every day."

Danielle extended her hand across the aisle and Mointz took it. She smiled. When the flight landed in Warwick, Rhode Island, Mointz dropped Danielle at home and then played the game that he needed to buy something at the market. He wanted to buy Danielle flowers as he did at least twice, if not three times, a week. She loved his little game.

Mointz did grab a few food staples and brought them home along with the flowers. His mother was bringing Rosie Marie back at six, allowing Mointz and Danielle an hour and a half by themselves. They made the most of it, immediately lighting a fire in the bedroom and getting busy.

"Okay, maybe you are fine after all," Danielle said out of breath after they had made love.

"Told you I can handle even a tigress like you. Why don't we take a bubble bath and wait for our angel?"

Danielle giggled, "If her grandmother gives us our Precious back."

Mointz worked out hard at the new Gold's Gym in Providence where they named their pool after him for shameless promotion. The owner, Jonus, did give him a free membership along with a nice fat check for the Providence Playground Fund.

Anthony Riggoli was actually working in the bakery when his friend walked in to see him.

"Jesus, look what the cat dragged in," Anthony cried out when he noticed Mointz.

He hugged Mointz, toning down his normal big squeeze in care of Mointz's healing back. His same crew was working instead of drinking espressos.

"I heard you finally took my advice and started a catering business. Nice trucks," Mointz told him.

"Heisman, I do my best," Anthony replied. He loved calling Mointz 'Heisman' since Mointz had won college football's best player award. "Feeling better?"

"Getting back to normal pretty much. How are you?"

Anthony and his guys spent an hour with Mointz before they headed off to a catering job. Mointz needed to speak with Anthony's uncle and stayed. He insisted Anthony promise to come down to DC for Columbus Day weekend.

Raymond Belvenie was in his restaurant and welcomed Mointz into the office. Belvenie was extremely proud of Mointz.

"Nice to see you, Mr. Hero. Glad you called me," Belvenie said with a grin.

"Thank you for all the letters and gifts to Rose Marie. We really appreciate it."

"I know you do. Believe me. I enjoyed the wine you sent me. Those Virginia wineries are a hidden jewel," Belvenie said. "Sorry you have to retire, I really enjoyed watching you play."

Mointz wanted to speak to Belvenie from the heart, and in Mointz's typical fashion, he had to tell it straight.

"Mr. Belvenie, you know I am more than an athlete, correct?"

"Certainly, son," he replied with a smile.

"I am glad, because I am here to warn you if you do not diversify your business, there will be major legal issues for you, if you can catch my drift," Mointz said. "When there are wiretaps, subpoenas, and a bunch of suborn people, people will sing like canaries."

Belvenie was stunned. Mointz had slipped him valuable information over the years and Belvenie could not ignore Mointz's words. "I will not bother to insult your intelligence by asking if you are certain because, knowing you, I bet you sat in the damn meetings at the Justice Department."

"All I ask is to keep Anthony in the catering business and out of the book business. He is not a good gambler."

"Thanks, son. I hear you."

"No, thank you. Anthony means a lot to me and you do, too. I promise you will be fine," Mointz said.

There had not been any problems for Belvenie for ten years and Mointz wanted it to stay that way. He really liked them both.

Mointz left with enough food to feed an army and returned to the beach house to eat lunch with Danielle. She set out two plates for them as Mointz held his daughter.

"This veal is fabulous," Danielle said. "Want me to take Rosie so you can eat?"

"Relax honey, I have her."

Danielle loved watching Rosie in Mointz's arms.

"I wish I didn't have to go tomorrow."

"Yes, sweetie, I know. Put it off."

"Nah, I would rather get it over with."

Chapter Twenty-Nine

Mointz worked out at the gym and let Danielle give him a deep tissue massage as soon as he arrived home Monday morning. He felt better than he had in days. His trip to Saudi Arabia was his first time away from home since returning from Iraq. Danielle had taken classes in muscle therapy during Mointz's rehabilitation for his back and knee injuries. She had miraculously alleviated a lot of his pain and he appreciated the efforts she had put in letting a friend of the Redskins' doctor, Dr. Nancy Romero, into the Georgetown home to teach her. Mointz appreciated Danielle more than ever for all she had done for him and, as he left the house in a town car with Lauren, his heart felt extremely heavy.

"Gets harder every time, eh?" Lauren asked.

Mointz nodded and sat quietly all the way to the airport. He continued to sit without a word until the plane had flown for almost 2 hours.

"Spill, Mointz. What exactly has you upset today?"

Mointz frowned and pushed his seat back on the private jet.

"Come on," Lauren told him. "Are you going to mope all the way to Saudi Arabia?"

"Don't start," Mointz said. "I guess the American gigolo is at it again. I read the agency report."

Lauren raised her eyebrows as if to scold him. "Stop it. Nobody said you needed to sleep with the king's daughter. The report mentioned maybe you could work some magic and make a connection for future reference."

"How would you feel if I threw you down and gave you the old high hard one?" Mointz said. "And don't tell me I am threatening you with a good time. I know you and Trent want to have children."

At first, Lauren didn't respond, but then she said, "Maybe, you have a point."

"But you don't really give a hoot and I know why. Save the world for everyone blah, blah, blah. However, if you do not have integrity, what do you have?"

Lauren knew this was not the First Parallel Mointz. His heart was always big and now he had the integrity to be what he should have been. The right woman behind him, a good family and great friends had allowed him to fulfill his potential.

"I am going to sleep," he said.

Lauren and Mointz slept a good six hours, arriving in Saudi Arabia early Tuesday morning. They showered on the plane and felt refreshed as the Saudi government had a big welcome for Mointz and Lauren. A large American military contingent greeted them as well.

Prince Kareem greeted them warmly while the state-run media took plenty of pictures and videos of Mointz and Lauren with the Prince. The American media also made a big deal about their arrival.

"So much for lying low," Mointz whispered to Lauren.

"When do you think you'll ever be able to lie low?" Lauren replied.

Mointz commented briefly to the media about playing hooky from law school and how honored he was to be with the Saudi people. Prince Kareem was star struck, as he had studied economics in the United States, at Northwestern University.

Mointz and Lauren were brought to the King's main palace for a state dinner in Mointz's honor that evening.

Lauren was escorted with Mointz to a guest wing in the palace. The Prince immediately invited Mointz to join him in his private quarters in an adjacent wing.

"Want a beer?" Prince Kareem asked.

"I thought alcohol was not allowed in the kingdom," Mointz replied. "However, if one is available, a beer would be splendid."

"Mr. Mointz, I partied just fine in College."

"I am surprised you actually had time to study."

The Prince laughed. "Why don't you allow yourself some relax time. I will have you brought to our spa. I'm sure you will enjoy some pampering."

Two blonde European women showed up almost the same instant the Prince picked up the phone.

Naked women washed Mointz, massaged him, dunked him in hot and cold tubs, then washed and massaged him again before dressing him in a bathrobe and sending him to meet the Prince in the Prince's elegant steam room. Relations between the Saudi Royal Family and the United States had grown stronger during the First Gulf War and US educated Prince Kareem led the majority pro-American part of the family. The pro-war, pro-American Prince wanted Lauren's ear later on in the evening. At first he had thought about putting a move on her, but he had learned from Saudi intelligence Mointz was her protector.

Mointz had read every piece of information on Kareem in both parallels and he had two choices. He could eliminate Kareem permanently or he could straighten him up like he had done to Raymond Belvenie.

"Nice place, Cristopher?" Kareem asked in the steam room.

"Fabulous. The attention to detail is amazing as well as the massages. Let me ask you, Prince Kareem, what are your plans for the future? I am sure you know about my interest in playing a major role in American politics."

"My kingdom has many long-term goals, but number one has to be the security of the kingdom. My father, the king, has old world ideals; I am closer to the West from my time there."

Mointz did not feel good about Prince Kareem; to him Kareem had only learned how to be a greedy, capitalistic pig. The good news was he sort of liked the Prince and he believed he was salvageable.

"Fine. No problem there. My question to you is, 'Why are you taking what we are selling to you and reselling it to other countries not approved to have these weapons, at unbelievable markups?'" Mointz was trying the Raymond Belvenie approach.

"I am sorry, Mr. Mointz. I do not know what you are talking about."

"Kareem," Mointz began. "I can call you Kareem, yes?"

Kareem nodded as the steam cranked up.

"The powers that be in the United States know about your projects; believe me, and so does Lauren Gabriel, who will soon become a United States Senator from the great state of New York. I plan on running for Congress and if you want continued support in this kingdom without Daddy knowing what you are doing, pay attention."

Prince Kareem Abdulaziz knew he had been caught with his hand in the cookie jar. What he did not know was Mointz's role in all of this. "I am still not sure how you came to that conclusion."

"Yes, you do, Kareem. Don't bull shit a bull shitter. Please don't ask how I know. Just know I know and if you want to eventually become the leader of this kingdom, you need to know this…play ball with Lauren and I and we will always support you. However, if you decide arms dealing is the way to go, the US will not allow you to exist."

"No one can tell me what to do."

Mointz slapped Kareem on the side of the head, "Say again?"

Prince Kareem Abdulaziz' eyes were as wide as a set of headlights as he stood up from the floor of the steam room. "I…I…could have you killed for that," he stammered.

Mointz slapped the Prince again for good measure, "No one is killing me anytime soon. Now, if you would like to discuss your survival, let's do it now. Because if you don't want this discussion, I will be glad to end it permanently."

Kareem realized Mointz was not fooling around. "Who are you?"

"A person who could be your best friend or your worst enemy. Maybe you think I am a bully, but I am far from it. Lauren Gabriel is my best friend and I know you know who her father is. Shall I say more, Prince Kareem?"

Kareem bowed his head. "I am sorry. The kingdom…"

"Forget the kingdom right now. Your proverbial ass is on the line. I can go to bat for you."

Kareem took Mointz's hand and pressed it against his own forehead. He begged Mointz to keep him safe. Mointz knew he had him then and there.

"What can I do to show you I am sincere? I will send women to pleasure you, money, anything," said Kareem.

Mointz stood up. "I want some pampering for Lauren and more than that I need you to be a decent human being and to only take one wife." Mointz threw the last request in for a little fun. "Believe me, you'll have the backing of the United States and more importantly, me. In the future, you'll need Lauren and me."

Lauren smiled after her spa treatments while Mointz sat with her in the hot tub.

"I have never felt so relaxed," Lauren said.

"Me neither. My back feels incredible. I probably could play three games in a row today of rugby, football and sumo wrestling."

Lauren slid next to him and whispered, "Did you turn him?"

Mointz winked. "Easy as pie. I think he almost shit himself in the steam room." Cristopher explained exactly what had happened.

Lauren tried to tap his knee. However she went a little left and felt the naked Mointz's manhood.

"Jesus, Mointz! You have no clothes on."

"And, when do I go in a hot tub with clothes on?"

She giggled. "Get on your side of the tub and put that thing away."

"Yeah, yeah, we need to get ready for dinner with the Royal Family."

Mointz stepped out of the tub and Lauren hardly looked away. He put on a robe and laughed all the way back to his room and changed quickly into his tux for the state dinner.

Lauren and Mointz were introduced and seated according to the strict Saudi government protocol. Mointz had Kareem pull strings to seat him next to Kareem's American-educated sister, Amina.

Mointz hoped the kingdom's faith would allow him to not get too deeply into his true feelings on the kingdom's treatment of women. Rose Marie was certainly never going to bow down to a male, Mointz thought as he finished his speech which drew much applause.

"That was a wonderful speech," Princess Amina Abdulaziz said to Mointz, when he sat back at the table.

"Amina, you really don't believe that. I bet you wanted me to get up there and tell all these chauvinistic towel heads to dip their head in oil," Mointz whispered to her and winked. Mointz squeezed the Arab beauty's knee under the table.

He already has turned her into putty in his hands, Lauren thought as she watched Mointz flirt with the Princess.

"Mr. Mointz, so not true," Amina replied with a small giggle.

"I promised to meet with your brother tonight, but I would rather meet you in my suite later."

"Heading to your suite would put me in serious peril if someone noticed me there."

"Didn't you go to Duke? There is no way you can tell me you are not proficient in sneaking out of dorms."

Amina grabbed Mointz's hand under the table and excused herself. Mointz had accomplished what he had needed to and he knew he was going to be in for a long night.

"God, Mointzie. I think she is all wet just thinking about what you're going to do to her tonight," Lauren whispered, as Mointz asked Lauren to dance.

"I hate you, do you know that?" Mointz replied. "I should've just stuck you in the hot tub."

"Promises, promises," Lauren said. She loved to tease him as Mointz teased other people. The song ended and the US Ambassador escorted them from the beautiful state dining room. Mointz and Lauren met the Ambassadors from surrounding countries and dignitaries from the kingdom. Mointz's head spun after he brought Lauren back to her suite and stopped at Kareem's wing. Kareem was throwing a party for Mointz with a few of his close friends and several gorgeous females. The Prince handed Mointz some champagne and Mointz handed Kareem a list.

"What is this?" the Prince asked.

"The people who need to go."

"Go?"

"Please, don't play ignorant with me. Everyone on that list is absolutely no good. You can cross these three off the list, they had a bad day."

Prince Kareem shook as he filled both his and Mointz's glasses. The Prince had never felt this nervous in his life. Mointz found this fact mildly entertaining and he tapped champagne glasses with him.

"Will you meet me for breakfast tomorrow?" Prince Kareem asked.

"Congresswoman Gabriel and I would be honored to have breakfast with you. I am a bit tired and I will have to excuse myself and retire for the evening. Thank you for the lovely and most interesting day."

The Prince thanked Mointz for "enlightening" him and Mointz returned to his suite. He dressed in a pair of khaki shorts, a Redskins' T-shirt and his trademark—a New York Yankees' baseball cap worn backwards. He was enjoying a Miller Light when Princess Amina Abdulaziz walked into the suite, dressed in a silver cocktail dress, which showed plenty of cleavage. The Princess was not leaving anything to the imagination and Mointz knew for certain she never wore the dress near her father or outside the palace in Saudi Arabia.

She was absolutely breathtaking, he thought, when her smile showed her perfect pearly whites.

"Beer is illegal in the kingdom," Amina told Mointz and he finished it in one gulp. The Princess grabbed two beers from the bucket and sat on the sofa in the suite. She patted the sofa for Mointz to join her and he readily accepted.

"How many cheerleaders did you fuck?" Amina asked Mointz.

"More than my fair share," he replied technically. He was not lying when he included both parallels in his answer.

"I know you are married to the beautiful Danielle. I watch plenty of American television and I spend a lot of time in France and the US. My husband is in the Saudi Air Force and we never see each other, nor do I want to see him. Most of my time here is spent behind the scenes, trying to help my country," the 29-year-old Princess said. "I would very much like it if you would have sex with me now."

The Princess was the most sexually adventurous person Mointz had ever tangled with in either parallel. Mointz's fascination with Kama Sutra boded well for him as he made sure to blow the Blue Devil's mind. Even at 24, the extra help he received from Davis's little green pills totally impressed Amina with his vitality.

"Praise Allah, a man who actually knows how to please a woman," Amina said as she lit a cigarette. "Want one?"

"Hell no. I am an athlete, for Pete's sake," said Mointz, desperately wishing the assignment was over so he could take a hot tub and get Princess Amina's smell off him.

Amina put out the cigarette and took Mointz in her mouth, bringing him to attention. The Princess was not done until she had straddled the former quarterback until he came in her again.

"I hope you're not planning on sleeping too much. There are not many times I get a real live American footballer here in the palace."

"Amina, what do you mean when you say you run the show behind the scenes?"

"Please tell me you are joshing. How could you believe my brother and father could run this country?"

Mointz hoped the little vixen was not behind her brother's arms dealing.

"I didn't really, but if you pull the strings, you and I have a problem."

Amina gave him a hurt look. "Why would we have a problem? We seem to be doing well here."

Mointz spared no detail on her brother's activities. It appeared Princess Amina could not believe what she was hearing, Mointz thought, but he needed to be sure. Amina tried to light another cigarette. Mointz grabbed her wrist and hit her with Davis's new truth serum drug. He immediately went and picked the lock on the door of Lauren's suite, waking her up.

"What are you doing here?" Lauren asked sleepily. "Tell me you didn't kill her."

"No, I didn't kill her, but I did drug her."

"What??"

Mointz told Lauren what had happened and then said, "The woman makes Samantha Jones in 'Sex and the City,' seem like a nun," referencing the well-known show they both remembered from the First Parallel.

"Seriously?" Lauren asked giggling.

"Shut up and come help me interrogate her."

"Okay, okay. I am not the one who drugged her."

Lauren followed Mointz into his suite and into the bedroom. She could hardly believe he drugged her.

"Cheese and rice, Mointz. You could have dressed her. She is gorgeous."

Lauren asked Amina numerous questions: about the kingdom, arms deals, her brother and her influence on her father and brother. Princess Amina was absolutely oblivious to her brother's activities.

Lauren had one more question for her. "How good is Mointz in bed?"

"Ass hole," Mointz said.

"The best lay I ever had," replied the Princess.

"How do you feel?" Lauren asked the next morning, as Mointz stripped off his robe and joined her in the hot tub.

"The girl didn't quit."

"She could not help herself," Lauren said needling him. "Poor baby, you just spent a night with one of the most beautiful women in the world."

"You still don't get it do you?" Mointz asked.

Mointz pulled Lauren to him and kissed her hard and with Lauren's naked body in the tub, he entered her when she put her arms around him and returned the kiss. Lauren moaned in ecstasy softly as her orgasm was powerful and had her hungry for more. Mointz complied with her wishes. Lauren and Mointz climaxed together and Mointz kissed her one last time before walking out of the tub.

"Now wait and see how what just happened makes you feel over the next few days," Mointz told her and left.

Lauren finally caught her breath and felt lightheaded from a combination of the water temperature and the sex with Mointz. She took a dip in the saltwater pool, a cup of water in hand. Mointz felt fantastic physically, but it did not take Lauren long to realize what he had been talking about. Lauren checked the time and raced to her suite to change.

Mointz came into the suite as Lauren finished dressing. "Almost ready, darling?"

"Yes, Mointzie."

"Holy smokes! You look amazing," Mointz said, when Lauren came out of the bedroom.

"Shut up, ass hole."

"Sorry. You look stunning. How can you be mad at me? Listen, Ms. Priss, I love you and will always love you, but sometimes you have not adjusted to this parallel. We are not the same this time around. What will hurt is when you and I sit down with Trent and Danielle and feel like a sack of rotten apples because we are so in love with them."

Lauren hugged him and started to cry. "Thank God, one of us figured it out." She released their embrace and stepped to the bathroom to fix her makeup.

"I love you too, by the way," Mointz said, as he followed her into the bathroom. "So, Blondie, what do you think of the Princess?"

"Besides the fact she has the hots for you, I definitely believe she knows what she is doing. I would suggest that you lay it all out at breakfast and let the cards fall as they may."

Mointz nodded, "I concur with you. It really would be nice to leave this blessed country and the nympho without killing anyone."

"I could not do what you do. Even though I begged to be the one, they did not pick me. I couldn't reboot my life like you did. What amazes me about you is you did it alone."

"I had your help."

"No you didn't. You returned at the age of eight and had to find your way to Danielle; plus, fulfill the wishes of the panel. I am so glad you're in my life, I really am and I'm not just talking about saving the world."

"Same here. We have made each other what we both should be. Now, are you still upset with yours truly?"

"I could never be mad at you," she replied with a giggle. "Danielle is a lucky girl. Now, I know why she is knocked up again. She loves you and you have one of the most loving and sexiest women on the planet. My godchild is a little angel. We're saving the world and because you love the women in your life, you do this. I get it now."

Mointz and Lauren met the Prince for breakfast in Prince Kareem's suite. Princess Amina waited for them with her brother.

"Please join us," the Princess said, sitting at the breakfast table.

Princess Amina smiled brightly at Mointz as he sat down. Mointz could only imagine what was going on in her mind. He tried to take out of his head some incoherent pillow talk she'd spoken after he had drugged her. She had said something to the effect about her and Mointz performing eugenic techniques perfect for good offspring.

"This looks wonderful," Lauren said to Princess Amina.

"Thank you Congresswoman. My brother and I know you are scheduled to leave later today. However, I would like to plead to your good heart and hope you would stay one more day so we could go over a few issues regarding the kingdom. We wish you could meet with the King of Jordan tonight."

"Why us?" Mointz asked. "Let me guess, his American wife and American-educated children are football fans."

"My sister and I believe you can make a difference here," Kareem said.

"I do not think I have any power to make a difference."

"Congresswoman, with all due respect, we are talking about Mr. Mointz," the Princess said.

Lauren wanted to crack the biggest smile. Mointz, at 24 years old, was regarded by our closest Arab ally as some sort of leader, for lack of a better word. He was a law school student as far as the world knew.

"Me?" Mointz exclaimed. "Why me? I am a dumb jock."

"Mr. Mointz, you are a member of the security community. We know this to be true. I also know what you told my brother came from the top. They had a problem and sent you to fix it," Amina said. "Please don't insult my intelligence as you were crystal-clear about your position and about my brother's activities."

"Fine. I will stay."

Lauren gently squeezed his hand under the table. She had never felt prouder of him than she felt right now. Every time she thought he could not do any better, he moved a mountain.

"Excellent, thank you," Amina said.

"We're still good, yes?" the Prince asked nervously.

Mointz nodded and could see Kareem's face turned back from white to olive.

"I would love a tour of the kingdom after I stop at the embassy. We had planned to see the troops before we left and I need to keep that appointment," said Mointz.

Lauren and Mointz reiterated what had worried Lauren's father at the agency about the uneasiness after the war in the Middle East. Princess Amina vouched the kingdom would operate 100% above board moving forward.

Mointz felt good after Lauren had grilled Amina last night after she was drugged.

Breakfast lasted over two hours and the foursome agreed to meet again later. Under heavy security, Mointz and Lauren were on their way to the embassy to call Director Gabriel. Lauren and Mointz fidgeted in the limousine because of the surveillance.

"Mointzie, I cannot believe how well you handled breakfast. Not only did you have them eating out of your hands, you have the Prince and the Princess believing you are one of the most powerful men in the United States. I didn't know a 24-year-old had a direct dial to The White House," Lauren said. "I take that back. You actually do."

"Hardy, har, har! Do you really believe I wanted to stay here with Amina?"

"I will give you a 'no comment,' Mr. Mointz. Last time I opened my mouth, I paid for it with an orgasm."

"Good girl."

The limousine pulled into the embassy and Ambassador Richard Bonner met Mointz and Lauren in the carport. He escorted them into the office section of the embassy.

"I hear that you are extending your stay," said the Ambassador as he led them into a conference room.

"We have a meeting with a few government officials," Lauren responded.

The Ambassador had planned to visit the troops with Lauren and Mointz in an hour and he excused himself to prepare for the trip.

Mointz called Danielle quickly to let her know of the change in plans. She was a bit disappointed. However, she tried hard not to give her feelings away. He knew she was disappointed and he promised to be at her mercy the rest of the week. Lauren called Davis and Mointz chuckled when she grew all mushy and emotional. She had finally learned the importance and power of love.

Lauren called the agency for a scheduled call with her father and she gave him a full report of what had happened yesterday.

"The Princess really does run the show. Who would have guessed?" Director Philip Gabriel said.

"Cristopher really straightened out Prince Kareem. He kissed Cristopher's ass so much, his lips are permanently now tattooed on it," said Lauren.

Mointz stuck his tongue out at her.

"Good job identifying the Prince as a workable asset, Cristopher. This is a major breakthrough," Philip told him.

"Thank you, sir."

"Dad, the Princess and Prince are totally convinced that Cristopher is the man in the know."

"Well, isn't he?" Philip replied.

American troops were heading home in droves and the troops who remained in Saudi Arabia were in good spirits. Their spirits were further enhanced when Mointz showed up and spent a few hours signing autographs and taking pictures.

Lauren also took pictures with the troops, which played well back home on television. Senate candidate and current Congresswoman Gabriel ran a good campaign and used Mointz's fame to her advantage. When Mointz's helicopter had gone down, Lauren had calmed the nation. "The citizens of New York trust her fully," the new poll in The New York Times reported, back home Wednesday morning.

The Ambassador joined them in the helicopter returning to the capital of Saudi Arabia. "Do you get nervous in a helicopter?"

Mointz smiled, "Nobody is shooting at us so I would have to say 'no.'"

Lauren laughed, "Thank you for bringing it to my attention, Cristopher Cathal Mointz."

She breathed a sigh of relief when the helicopter returned to the capital. Mointz didn't mind being back on the ground either, for that matter. He noticed the inflection in Lauren's voice when they walked to an awaiting limousine.

"Do you really want to head back to Princess Amina?" Lauren asked, even though Mointz believed she knew he had to. She was trying to show empathy for him, knowing it was hard for Mointz to do what he needed to do.

"No, sweetie. I do not want to go to Princess Amina. We need a solid ally here, so it is what it is, I am afraid. I wish we could go boozing it up in Riyadh for a while and wait for King Hussein of Jordan to share his infinite wisdom of the Arab world," Mointz said. "Problem is, there is no effing booze here."

Lauren laughed and rested her head on Mointz's shoulder as they walked to the cars the embassy provided.

"I am beat," she said.

"Please tell me you are not complaining about lack of sleep."

"Absolutely not, sir," Lauren said and laughed again. She had a sexual attraction to Mointz she could never understand. He was 'People Magazine's sexiest man alive', yes and he was sweet, but she loved him as her brother and best friend so much more. Mointz had changed the former miserable bitch forever.

Mointz smiled at her.

"Our boys have really enjoyed your visit to them," said Lauren. "I wish you could jump into politics now."

"Why, pray tell?"

"Because if you were older, you'd already be in the house on Pennsylvania Avenue and I could breathe."

"I know what you are trying to say, Lauren. Thomas and Patrick together with Rosie and our new baby would be great. Patience is a virtue and I will just have to keep in my mind: patience, patience, patience."

"Mointzie, you have the patience of a gnat."

"Okay, good point. Can we just kill Bin Laden now instead of waiting?"

"Absolutely, if we knew where he was. Maybe during Bubba's time in The White House, we could get him in Somalia when we have the chance."

"Glad you agree, because I put his name on the list I gave Prince Kareem."

Lauren could not believe it. Mointz had finally risen against Davis in clear defiance of him. Davis had been adamant not to get rid of Bin Laden at this time.

"Trent will be really aggravated with me. But, I was the one sent back as President. All of you joined in. If I were here alone, like I expected, I definitely would have offed him long ago."

"I am out of this one."

"Getting rid of Bin Laden now is a smart move. I made an executive decision and it's the right way to go, capiche? "

"Yes, sir. I agree," Lauren said.

"Don't patronize me, cupcake."

The two Marine soldiers driving the limousine asked Mointz for his autograph as they parked inside the compound of the King. Mointz gladly complied.

Palace staff escorted Mointz and Lauren to their suites. The Princess's personal assistant had received instructions to bring Lauren for spa treatments and Mointz to the Princess.

"Go ahead, say it," said Mointz.

"I am keeping my comments to myself," Lauren told him and kissed his cheek.

Princess Amina was surprisingly dressed when Mointz entered her living quarters, which were the size of an airline hangar. Mointz kissed her cheek and the Princess smiled.

"How goes the day?" Mointz asked in Grandpa Leo fashion. The Irish greeting made the Princess week in the knees.

"Fine, Mr. Mointz. I am glad you agreed to stay, we have about four hours before we meet King Hussein at eight and I have some serious plans for those four hours."

"Tell me."

"I would rather show you."

Amina kissed him passionately and led him into her bedroom. Her first plan was to attack Mointz like a lioness pouncing on her prey. Hours two and three were all about pampering Mointz: dual massages from her wellness staff, a facial, manicure, and a pedicure with a couple of cocktails to go along. The final hour with the Princess took Mointz into a hot tub, which could have held ten people. Candles, rose petals and champagne decorated the tub.

"Did you enjoy yourself so far?" Amina asked.

"Patently! I am going to assume this is some sort of business meeting."

"My, my, Mr. Mointz. What kind of girl do you think I am?"

"An under-sexed one, I would say. I hope I am satisfying you just a little."

"Ouch, you're tough," Amina replied giggling "Since you uncovered my motive to keep you here, I would like to ask you to be upfront with me."

"I will try."

"Fair enough. How much pull do you have with the British?"

"I bloody wouldn't know. But I did save Commander Harris, so he has given me some good gin."

"You've received an honorary knighthood, for Pete's sake."

"And your point, Princess?"

"The kingdom needs British Petroleum to drill more to make up for production we lost from Kuwait to keep OPEC's price down. The Brits will not comply with our requests. They want to punish us for our value system. These are not my values."

Mointz was puzzled why the real leader of Saudi Arabia was a woman, in a country who requires women to wear Burqas and forbids them to drive.

"Can you blame them?"

"It is not going to be addressed anytime soon. Maybe in another twenty years."

"Maybe more like 25, but that is just a hunch."

"OPEC cannot meet their quota for the rest of the year. Oil prices will skyrocket and we will lose any goodwill. Commander Harris being shot down has inflamed British anti-Arab sentiment right now."

Commander Harris had told anyone who would listen when he returned home to England how terrible the Mideast was and how Mointz and Ronnie had acted heroically in Iraq. These actions changed the game, as Harris had never voiced his opinions in the First Parallel. The Enron folks were on the BP board and owed Mointz a big favor or two.

"What is in it for me?" Mointz asked and immediately wished he hadn't, as Princess Amina slid on his body and started to excite him by kissing his neck. She was riding him in the tub within seconds.

"Satisfied?" the Princess asked after he finished.

"It was more for you than me. Seriously, what is in it for me?"

The Princess pouted. "What do you want?"

"Princess, you come to me for help. You are asking a lot considering your moron brother's arms activities in the kingdom. Again, what is in it for me?"

"Undying love and respect. Plus, you will have an ally in the kingdom always, and me here naked every time you see me."

"Okay, cupcake. I will make it happen."

"Seriously? I was taking a shot in the dark," Amina said.

"I am a 24-year-old ex-swimming quarterback, but I have friends in high places. You owe me, Princess Amina."

She kissed him. "I will start working on payment after dinner."

"King Hussein was interesting, eh?" Lauren said on the plane ride home.

"Lauren, I have a whole new appreciation for him. I wish we could have told the King if he didn't trust the West, there will be no kingdom."

The King had married an American for his second wife and respected women greatly. He was totally enamored with Princess Amina.

Mointz had made a call to his Enron connections, who in turn called British Petroleum right before Mointz's meeting with King Hussein. Amina and Kareem, "the moron," as he was now known, were blown away that British Petroleum reversed course and agreed to increase oil production in their own oilfields.

"Back okay?"

"Amina abused me after every massage; she is a contortionist, for the love of God."

Their flight attendant served them a meal about an hour from TF Green Airport.

"I miss pizza," Mointz said. Pizza was a Mointz food staple.

"Mointzie, I promise to buy you one tomorrow."

"You should for my discovery of the Augean stables in Middle Eastern government."

"Huh," said Lauren.

"Augean stable, you know—an accumulation of filth and corruption."

"The vocabulary you use befuddles me."

Mointz smiled, "I do my best."

"We're returning the same time as our departure. It is noon again."

"Danielle is here to pick me up. Have fun going to Washington DC today. Tell Philip I said 'hi.'"

Lauren giggled. "I will be sure to do that. I cannot believe you are blowing off school to spend the rest of the week here in Rhode Island with the beautiful fall weather."

"Lauren, I need my rest to stay strong."

"There is going to be limited rest when Danielle delivers your second angel. Get all you can now."

"Maybe you can tell Phil I am on a permanent vacation."

"Sure, Mointzie."

Mointz gave Lauren a long hug before he deplaned. Lauren stayed on the plane to head down to DC. Danielle, as promised, was waiting for him with his Rosie Marie. Danielle kissed him immediately and Rosie Marie smiled at her "Dada."

"Nice trip?" Danielle asked, as Mointz took his daughter.

"Better than usual."

"I won't dare ask or maybe I should."

Mointz told Danielle all about his trip, leaving out his private time with Amina and Lauren. Guilt was a given, but he refused to let it ruin his life or his family's.

Rose Marie's nap gave Danielle and Mointz ample time to properly say 'welcome home' to each other. Danielle loved the idea of him staying for the next ten days, especially when Gennifer and Ronnie were going to have a C-section birth in five days.

"Do you worry Heidi Lynn will know you as 'Auntie,' instead of 'Grandma?'"

"Sometimes, but I will never not be there, so a name is a name," Danielle said with a smile. "Remember, she will be your goddaughter."

Mointz kissed her. "I love her already."

Chapter Thirty

June 1992

"Senator Gabriel," Mointz said.

"Where is your new daughter?" Lauren asked.

"Ashley Megan is in the nursery. You just missed everyone. Mum took Rosie Marie for the night and Ronnie and Gennifer relieved Gennifer's mother, who was watching baby Heidi Lynn."

"Where is my husband?" Lauren asked.

"Trent is going over Ashley Meg's lab results."

"Anything wrong?"

"Not at all, thank the Lord. Trent is doing his sci-fi crap. What delayed you?" Mointz asked and then regretted it. "Ah, shit. I see that look in those baby blues."

Lauren hated to ask Mointz for anything as Mointz looked so overjoyed with his new daughter. He had finally stayed out of the spotlight for the previous eight months. Danielle and Mointz were enjoying their summer in Barrington away from Georgetown's law school. Danielle had graduated law school for the second time just before giving birth to Ashley Megan.

"I have a problem I need help with. It is not an emergency, but it is high priority."

"When isn't it high priority? Tell it to me straight," he began as they walked to the nursery, "when and where?"

"Most likely in two weeks. The 'where' is India."

"Can we just go to a seven…"

"Don't say it, Mointzie. My friend, aren't you the poster boy for their largest tech company?"

Mointz laughed. "Actually, yes. I love India very much. Remember I used to date someone from India and…"

Lauren cut him off again, "I know, her parents did not approve of you and she did not disobey them by continuing the relationship. She was the first person you let in after Deidre."

"Hello, McFly, I just had a new daughter; ease up."

Lauren giggled. "Sorry, Mointzie." Mointz gently picked up Ashley Megan from her bassinet and introduced her to Lauren.

"I know, the blessings keep coming in for me, and my best friend is here to rain on my parade."

"She is an angel. I hate raining on Ashley's parade," she said and put her head on Mointz's shoulder. The two friends smiled and admired Ashley Megan.

"Ready?" Mointz asked.

Lauren nodded. "I will buy you a cup of coffee and find my beloved."

"Really now," Davis said from behind them. Lauren stepped up to Davis and kissed him. They held hands as they took a final peak at Ashley Meg and headed to Starbucks for coffee.

It was past midnight and Mointz was still wide awake and would be for a while after he drank the hot Java he loved.

"Anyone want a sandwich?" Davis asked.

Both Mointz and Lauren declined. Davis ordered a tuna melt from the cashier and paid for his sandwich and the coffees. The three sat at a table.

"Blondie over here wants to send me to India for God knows what. Make her stop, Trent."

"Actually, there are good reasons for this trip, my friend. I am convinced that in the next few weeks, the Pakistanis will steal India's nuclear secrets."

"Trent, you want me to stop nuclear secrets trading? Hell, man, what a piece of cake."

"No, this is not a piece of cake. However, I believe you and Ronnie can handle this project. Dr. Epen Chandy gives Dr. Abdul Qadeer Khan the nuclear secrets."

"What a bunch of wankers you two are. This is a scam and I now know a woman is involved. I also know in 2004, Khan gave the Iranians, North Koreans and others nuclear secrets."

Lauren smiled. "I hate that word 'scam,' but you are right. A woman is involved. Epen's sister is a Bollywood actress, Ashira Chandy. A week ago, she said her first on-screen kiss should be with none other than you, Mointzie. CIA assets in New Delhi have pressed her on this and she said she could 'eat you with a spoon.' Her quote, not mine."

Mointz shook his head. "PLAYBOY Magazine voted Ashira Chandy the second most beautiful woman in the world."

"Who was the first?" Davis asked.

"Danielle," Lauren said.

"Why don't these women know I have a wife?" said Mointz. "And yes, she is PLAYBOY's number one this year and after child birth. By the way, you were named sexiest politician ever, Blondie."

Lauren giggled. "I received the copy of PLAYBOY you sent me, Mointzie. Thank you. Most people in the United States don't know you are married, let alone people who live overseas."

"I guess you are right. I know we keep Danielle and the children out of the limelight. People who want to eat me with a spoon are pretty disturbing. Please tell me three days is long enough to use and abuse me in India. I have to visit India anyway for a tour of the tech company."

"Without kicking and screaming this time," Davis said.

Mointz shrugged. He had made peace with what he had to do and had stopped fighting it. Mointz also knew the President was about to lose The White House to Bill Clinton, who Mointz actually admired a great deal. However, the Middle East needed to be calmed. Middle Easterners hated changes of political parties at the top of the government. The only way to keep the Saudis worries to a minimum was to visit with Amina and Prince Kareem. Mointz figured he could kill two birds with one stone and visit both India and Saudi Arabia.

"I have to visit the Princess, so says Philip, even though she visits DC every few weeks now," Mointz said to them, sipping his coffee. "Lauren, your father is convinced Bush loses."

Davis chuckled. "The two of you have convinced him Clinton will win and he is worried. He tells me things. Senator Ellis has also told him Clinton will win."

"Wake his ass up," Mointz suggested.

"What?!" Lauren asked.

"Valmer Ellis needs to join us in this fight. We have changed an awful lot, no? We are doing this by trial and error and we might as well add him," said Mointz.

"I could live with it," Davis agreed. "Cristopher did more in the previous 16 years than anyone could have even imagined."

"The key was Lauren. She made the biggest difference in those roadmaps, Trent, not me."

Lauren blushed at the compliment. "Thank you. We have had plenty of time together pulling off miracles and you, yes you, have blown away even my husband over here. Vice President Ellis probably will help, but he has to know Mointzie is the lead. No offense Trent, but he has been amazing so far."

"None taken, honey. I am here to advise and counsel."

Mointz almost burst out laughing. "Can I get that on tape somewhere? I love both of you. However, I am already agreeing to go. The two of you don't have to butter me up."

"We are not buttering you up. I want it on record you are in charge here. Valmer is going to have to respect that."

"I am woman; hear me roar," Davis said. "I will, as Dr. Cris says, wake his ass up."

Turning to Danielle, he said, "Honey, I believe you are about to meet *The Man*."

Danielle kissed his cheek and placed baby Ashley Megan in her bassinet. Mointz led Danielle and Rosie Marie to the deck. Lauren held a bottle of wine and flowers.

"Son, I am so proud of you," present-day Senator Ellis told Mointz. Tears in his eyes, he hugged Mointz.

"Sir, I would like to introduce you to my wife, Danielle, and my daughter, Rosie Marie."

Danielle and Ellis embraced and then the Senator picked up a smiling Rosie Marie.

"What a pleasure it is to meet both of you," the First Parallel's Vice President said.

"I will help Danielle get some snacks. Why don't you reacquaint yourself with Valmer?" Lauren said to Mointz and left with Danielle.

"Am I losing it or is Lauren Gabriel in your kitchen making sure your wife is comfortable while she gets snacks? What the hell did you do to her?"

Mointz chuckled and took Rosie Marie from Ellis. "We sort of became best friends."

"Hell, she loves him more than me," Davis said laughing. "I had to witness it myself at his wedding."

"Son, I have only started to learn about everything you have accomplished. I can't even begin to understand how you became a superhero. Correct me if I am wrong, but didn't I tell you to be careful?"

Ellis was shocked to learn the measures Mointz had taken to save American lives. He certainly was not pleased about him getting shot at, or shot, and crashing in the desert of Iraq after his rescue of a M*A*S*H unit.

"I have tried to do exactly what I thought best. The truth is, I have never really wanted to complete anything as badly as this mission. I even had some fun."

"Winning gold medals and playing football for my Redskins must have been a blast," Ellis said.

"Well, it helped my image."

Davis and Ellis laughed as Danielle and Lauren came out of the house with plenty of snacks.

"Mointzie, your parents are coming over with Grandma Rose and Grandpa Leo. They are going to get a kick out of meeting two senators at their beloved Cristopher's house," Lauren said.

Mointz threw a grape at her. She giggled and threw a carrot back.

"These two never quit, sir. They are like two teenagers," Danielle said.

"Danielle, please call me Valmer. I am just a friend here," said Ellis.

"I enjoyed the videos featuring you and Lauren. My first mission resulted from your video about Lord Ferguson."

"Rumor has it you outed Lauren at the CIA transition class," Ellis said with a smile.

As predicted, Mointz's parents and grandparents enjoyed meeting Senator Ellis and were as proud as peacocks over their new grandchild. Ellis needed to get back to his holiday and agreed to come here with his wife soon.

"I cannot believe you pulled this off as well as you have so far. The successes are mind-boggling. I still must digest them now that I'm here. Imagine my surprise when I learned that Dr. Moore was Mrs. Ronald Mahoney Jr."

"Did you expect Danielle and I to be together?"

"Yes, I did. Not for nothing, but I am in awe of how you handled the Flaherty situation."

"They were wretched people, but did not deserve to die in the terrible way they perished."

"The way you took care of retribution was a thing of beauty. Were you glad you did it?"

"Hell yeah, I was. Sir, I can never imagine being in a Flaherty situation with Danielle."

"Son, I would not wish what you went through on my worst enemy. The little lady you have there is incredible. She has really been your other half."

"Would you like to head to India with Ronnie and me? You might get a firsthand look at what all of you put me through. No offense, but I am kind of upset you didn't tell me how this would change every second. I understand you wanted me to create my own identity and to fall in love with Danielle. However, Lauren could have just come to me. This all doesn't happen without her, she gave me the confidence I needed with Danielle and for every mission or task."

Ellis smiled, "So far it has worked out and, to be honest, I believe you would have done it with or without her. I am glad you advocated for me to get my memories back. I believe in my heart I can help."

Mointz shook his hand and Ellis agreed to accompany him to India and to Saudi Arabia.

Ashley Megan enjoyed the bottle her father fed her at three in the morning.

"Thank you, sweetie. Give me a kiss," Danielle told him when he crawled back into their bed.

"I love getting my daughters changed, fed, and happy," Mointz said and kissed his wife. He held his wife tight and fell asleep holding her contentedly.

Rosie Marie, the little baby alarm clock, woke up before Ashley Megan at 4:30 and Mointz arose in a flash before Danielle and the baby opened their eyes.

Mointz sang and danced with Rosie Marie in the bedroom, totally forgetting to shut off the baby monitor. "Rosie Marie swinging on a rope on a tree as Daddy has to make sure she is happy playing with her puppy," he sang.

"Oh, my God, you have lost it," Danielle said as she came into the nursery. "I can hear your terrible tunes in the bedroom."

"Ooops, I forgot to shut the monitor off."

Danielle kissed her husband and took her daughter, "Have you finalized your India trip? I am going to miss you every second."

"Next Monday. Three days is all I gave them. I am sorry, sweetie."

"Please do not say sorry. Cristopher, you are saving the world for our babies. Never apologize for it."

Rosie Marie fell back asleep and Mointz forced Danielle to stay under the covers and rest until Ashley Megan woke up for her next bottle.

Mointz rocked Ashley to sleep after her bottle and decided to go for a run, while his three angels slept. His back felt as good as new, finally. He normally ran six miles on a Sunday, but today he felt a half marathon was in order. He arrived home feeling good and drenched in sweat.

Mointz stripped out of his red running shoes, shirt and Brown University hat and dove into the ocean. Danielle covered Rosie Marie with sunblock and held her under an umbrella on the deck, while she drank coffee with Lauren and Davis.

"Coffee for you," Danielle said handing her husband a hot cup of Java.

"Cannot wait to get my Keurig machine," Mointz said when he took the mug.

"I have heard about this thing forever it seems. I will put one in every room," Danielle told her husband and kissed him.

"Nice to see you even more buffed than you were. Pretty soon you'll be almost as big as Trent," Lauren said.

Davis chuckled, "Yeah right, Cristopher gets bigger every time he wakes up." He had started to inject Mointz with low levels of HGH to heal his injuries and Mointz felt vibrant. Danielle still had the longer-acting drug working on her. She felt her body grow younger every day. Lauren and Trent took the same doses as Mointz. Everyone but Davis spent the requisite hours at the gym to get the full benefit.

"Cristopher works out all day long, sweetie. You do not."

"I work out," Davis said biting into a Boston crème doughnut.

"What is the plan for this beautiful Sunday?" Mointz asked.

"We've all decided to barbeque this afternoon. Ronnie and Gennifer are bringing Heidi. I am the new mother and I decided to have a BBQ here with my family today all together relaxing. I do not want to hear one thing from any of you: no plotting, nothing but food, beer and wine and our little blessings. The weather is beautiful, not a cloud in the sky, and take what I say as an edict," Danielle said.

"You go girl," Lauren added.

"No argument from me," Davis said.

Mointz, still wet, hugged her, making Danielle giggle. "Honey, you are the master of my domain."

Ronnie, Lauren, and Mointz circled the grill with beer and pounds of steak tips, pulled pork, chicken and shrimp. Mointz had asked permission from his wife to tell Ronnie he needed him to go to India and Saudi Arabia.

As they grilled delicious shrimp, Mointz told Ronnie he needed a wingman for India and Saudi Arabia. Lauren explained why she needed Ronnie on this mission. Even though Mointz objected, Lauren impressed on him the importance of Ronnie's presence.

"Man, this sucks," Ronnie said. "I know there is no other way. Now I realize why you hate going on these little adventures overseas. What the f…" he was about to say.

"There is always a reason I try to keep people short on the details," Mointz interrupted. "Lauren says it will save lives and so does Trent." He put some steak tips the grill.

"I don't want Cristopher to do this alone," Lauren said. "This could be a dangerous mission."

"General Perry knows about this? I was supposed to be in a class before heading back to the Pentagon."

"I already cleared it with him through my father," Lauren said. General Perry had taken over the Navy's Criminal Investigation Service at the Pentagon and Ronnie was one of his investigators, a very good one, thought his superiors. Mointz had retired after his accident, but still held Defense Intelligence credentials and was assigned to General Perry under direct orders from CIA director Philip Gabriel.

"Danielle would flip out if she knew the details of this. A mission of seduction? Geez, Louise," said Ronnie. "So Blondie, what do you do?"

"Nothing," Mointz said defensively. "She is a United States Senator; her hands will never get dirty. Watch the grill, Ronnie, will you? I have to get some more marinade." He handed Ronnie the grill tongs and entered the house.

"Did I hit a nerve?" Ronnie asked.

Lauren frowned, "For an investigator, you are slow at times."

"What do you mean?"

"Cristopher protects your mother, you, me, Trent and Gennifer. And watch how he takes care of his children. Do you think he wants me involved with this? How about some guy having his hands on me?"

"Hey, I would never let that happen to you. I would ring someone's neck first."

"I know you would."

"Catch," Mointz said, flipping Ronnie a piece of meat off the grill after he returned with the marinade and three cold beers. He laughed as he threw the meat to break the tension.

"Ouch, this sucker is hot."

Lauren told Ronnie to put it on the plate on the grill. She could not help herself and laughed at the image of Ronnie playing hot potato with a steak tip. Lauren could not wait for this trip; a mission with these two was going to be a blast.

###

The Central Intelligence Agency owned several Gulfstream IV business jets for agency use. Philip Gabriel had authorized Senators Davis and Ellis to take Mointz and Ronnie in the most updated G-IV for their trip to India and Saudi Arabia.

"Any chance we can go for a burger with egg salad and bacon in London?" Ronnie asked.

"I love the tutti-frutti ice cream," Ellis said. He no longer wanted the title of Vice President.

Mointz chuckled, "I went to Harrods and ate it when I went to meet Lord Ferguson and then again when Danielle and I traveled to London on vacation. I remembered you, Valmer, on the Ferguson tape telling me to try it."

Ellis laughed and shook his head. Mointz, Ronnie and Lauren acted like teenagers at a frat house. They gave Ellis a full account of the seventeen years since Mointz's return.

"I hated making those tapes," Lauren said.

"That is because you had the personality of a rattlesnake. Blondie, you're so much more fun now. Valmer, you should see her partying in Saudi Arabia."

"I would never have guessed Princess Amina wielded such power," Ellis said. "How you came to Amina and squashed her brother is amazing, Cristopher."

"Nothing is easy. However, Amina didn't put up a big fight," said Lauren. "Mointzie over here scared her brother into submission and she caved quickly. They both believe Cristopher is the pulse of the United States. Then, twenty-four-years-old and he gets British Petroleum to pump more oil. Mointzie has the Saudis and the Jordanians eating out of the palms of his hands."

"Patently," Ellis said. "I look forward to meeting the Princess and Prince Kareem."

"She called me ten times this week wondering why we were coming. A visit from not one, but two, US Senators has her curiosity up," Mointz said.

"I am only on my second term," Ellis said. "We don't carry the weight we will yet."

"Valmer, you were a Navy doctor. In your first eight years in the Senate the country sees your star rising. The Saudis are not stupid. I am the one everyone besides Amina and Kareem believe knows nothing."

"Hello! Everyone still remember I am still on my first shot at life as far as I am concerned. What do I know?" Ronnie asked.

"More than most," Lauren replied.

Ellis switched topics. He started to discuss the Indian nuclear-secret swap with the Pakistanis. Dr. Epen Chandy was the target and Ashira Chandy was the way to Chandy's inner circle. Mointz would masterfully use everything at his disposal to obtain positive results. Women just happened to be his quintessential result gainer, unbeknown to Danielle, thankfully.

Mointz had joined the Senators on their trade mission to New Delhi. The Indian government had invited Mointzie a year ago to their new technology center and he finally accepted their offer. Mointz was the face of New Delhi Technologies in America and Europe. The Indian company was celebrating their spokesman's trip even before he stepped on Indian soil.

Mointz's financial portfolio had continued to grow over the last four years. He was very careful where he invested his funds and kept to moderate gains except for his Microsoft, Oracle, and Apple stocks. The next ten years would bring big profits for him because tech stocks would skyrocket and he planned to use his technology industry backing to further him politically.

"After our meeting at the company, we are going to a screening of Bollywood's new Ashira Chandy film," Mointz said. "Rumor has it I will get a chance to meet Ashira's brother, Epen, tonight. Oh happy day!"

"The movie and party are not all you get to do," Lauren said. "Your wife set up a photo shoot for you."

"I love having my wife as my agent."

Ronnie nodded and smiled. "Once I realized she smiles every day because of Cristopher, it was not difficult to want to be part of this; I thank you, Senator, for believing in Cristopher."

Ellis instantly knew what the young man meant. Mointz did exactly what the panel wanted him to do. They wanted him to follow his heart and be the person he was destined to be.

New Delhi's international airport held a celebrity welcome for Mointz and his entourage when they deplaned. The world news media covering Mointz's first trip to India showed Mointz's rock star treatment.

India's Prime Minister welcomed his guests and, after plenty of photo opportunities, he escorted Mointz and the Senators to the technology company's headquarters. Ronnie blended in as a member of the security team.

The technology company plastered photos of Mointz's face all over the airport in several ads and on plenty of billboards as the company displayed his likeness in every one of their ads.

The Prime Minister left after an hour at the company because of a meeting at the capital. He planned to meet with Mointz and the senators the next day at his office.

Mointz was still socializing at the company four hours later with the Senators and Ronnie. The visitors found the Indian cuisine fabulous. Every single employee of the company had their picture taken with Mointz.

"He is incredible," Ellis said to Lauren and Ronnie as Mointz mingled with employees.

"Our boy is in his element right now," Lauren replied.

"Cristopher actually loves this," said Ronnie.

Ronnie was in charge of security for Mointz and the Senators on the trip. Philip Gabriel had made sure President Bush's National Security Adviser okayed security before Mointz left the country and the Senate's Security covered the two Senators as well. Ronnie excused himself to prepare for their departure.

"I am all set, Senators. I think they like me," Mointz said five hours after their arrival. "I promised to come back tomorrow night for a cocktail reception."

Lauren smiled, "Of course you did. You wouldn't be who you are if you didn't."

"Sorry, be…"

Lauren interrupted, "Yeah, yeah, yeah. Be careful what you wish for. We brought you here."

Ellis chuckled, "I need a drink. Why don't we go back to the hotel for a drink before the movie premiere? I believe the premiere starts at eight."

"A scotch would be great," said Lauren.

###

"Cristopher, I would be honored to introduce you to the star of our show, Ashira Chandy," one of the producers of the show said. He was introducing Mointz to the cast at the after-show party.

"A pleasure to meet you, Ms. Chandy," Mointz said, taking her hand and kissing the back of it.

"The pleasure is all mine," the beautiful star replied.

Mointz escorted Bollywood's leading lady to the bar and ordered a couple of martinis. The Senators and Ronnie left Mointz alone, allowing Mointz to perform his magic.

"Tell me what the real Cristopher Mointz is like up close and personal," Ashira said as she sipped her cocktail.

"I am here to support my friends and was graciously invited to your premiere," Mointz said, playing coy. "Funny, I do not see your leading man here."

She giggled. "And I do not see Mrs. Mointz here. I won't tell if you won't."

They clinked glasses and eventually skipped out of the event to return to her hotel suite. Ashira, stunning now in a pink silk nightgown, handed him a drink and asked him to sit by the fire with her. As soon as he did, she planted a kiss on his lips. Ashira was extremely seductive and gorgeous, but still second on PLAYBOY Magazine's list to Danielle.

"Thank you for the kiss," Mointz said. He took her glass and set it down on the coffee table. Mointz went in for his conquest and Ashira Chandy readily gave herself to Mointz.

India's number one star could not get enough of her new lover in the bedroom. It was almost four in the morning before they fell asleep. Mointz's alarm on his watch went off after he had only two hours of sleep.

"Sorry," Mointz said and kissed Ashira. "I have an early meeting at the university with a Dr. Epen Chandy and then with the Prime Minister."

"Epen is my brother," she exclaimed giddily, "I would love to accompany you."

Mointz smiled. "Only if you will accompany me to a cocktail party later."

Ashira giggled and kissed him. "Absolutely, but remember we cannot be seen canoodling in public. I know your reputation is as important as mine."

The girl obviously pays attention to the media, Mointz thought.

"Agreed! I need to change back at my hotel. My driver will pick you up. I am sure my security is downstairs."

"I will meet you in two hours. If you have to be at my brother's at nine, it will take about 20 minutes from your hotel."

Mointz kissed her goodbye and rode the elevator down to the lobby where Ronnie was waiting.

"Do I dare ask how you made out?" Ronnie asked, regretting the words as soon as he opened his mouth. He could see the tears in Mointz's eyes and the pain in his face, as Lauren did.

Mointz nodded.

"Buddy, I am glad they picked you and not me," Ronnie said, putting a hand on Mointz's shoulder while they walked out to the car. Ronnie opened the car for Mointz and the security detail drove them back to the hotel in silence.

"I love her, you know?" Mointz said in the elevator back at the hotel. "Danielle, the girls, and your family are the reasons I am so dedicated to succeeding in this mission."

"Stop believing I am looking down at you for this. I love you and I know how you feel about her. Do not apologize for saving the world, especially to me. My mother will ask me about what we did and I will never divulge what you have to do."

Mointz hugged him quickly before returning to his hotel room to shower. Ronnie had room service bring breakfast foods into the room while Mointz showered.

"Did you sleep last night?" Mointz asked Ronnie when he sat down to eat at the table in his room.

"I had just arrived when you came down. Are you always up at six when you travel?"

He nodded.

"Thanks for getting Ashira here so she can accompany us to see her brother. Good times."

"Forget her, I am more worried about the nutty professor gone bad. These mission activities make the day go by very quickly."

"I want to kill this guy, Chandy. He single-handedly causes almost a billion deaths when he gives over these secrets. We are going to have to shake down this Chandy and I will use his sister to make it happen."

"Do you have an idea outside the thoughts of Lauren and her father?"

"Absolutely," Mointz responded with a smile.

The meeting with Dr. Epen Chandy at the University accomplished exactly what Mointz had hoped. Epen invited Cristopher and Ashira for dinner at a popular Indian restaurant. The doctor rarely left the lab and, with Chandy out with Mointz, Ronnie and the newly arrived CIA duo of Adam Chace and Charles Atwood would break into the lab, remove all the equipment and supplies and have them shipped back to the United States.

Ashira, Mointz and the Senators met with the Prime Minister. Ashira kept the Prime Minister laughing and smiling while he entertained Mointz. She laughed and flirted, almost ignoring Lauren and Valmer. The exchange of pleasantries was about all the team accomplished there.

The cocktail reception at New Delhi Technologies went off splendidly, especially when the beautiful Ms. Ashira Chandy escorted Mointz. They were both a big hit, and the company was even more enamored with Mointz than ever before. That happened a lot when people met him in person.

Ashira begged Mointz to make a quick detour to her hotel before meeting her brother at nine for dinner. Mointz complied, informing Lauren at the cocktail party he would be going back to Ashira's heavily guarded suite. The CIA had given Mointz plenty of reasons to return to her place, the main one being Ashira Chandy had hidden many secrets there and Mointz needed to photograph the inside of the building and her apartment for the agency. Once Mointz had bedded Ashira and she went to change, Mointz snapped away.

"My brother hates lateness," Ashira said with a smile in the limousine.

"He will live," Mointz said curtly. His tone surprised Ashira.

"That sounded not very nice," the pouty actress snapped back.

"Meaning I am rude? I am not nice. What do you expect? Your brother is a traitor, Ashira. He is trying to sell India's nuclear secrets to Pakistan."

"Epen would not dare do such a thing. And even if he did, there is no way you could know about it," Ashira said.

"I know all about your scheme. I drugged you last night and you sang like a canary. Imagine my surprise one as beautiful as you could be involved in such treachery. Right now, your brother has been told to join a couple of agents as we were supposedly in an accident. He will be meeting us at the safe house the CIA operates to get the truth out of the both of you."

Ashira was speechless as the limousine pulled into an underground garage. Two agents immediately placed her in cuffs and brought her to an interrogation room. The actress's brother was already in the room cuffed.

Mointz stepped into the adjoining room behind the two-way mirror to join Lauren and Valmer.

"I still cannot believe Ashira made her brother give up the nuclear technology," Lauren said.

"She didn't have to push too hard. The Pakistanis contacted her. Dr. Chandy, the greedy wanker he is, easily agreed. Now what does dear old dad want done with them?"

"We didn't call him," Ellis said. "This is your show, what do you want to do?"

"Get all we can out of them and let Philip clean up. No offense, but we're trying to make our life easier in the future," Mointz said. He winked at them before entering the next room for the interrogation.

Chapter Thirty-One

Mointz had nodded off on the plane to Saudi Arabia and when he woke up, Lauren handed him a cup of Java.

"How are you feeling?" Lauren asked.

"Better now. I was exhausted," he replied.

"Lauren and I spoke with her father. The agency will prosecute all of the people whose names Ashira and Epen gave up," Ellis said.

"Where is Ronnie?" Mointz asked as he sipped on his cup of coffee.

"He is in back with our two unexpected guests. The Chandys are still quivering back there," Lauren said. "The limousine accident Atwood and Chace caused, effectively killing the Chandys, is all over the news back in India. They are getting a hero's mourning. I am still trying to figure out why we kidnapped them and provided cadaver bodies for them. Why did we do all this, Mointzie?"

"I wanted to make a point with Princess Amina. Do I trust her? Only kinda sorta."

"Jesus, when did this action-hero person come about?" Ellis asked.

"Whoa, wait a minute. The two of you and Trent put so much crapola in my head I had to follow my instincts. I studied a lot about human nature in this parallel. Gennifer has told me over and over the visual is more important than the suggestion. Amina needs a visual and so does India."

Lauren looked at Ellis and shrugged. "He seems to know what he is doing most of the time; however, I am not seeing where he is going with this."

"Kidnapping Bollywood's number one actress and faking her death will not endear you to the country," Ellis proclaimed.

"No, it will not. However, being on every billboard and ad won't hurt because I am going back to publicly mourn with the nation. There will only be about 800 million people in India to hear my heartfelt goodbye to their star."

Ellis now realized Mointz's brilliance. "Nice, bloody brilliant."

"I will take a plane over with Ronnie, as you two need to return to DC. It will only take an extra day."

Princess Amina didn't know what to say when she was brought into a conference room at the US Embassy with her brother to meet the Chandys. Mointz and Senators Ellis and Gabriel greeted her before introducing her to the Chandys.

"Is this some sort of joke?" Amina asked.

"Hello, Amina," Mointz said and winked. "No joke at all, cupcake, but I wanted you to hear for yourself what my friends here did. Tell them, friends, and remember your life depends on it."

Ashira and Epen Chandy gave a full account of their scheme to enrich their bank account by selling nuclear secrets. Princess Amina noticed the anger in Mointz's face and made a mental note of it.

Mointz called in security personnel, who led out the doctor and his vixen little sister. Their petrified expressions hammered home Mointz's point perfectly.

"I visited India as I believed it was a perfect paradise for three days of tranquility. Boy, I could not have been more wrong."

"What will happen to the Chandys?" Princess Amina asked.

"I wouldn't have the foggiest idea." The statement was not exactly true. Mointz knew they were traveling to a secret American prison in the mountains of Colorado.

"The Senators are going to visit the troops today and I hoped you would spend the day with me going over some ideas I believe need to be passed up the ladder. We are not too sure Clinton can win the election easily," Amina said.

"Clinton will win. Bush's 'read my lips' no new tax pledge from his last campaign has the Bush team lost in the desert, no pun intended. I will obviously make sure your feelings and wishes are made known."

Mointz joined Princess Amina and Prince Kareem in a light lunch at the palace. Back in Mointz's suite, Amina attacked him with zest and vigor. Mointz knew it was coming and Princess Amina did not even try subtlety.

Amina's powerful fingers really dug into Mointz's deep tissue and Mointz had to admit to himself she knew how to give him the perfect massage. The other things she did to him he could do without.

"The kingdom cannot afford a drop in support with a new administration. Iran, Iraq and Israel still pose a threat."

"Israel poses no threat and you know it. Muslims and Jews could live in peace if you allow a frank discussion."

Amina pinched him hard.

"Ouch! What was that for?"

Princess Amina laughed. "Your delusions sometimes scare me. Jews and Muslims will not live in peace in our lifetime."

"We'll see about that."

###

Senators Gabriel and Ellis entered the embassy limousine to drive to a meeting with the Saudi Council on Energy. The Senators were both members of the Senate Intelligence Committee and the Senate Committee on Energy & Natural Resources. The Republican, Gabriel, and Democrat, Ellis, wanted to use the trip to make political headway back in the Senate at home.

"Princess Amina has Mointz to lean on, yes?" Ellis asked.

"Absolutely. The Princess is in love and Mointz is her protector extraordinaire. I agree with Mointzie; she is definitely the brains behind the crown."

Rumors ran rampant in the First Parallel Amina had a powerful influence later in the second Gulf War, especially in lifting restrictions on women. Ellis believed this was another major game changer. He also wanted to push Mointz to visit Ko in North Korea, who had been itching to see Mointz again, and to help her son who was doing well in swimming. Mointz agreed to visit North Korea after the holidays for a few days at most.

"What was that?" Lauren asked the driver, a Marine.

"A Mercedes hit us from behind," the young Marine said. An explosion rocked the limousine and gunfire broke out in the street. Five hooded men tossed C-4 on the door of the limousine and blew the door open, shooting the driver in the head. They quickly manhandled both Lauren and Ellis, tying them up and gagging them before shoving them into another vehicle.

Ellis's eyes showed fright as the vehicle whisked them away from the scene. Lauren did not panic. Instead, the former CIA agent took a deep breath and cleared her head. She knew she was going to have to help Mointz find them and she needed to think logically.

Director Gabriel mobilized all of the agency's assets. Mointz and Princess Amina arrived at the embassy to meet Hasan Kabir, Head of Royal Security, the Saudi version of the FBI. Kabir briefed Mointz and Ronnie fully on the details of the kidnapping. Mointz looked like a wounded bear.

"Jihadists did this; I assure you," Hassan Kabir announced in the US Embassy's conference room.

Mointz lifted the five-foot-five Kabir off the ground and fire shot out of his nostrils like a dragon. Ronnie and Amina pulled Kabir from Mointz's hands.

"I don't care if the King did this; I am going to crack heads. Where are they? Anyone who does not give me full disclosure, I am going to destroy them."

"Cristopher, we need a cool head," Ronnie told him. He then turned his glare towards Kabir. "Hassan, where do these jihadists live?"

Hassan Kabir's hands shook as he opened the folder. The kidnapping had taken place over three hours ago. Kabir handed Mointz photos from the Royal Bank that had captured the attack. Philip Gabriel, feeling helpless, had already faxed them to Davis. The CIA images were not even close to picking up anything significant. Mointz had promised Davis, Philip and Danielle he would get Ellis and Lauren back when he spoke to them earlier.

"These Jihadists live in a very isolated area in the city. We have probably 72 hotspots, which could have information on this group. The Mercedes pictured in the stills from the bank was stolen from one of these spots, I would assume," Kabir said. "I suggest we send in the security force under my control and find them."

"Negative," Mointz said. "The four of us are going to find them."

Amina and Hassan Kabir looked like they had seen a ghost when they heard a knock on the door.

"Come in," Ronnie said.

A young Marine staffer came in and said, "Sir, a phone call came into the embassy a minute ago. They said they are the kidnappers who swiped the senators. Press line one on the phone."

Mointz nodded and Ronnie gently pushed the soldier out of the room.

"You start speaking to them," said Mointz. "I will jump in when necessary."

Kabir agreed and Mointz pressed "one" on the phone and put the call on speaker. The speaker's voice was raspy and unsure as he asked who he was speaking to. Kabir introduced himself.

"We have the Americans," the man said. "Our group demands the immediate withdrawal of all troops from our country. You have 24 hours before we behead the hostages," he said in Arabic.

Mointz, in Arabic, asked for more time as it would take a miracle to get everyone out. The caller balked at any extension and Mointz winced at the time he was given.

"I want to hear the woman's voice," Mointz said in Arabic. He spoke sternly and crisply.

"Pierce, Garnet, and Parrish," a sobbing Lauren said, giving Mointz exactly what he needed.

"Satisfied?" the caller asked.

"I will bring this to the King immediately," Mointz told the caller. "I don't like the foreigners either. I will do my best, if you give me a chance."

The kidnapper thanked him and praised Allah before he disconnected the call. Mointz at least had hope they would not jump the gun and hurt Lauren and Ellis.

"What is Pierce, Garnet, and Parish?" Amina asked.

"34,500 Mississippi's. The kidnappers took Lauren and Senator Ellis 57 minutes and 50 seconds away," Mointz said. "Lauren knew to count one Mississippi, two Mississippi, three Mississippi, if she was ever taken. Where does it put them?"

Mointz grabbed the phone and called Davis as Kabir fooled with the map to find out possibilities. Mointz took out a Sharpie and within ten minutes he had whittled down the location of the Senators to the two most likely locations.

"Put on your burqa, cupcake. We are going ourselves," Mointz said and quickly called an aide to the ambassador who brought in a wide variety of Arab clothes.

Celeste Philip's training in their memory banks, Ronnie and Mointz quickly became Arabs.

"Ready to go?" Ronnie said in Arabic.

Mointz nodded and before he left he gave specific instructions to patch calls into the armored Mercedes's satellite phone. Mointz had Amina by the arm as she was not sure what she was in for as they reached the carport in the embassy.

"Nice," Ronnie said. "Here comes a God-bless-the-wishbone moment."

"What is that?" Amina asked as they pulled out of the embassy.

Ronnie turned to Amina and Kabir in the back. "The 'wishbone offense' is our style of American football in high school and college. When Mointz goes on the offense, he picks names and lets God sort them out."

The kidnappers had not hurt Lauren or Ellis, but the Senators didn't doubt if the kidnappers' demands were not met, Lauren and Ellis would suffer serious consequences. Their hands were tied behind their backs and their legs tied to wooden chairs in the abandoned apartment. There seemed to be only one man outside the door. When Lauren asked to use the bathroom, he did not answer…

"Why aren't you nervous?" Ellis asked.

"I gave Mointzie our location. He will be here," Lauren replied. Her confidence was not lost on Ellis.

"How will giving the names of basketball players help?" Ellis whispered.

"Mointzie can deduce how long it took for us to get here. He knows approximately how far we traveled."

Lauren explained the significance of the players she had picked. In her heart she believed Davis would narrow it down and Mointz and Ronnie would burst in, guns blazing.

"Somebody whose life has changed in this parallel decided to take us," Ellis told Lauren. "He can find us from there, no?"

Lauren frowned. "This whole place has changed with Cristopher turning Prince Kareem into a better person. Anyone connected to him could be a culprit."

"There goes my idea. It is almost like Mointz has changed the world already," said Ellis.

"Valmer, he has and it is why we should have never come back. I realize now we needed him to do his own thing."

Ellis nodded. He was experiencing rope burn from the tight nylon rope around his hands. "Maybe Danielle and he would not have become a unit."

Lauren shook her head. "The two of them were in love before I entered the picture. We cannot think they wouldn't be together. We are in this predicament because of our own fault; we have to be more careful."

"That is, if we ever get out of here."

"Guess you have not read the memo yet?"

"Memo, what memo?" Ellis asked

"The memo Cristopher Mointz does not know how to fail."

"Are you sure this is the place, Hassan?" Mointz asked when he pulled into the neighborhood that Trent said to try first. Trent believed there was a 90% probability they would find Lauren and Ellis here.

"Positive. This is where we had some serious resistance to the kingdom."

Davis had confirmed to Mointz that there were plenty of extremists in this region as the Saudis had battled with them for years here. Mointz knew Davis was almost always right about these things and Mointz was hoping this was one of those times. His gut said 'yes' anyways.

"Thoughts?" Amina asked, sincerely concerned for Lauren as Mointz and Ronnie looked around at the neighborhood behind the tinted glass.

"The buildings which are all broken down, what are they?" Mointz asked.

"A riot happened here when the war in Iraq broke out," Kabir replied. "This whole section is about to be rebuilt."

"Let's go," Ronnie told Mointz. "We know who to ask for help, right Cristopher?"

"The boys on the street playing. Blondie is going to be making me her lasagna for a month."

Mointz told the Princess and Hassan Kabir to sit tight. Kabir had plenty of firepower in his possession as did Princess Amina, who knew how to, at the very least, fire a weapon.

Ronnie and Mointz got out of the car, each with two Glocks under his robe as well as weapons in the belts of his shorts. Mointz grabbed a boy running in the street and handed him a few banknotes with the King's portrait on it.

"Son," Mointz said in Arabic. "Have you seen a couple of white people being held here somewhere?"

The boy, about twelve, didn't answer right away. He held out his hand for more money.

"You little shit," Ronnie exclaimed and pulled out his weapon. "Answer the question!"

The boy's eyes turned wide and he pointed to the apartment building on the corner.

"They are in there. I saw them brought up to the third floor."

"How many were brought up?" Mointz asked the boy and handed him more of the King's money.

"Two, a man and a woman," the boy replied.

The boy went on to tell them the third floor was empty. He and his friends had played up there until the kidnappers kicked them out. Mointz gave him the rest of the money and Ronnie kicked him lightly on the bum as he ran off.

"Son-of-a-bitch," Mointz said softly. "The Mercedes that took them just showed up. They are about 300 yards away."

"What do you want to do? I say we go get them out now, but we need a diversion."

Mointz looked at Ronnie. He noticed it was approaching nightfall. "If we make a mistake, they will shoot them, no question in my mind."

"I agree 100%. A diversion will work. I say we blow up the Mercedes and make them come out," said Ronnie.

"Hassan says they are going to get this place restored. I say we burn it down and smoke them out. It will increase our odds. We will be like Al Pacino taking a 'flamethrower' to the place.'"

"From what movie is that?"

"When it comes out, I'll see it with you."

"Fire, fire!" one of the extremists screamed when he looked outside to see half the block ablaze.

"We need to get out of here," another said. "Leave the Americans, hurry, hurry. The police will find them."

Ellis wondered why Lauren was laughing through tears. "Did you crack up? We are about to burn to death."

"We are saved. Mointz is here," she said as smoke billowed into the room.

"How do you know that?" he asked.

"Pardon the cliché, but where there's smoke, there's Mointz's fire," Lauren said. At that moment, Mointz and Ronnie kicked in the door. "About time you two got your asses here."

Mointz stuck out his tongue at her and quickly cut Ellis loose. Ronnie cut Lauren's ties. She immediately dropped into Mointz's arms and, as the tears flowed, he held her tightly.

"We have to get out of here. Amina and the head of Saudi Security Service are out there in an embassy Mercedes," Mointz said. He handed Lauren a Glock. I don't think there is anyone left." He winked at Ellis. Ellis and Lauren shook off the cobwebs and cramps from the tight ropes.

Ronnie handed the Senators his canteen so they could try to rehydrate. The four friends hustled downstairs. Mointz ran up the street to grab the Mercedes.

"Get in the trunk," Mointz ordered Amina and Kabir.

"What?" Amina screamed.

Mointz popped the trunk and practically threw both of them in. He gunned the Mercedes, picked up Ronnie and the Senators and sped from the neighborhood before they became burnt toast.

"You locked them in the trunk?" Ronnie asked.

"Yep. I could not think of a safer place. I'll get them out in a minute."

"Considering you have no idea where the hell you are, it would be a good idea," Ronnie said chuckling.

"Lauren knew you would save us. Me, I was not so sure. Going from college professor to Rambo, who would've thought?" Ellis said. "How did you find us?"

Mointz told them how Davis calculated where they could be and how Ronnie scared a 12-year-old child, who was trying to shake them down for money, but knew Lauren and Ellis's location. Mointz said he took gas from the Mercedes and lit the block on fire to smoke the assailants out of the building. Ronnie said they picked them off one by one as the extremists ran out of the building.

"Sorry it took nine hours to get the two of you back in a foreign country! I have to let our hosts out of the trunk."

Lauren slid into the front seat and kissed both Mointz and Ronnie on the cheeks. Amina and Hassan got into the car. Lauren rested her head on Mointz's shoulder.

"Why did you put us in the trunk?" Princess Amina asked, after welcoming back the Senators and apologizing profusely.

"To give you plausible deniability in case I had to blow one of those wankers' heads off," Mointz declared.

"Oh, okay then," was all the Princess could say.

Lauren called Davis on the car's satellite phone and as tears rolled down her face Mointz gently gave her arm a squeeze as Ronnie put an arm around her.

Exactly fifty-nine minutes after they rescued Lauren and Ellis, Mointz pulled into the embassy. The American Ambassador, Richard Bonner, greeted them enthusiastically. Mointz agreed to meet the Princess for food and massages—her words—later in the evening. Ambassador Bonner handed Mointz a beer as Lauren, Ellis, Ronnie, and Mointz asked for a minute alone in the conference room.

"We all need a bath," Ronnie said.

"Got that right. Then, I have to greet Amina and Kareem."

Mointz slouched in a leather chair and put his feet up on the conference room table. Ronnie did the same and sipped a beer.

"Comfortable?" Lauren asked with a grin.

"Not yet, but very soon I will be," Ronnie said guzzling his beer.

"So, Senator Ellis, welcome to 'life sucks and we make it right,'" Mointz said and tapped beers with Ronnie and Lauren.

Senator Ellis laughed, "Jesus, the three of you are actually having fun at this."

"Fun, what is fun?" Lauren asked. "You have been living life hard. We have been working hard." Lauren hugged Valmer Ellis and handed him another beer. "Thanks for joining the club."

Princess Amina handed Mointz a glass of champagne in the tub. She had forgiven him for throwing her in the trunk after her first orgasm.

"I have a present for your new daughter," Amina said innocently.

"Thank you. I appreciate it. I want you to give me a present."

"Anything, you know that."

"Clean up these extremists, please, before I have to. This is a great place to visit and we certainly satisfy each other's needs when I drop by, but I have to move on with my career and I am too busy to clean up your messes."

"I watched you handle those men with ease. Hassan was shaking in his boots and you lit the place on fire. The Chandys are no longer a threat and you came here to supposedly ease my fears about a change in the administration. You are a wild one."

"Among other things," Mointz told her and pulled her to him and entered her before Amina became fixated on why Mointz really came here, which was to keep her and her brother on the straight and narrow or they would end up like the Chandys.

Mointz finally wore out Amina and for the second time he injected her with a Davis concoction to find out the Princess's actual activities in the kingdom. Amina admitted she had not been with anyone since Mointz had sex with her the first time and she was still on the level about keeping the economy in her country moving forward. She also kept her brother on a short leash. Mointz believed if he could keep the Saudis moving forward peacefully, the world would follow.

"I am going to the states between Thanksgiving and Christmas. I hope we will spend time together," Princess Amina said after a deep sleep.

"That is awesome and a surprise," Mointz said, "I, of course, will have time for you, but why the excursion to the states?"

"Shopping, Mr. Mointz. A woman needs to shop."

Mointz chuckled and had sex with Amina before he showered and prepared to head to India to mourn the deaths of the Chandys. He hated the farce he lived while he was away.

Princess Amina and Mointz said their goodbyes. The Prince escorted Mointz to the airport. Prince Kareem wanted to hear every detail for himself on what had happened to the Senators. Mointz left out no detail and really put a guilt trip on the Prince for the criminal element that eventually would splinter off to become the group who would take the towers down. Mointz was laying the groundwork for the moment he and friends would need to come and eradicate the terror cells.

"I expect you and your security people will keep these radical Islamists out of the mainstream," Mointz said as he shook the prince's hand.

"Indeed I shall," Prince Kareem replied emphatically.

Mointz departed from the Prince's limousine and entered the Gulfstream where Ronnie, Lauren, and Ellis sat buckled in.

"Nice of you to join us," Lauren said as she sipped her coffee.

"Been partying with the Prince all night and probably have a blood alcohol level three times the normal limit. So much for no alcohol in the kingdom."

Lauren knew exactly what Mointz was doing last night and knew he was not drinking with the Prince. Mointz drew a fine line between what Ronnie needed to know and what he did not need to know. In the First Parallel, Mointz never passed up a chance to be with a beautiful woman. His behavior in the Second Parallel was different. Mointz needed Danielle and only Danielle. No relationship could rival the intimacy they shared. Lauren knew Mointz made himself sick when he had to be with anyone besides his wife and she hated to put him into the bed of Amina. The lesson Mointz had taught her last year had changed her understanding of terms of the heart.

"Well, you look as though you were hit by a bus," Ronnie said laughing.

"More like a hurricane, I am going to sleep as soon as this bird goes wheels up."

Mointz swallowed two aspirin and drank a large glass of juice before the Gulfstream leveled off enough for Mointz to fall asleep.

"He freaked when they grabbed you," Ronnie said to Lauren. "I thought our friend was going to burn down the kingdom before the kidnappers called. I have been there when he has been in tough spots, but this was totally different. Those bastards came out of the building like rats and we sent them to their date with the devil. Come to think of it, he actually *started* to burn down the kingdom."

"I hear you were just as stoked up to find us," Ellis said, "Thank you, son."

"No 'thank you' necessary. The two of you sent me my wife and my best friend saved me from myself. It is an honor to help in any way I can, sir."

Ellis smiled and sat back in his chair, "I hope I will not be kidnapped in the future."

Lauren giggled, "Valmer, it builds character."

Mointz practically healed the nation of India with his soothing words at the funeral for the Chandys. The nation mourned and even the Prime Minister was astonished by the power of the 25-year-old's words during the funeral.

Senators Ellis and Gabriel attended the funeral and were dumbfounded how Mointz held India in the palm of his hands.

"Mointz is brilliant, simply put. It was the best eulogy I have ever heard," Ellis whispered to Lauren.

Lauren nodded and whispered back, "Yes. Mointz is brilliant."

Mointz, Ronnie, and the Senators only spent ten hours in India before returning to the CIA jet to head home.

Ronnie and Mointz hitched a ride home in Lauren's limousine back to Rhode Island from Hanscom Air Force Base in nearby Massachusetts, while Ellis flew back to his home in Virginia.

Danielle melted in his arms when Mointz walked in the door. "Why do you have to play John flipping Wayne all the time?"

"Me? What the heck did I do?" Mointz asked Danielle.

"Lauren and Valmer got kidnapped and you, as well as my son, burned down the neighborhood to save them and here I am changing diapers and cleaning up burped baby formula while I work," said Danielle. Her smile was pure and loving.

"Want to trade, darling?"

"Heck, no. I would not want your job; all I really want is another year of peace."

"Done."

"Seriously?" Danielle asked.

"Absolutely."

Chapter Thirty-Two

November 1998

Danielle received her wish and received six years of mostly peace and tranquility. The 31-year-old Cristopher Mointz had only visited Bosnia a couple of times, North Korea a few times and of course Saudi Arabia several times. Today was the first Tuesday of November and a seven-year-old Rosie Marie and six-year-old Ashley Megan sat on their father's lap at the Madeira Restaurant in East Providence waiting for election returns to come in.

Attorney Cristopher Mointz ran for district one's United States Congressional seat from Rhode Island and Providence Plantations, the official name of the state. Polls predicted Mointz would receive over 78% of the vote. The Raymond Belvenie restaurant held all of Mointz's family and friends except Grampa Leo, who had passed away on May fifth of 1996. A five-month–pregnant-with-twins Gennifer, handed a napkin to Mointz to wipe the cake frosting off Ashley Megan's full mouth.

"Where is Danielle, Gennifer?" Mointz asked. "Channel 10 is about to make me a Congressman."

"I will get her," Gennifer said. "Sit and enjoy the moment."

Gennifer brought in Danielle, who led Heidi Lynn by the hand. Gennifer turned up the big-screen television. Kathy had Seanie on the phone from Seattle where the All-Pro tight end was ready to celebrate his brother's election. Colleen picked up Kathy and her two-year-old daughter, Aleixa, from Grandma Martha. Kathy had conceived baby Aleixia via a surrogate father.

"Here it comes!" Lauren cried out handing her son, Kevin, to her husband, Trent, and Kevin's twin, Keith, to Mointz's father, Robert. The one-year-old twins slept soundly.

"Patrice, can we pick a winner in the district one Congressional race?" *Dan Henning asked his anchorwoman partner Patrice Wood.*

"Indeed we can, Dan. Not much of a surprise here. Channel 10 News has projected Rhode Island's native son, Cristopher Mointz, has won by a landslide in the race for Rhode Island's first congressional district. The former Olympian, NFL MVP and war hero will represent Rhode Island in Congress."

"No one believed this race was ever going to be close, Patrice," *Dan interjected. "The new Congressman-elect is one of the most recognized people on the planet."*

"Let's go to Elizabeth Hurley at the Madeira Restaurant in East Providence with Cristopher and Danielle Mointz," *Patrice said.*

"Thank you, Patrice," *said Elizabeth. "Congressman-elect Mointz, Mrs. Mointz, I can see the celebration has just erupted here in East Providence."*

Cristopher and Danielle smiled into the camera.

Elizabeth continued. "How does it feel to know you are heading to Congress?"

"Representative Silveira graciously called a minute ago and offered his congratulations. I would like to thank everyone who took part in my campaign, especially my wife, Danielle, and my sister's partner, Colleen, our campaign manager, who brilliantly steered me in the right direction when I was learning to crawl before I could walk. This race was about change and showing the people of Rhode Island they have a loud and proud voice in Congress. I will be the voice for the young and old, the strong and the meek, whether you voted for me or not, I will work hard to earn the trust of the people who didn't and deliver for the people who supported me. No one will ever feel they do not have someone who will fight for them in this state. I humbly accept your trust and faith in me and I promise not to let the people of Rhode Island down."

"Thank you Congressman-elect Mointz," reporter Hurley said. *"Patrice this place is now one big party as Cristopher Mointz heads to Congress."*

The party continued late. Mointz's Mother and Father had earlier brought home their grandchildren and Heidi Lynn, allowing their parents to enjoy the evening. Davis took the twins home, letting Lauren out for the first time in a while.

"Have you accomplished what you had hoped?" Kathy asked her brother, sitting at the bar with him.

"This is pretty special, but I have some lofty goals. Colleen did a great job in the campaign. I think she will enjoy being my Chief of Staff."

"What are you going to do with your law firm? Is Danielle planning on absorbing the office here into the one in DC?"

"Honestly, I'm not sure. She travels all over the place with her work. Our firm here in Rhode Island has done some really great things."

Kathy gave her brother a hug before she went looking for Colleen. Lauren and Danielle came over to sit with the Congressman-elect.

"Ladies, nice to see you can finally sit with me."

Danielle kissed her husband softly, "Way to go, stud."

"Awww, you two are so cute," Lauren said. "Enjoy the night Congressman. There is a lot of work to do on the hill."

"The good news is we have our Georgetown house. The really good news is I get to come home on the weekends and the super good news is, I can get my hands dirty again. Ronnie, where are you?" Cristopher called out, searching for his friend.

"Just because you are some hotshot now does not mean I am not going to monitor your activities with Lauren," said Danielle.

"Danielle, I promise to keep him away from my father the best I can, but you know we are getting into the point of no return," Lauren said.

"I know, I know, Lauren. The risks he takes puts in danger all he has accomplished so far. Twenty-six years from now, this will all be over for us. I see light at the end of the tunnel," Danielle said.

"Sweetheart, we can enjoy this now and I promise the pot of gold is still under the rainbow," Mointz said and kissed her.

"Mointzie, the blarney of the politician of Irish descent is perfect for America," Lauren said and hoisted her glass in the air.

"Cristopher, don't miss the vote," Colleen shouted at the newly sworn-in Congressman as he walked into his office.

Mointz turned thirty-two years old today on a snowy fourth of February, 1999. He shook off the snow onto the floor of his office. Colleen ran him to the chamber and he made his selection on the amendment to the amendment of the appropriation bill. His committee meeting on Iran was about to commence.

Speaker Hastert had selected Mointz to sit on the House Intelligence Committee on the recommendation of CIA director Philip Gabriel, who had shared with the Speaker most, if not all, of what Mointz had done for the agency.

Secretary of State Madeleine Albright was on the hill today discussing Iran's boarding of international ships in the Persian Gulf.

Mointz rolled his eyes at the malarkey spouting from both the committee's and the Secretary's mouths. He had a better understanding now of why nothing was ever accomplished here on the Hill. He was about to rock the boat.

"Madam Secretary, I have not heard one statement from anyone that gets to the root of the problem. The Iranians are collecting arms in the region and are using these fake boardings to disguise their means of unloading the weapons from the ships. We are wrong in saying the real problem is the boarding of ships. The Iranians are masking their true intentions and we took the bait."

The Secretary of State tried to backpedal and explain the State Department's intel. However, Mointz's knowledge of the subject resulted in a boxing match with Albright. The spirited debate finally ended, but not before the Secretary agreed to return to the Hill in a month on the premise she would have better intel.

Both the Democrats and Republicans on the Hill were astonished at the knowledge the new Congressman from Rhode Island displayed on this and every other subject regarding intelligence. They knew he had worked with

359

Senator Gabriel, the senior senator from New York, when Mointz was not fighting battles in court for the underdog. The biggest surprise to the committee occurred when Mointz's Defense Intelligence Agency record was partially released.

Lauren sent Mointz an e-mail asking him to meet her for coffee. They loved having their e-mails and cell phones back and Davis gave them palm pilots with full capabilities.

"Blondie, how are you, love?" Mointz said embarrassing her at their favorite coffee spot, Mario's Specialty Coffee, next to the Capitol.

"Happy birthday, old man," Lauren said, giving him a kiss on the cheek.

"I will give you old," he said as they received their coffee after first signing an autograph. Mointz could never refuse an autograph seeker. He always signed and gave a big smile when he did it.

"Trent and I look forward to dinner tonight. My parents have graciously agreed to watch the babies."

"Colleen and Kathy have baby duty tonight for us; I hope Colleen gets over me ripping into the Secretary of State."

"I thought you were wonderful. Maddie Albright knows what is going on. Now Maddie knows someone else does, too. She called me ten minutes after the hearing. Good job, Congressman."

"Director Philip told me to get into it with her. He loves me being the bad guy."

"Father likes it because no one dislikes you. The hearing is all over C-SPAN already. The headline on CNN's says 'no one pushes around America's hero.'"

Mointz had arrived at the Hill with moxie and big expectations. He didn't come here to fail. Clinton was in the lame-duck stage of his Presidency and Mointz and Lauren had helped Clinton behind the scenes to keep the Monica Lewinsky affair from throwing him out of office.

Mointz wanted to help pass an economic affairs bill and a few intelligence bills before George Dubya entered The White House. Mointz wanted to increase his personal stature inside the chamber because outside of it he was America's darling as well as Danielle's.

"Promise me you will have the economic affairs bill ready when Bush has the nomination in sight. I like McCain, but we need the man with the bullhorn when we go to battle with the terrorists. Sorry to steal your thunder now that I am here, Lauren," said Mointz and sat down with Lauren.

"I do not care what you do and you know it," Lauren said. "What I don't know is why you are so forceful over economic regulations and tax cuts now."

"Tax cuts work. The dot-com bubble needs a scheme to keep it from popping. I will be the one Congressman to say at the end of the day 'I warned you.' I used to teach students if you don't make a product you can put in a box, it is not worth investing in."

"Congressman Mointz, what an astute observation. It must be nice to know you were right more often than not."

"Sounds a bit sarcastic. Then again, when aren't you sarcastic?"

The two popular elected officials finished their coffee and ordered seconds to go. Mario's Coffee rivaled Mointz's favorite coffee shop back in Rhode Island.

"Will you walk me back?" Lauren asked.

"Certainly, my lady. One second, okay?" Mointz asked as he noticed a late 30-year-old homeless man begging for change. Mointz always carried several bills in his front pockets stapled to an address of a shelter he supported financially to help the less fortunate. "Here is a $20 bill, go get warm and get some food. There is a wonderful place at L and 15th. Ask for Ms. Edna and tell her what you need. She will do her best to help you." The DC homeless foundation to which Mointz had given $1million was designed to restore a person's pride and dignity.

"Congressman Mointz, I need to speak to you in private, please. I am not a homeless man, obviously," he said as he pocketed the twenty.

Lauren gave Mointz a puzzled look.

"Who are you then?" Mointz asked.

"Please, Congressman and Senator Gabriel. I am an NSA employee; my family and I are in serious danger. We need help," he said.

"I will call you later, Lauren," Mointz said, nodding to her to step back. "Walk with me, sir."

The NSA man walked next to Mointz, "My family, sir, please."

"No one is going to hurt your family. Meet me at the shelter in an hour. There are plenty of places to speak freely there."

"What is your real name?" Mointz asked in a back room at the shelter. The Congressman had already hidden on his person an earpiece, a microphone and a camera that beamed back to Davis. Davis and his team had built a 2016 capable private Net and two NASA satellites allowed Davis to use the technology as his own private information superhighway.

"My name is Douglas Porter."

"Mointz, Doug Porter is telling the truth about that," Davis said as he searched the NSA database at Langley. He now split his time between MIT and CIA headquarters.

"Okay, Doug Porter. I am here, what can I do to help you and your family?"

"I am head of the task force investigating corrupt politicians. The task force, all six of us, received information a certain Senator had gotten into bed with people in Hungary. These people had connections with human sex trade pirates. The Senator loves young girls and when we confirmed this, we were about to go to the Deputy Director of the NSA. A day later, five members of the task force were missing. My family and I had left our house to have it exterminated, so we were at the neighbors'. I saw men enter my house and when I started calling the five other members of the task force, no one answered. My wife and children are safe for now, but I had no idea at first who to go to until it dawned on me—you were a Defense Intelligence Agency member and if there is one person in the country who cannot be bought, it is you. Please help me."

"Trent, is he telling the truth?" Mointz said, startling Porter. Mointz put his hand up to settle him down.

"From what he says, it adds up," Davis said.

"Mr. Porter, I have a trusted friend in my ear. Your family will be safe; believe me. I will protect them as if they were my own. Do you know who Ronald Mahoney is?"

"Yes, of course, sir."

"Great. That helps because he will be protecting your family personally. Who is the senator?" Mointz asked. Almost simultaneously, Davis and Agent Porter announced it was Senator Mark Nicholas, the Republican Senator from the state of Washington who ran on a pro-family platform.

Porter filled Mointz in on the information the task force had compiled on Senator Nicholas and his cronies. The criminal organization Nicholas headed with Victor Caroli, mayor of one of Hungary's largest cities, was exerting more influence in Eastern Europe every day, according to Porter.

"Where is all the information you compiled?" Mointz asked.

"At my house. I have copies in my safe. I had it on our secure servers. However, the servers are no longer there. I'll bet they have been erased."

Mointz nodded. At that moment, Ronnie walked into the room, Ronnie introduced himself to Agent Porter and Mointz could see some tension die down in Porter. Not much, but some. Some was always better than none.

"NSA Deputy Director Barbara McNamara has to help, right?" Porter asked nervously.

"Lauren can crack that nut. I will see what we can do about Senator Nicholas. Agent Porter, my friend here and I will personally get you and your family to safety so at least you can have some peace of mind. If there is a leak, I do not trust anyone."

"Where am I going to go?"

Mointz smiled. "Barrington, Rhode Island, is a great place this time of year."

Danielle had given Ronnie her old house near Mointz's parents and the Porters would be safe there with Ronnie and a few agents hand-picked by Ronnie.

The relief now on Porter's face was crystal clear to the Congressman.

"I have to run an errand," Mointz told Danielle as he grabbed some firepower from the walk-in gun safe in his closet. "I might be late tonight."

"Nice try, but I am going with you," Danielle said sarcastically. "The Porter family needs a woman's touch. I promise to be at the airport waiting for you."

"Last time you said that, I found you in a pub in Ireland. This time I want you to come, they will need you," Mointz said.

Ronnie rang the bell and Mointz let him in. Ronnie hugged his mother, who now looked younger than her son.

"I put Doug Porter in your favorite place," Ronnie said with a smile. "Happy birthday, buddy."

Mointz chuckled. "You put Porter in the trunk? I hope you let him shower."

Danielle smiled and told Ronnie she would meet them at the airport and take Porter with her. Ronnie had called in agents Chace and Atwood to assist with the security for the Porter family. Mointz was going to send Danielle with Adam Chace and Charles Atwood along with Porter to the airport. Porter begged to go with Mointz, but Mointz did not want Porter with him in case of a problem at the house. Mointz did not need to watch out for a tired agent in the event of a firefight.

"Congressman, are you wearing your vest or are you bench pressing more?" Ronnie asked, getting in Mointz's black Jeep Wrangler.

"Yes, dear. I am wearing a vest," Mointz replied. "Do you know where this place is?"

"Porter gave me good directions. Supposedly, this cabin belongs to one of our friends and he knew they were on vacation. It must be cold in the woods of Virginia."

"Valmer is incensed at all of this, he is close to Senator Nicholas. Valmer told me he had no idea."

"That is awful. Agent Porter's wife and two young boys don't deserve this. The idea of five lost agents blows my mind."

Mointz pulled into the cabin's long driveway and turned the engine off, rolling the six speed. Mointz and Ronnie both got out of the Jeep and immediately noticed a Ford Taurus Hertz rental car in front of the cabin.

"Shit, someone beat us here," Ronnie said.

"We need to look in the cabin," said Mointz.

Mointz followed Ronnie around the back of the cabin and peered into the side window. Two white males, both in leather jackets, held pistols: one pointed his in Jackie Porter's face and the other pointed a gun at her two little boys. They were both speaking Hungarian.

"Shoot to kill. I will hit the one on the right; you get the one on the left," Ronnie said as he steadied his M4 and Mointz steadied his.

"Three, two, one," Mointz counted down and they both fired. The two men went down like sacks of potatoes.

"Go, go," Ronnie screamed and rushed into the house with Mointz.

Jackie Porter grabbed her sons, Evan, who was six, and five-year-old Paul. Sobbing, she let Mointz and Ronnie help her to her feet and out of the room with her sons.

"Congressman Mointz," Jackie said sniffling. "Please tell me Doug is fine, please."

Mointz's trademark smile dissipated her worries quickly. "Yes, he is fine. My wife is with him. We need to leave quickly; I will take you to him."

"Ready, boys?" Ronnie asked as he picked up Paul. Mointz picked up Evan and held him in one arm, holding Jackie's hand with the other.

Ronnie called Davis to have the agency pick up the two men with bullets in their heads. Mointz buckled up the two boys in the back.

"Everything okay, guys?" Mointz asked driving away.

"Yes, Congressman. My husband and I thought finding you was the best bet. I guess he found you," Jackie told him. "He is definitely fine, correct?"

"Definitely fine," Ronnie said, turning his head toward the back seat. "Are you boys ready to go on a plane?"

The boys nodded and gave shy smiles. Their smiles became bigger when their mother told them they were going to see their father.

The Jeep pulled into the airport at 5:20 PM where Danielle and agents Chace and Atwood waited for them. Dulles Airport's private runway personnel had prepared the private plane for its flight to Rhode Island. The Porter family reunion put tears in Danielle's eyes. Agents Chace and Atwood boarded everyone as rapidly as they could.

Mointz pulled Doug aside and gave him an overview of what happened at the cabin. The poor agent didn't know what to say.

Mointz sat next to Danielle and held her hand and kissed it.

"I have a present for you," Danielle whispered to Mointz.

"Oh yeah, what is it?"

"Lauren is taking our little angels to Barrington."

"I love you, sweetie. I love you, I love you, I love you. It is the best present I could ask for. My parents will be so happy."

Mointz's phone rang. It was Davis, who informed Mointz an elite CIA anti-terror group had stopped at the Porters' home. As they tried to enter, the house had exploded into confetti and three agents had been killed. Mointz figured he would hold off for a calmer moment before telling the Porters everything they owned was charcoal.

The hour plane ride had more bumps than normal. Evan and Paul felt a bit nervous until Mointz started to sing.

Two of Belvenie's limousines whisked the party away to Ronnie's as soon as the plane landed. The Porters settled in nicely and Mointz and Danielle walked over to Mointz's parents to surprise them.

Robert, Martha, and Grandma Rose were about to eat as Mointz walked into the house with Danielle.

"Hello family," Mointz exclaimed.

"Grandson," Grandma Rose cried out and hugged the birthday boy. "Are the children here?"

"On the way, Grandma Rose," Danielle replied.

Mointz explained what had happened and the reason for their Barrington visit. Robert and Martha felt heartbroken for the Porters, but glad to see the birthday boy.

At that moment, Lauren and Gennifer brought in Rosie Marie, Ashley Megan, Heidi Lynn and Lauren's twins, Keith and Kevin. Each carried presents for Mointz and he hugged and kissed all of them.

"Thank you," Mointz told Gennifer and Lauren as he embraced both of them at the same time again with his long arms.

Ronnie came in and gave the last of clothes and incidentals to his mother and kissed his seven-and-a-half-month-pregnant wife Gennifer. Gennifer told Ronnie after this was all over, her husband needed to take a sabbatical and Mointz promised Gennifer he could make it happen.

Everyone, including Grandma Rose, who needed a wheelchair, decided to head to the mall to shop for the Porters.

"This is a good idea?" Ronnie asked. "Suppose someone sees us shopping and notices we're buying clothes for a family of four."

"We are going to Dave and Buster's Arcade restaurant and my mother is going to give a list to her friend at Macy's to gather it all," Mointz said as they walked behind the others.

Mointz woke up with Danielle in his arms at the beach house. Martha and Robert watched the girls and Danielle gave him one heck of a birthday present.

"Good morning, Congressman. I hope you do not miss any votes today."

"Danielle, I am almost positive we do not have any until next Tuesday, but I have to get back to solve this Doug Porter – Senator Mark Nicholas problem. Lauren is going to take a run at Barbara McNamara, the Deputy Director of the National Security Agency. I cannot wait to sit in on that meeting."

"Mointzie, if it is true human trafficking is going on in Hungary, you need to shut it down."

Mointz kissed her. "We know it is happening and I promise I will shut it down."

Danielle stared into Mointz's blue eyes. "This happened in the First Parallel, didn't it?"

He nodded. "These bastards absolutely preyed on young girls. Believe me; I will do what it takes."

She kissed him hard and they made love again. Mointz wore the brightest smile.

"I know in my heart, you will stop it. Go for your run and I will make you breakfast," Danielle said. "Dress warm; it is frigid outside."

Danielle cooked breakfast and Mointz ran a hard eight miles in between waving at honking cars. Mointz ate plenty of sausage, egg and cheese casserole when he returned home.

"Go shower and I will take you and Lauren to the airport," Danielle said as Mointz kissed her, all sweaty. "Martha is watching the children with Gennifer and we are dropping off Lauren's boys."

Light traffic on the way to the airport at ten in the morning made the ride easy for them. Danielle wished them luck and received a big hug from her husband before he left with Lauren for the private hangar for the trip back to DC.

"Are we going right into Barbara McNamara's office?" Mointz asked, once they became airborne.

"Hell, yes. We owe it to the Porters and the families of the other agents. I will let you be your total self."

"Thank you, dear."

The two politicians went over their strategy on double teaming Deputy Director McNamara. When they landed, a town car drove the politicians immediately to the NSA headquarters.

A young female NSA employee stopped Lauren from entering the building. "Excuse me, ma'am," said the employee.

"Yes, what can I do for you?" the 41-year-old Senator replied all fired-up, as she took her sunglasses off.

"Oh, sorry, Senator. I didn't recognize you with your sunglasses."

Any other day, she would have laughed it off because everyone froze and stared at Mointz and ignored her. Today was not a laughing day. However, Mointz bailed her out.

"Don't worry; her bark is worse than her bite. She is normally pleasant on Tuesdays, believe me." Mointz's wink made the young woman smile.

Lauren did not wait to be buzzed into Barbara McNamara's office. She walked right in, with Mointz following.

"Lauren, Congressman Mointz, what is wrong?" Barbara said, shocked they had interrupted a meeting with two agency employees.

Mointz grabbed both men by the collars and threw them out of the office. "What do you know about Doug Porter's task force?" Lauren asked.

"Not much, why?"

Lauren told her friend the full story and as expected, Barbara had no idea what Lauren was talking about.

"Jesus, Congressman Mointz shot them in the woods?"

"Barbara, please call me Cristopher. I know you are not involved in this, but someone is. Who is the person who oversees this particular task force?"

"William Kitt is the lead."

"Bring in Willie," Lauren demanded. It was not a request; it was an order.

Kitt entered right away. As soon as he walked in, Mointz buried his right fist in his stomach. Barbara McNamara did not know what to think.

"What?" Mointz said as he shrugged "I do not think I am going to get arrested anytime soon."

Mointz picked up Kitt off the floor and set him in a chair next to Lauren, while giving him a sadistic smile.

"Can someone tell me why the Congressman is so livid?" asked Kitt.

"First, tell us about Doug Porter's task force."

The Deputy Director nodded to Kitt. She couldn't do anything else as she knew Mointz's reputation and most of his deeds. Mointz looked like an angry wolf, McNamara thought.

"He is leading a task force on human trafficking in Hungary."

"When was the last time you saw him?" Lauren asked.

"Late last week, if you must know. What the hell is going on here? I demand an answer."

Mointz slapped the back of Kitt's head and Deputy Director McNamara rolled her eyes. She had never seen Mointz in action before.

"Asshole, his team has been wiped out. The Eastern European mafia members have been identified; they were shot when they held guns in the face of Doug Porter's wife. How do you not know about this?"

"We speak almost every Friday. I do not micromanage my people," Kitt proclaimed. A slap from Mointz gave him an extreme attitude adjustment. "Congressman, he is in the field, it is not unusual."

"This is unacceptable to me," Lauren said. "I have spoken to the Director and he has agreed to let the Congressman, Senator Ellis and I work with Deputy Director McNamara to get a handle on all of this."

"A Senator and Congressman should not run an internal NSA investigation," Barbara McNamara said to her friend.

Mointz picked up Kitt by the collar and said, "Get me every file on Porter's team, now."

Kitt high-tailed it out of the Deputy Director's office to complete Mointz's request. Kitt felt scared to death of the Congressman after this manhandling—not many people weren't.

"Barbara, this goes no further than right here," Lauren said.

"Please, tell me what the hell is going on?" pleaded Barbara.

Davis had run everything on Deputy Director McNamara in both parallels. Lauren, as well as Trent, knew she was above reproach. Lauren explained to the Deputy Director the activities of Senator Nicholas and Victor Caroli.

"Understand why we are involved?" Lauren asked.

"Obviously, there is a leak in here somewhere," Mointz said. "No one needs to know I was there when the two men accosting the Porters were killed. There needs to be a two-part investigation here. Director, you, Lauren and Valmer Ellis need to work on the Senator Nicholas issue and someone needs to go pay a visit to Hungary."

"Who can we send?" Barbara asked.

Lauren grinned, "Barbara, Cristopher is going to go figure out what our friend Victor is up to."

Deputy Director McNamara slumped in her chair and took in a deep breath. "Congressman Mointz is going to Hungary? How can we protect him over there?"

"Barbara, the real question is who is going to protect Eastern Europe from Cristopher?" Lauren said.

"Heaven help us," the Deputy Director declared.

Mointz and Lauren headed over to Ellis's office where Davis studied all the NSA's information on Agent Porter's team. William Kitt personally delivered the material to Senator Ellis at the Capitol.

"Ticked off, eh?" Davis asked Mointz. "Sorry I missed your party yesterday."

Mointz chuckled. "Where did you ever get that idea?"

"Throwing people out of the Deputy Director's office is extremely statesmanlike," Ellis said as he shook his head with a smile.

"Valmer, I would have done it if Cristopher didn't. I do not like this William Kitt," said Lauren.

"My wife makes a good point. Cristopher needs to have an aura about him of being exactly what the public perceives him to be. The intelligence agencies need to fear Cristopher as 9/11 is approaching; they need to fear him when he goes before Congress and America and tells the world it was him and my father-in-law who knew the extremists were coming to kill American citizens."

Ellis raised his eyebrows. "Sometimes I wonder what people did right under our noses in the First Parallel. It not only keeps me up at night, but it also saddens me I personally did not do enough to stop these creteins."

Mointz stood up and paced. "Valmer, you cannot blame yourself. Coming here and doing a retake of our lives makes it easy to second-guess ourselves. I came back at the age of eight and Lauren at eighteen. When I sat in my room or my clubhouse for that matter, I tore my whole life apart, begging God to not let me make the same mistakes twice. I still do not get it right all the time. Having Saudi Arabia, North Korea, and India on my résumé makes me feel my integrity is not what it seems. We are here to save the world and in between, we certainly can make the world a better place. We owe it to the world to meddle."

"Set your eyes on this young girl," Mointz said, holding up a picture of a 15-year-old girl from Hungary addicted to heroin. "How many men has she had to sleep with to eat? We need to keep moving forward and not back and we must keep getting better all the time."

Ellis, Lauren, and Davis knew this type of lecture from Mointz came right from his heart. He believed what he was saying completely. The 15-year-old needed a man to stick up for her and Mointz was the man to do it.

"I have William Kitt monitored and we will know…" Davis started to say as Senator Mark Nicholas was buzzed into the office.

"Senator Nicholas how are…" Ellis tried to get out before Mointz broke the 46-year-old's jaw in several places.

Davis and Lauren quickly stepped in front of Mointz before he finished off the Senator. Ellis called in the CIA's medical team to get the unconscious Senator out of the office.

"Get to your office," Lauren ordered Mointz who could've easily kept hurting Senator Nicholas. He obeyed and stormed away.

"What the hell was that?!" Ellis screamed at Davis as Lauren closed the door after Mointz left.

Davis examined Nicholas who was waking up. "You will live, Senator, only because the Congressman left and did not finish the job."

Ten minutes was all the CIA needed to get their paramedics to bring the Senator to the hospital at Langley.

"Can you tell me why he did that?" Ellis asked.

"He did it because he sees Nicholas as an abuser of children. I knew exactly what he was going to do. It is why I sent for Senator Nicholas to come here," Davis said.

"Jesus honey, what would have happened if Cristopher had killed Nicholas?"

Davis frowned. "Then he would have killed him. We will get to the bottom of this sex-trade issue at the NSA now without Senator Nicholas' help. The main issue is calming down, our boy."

"Who can calm Cristopher down?" Ellis asked.

Davis chuckled.

"What is so funny? Man, you two and the bull who just left here sure confuse the hell out of me at times. Remember, I've not been back as long as you."

"Valmer, Danielle is in his office," Davis said. "I told her to follow him here without him knowing and before he knows it she will have turned him back into a pussycat."

"God, I love you," Mointz said holding his wife.

"Trent said you might need a big hug today and if I could be in the neighborhood, I might be able to help," Danielle said. "I brought you a hot, delicious, coffee."

Mointz kissed her. "Liar, it is ice cold, but I will nuke it in the microwave."

The Congressman set his coffee in the microwave and once the coffee was heated up, Danielle handed it to him and sat in his lap. An aide let Lauren, Davis and Ellis into his office and Lauren cracked up.

"Oh, shit I am in trouble," Mointz said and hugged Danielle tighter.

Danielle smiled. "What did you do now, Mointzie?"

"Blasted Senator Nicholas in the jaw as I figured he would," Davis said. "Why do you think I called you?"

"Cool beans," Danielle said which got her a kiss on the cheek by Mointz.

Mointz grinned boyishly. "Sorry, sorry—I lost my head when I imagined those girls. I promise to behave when I go to Europe."

"Maybe a babysitter will keep you in line," Lauren said.

"No way, your blonde ass is staying here," Mointz said.

Lauren chuckled. "I didn't mean me; smart aleck. I'm thinking more in the lines of a Ronnie than a Lauren."

Mointz shook his head. "I want him to help Chace and Atwood here to protect the Porters. I have someone who can help. Actually, he would love to get into this business, although we might need to get him some credentials. My Rhode Island buddies are more effective than anyone."

Danielle smiled. "Anthony is perfect for the job and I bet he would love to help." Danielle knew that Anthony Riggoli would do anything to help Mointz.

"Anthony Riggoli?" Davis said, then he nodded. "I would have to say, besides Ronnie, he could be your biggest supporter."

"Let me think about this," Lauren said. "You want to take the former Mafia Don's nephew and make him a part of the agency? My guess is you want my father to approve this."

"Sure, why not?" Mointz said. "Let's fight fire with fire."

"Speak," Anthony said into his cell phone at his bakery.

"Anthony, are you sure I am allowed?" Mointz replied.

"Congressman, oh hell, sorry. How are you?"

Mointz always enjoyed uncouthness from Anthony. "No worries, Buddy. I need a big favor."

"Anything you need. You need me to cater an event?"

"Not this time, buddy. I would like you to go with me to Hungary and join the CIA."

Anthony at first laughed and then figured Mointz might be serious when Mointz didn't give him his famous chuckle. "Tell me you are pulling my leg."

"No leg pulling at all. Look out your window. Do you see a limousine?"

"Yes, I see it."

"Hop in and I will see you soon," Mointz told him and hung up.

Mointz had already called Anthony's Uncle Raymond Belvenie to propose his idea for Anthony. Belvenie had never felt prouder of his nephew and even offered to accompany Mointz if Anthony turned him down.

Danielle was listening to the conversation between Anthony and Mointz in her husband's office. She had been searching Davis's web for information on Hungary and Victor Caroli.

"Congressman, Director Philip Gabriel is here," Colleen said over Mointz's intercom.

"Send him in, Colleen, please."

Philip Gabriel, 66 years young, entered Mointz's office and embraced Danielle and kissed her on the cheek.

"I will leave you two alone," she said smiling at the director.

"Why?" Director Gabriel asked with a smile. "He's going to tell you anyway."

"True," Mointz said. "How much trouble am I in?"

"None with me, but it isn't easy to keep this from the President. Lucky for you, Nicholas is a Republican. Please do not punch out any more members of Congress."

"Sorry, Director. I lost my head."

"Lost your head at the NSA today maybe as well?" Danielle giggled and caught herself. "Oops, sorry."

The Director smiled at the beautiful attorney, whom he respected greatly as she was a pit bull in court or in a negotiation. He also admired how the two of them acted like love-struck teenagers.

Mointz grinned like a child with his hand caught in a cookie jar. "I was not sure how to handle the Deputy Director so I went in guns blazing."

"So your solution to the problem is Anthony Riggoli, correct?"

"He is a standup guy, believe me."

"Director, we can trust Anthony no matter what. He won't be afraid to get his hands dirty and we need his fearlessness as trouble finds my husband and most of the time my nephew is involved. Agents Chace and Atwood as well as

General Perry are wonderful, but Cristopher needs a roll-up-your-sleeve type of person when the agents are not around, if you know what I mean."

Gabriel did and the Director felt Danielle had made a great case for Anthony Riggoli. Gabriel had already decided he was a go.

"Danielle, the Congressman is like a son to me and you are like another daughter. The day my daughter met Cristopher was the day she came to life. He backs Lauren, she backs him and henceforth, I back them both unequivocally."

"Thank you, sir," Danielle said with sincere appreciation. "Those words mean a lot to me."

The Director chatted for a bit longer before standing up to say his goodbyes to the Mointzes. Shaking his head with a grin, he left the new Congressman's office, which was as big as a senior member's. Freshman Congressmen are normally squeezed into a small office, except this freshman Congressman was special. No one on the capitol staff wanted to be the one responsible for giving Mointz a small office. Unless you were living under a rock in Washington DC, everyone knew Mointz was going places and to be associated with him meant job security. Director Gabriel trusted his daughter and Mointz to take the mantle from him someday. He would never say it, but he was proud of Mointz for knocking Senator Mark Nicholas out cold. Toughness did not need acknowledgement, but integrity did. Mointz and Lauren both had integrity and the direction to do what it would take to fix this Eastern European problem.

Davis checked out Senator Nicholas, who had just undergone surgery to repair his jaw in the CIA's hospital. Nicholas' wife had learned he needed to leave on a top-secret joint operation with the Pentagon and that the Senator would call her soon. Philip Gabriel was waiting for Davis when he left the Senator's hospital room.

"How is the daft prick?" Gabriel asked.

"He will be eating out of a straw for a year," Davis replied. "Did you see Cristopher?"

"The Congressman is doing well. Danielle visited the office and calmed him down. How she can snap her fingers and have him shut down the anger is amazing," the Director told his son-in-law. "I certainly would never want him to hit me; no wonder the Senator is not saying anything."

Davis added, "He knows he has been outed. Senator Nicholas' eyes kept looking at the door, probably hoping Mointz did not walk through. I am inclined to let Mointz take another run at him."

The Director chuckled. "The Congressman might castrate him. I am having enough problems keeping this quiet."

Davis immediately became nervous. The last thing he wanted was Mointz to have a black mark on his record. Leaks were notorious in the Clinton administration. "Should we worry?"

"Son, do you think I have lost my fastball? Let me remind you I know you and my lovely daughter want Cristopher to sit in the Oval Office. Lauren and Valmer either want my job or want to be Vice President with Cristopher at the head of the ticket. Either way, I am going to protect Cristopher because we created him. The young man holds the key to America's future."

"I agree, Philip," Davis said. Davis's father-in-law had always been impressed with the man who stole the heart of his daughter. Physician, scientist, and friend of Mointz, Davis was his daughter's and Cristopher's rock. Philip Gabriel watched the young doctor run the scientific community with his all.

"My daughter needs to watch herself as well. The two of them love getting into everything they can get their hands on. I turned the both of them into troublemakers and I have to protect my daughter. Mointz has never failed her and I will not tie Cristopher's hands. I owe it to my daughter."

"I understand what you mean, sir. She loves him and she protects him as much as he protects her. My wife and the Congressman had already started their mischievous ways when I met them. I also feel the two of them are my main priority here at the agency. I agree with you, Phillip. They are the future of our nation."

"Then we will help them the best we can at all costs. This country needs politicians who actually practice what they preach. I am proud of the two of them no matter what they do or how they do it."

###

Lauren brought Anthony Riggoli to Mointz's office. Anthony gave Danielle a big bear hug. The new agency employee spent three hours undergoing agency processing. When he passed his firearm target shoot, he received a weapon, a legal one, a CIA identification card, as well as a badge.

"Look at who the United States made a spook. What the effing hell were they thinking?" Mointz declared.

"Excuse me, Congressman; I believe you were the one who requested my expertise."

Mointz got up and shook his friend's hand. "Thank you for joining us."

The wide-necked Riggoli laughed. "I hope you know what you are doing, God bless America. They will give anyone a gun and a badge."

"Anthony, you're going to be an asset," Lauren told him.

"I agree," Danielle added.

The big man blushed. "No worries, ladies. I can play bodyguard."

Mointz smiled as the only protection he knew about was acting as bodyguard for his uncle, Raymond Belvenie.

"Since you are part of our little community, why don't we go over the reason we recruited you?" Lauren suggested.

Riggoli's face reddened when he studied the folder of the young girls Victor Caroli and his organization preyed upon. Lauren knew immediately Mointz had hit a homerun by signing up his goomba buddy.

"Thoughts?" Danielle asked.

"When do we leave for this place?" Anthony asked.

"Tomorrow morning," Mointz replied. "The Sergeant at Arms is supposedly trying to secure my trip, but the Director, your new boss, is taking it over from him. We will have agents with us."

Anthony accompanied the Senator, Congressman, and Attorney Mointz to the Old Ebbitt Grill for dinner. They finished by 9 pm and headed home as Mointz and Anthony planned to be at Langley early in the morning. Their destination was a US Consulate in Hungary.

Chapter Thirty-Three

The House's head of security, the Sergeant at Arms, settled his worries about Mointz's security when CIA Director Gabriel agreed to allow two of his agents on Congressman Mointz's trip. Eight CIA agents joined them on the CIA plane to Hungary with the House security and Anthony Riggoli. Anthony was all ready the 'go-to' guy within the security team about anything related to security. Little did they know, it was the big man's first day on the job and his family had formerly run the Mafia in New England.

Every person on the plane revered Congressman Mointz. Half of the team were women and, agent or not, Mointz's smile was still infectious. All of the agents knew Mointz's real motive of this trip was to uncover the extent of human trafficking in Hungary. They also knew Mointz had at one time belonged to the DIA and was not afraid to dirty his hands. Director Gabriel expected and encouraged them to follow Mointz's lead.

The long flight finally landed in Miskolc, Hungary. The American Consulate in Miskolc was not as big as the one in the capital, but a very functional one for any part of the world. Ambassador John Turcotte met the Congressman at the airport and was impressed that he commanded so much security. Hungary's president was going to meet Mointz in the capital tomorrow night. The President, a supposed reformist, could not wait to meet Mointz for dinner.

The Congressman settled in at the consulate by 11 pm after a quick dinner with the Ambassador. Mointz had a plan and he wanted to get in and out of Hungary quickly. He knocked on Anthony's door as soon as he had changed into jeans, a collared shirt and a black leather jacket.

"Ready to go?" Mointz asked when Anthony opened the door.

"Heisman, are you sure you can just walk out of here with me?"

Mointz chuckled. "I do it all of the time. Quit worrying and let's get out of here."

They moved down the hallway quickly, but not quietly, as nothing about Anthony's big feet were quiet.

"Congressman, where you going?" CIA agent Janet Klein asked.

"A little field trip. Please keep your voice down," said Mointz as CIA Agent Tabatha Nassif peeked her head out of the room she shared with Klein.

"What is going on?" Agent Nassif asked.

Mointz rolled his eyes and used a hand gesture to push them back into the room to join another agent, Dan Collins, from the House Security detail.

"Listen, I am going out to discover for myself what the country is doing about drugs and prostitution. I don't need a big posse of people. Agent Riggoli and I are heading out now. If you follow me, stay out of sight."

The three had no choice but to agree. They followed the Congressman and Riggoli out of the consulate and into a cab. Mointz laughed at Riggoli as he turned to watch the agents scramble to hail down their own transportation.

"I never follow advice," the Congressman said and asked the cabbie in English to take them to the seedy club that Senator Nicholas frequented. Doug Porter's team had visited the club and Mointz hoped they were onto something.

"No shit, you never follow advice," Riggoli remarked.

Mointz shrugged. "People will not recognize me anyways."

"Somehow, I think you are pulling my chain."

"I am unequivocally pulling your chain. People here will know me. I am the face of many American products as well as European goods and services."

"You mean all those fairy clothes you wear make you popular?"

Mointz paid the cab driver and the three agents pulled up right behind them. "Our escorts are here," said Mointz.

Anthony laughed and followed Mointz to the head of the line at the club, which was noisy from the music and as bright as day from the lights, which illuminated the clear nighttime sky.

"Where do you think you are going?" The doorman said in broken English.

"Inside."

The man looked over Mointz and Anthony and softened his brazen attitude. "You are the man from the magazines, the Olympian."

Mointz smiled and handed him a $100 American bill. "Yes, sir. Zsolt Brokai told me to come here if I was ever in the city."

Brokai was the 1988 Olympic champion in gymnastics, who Mointz had a few beers with in Seoul and he had kept in touch with his fellow gold medalist. He was now living in Florida with his family running a gymnastics school.

"Please come in. We proud to have superstar," the man said. He called over a buxom, blonde woman to escort Mointz and Riggoli. The door man also called over a slender, tuxedo-wearing male and told him to give word to the bosses of the new arrival.

"Please sit, Mr. Mointz. We will have champagne brought to you immediately," the hostess said.

"You know who I am?" Mointz asked.

"Yes, of course I do. Every western boutique has your picture in it."

Anthony shook his head when she left. "This is blowing my mind how thousands of miles away from home, people still kiss your ass."

Mointz shrugged and said, "We're getting company."

Several men in suits accompanied a long-haired Russell Crowe look-alike, who Mointz recognized from his dossier. Tibor Papp, former member of the

KGB before settling into a life of drug dealing, selling sex and running nightclubs, introduced himself to the Congressman and sat down at his table. Mointz told him he was meeting the country's President tomorrow and he would like to have some fun tonight.

"What kind of fun are you trying to find?" Papp asked in almost perfect English.

"Maybe some companionship of the female variety. A colleague of mine, Senator Nicholas, told me this was a must stop," Mointz said and handed him an envelope stuffed with $10,000 cash.

"My good friend, Senator Nicholas. You Americans love your young girls," Papp laughed.

Mointz gulped his champagne to hide his disgust. "The two of us would be forever in your debt. Multiple girls are always appreciated."

Mointz's new friend, Tibor Papp, excused himself and instructed one of his men to take Mointz and Anthony to the luxury hotel where they would be well taken care of.

The stretch limousine was full of alcohol and Mointz grabbed a beer. He typed a message to Davis on the way to the hotel on his Palm Pilot.

Trent, on my way to the hotel. I lost a few of my friends somewhere: I would really appreciate a footprint of the hotel. Send me a group to take these girls. Thanks

Mointz

Received. Be careful. Agency personnel will wear windbreakers with "USA Polo" on the back.

Davis

"What the hell is that thing?" Anthony asked in the limousine.

"Fancy Palm Pilot," Mointz answered with a grin. "Excuse me, driver, is there a room already for us?"

"Yes, sir. There is a whole suite," he replied.

The driver made Anthony and Mointz look like dwarves. Once they arrived at the hotel, he opened the doors for Mointz and Riggoli.

"Thank you," said Anthony and handed the man a $100 bill.

Two hotel workers led the Congressman and his friend into the hotel and handed them champagne, which to Mointz seemed to be the drink of choice in Hungary.

One of the employees handed a key to a bellhop, who escorted the two men to a room and handed Mointz the key.

"Jesus, Mary and Joseph," Mointz cried out softly when he opened the door. Six girls, between the ages of twelve and fifteen, Mointz guessed, were about as frightened as one could get

"Heisman, what the effing hell is this?" Anthony asked, calling Mointz by his favorite nickname.

"We make you happy, no?" said a girl about twelve wearing a red dress. She was heavily made up and started to take off her dress.

Mointz stopped her with his hand.

"Mister, if you don't like, I in big trouble," she said.

"Sweetie, I am here to take you to America so you do not have to do this anymore. I want to help all of you. Maybe you can help me."

The young girl was not sure what to think. However, Mointz sat them all down and did his best to explain why he needed some help.

Another girl, about twelve, in a blue dress asked, "We will really not have to do this again?"

"No, honey, never ever," Anthony said softly.

She started to sob, "Thank you, Mister."

Mointz asked if they knew where the men lived and how many men were there. These six sweet frightened girls knew exactly who had captured them, where they kept them and how they enticed young girls with the promise of designer clothes and modeling contracts if they came to live with them.

Several of the girl's captors were arrested in and around the hotel. Mointz called in the team Davis had promised to send to take the girls away. A girl in blue came over and hugged Mointz, crying, just as she was about to follow the female agents.

Every member of Mointz's security detail met him at the nightclub within a half an hour.

"Absolutely not!" Anthony exclaimed, when Mointz told him what he wanted to do. "I am here to protect you."

"They won't shoot me," Mointz declared. He walked right into the club and straight to Papp's table.

"Did you enjoy yourself?" Papp asked standing up to shake his hand.

Mointz quickly shoved his Glock in Papp's mouth and screamed, "Back off, just back off!"

Anthony covered the Congressman as agents flew into the club with guns pulled to cover him. Mointz and Anthony pulled Tibor Papp out of his lair and into a limousine.

Mointz smiled and then punched Papp in the face. "Not so tough now, are you?"

"What are you doing? Do you know who I am?"

Mointz belted him again.

"Tibor," Anthony said. "I don't think he gives a shit who you are."

The limousine driver drove the three men to a heavily guarded compound. Davis had sent over satellite images of the compound. Anthony pointed a gun in Tibor's face and instructed Tibor, who called his bodyguards over the intercom to open the gate. Once they parked, Tibor walked into the house with Mointz and Riggoli.

"We are in," Anthony called into his two-way walkie-talkie.

An elite CIA team popped out of the trunk wearing thermal imaging goggles designed to detect human bodies.

Mointz pushed Papp into an office and shot him with the silenced Glock. Anthony's eyes almost popped out of his head.

"You're in the big leagues now, buddy. I need to do what I need to do," Mointz said.

Power was cut to the compound. Mointz and Anthony put on pairs of night vision goggles and pulled out unlit flashlights.

"Let's finish this," Anthony said.

One by one, Papp's men went down all over the property. Mointz and Anthony eventually found two rooms with almost 50 girls cramped inside.

"My God," Mointz cried. The girls hugged each other when Mointz and Anthony shone their flashlights in the room.

"You can say that again, Heisman." Anthony was too choked up to say another word.

The next morning, Director Gabriel and President Clinton spoke with Mointz before he met with the President of Hungary. Mointz was told to immediately ask the President for permission to arrest Victor Caroli. He agreed with the Congressman. However, he would learn, after Mointz left, the mayor was already dead. Mointz and Anthony had taken him out.

When Mointz left for the United States at 11 pm, it was early in the evening in DC. Danielle sat with Lauren at the Capitol building where several Senators, Congressmen and Congresswomen read the reports from Hungary.

They processed how Senator Nicholas's "friends" in Hungary had offered Mointz female companionship. Republicans and Democrats alike hugged Danielle and Lauren. They read Mointz had called CIA Director Gabriel and followed the trail to a hotel and then to a compound of former KGB operative Tibor Papp. The report stated Mointz, taking his own initiative, had stormed the compound with a few CIA agents and saved over 50 girls aged 15 and under. Lastly, members of Congress were informed Senator Nicholas had been taken into custody and Mointz would be addressing a joint session of the Intelligence Committees of the House and Senate.

Danielle and Lauren sat with a bottle of wine in Georgetown at Danielle's place when Cristopher came in shortly after midnight, D.C. time. Both women hugged him.

"Where is Anthony?" Danielle asked.

"He went to Langley to meet with Trent and Lauren's dad to review every detail. Anthony is eating this up. I am really glad he came."

Danielle poured him some wine and sat next to him by the fire. "The reports I read made me sick."

"How did Congress handle it?" Mointz asked.

Lauren's face turned purple from anger. "Every member wanted to take those girls home. I see you hot-dogged it as usual."

"Don't give me a lecture, please," Mointz said.

Danielle held her husband. He held out his hand and brought Lauren next to him as well. They comforted him the best they could before he walked upstairs to shower and get ready to eat a big pizza pie and some Caesar Salad.

"I should probably leave," Lauren said.

"Why don't you stay? Trent is at Langley tonight and the children are coming home in the morning. He wants you here."

"I wish I never said, 'hot-dogged it.' He just drives me crazy at times."

"Tell me about it," Danielle agreed.

Mointz handled question after question during the joint session. He held nothing back for the first time, rapidly unraveling the investigation into the NSA. William Kitt, although not personally involved in the trafficking, had leaked information about Porter's investigation to Senator Nicholas, who had passed on the information to Victor Caroli. Kitt was arrested and would eventually spend some time as a guest of the Federal Bureau of Prisons. The only thing that would save Kitt a bit was the fact he had not taken money from Nicholas. Papp had paid Nicholas well over the years for information.

"Congressman," Senator Richard Lugar said, "you were with Captain Mahoney when Agent Porter's family was under duress, correct?"

"Yes, Senator. We saved the Porter family."

"Care to give us more details on how you saved them?" Senator Feinstein asked.

"No, ma'am," Mointz said with a smile and the California Senator got the point.

"Congressman, who authorized you to enter a compound of foreign citizens and start a shoot-out?" Senator Edwards asked.

"Me," Mointz said.

"Again, on whose authority?" Edwards asked.

"And I will repeat it again. Mine, as a private citizen."

Mointz stared down the future Democratic Vice Presidential nominee. Edwards learned that Mointz was not going to kowtow to the senator. "I gave him the authority," Director Gabriel said. "On the President's order, by the way. The Congressman is still a member of the DIA and if Congressman Mointz won't say it I will; he stopped being a politician and started being what he always is—a hero. What would you have done?"

Edwards said nothing further.

"Congressman, is this going to be an issue we need to waste valuable resources on?" Senator Feinstein asked.

"Would you want your daughter to be a sex slave because of valuable resources?"

"Well, I…"

"Exactly, Senator," Mointz said.

"I, for one, believe you are not only courageous, but a hero. Your quick thinking saved these girls from a grotesque situation. Congress needs more people like you," Senator Ellis said, wishing he could tell them Mointz had broken Nicholas' jaw.

"I second that," Senator Lugar added. "Congress needs more heroes."

"Add me to the list of people who believe the Congressman is a hero," said Speaker Hastert.

Danielle, who represented Mointz and Ronnie legally at the hearing, smiled as Doug Porter lavished praise on both her husband and son. Deputy Director McNamara promoted Porter to William Kitts' position to help to get a handle on Senator Nicholas. The Porters were staying in a secure location, while they rebuilt their home. They felt extreme gratitude to the Congressman and his family for saving them.

Senator Gabriel, to no one's surprise, spoke glowingly about the mission to the committees. Lauren's father and Barbara McNamara also praised Mointz. McNamara could not wrap her head around how Mointz had wasted no time to find a positive solution.

"Last question, Congressman; should we expect this type of action from you again?" Senator Lugar asked. "No offense, sir, but you have been in office only a month."

"I hope not, Senator. It would be an effing nuisance."

Chapter Thirty-Four

September 10, 2001

"Mr. President, I am positive on this," Congressman Mointz told President Bush. "Our towers are going to go down if we do not act."

"I agree," 68-year-old Director Gabriel said. "The Congressman has some good intel on this."

"Director, Congressman Mointz, I understand, but do you think catching them in the act is the way to go?" President Bush asked.

Mr. President, we need to show the American people this is going to be a terrible day barely avoided," Senator Ellis said.

Lauren gave a synopsis of the dangers about to be faced by Americans and won over Vice President Cheney and the President.

"Sir, we need agents on planes starting at midnight, especially four specific flights," said Lauren.

"It baffles me how Congressman Mointz, Captain Mahoney and Anthony Riggoli tracked this down. We only have half a day before this happens," the President said. "I am supposed to read a book to children tomorrow; we'll have to cancel."

"Mr. President, you should go. I believe it is best we do not cancel anything," Director Gabriel declared.

"Get it done," the President ordered and with that the meeting was over.

Lauren, Ellis, Director Gabriel and Mointz met Davis and Danielle at Langley. Ronnie and Anthony were about to leave for Boston to get ready for Flight 11 tomorrow. Several teams were assigned to specific flights.

"All of you are sure we have this right?" Director Gabriel asked. "I realize that all of you have researched this for six months, but you have to be sure we have every base covered."

"We do, Director. I bet my reputation on it," Mointz said, knowing the hijackers were watched and did exactly what they had done in the First Parallel.

"Lauren?"

"Yes, Father."

"Trent?"

"100 percent?"

"Ronnie?"

"Absolutely."

"Valmer?"

"No doubt in my mind."

"Danielle, Gennifer?"

They both nodded.

"Anthony?"

"No question, sir."

They all affirmed. The director cleared his throat and said, "Then, God bless you all, but I need to make an adjustment. Cristopher will not be on a plane. I spoke to the President and he wants you to break news of the attack to the public."

"Why me?" Mointz asked.

"It is your handiwork that discovered this event and with you informing the agency and NSA Director Hayden providing the details, we've put security in place and the reward is that you get to break the news."

Mointz had a feeling someone named Davis had stabbed him in the back. "Fine, I will do as you say."

"Can someone tell me what my husband drank today," Danielle asked. "Did he say 'fine?'"

Director Gabriel smiled. "America needs to be convinced of the seriousness of this. My daughter and I spent time talking about it over the last day or two. I believe Cristopher will best serve the nation this way. Ronnie and Anthony, Godspeed to you."

Lauren nodded at her father. "Congressman, thank you for being a voice of reason and bringing this attack to light."

"Hmmph," Mointz said. "It is what it is."

Davis stayed at Langley while Ronnie and Anthony headed to Boston after the meeting. Director Gabriel and Ellis headed to The White House to work on the next day's action plan together with NSA Director Hayden. Mointz, Danielle, Lauren, and Gennifer stopped by the Mointzes' to eat pizza and watch videos of 9/11 in the First Parallel.

Danielle sat stunned at the images on the television and squeezed her husband's hand tightly. "This video is one of the most heartbreaking things I have ever seen."

###

A hijacker went up to the cockpit, box cutter in hand, only to find Ronnie Mahoney waiting with gun in hand. Mahoney shot the hijacker as Anthony and the rest of the team took down the rest of the hijackers. The passengers' screams turned to cheers when the agents flashed badges and comforted passengers.

Passengers immediately recognized Ronnie, who announced on the intercom that planes had carried security personnel over the last year.

Flight 11 was diverted to LaGuardia Airport and the other flights which went down in the First Parallel were also diverted. All pilots in the sky brought their birds to the ground.

"He called it, didn't he?" Anthony asked Ronnie, as they cleared out the first-class cabin and converted it into a makeshift jail.

Anthony smiled, believing Mointz could predict the future. *Little did he know he could*, Ronnie thought.

"Cristopher understands terrorists and as a leader, not only is he predicting the future, he's changing it," said Ronnie.

"I'll say. What a genius!"

"You only feel that way because he made you an agent."

One of the hijackers complained about being cramped and Ronnie smacked him in the back of the head.

The pilot announced the initial descent into LaGuardia. After securing the plane at the gate, authorities and rescue personnel entered the cabin.

Rudy Giuliani calmly shut down the city and amazingly did so after he received the call from Congressman Mointz. The Mayor did not realize the scale of the operation until Mointz started his news conference at the Capitol.

Congressman Mointz stepped up to the podium in the Capitol's media room with Philip Gabriel and NSA's Director, Lieutenant General Michael V. Hayden, as well as politicians from both parties.

"Good morning; President Bush has asked me to deliver a news update on the attempted hijackings of American commercial aircraft this morning. All

flights in the air right now are being diverted to their emergency locations. I can confirm radical extremists from the Middle East attacked four flights, two from Boston, one from Newark and one from Washington, D.C.; however, those attempted hijackings were foiled.

A few weeks ago, I received a copy of a security alert from the CIA and as a member of the Intelligence Committee, I took it seriously. I noticed some similarities to chatter before the election. I contacted Directors Gabriel and Hayden as well as the President. Senators Ellis and Gabriel notified the Senate Intelligence Committee and, in a joint effort, put emergency funding in place to ensure the safety of the United States.

President Bush executed an order to add marshals to flights. I have some information to share from two of the flights where hijackers have been interrogated.

The hijackers had planned to take Flight 11 from Boston hostage and fly it into the North Tower of the World Trade Center and United Airlines Flight 175 into the South Tower. The hijackers, who have given up their plan, stated the two other flights would have crashed into The White House and the Pentagon.

As the President is about to land back at Andrews Air Force Base, let me make it clear that we have secured every flight now in the air. The President will decide how to move forward...

Ladies and gentlemen, an extremist group linked to a man named Osama Bin Laden tried to bring destruction to the United States as never seen before. This action is a declaration of war. Over the next day or two, there will be anger and sadness all over the world. I am pleading for calm. Remember, extremists linked to Saudi Arabian leader named Osama Bin Laden committed these acts, not Muslims all over the world. We know this extremist leader took part in the attempted bombing of the USS Cole. The United States will not bow down to terrorists; these actions will not be swept under the rug; we will not have our resolve shaken and we will not tolerate these acts of violence."

Congressman Mointz did not answer any questions. An immediate session was called in both the House and the Senate's Intelligence Committees, where Director Gabriel and NSA Director Hayden filled in the members of Congress; the Vice President and the President joined in via teleconference.

"Congressman Mointz, you are to be acknowledged for picking up on this. Well done," the President proclaimed.

###

Princess Amina greeted the Congressman with a kiss when he entered the palace. She had arranged for private time for the two of them this morning.

"God, I missed you," Amina said as she rolled off Mointz in bed.

"Gave up the cigarettes, I see," Mointz said with smile.

"I had to. This beautiful face does not need wrinkles."

"My wrinkles come from your co-patriots. Amina, this is a very serious matter."

She kissed him and said, "I know you are here for a reason and it isn't just to help me get off, although it is a major benefit for me. What does the President ask of us?"

"There is a war coming in Afghanistan. The Taliban have taken over the political scene there and they have lofty goals. I am worried this could spill over into the rest of the Arab world."

"Who else believes this?" Amina asked.

"Everyone in the know."

Mointz's statement worried Amina. She appreciated how he always told it to her straight. Amina had as much, if not more, influence now than in the past.

"Can you help me talk to my brother about this? He respects you greatly."

"Amina, Kareem is afraid of me. I want you to go to your father for his support."

"My brother and you can speak to him."

He shook his head 'no.' "All three of us will speak to the King. No way will I allow you to stay in the background. Time to step up to the plate."

"I…can't…you know that."

"No, I don't know it. We buy your oil, we keep you safe and no longer am I going to pretend I don't seek your counsel. Sorry, dear, but you have to step up, here and now."

Amina pulled the covers over her head. She was actually petrified of the plan Mointz was pushing. "Please, this is not a good thing."

Mointz smiled. "C'mon. I promise to protect you."

The Princess snuggled next to him. "A promise is only as good as the person behind it. I will trust you. Don't let me down, please."

"Have I ever let you down?" Mointz asked. A tear rolled down Amina's cheek.

"You cannot love me freely. I understand it, but it does not mean it doesn't hurt to the bone. Danielle has you and your heart. There might be a place for me in it, maybe."

Congressman Mointz could feel her pain. "Amina, you have a big place in my heart. Unfortunately, our worlds are not one. We are both married and have many responsibilities to our respective nations. It does not mean I do not love you back or that you are not in my thoughts."

Mointz was stretching it big time, but she did not need to know.

"Really?" Amina asked.

"Yes my love, really."

Amina smiled and Mointz knew in her mind and heart she was making love to him. He had to keep her strong in mind and heart if he was to get the Saudis to play ball better than they did in the First Parallel.

Mointz won over the King with his strong, powerful words and demeanor. Mointz complimented Princess Amina and Prince Kareem profusely. The King agreed with all of Mointz's requests.

Prince Kareem and Princess Amina spent the rest of the afternoon with Mointz making back channel calls. The three of them accomplished exactly what the United States needed.

"Thankfully, your father readily agreed to allow us to use our bases here for the attack."

"Cristopher, he is worried about the Taliban taking over the kingdom. My father has to believe in you," Prince Kareem said.

"We all believe in you. Kareem and I watched your press conferences and we are so proud to be called your friend," Amina said.

They ate dinner together and when they finished, Kareem retired to his quarters. He promised to visit Mointz in DC soon. Amina changed into something more comfortable. A purple lace negligee had the Princess feeling sexy. She sat down on Mointz's lap and kissed him passionately. Just as Mointz was getting her out of her negligée, alarms went off in the palace.

"What the hell is that?" Mointz asked.

"Come, come" she screamed and he followed her into the bedroom. "The palace security has been breached."

"Uh, what does it mean?" asked Mointz. "Ah, shit," he said and opened his security compartment in his suitcase.

"How did you get weapons in here?" Amina said looking at the weapons.

Mointz kissed her. "Shh, Princess. Where is your father?"

Amina was too stunned to speak and Mointz threw her clothes at her and smiled, telling her to get dressed.

Prince Kareem came flying into the bedroom winded. Mointz noticed his forehead was bleeding.

"There are several commandos running around," Kareem said. My father is in the downstairs bunker. I don't think there are enough guards."

Mointz pulled out his BlackBerry and sent a text to Davis and Lauren about the situation before pulling on his sneaker boots and his favorite college team's hat, backwards.

"The two of you have two options: option one is you can stay here or you could follow me. I suggest you lock yourselves in the bathroom and stay here," said Mointz. "Kareem, are you all right?"

He nodded. "Please take us with you. I ran into a door and cut myself."

Mointz almost laughed, but the situation was a serious one. He knew Amina and her brother would follow him. Kareem was, if nothing, a coward.

"Fine. However, when I say jump, you say 'how high?' Understand? I will get us out of this and save your father."

Mointz's phone rang. It was Davis. The Congressman quickly filled Davis in on the situation.

"How could this have happened?" Mointz asked Davis on the phone.

"I don't know. I would guess the people who had ties to Kareem acted on their own," Davis replied.

"Great!" Mointz exclaimed. "Get me some help will you, please?"

"Okay, okay. I'll do what I can. I promise," Davis said.

They hung up and Mointz handed Amina and Kareem each a nine millimeter handgun.

"Shoot straight, love," Mointz said. Within a second, two commandos burst through the door of Mointz's suite.

"Shhh, get in the bathroom. I will take care of this," Mointz shouted.

Mointz waited for the men to get close and then he fired his silenced Glock into the two of them, killing them instantly. Mointz then took their US government-issued M-4's.

At that moment, the lights in the palace went off. Mointz pulled out a pair of night vision googles from his bag. He took the dead men's night vision goggles and handed them to the Prince and Princess.

"They are dead, aren't they?" Amina asked.

"No sweetie. They are just incredibly sleepy."

Prince Kareem stared at the two Arab men and Mointz gave him a little shove to get him into the game. Mointz asked them to follow him. The Prince described the locations of his father's bunker and two panic rooms. Mointz decided to hide the Prince and Princess in the closest panic room and finish off these extremists.

Mointz led the way out of the suite and started down a hallway the size of a football field. Three commandos jumped out of a small sitting room in front of them and Mointz gunned them down instantly.

"Jesus, help us," Amina cried out.

"Now you pray to Jesus?"

"I can use all the help I can get," she replied.

"Kareem, still with us?" He asked his friend.

The Prince nodded and muttered something inaudible. Amina whispered to Mointz the directions to a panic room.

Mointz threw the Prince and Princess behind him when he heard footsteps. He gunned down two more men.

"Where the hell are all of your guards?" Mointz asked.

"They are dead. Everyone has to be dead," Amina said.

"Lucky for the two of you, I am not. So we have a chance."

Mointz gunned down two more men before they reached the royal offices. Bodies lay everywhere as the extremists seemed to have slaughtered everyone in their path. The two royals and the American Congressman made it to the panic room.

"Get in there," Mointz said.

"Save our father, please," Kareem begged.

"The two of you will owe me beer for life, but I will not let you down."

Kareem closed the door and Mointz slid the panel closed.

The palace was the size of the Pentagon. Mointz put in one of the Bluetooth ear pieces Davis had given him. He needed to figure out his location in this monstrosity before he called Davis.

"Status," Davis cried out into the phone.

"With all apologies to Mel Brooks, it is not good to be the King right now. I just put the Prince and Princess in a panic room. The lights are out and I have shot several men. Oh, yeah. One more thing, I have to find the King in some bunker and I really don't know where it is."

"Hold on, the Princess called into The White House and they patched her in to us," Davis said and conferenced in Amina. She explained that there was an emergency phone in the panic room. With Davis in The White House situation room full of government officials, there was a panic on both sides of the line.

Mointz fired an M4 into four men, dropping them instantly as he tried to reach the King. Amina and Kareem gave him directions to a bunker in a room adjacent to the King's office.

"I can't see a thing off the cameras in the palace," Davis said. "The cameras are not IP and we need to get the feed."

"Figures, right? This place is in trouble. I do not have a good feeling about this."

"Cristopher, there is a fire fight on the grounds. There is no one to get there for another hour. You are it, my friend. Go get into a panic room," General Walter Perry ordered.

"Yes, dammit," Lauren said.

"Hi, Blondie. Where the hell did you come from?"

"Listen, Mointz, I was here. Amina, is he close to a panic room?"

"Yes, there is one…"

Mointz interrupted. "The King is in danger. Get me eyes somehow, Trent, or we are all dead."

Several Saudi Royal Guards outside the palace managed to uplink a feed. Watching carefully, Davis calculated only twelve terrorists left inside. Amina was taken off-line. Ronnie, as well as Anthony, joined Davis and Lauren with the group in the room.

"Nice outfit," Ronnie said. Mointz gave him the middle finger salute into the camera.

"Cristopher, there is a weapon stash about 100 yards to the left of you," Davis said. He spoke over the phone to one of the King's guards, who was out on a holiday.

"Okay, boss," said Mointz.

Mointz grabbed what he needed. He popped a grenade into the King's office, instantly putting down four commandos.

"Nice," Anthony said.

"Four down and eight to go," Lauren said. "They are trying to blast their way into the King. Be ready; three heading your way in an all-out sprint."

Mointz lay on the floor and fired. All three were put out of commission permanently.

"Any treaty with the Saudis will be abrogated if it is not to our advantage. Tell Rummy I have his bases available."

The Secretary of Defense chuckled. "Rummy hears you, son."

"Oh, sorry, sir," Mointz said, embarrassed. "Only five left, correct?"

"Yes, buddy," Ronnie replied. "FYI, your wife is here. We were eating dinner together. Your mum and dad have the girls."

"Trent, the video feed," Mointz said in a panic.

"Don't worry, Mointzie," Lauren interrupted. "I have it ready to get cut and I mentioned it to your friend."

"What is wrong?" Danielle asked nervously as she looked at the-70 inch flat screen on the wall to see her husband in shorts, a Redskins T-shirt, and night vision goggles holding an M-16.

"Hi babe," Mointz whispered.

"Get the hell out of there," she screamed.

"No worries love, I am saving the King."

Lauren explained to Danielle what was going on as Mointz made his way to the entrance of the King's bunker room. Mointz pulled two grenade pins and threw the grenades into the bunker's entrance way, hopefully turning the remaining commandos into human confetti. Bodies lay all over the place. There was no movement.

"Anyone left?" Mointz asked.

"The President is here, watching this," Davis said.

Mointz chuckled and waved into the camera.

"Stop being a wanker," Danielle yelled at him. "Pay attention."

"Mointz!" Lauren screamed.

Mointz turned on a dime as one of the terrorists aimed a gun at him. The terrorist went down as Mointz shot him between the eyes.

"I saw it," he said and checked the other four bodies. Mointz could not believe someone had survived the blast. "All clear."

"Jesus, you scared me," Danielle said.

"Army Rangers are on the way. Do not shoot. I repeat, do not shoot," said General Perry.

"No shooting, check," Mointz said.

"Congressman Mointz," President Bush said.

"Sir, how are you?"

"Nice job, Congressman. Nice job," the President said as an emergency power supply kicked in.

"Hello, honey," Mointz said. "Sorry, Mr. President. She is cuter."

President Bush chuckled. "Be safe coming home, Congressman."

The American Rangers reached Mointz and he signed off on the audio and video feed. The Rangers with the Royal Guards had finally made it into the palace and helped extract the King from his bunker. Mointz retrieved Amina and Kareem from the panic room. They both hugged him and would not let go.

"Thank you, thank you, thank you," Amina said kissing him all over his face.

"Ummm, Kareem, you can let go now," Mointz begged.

###

The King did not stop praising Mointz for saving his life and the lives of his children. Amina wanted to leave the palace for the night and she asked her father if Kareem and she could take Mointz to their resort home in the south of France while the King got his house and his generals in order. Amina promised to keep in touch with her father by phone. The King was only too happy to oblige his beautiful daughter. He immediately summoned a jet for their flight.

Mointz convinced the Princess that she would have to "settle" for his jet and when the agency's bird was in the air, Mointz nodded off as Amina snuggled with him. She couldn't care less what her brother thought as they flew to France.

"He saved the kingdom from a coup d'état," Kareem whispered.

"Mointz is the man. We owe him not just our lives, but we also owe it to him to help him as long as we have air in our lungs."

"You love him, don't you?"

"Who wouldn't? We are both not available and it will never change."

"Sorry, sister," Kareem said. He knew she loved Mointz and her own husband was no American hero.

Amina spent the next 24 hours in bed with Mointz before he headed home to deal with America's problems.

Mointz sat on the bed and pulled Amina into his lap after he had packed for home. "Why so blue?"

She cried and buried her face into his chest. "I can't be with you again this way. You are about to have your third child and I am going to have to get over this part of our relationship. I cannot have children, as you know, because of damaged fallopian tubes, but my husband and I will conceive through invitro fertilization at your Mayo Clinic this summer. I have not been with him since I met you and I never will be with him again."

Mointz held her tight. He was relieved a bit, but his heart went out to the Princess. Amina, in another time or parallel, would have been his, Mointz felt, and he was sure they would have made a go of it. She was beautiful, intelligent, funny and sexual. In her, was a woman who would adore a man like Mointz.

"I will always be a shoulder to cry on and you can get me anytime, you know that."

Mointz kissed her tears and then gave Amina an image to keep ingrained in her mind for the rest of her life. Amina felt Mointz inside her like never before and as he brought her to climax, he held her tightly.

"I love you, Mointz," she told him, believing the love of her life had touched her in this manner for the last time.

Chapter Thirty-Five

Danielle met her husband as he walked off the jet at Andrews Air Force Base. Lauren and Vice President Cheney accompanied her to welcome home the Congressman. Mointz hugged his wife and Lauren before shaking hands with the Vice President. Lauren loved the fact he always kept his priorities straight.

"Incredible job, son. I am so proud of you," the Vice President said as they walked to an awaiting convoy.

"King Fahd has professed undying support for us, thanks to you, Congressman. This was a big win for America on so many fronts," Lauren told him, getting into a limousine with Mrs. Mointz.

The Vice President shook Mointz's hand one more time before leaving for an overseas trip to meet with allies in Europe now that Saudi Arabia trumpeted a strong alliance with America.

"Can you imagine no more pushback from the Saudis and their allies? This is unprecedented. You did it!" Lauren said as Mointz entered the car.

"We all did it," Mointz replied and took his wife's hand.

"So not true, my friend. The Saudis are all on you. The Prince and Princess feel like you are one of their family," said Lauren.

"She has been so nice to the girls. I only met her a couple of times, but Princess Amina seems to be a sweetheart."

"She has her moments."

Lauren smiled. "Your parents are here to watch the children. They promised to bring them to the office later. We have hearings today that need us."

"I am going to the office as we have to get ready for several lawsuits at the airlines for ignoring safety," Danielle said. "Mointzie, do not roll your eyes at me. They do not deserve to get away scot-free. If you did not stop these events, imagine the lives lost. It would have been the fault of the airlines and lackadaisical security at the airports." She immediately covered her mouth, forgetting they had already lived the experience.

"No, you go, girl," Lauren said.

"I agree with Lauren," said Mointz. "Honey, you are absolutely correct."

"Sweetie, you filed the bill to overhaul airport security and no one listened," said Danielle.

"I put it in an appropriations bill I knew would fail and it did."

Danielle handed him the 'Wall Street Journal' from this morning that Colleen had left on his desk. The headline had been strategically placed across the top of the page.

Congressman Mointz filed a bill to strengthen airline and airport security, only to be denied by the administration in 1999.

"They could have used a better picture. My face looks like I'm getting goosed in my rear end."

Danielle and Lauren laughed as the limousine pulled up to his office. Reporters clamored outside in full force and Mointz, always the media darling, answered all of the questions before entering the office. Lauren and Danielle giggled as the press followed Mointz into the building as the limousine drove away.

Chapter Thirty-Six

January 2006

"Grandma Rose was the biggest backer anyone ever had. She taught my mother how to love a child and how to be a mother and grandmother," said Congressman Mointz in Barrington's Saint Patrick's church as he eulogized his beloved grandmother. "My three daughters, Rosie, Ashley, and Marissa, as well as my niece Aleixa and our extended families' little ones, loved to listen to Grandma's Irish lullabies."

"My beautiful wife, Danielle, is about to give birth to our first son, Thomas, in February. My mum and Danielle will sing lullabies with Grandma's love."

Mointz finished his eulogy and sat down in the first pew. Father O'Brien resumed the mass. The past four years had continued to propel Congressman Mointz forward as a force to be reckoned with in American politics. Seanie had married his supermodel girlfriend, Holly, and Kathy, Colleen and Aleixa were happy and healthy, loving life.

Lauren and Davis, as well as their babies, Keith and, Kevin had been full of love and smiles over the last three years as had Gennifer, Ronnie, and their three children. Friends and family had gathered here to say "goodbye" to Grandma Rose.

The Madeira hosted the mercy meal for Grandma. Sadness veiled the Congressman's face until his baby girl, Marissa, sat in his lap and hugged her father. Marissa was one hundred per cent Mointz—even more of a little diablo and more mischievous than her older sisters.

Rosie Marie, Ashley Megan, and Heidi Lynn joined their parents and grandparents at the table, cheering up the mourners easily.

"Dad, someone told me you are running for Senator," Rosie Marie asked.

Mointz smiled. "Maybe, sweetie. Why?"

"Senator Mointz," Lauren called out and took Cristopher and Danielle by the hand. "The cat is out of the bag."

Chapter Thirty-Seven

July 2, 2006

Baby Thomas turned six months-old and both his parents were proud as punch at his christening in St. Patrick's church. Danielle announced she was pregnant again, shocking her close friends and family.

The Madeira catered a big party at the Mointzes and the Senate candidate enjoyed the day with family and friends at the beach house. The polls had Mointz at almost 90% and the Democrats could not field a candidate to run against him.

Davis handed his friend a cold frosty beverage and slapped him on the back. "Ready to face the Russians and Chinese?"

"All these months we have been investigating al-Qaeda links and I can finally fix this," Mointz said as Ronnie walked over.

"What are we talking about?" Ronnie asked.

"Cristopher's trip to China and Russia."

"Oh shit. I will come back later," Ronnie said.

Mointz chuckled. "Man, you are going with me. Pay attention."

Ronnie more than paid attention to this al-Qaeda crisis. As head of the Naval Criminal Investigation Service, Ronnie had his hand in all Mointz's affairs.

"So what is going on?" Ellis asked. "My wife is chatting with Danielle and Lauren somewhere."

"We are discussing our trip," Mointz said

"Yikes," Ellis said. "That is not good; this is a party."

"I know. The Princess was in DC last week and had nothing new for us. We are about to embark on an odyssey where we might not return the same way we went in," Mointz said.

"My man here is getting too much sun," Ronnie said. "Putin and Hu Jintao love you."

Davis chuckled. "If you say so. I bet they love Danielle more, though. Her popularity has spiked in China. When she represented China against the International Olympic Committee, she defended holding the Olympics in Beijing."

"She cannot believe she has to go to China with you," Ellis said laughing.

"My wife cannot wait for this trip. Her only drawback is spending a week away from Marissa and Thomas," Mointz stated. "I will not be in any shootouts, believe me."

"My mom only passed away last year, if you go by the First Parallel, in her name only. In reality, she is more alive, vibrant and wonderful this time around. Nobody puts Danielle in the corner."

"Nice 'Dirty Dancing' reference," said Davis.

"Well, Jennifer Gray cleared channels to get you in, Ronnie."

"She did?" Ellis asked.

"Danielle convinced the Chinese her nephew, while head of NCIS, is too close to Mointz and Danielle to leave home," Davis said.

Ellis was shocked. "Really, she is that popular?"

"We had manipulated the Olympic Committee to believe China was not ready for the games and should look elsewhere. Mointz's popularity and Danielle's brilliant idea to sue to help the Chinese has made her indeed more popular than Mointz, with the Chinese officials at least," Davis said. "Lauren can't believe it."

"What about Russia? Do we have an angle there?" Ellis asked.

"It is all about soccer, Valmer. The girls are going to play soccer in Russia, while I sit down with Vova. My beautiful girls obtain an education and I pick Vova's brain—win-win. Gennifer is going to go with Heidi Lynn and my Mum will babysit the twins. We are bringing Aleixa. My sister only let me take Aleixa because Danielle is going."

Lauren and Genny joined the men, glasses of champagne in hand to toast the baby's christening. They loved passing out champagne at the Mointzes's expense and Mointz filled glasses to the brim around the party.

Mointz gave a wonderful 'Grandpa Leo' toast. The day started out with the christening and ended as a celebration of life.

"How hard do we press the Chinese?" Lauren asked.

Mointz shrugged. "We'll have to find a person who is willing to work with us, I have ideas."

Immediately Lauren's mind thought of about six women he could use, but Danielle was going so that idea wouldn't work.

"I know who you are going to get," said Danielle.

Mointz smiled. "One of the team statisticians for the football program at Brown. He and his father are members of the Chinese hierarchy. We have always kept in touch over the years. Fu cannot wait to see me again."

"I love him," Danielle declared. "He was so cute and always happy at the games. What do you think he can do?"

"Fu could guide us in the right direction, at least. We have followed his online chatter for years. He hopes to make China an open and free society like the good old US of A." Mointz said.

"Tell me you and my husband will not kidnap Fu," Danielle remarked directly to Lauren.

"Nothing like that, right, Lauren? My wife here does not believe in kidnapping people."

Danielle giggled, "Thank you for respecting my wishes."

Mointz e-mailed Fu Wong from the plane on their way to China. Lauren had convinced Mointz she should accompany them and Danielle agreed. Rose Marie, Ashley Megan, Heidi Lynn and Aleixa joined the Congressman, the Senator and Danielle as did Gennifer and Ronnie. The Secret Service planted a few friends on the 777-200LR for security purposes as the President took Mointz and Danielle's security seriously.

"Our first trip without worry," Mointz said.

"It had better be," Danielle remarked and then smiled at her husband and kissed him.

Rosie Marie looked at her father with a big grin. He immediately knew she was up to no good.

"Father, Ashley Megan and I have been told Chinese food in China is not the same as Chinese food at home. This concerns us greatly."

"Yes, Father. We need proper nutrition for our soccer all-star games in Russia."

"What do you think, Heidi? How about your and Aleixa's nutrition?"

Heidi and Aleixa giggled.

"No way can you blame me for trying to convince you to get us a private chef," said Ashley Megan.

"Thank you for agreeing, Dad. Mother said the embassy chef would be glad to help," Rosie said.

"Rose Marie!" Danielle exclaimed. She was always Rose Marie when she was in trouble. "I do not believe I told you to approach your father like this, nor did I say you would have a private chef. What I said was..."

Mointz took his wife's hand and interrupted his wife. "I would imagine you said that if the food was not up to speed, the embassy chef would not let them starve."

Danielle giggled. "Nothing gets by you, Congressman."

"Exactly right, Attorney Mointz," Mointz replied.

"Hey, Auntie, how come nothing gets by Uncle?" Heidi Lynn asked her true grandmother. Heidi Lynn loved Danielle; Heidi Lynn and Danielle were the spitting image of each other.

"Yeah mom. What gives?" Ashley Meg asked.

"Let me take this," Gennifer said. "Kids, the adults will always be a step ahead of you, based on the fact we all have done the same things you all try to pull on your father. Ashley, he just happens to have more experience than all of us combined."

"I give credence to what you say," Ronnie added.

"Well, it stinks," Rosie proclaimed. "This is going to take more of an effort on our part."

A couple of agents on the plane laughed. They could not help themselves as the girls were too bright for their own good.

The girls went back and forth with the adults for a few hours before they finally settled down with their laptops. Gennifer and Ronnie watched a video of the movie 'The Patriot' starring Mel Gibson before his major meltdown. Mointz and Danielle snuck into the office on the private plane while Lauren snored away.

"Mile-high club?" Mointz begged as he took Danielle in his arms and nibbled at her neck.

"Down, big boy," Danielle replied giggling. "The kids could come in."

Mointz frowned. "Okay, rain check then?"

She giggled again. "Do I ever say 'no?'"

Mointz smiled. "You are saying 'no' now."

"Good point," she said and locked the door.

Danielle giggled the whole time they made love and when they dressed, Danielle sat on the desk and pulled her husband close to her. "Tell me what is going on in your mind about the 2008 election."

"Politics, what a buzz kill. I am going to run for Vice President. I believe I can do so much as Vice President in eight years because I will have free reign to travel the world. Whoever wins the Republican nomination will be a big help to us. I can swing my support to anyone."

"What do Trent, Lauren and Valmer think?"

"They are all over the place and go back and forth all the time. I will tell them what I decide soon enough."

She smiled and looked into her husband's eyes. "Why wait to share?"

"Because I might just have to run and fix this now. Sweetie, if I find out on this trip the Chinese and Russians do not want to play nice in the sandbox, I will run and Lauren after me. Lauren needs to be President in 2024 and re-elected in 2028 so our children can take over down the line."

"Honey, this is really brilliant. Who decides what route to take?"

"Ronnie, you and I will discuss it with Trent, Lauren, and Valmer."

"Why does this seem all too easy? What am I missing in all of this?"

"The world is one cesspool of negativity against the good. Believe me, there are jihadists and extremists all over the place. We have plenty of bad guys to stop before we can all breathe easy. World peace will be obtained when countries can all participate in a world economy where everyone plays a part, not just select countries. Honey, Trent and I spend hours talking about this. The world is not what it was when we first came back. I certainly was not what I call 'a good person' in the First, I was…" Mointz said with his voice cracking, as he could barely breathe.

Danielle hugged him. "Stop, sweetie. You are so much a part of what is good in the world. The children, and for that matter the world, loves you and believes in you."

Mointz held her tightly. "If you believe in me, then I know things will be well. I hate this gig. I hate what I have done and still have to do and I hate not being the man I am portrayed to be."

"Stop it! Darn you!" Danielle proclaimed and slammed her hand on the desk. "The world wouldn't be in such a good position without you busting your ass to keep it where it is. F-off, Mointzie, and finish this." Her smile melted him.

He smiled back. "Okay, love. I hear you."

Beijing International Airport rolled out the red carpet for the Mointz family and friends. The Chinese Premier, Hu Jintao, and Mointz's friend, Fu Wong, greeted them upon their arrival. A band played the Olympic theme song of the 1988 games in Mointz's honor as people waved Chinese and American flags. United States Ambassador Clark Randt greeted Danielle, Lauren and Mointz before introducing the Mointz family to the Premier.

"Senator Gabriel, Congressman Mointz, I am honored to welcome you to the People's Republic of China," the Premier told them.

"The reception we have had here today is a memory which will last a lifetime," said Danielle.

Mointz shook hands with the Premier and embraced Fu Wong.

"So nice to see you, Mr. Heisman," Wong said.

"I could not be happier to be acquainted with you, my friend," Mointz announced.

Danielle hugged the former Brown statistician and, after sharing some pleasantries, the group left for the Premier's home for lunch.

Mointz whispered into his giggling girl's ears.

"Dad, only you could think like that," Rosie told her father as they entered one of the armored limousines.

"Can I get the big eyeballs?" Ashley asked.

"Me too, Uncle," Aleixa cried out.

"Me too, what?" Danielle asked, knowing something her husband had said had the four girls laughing out loud.

"Dad said we were having snake eyeballs for lunch," Rosie told her mother.

"Cristopher, you are so bad. Luckily for you, Gennifer and Ronnie are in the other limousine because they would be asking for the big eyeballs," Danielle said, laughing with the girls now.

It took the limousine almost 45 minutes to reach the Premier's residence. However, the Mointzes laughed the entire ride, passing time quickly. The four girls, all on top of their respective classes, marveled at the beauty of the country between giggles.

"All bums out," Mointz announced, when the limousine stopped in front of a Ming Dynasty-designed residence, which looked more like a palace.

The girls laughed and all four hugged Mointz and Danielle, thanking them for bringing them to China. Ronnie, Gennifer and Lauren joined the mix as Fu Wong guided them into the residence. The Chinese and American Secret Service followed closely.

"I want a pu-pu platter for four," Ronnie whispered into his mother's ear.

She giggled. "You're as bad as the girls and Cristopher."

"I am so proud of you," Ronnie said, "This is amazing and so are you."

"Ditto, my son," she whispered and kissed his cheek.

The group entered a living room the size of a football field. The Mointz family looked forward to three days of jam-packed events in the country and Mointz planned to keep Fu Wong close to him.

Danielle gave a rousing speech at the lunch, congratulating the Chinese for their Olympic preparedness and commending them for bringing the country together to fight human rights abuses.

Mointz sat alone with Fu Wong, while Danielle paraded the girls around the great hall. Rosie Marie and Ashley Megan whispered to each other, amazed so many people rushed to greet their mother.

"Your wife has certainly turned these tough Chinese gentlemen into putty in her hands," Fu said, sipping some Chinese beer.

"I hear you can do the same thing."

"I am just an economist here; my father is the number two man in the Chinese government."

"My sources tell me you are more than an economist."

Fu Wong smiled, "My sources tell me you might be president soon. Everyone here knows that."

"Fu, we have been friends for almost 20 years, so let me be extremely blunt. The Chinese economy is tied to America's. I know you are aware that al-Qaeda is destroying the Middle East and has tied itself to factions here in China," Mointz said softly.

Fu pondered how to answer Mointz's question. Fu nodded to an exit for Mointz to join him outside the banquet hall. They walked down the long corridor and out to a botanical garden.

"This is beautiful."

"Indeed it is, Mr. Heisman. Tell me, Mr. Heisman, how much do you know?"

"Probably most of it. I know you want your country to be a human rights leader and that you believe your association with al-Qaeda and North Korea hurts China financially. Plus, you miss your Brown football team."

"Are you spying on me, Mr. Heisman?"

"But of course, my friend. Why do you think I came here?"

Fu explained to Mointz how the top level officials of the Chinese government were now businessmen and not the old hardline communists. The government, however, did not know just yet how to control the military or their spook agencies.

"I can help you deal with them. We have to contain al-Qaeda and I will do what I need so the region will not be destabilized."

"Agreed. However, I do not have the clout, even in my own country, to persuade the people I need to yet."

Mointz smiled. "I have ideas."

"Like playing defense against Navy?" Minister Wong asked.

###

"Father, the food was quite lovely," Rosie Marie said in a debutante's voice in the embassy. Chinese business leaders were hosting a formal dinner and the family prepared to attend. "I hope the cuisine is duplicated at the shindig."

"Hear, hear, sister," Ashley added.

"The two of you sound like two old ladies," Mointz told his giggling girls.

"Well, these two old ladies had better get their butts in gear before we are late," said Danielle.

"Boo, Danielle boo," Ashley cried out and giggled as she kissed her mother. "We want to pick on our father."

"Yes, mum. Picking on Sir Cristopher is a time-honored tradition," Rosie claimed.

Mointz was about to start a pillow fight with the girls. At that moment, Ronnie walked into the room looking very nervous.

"Helloooo, Uncle, what's up?" Ashley said, laughing before she noticed something was wrong.

"Hi, sweetie," Ronnie said softly. "Buddy, we have a big problem."

Ronnie hugged Ashley. A second later, deafening explosions startled the group. Gennifer ran into the room with Heidi Lynn and Aleixa from the suite next-door.

"People are firing at the embassy," said Ronnie. The Ambassador and his staff are at the dinner already. We are trapped. The snipers have taken out the officers of the embassy. Our security is wiped out. It is what I came to tell you. Lauren is out with the Ambassador and he got an SOS call. Where is your cell?" Ronnie said looking out the window.

Mointz frowned. "We both ran out of juice and did not plug in our phones."

Mointz grabbed his bag and pulled out weapons for himself, Ronnie and their wives.

"Dad, what is happening?" Ashley asked nervously.

"Come, sweetie," he replied and grabbed her out of her Uncle's embrace. "We need to get out of here. Follow us, ladies."

Gennifer and Danielle had never been in this situation before. They were now in a firefight. To Mointz's astonishment, there were people storming the embassy.

Ronnie called Davis, who was sleeping as it was 5 am back in Rhode Island. Trent immediately confirmed he would get help.

Ronnie and Mointz opened up the suite's door to see the embassy ablaze. Mointz fired at two men dressed identically to the men who had stormed the palace in Saudi Arabia.

"Fudge!" Mointz exclaimed. "These are the same al-Qaeda jihadists who stormed the Saudi palace!"

Two more men ran down the hall a split second before the hallway collapsed from the fire. Ronnie took both of them out. As the fire engulfed the hallway, Ronnie and Mointz quickly escaped back to their room. Mointz looked outside and knew they were vulnerable.

"Mointzie, get us out of here!" Danielle stared at the fire exit.

"Babe, look out this window. Ronnie and I will get us out of here. We will make a path. No one should come up from behind you because of the fire. If they do, shoot the sons-of-bitches."

The four girls' eyes were as big as snowballs. The girls kissed Mointz and Ronnie and nervously watched while the two men went outside.

It took only two minutes for Mointz and Ronnie to kill 16 terrorists. Danielle, Gennifer and the girls watched the firefight before running outside just in time to beat the flames.

The girls ran into the arms of the men outside, kissing and hugging them.

"Dad, you are bleeding badly," Rosie Marie told her father.

"That is because I have been shot, kiddo," Mointz said. "I hate getting shot."

###

The official story was the American Embassy in China had a small fire; however, the Mointz family was not there. The unofficial story was America was really irate at the assassination attempt on the Mointz family.

Fu Wong had China's best American-trained physicians take care of Mointz's bullet wound. Fortunately, the bullet had entered and exited his arm, so he would be able to recover quickly. A case of the stomach flu had been blamed as the reason Mointz missed two of his scheduled appearances.

The Chinese Premier had promised Lauren and Danielle he would get to the bottom of the attack. Neither the Premier nor Wong's words gave any comfort until word came that Mointz was out of surgery.

"Tell me you were able to lift some of their fingerprints," Mointz told Ronnie, as Danielle entered the hospital room with Ronnie and Mointz's two daughters.

Ronnie chuckled and received a look from his mother, "We got 'em!"

"Dad, are you all right?" Rosie asked, extremely upset.

"I love you," Ashley Megan said. "You and Uncle saved us.

Mointz swallowed and pointed to the ginger ale on the table. "Yes, girls. I am fine. How are the other guys?"

Rosie and Ashley smiled brightly. Their father always seemed indestructible and now he seemed more so than ever.

"Girls, your father needs rest. You can come back in the morning," Danielle said. Both girls kissed their father good night and left the room.

The door had barely shut before Danielle broke down in tears while Ronnie held her.

"Babe, I am fine. Really I am," said Mointz.

"F-Off, Mointzie," she shot back.

"Mother, he did stop the bullet that was bee-lining for my head when he dove in front of me and knocked me down."

"That makes me feel soooo much better, Ronnie."

"How are the girls processing this?" Mointz asked before Danielle helped him take a drink of ginger ale out of the straw."

"They are their father's daughters and Aleixa is all Mointz. They believe you are Batman and Superman all in one."

"I do look good in a cape," Mointz said.

Danielle giggled, "Stop, will you! I am still mad, but I love you. Lauren and I spoke to the President and Vice President. The President is livid and he gave you a green light to find out who they are and take them out."

Mointz smiled and chuckled. "Now, baby, give me a big smooch."

Danielle complied with his request. She could not stop herself from giggling. "You are so lucky, I love you."

"I know I am irresistible. Now, Ronnie, we have a problem, yes?"

"Buddy, when don't we? People tried to kill us."

"We're so concentrated on 2016, we forget that we ticked off a lot of people," said Mointz. "I need to get in fighting shape and figure out who from al-Qaeda has links to the Chinese. Then we need to eradicate the problem. I want to start now. I am out of here."

"Hell, no!" Danielle said. "Trent is on his way and will be here soon. Let him give the okay."

Mointz nodded and fell asleep quickly, leaving Ronnie and Danielle in the room by themselves.

"Mom, he took a bullet for me," Ronnie whispered.

"I know, sweetheart. Believe me; I know."

"Cristopher has to stop being the one in the fight."

Danielle looked into her son's eyes, "And so do you. What could he do if you went away? Cristopher would never recover if either of us left him. Help him do what it takes to save the world so I can have my family to myself, please."

Ronnie wasn't sure where she was going with this. "Meaning what, Mom?"

"Meaning I want my family to stop giving all they have to save the world and keep giving and giving until they can't give any more. Your sisters and my granddaughter and niece wanted to go out and help you two. Take the gloves off my son and do what you can."

"I told Cristopher," Danielle continued. "Now, I am telling you and anyone who will listen. Danielle the bitch has been born."

"That a girl, Mum."

Fu Wong met with Danielle and Lauren when Davis arrived. The two women expressed their displeasure with the Chinese government for having ties to al-Qaeda. Minister Wong promised to bring the Premier up to speed.

Lauren and Danielle entered the Congressman's room after the meeting while Davis shot medicine into Mointz's IV.

"Better not be a placebo," Mointz said.

Davis smiled. "No placebo, just a little helper," Davis said. Lauren and Danielle said "hi" to Mointz, then followed Davis outside while a nurse changed Mointz's dressing.

"Is my husband all right?"

"Honestly, the surgeon did a fine job. Cristopher is built like a tank, thankfully."

"The bullet he took was heading for Ronnie's head. I thought they were both goners," Danielle told him.

"All four girls witnessed him save Ronnie. They believe he is a hero," said Lauren. "Who was responsible for the attack?"

"My guess is some Middle Eastern prince paying big money to Chinese officials to help his al-Qaeda contacts," Davis declared. "Proving our hunch will be difficult. Cristopher is going to have to heal and take Ronnie and Anthony to the kingdom."

Lauren raised an eyebrow, "That is a very specific guess."

"Yes, Trent, a very detailed guess," Danielle said.

"Cristopher and I have an idea who this is, but we have to be careful how we handle it."

"Who is it, for the love of God?" Lauren asked.

"Amina's husband, Khalib."

"Oh, shit. What do we do?" Lauren said.

"Valmer and Cristopher believe the best way to handle the situation is to have Cristopher and Ronnie do what they do best."

"Good," Danielle proclaimed. "I want them to kill the son-of-a-bitch."

"Atta girl," Lauren stated. "Don't mince words."

"They went after my girls, my son, my granddaughter, my niece, my daughter-in-law and my Mointzie. Let Cristopher, Anthony and Ronnie do whatever it takes from now on."

Lauren looked at Trent and smiled. "You heard the girl. Heal up Cristopher so he can get the son-of-a-bitch."

Fu Wong promised Mointz he would work behind the scenes to sniff out who among their government officials as well as their business partners were involved in the attacks. He had the full backing of the Premier and his close associates. The Mointzes were very special to the Chinese for their support in bringing the Olympics to China. The Chinese people had such a special feeling for them, it was almost like they were one of their own. Chinese business leaders certainly did not want a pissing contest with the future leader of America.

Mointz, two days out of surgery, attended a few events before leaving for Russia.

"Wear your sling, will you?" Danielle whispered in his ear at an outdoor Chinese dance recital.

"Shhhh, I am watching this," Mointz replied, smiling at his daughters, Heidi Lynn, and Aleixa. All four girls were all over Mointz to make sure he was all right.

Mointz found the recital extremely well done. The party hurried to the airport afterward to arrive in Russia on time so the girls could join their soccer team. New agents were brought in and Davis decided to follow them to Russia with Lauren.

Minister Wong accompanied the group to the airport and again stressed how badly he wanted to make this right. Mointz promised to return soon, before the Olympics. Wong knew if and when he did return, it would not be to visit a dance recital.

Mointz's eyes closed as he sat back in the plane on the way to Moscow. Rosie Marie sat on one side and Ashley Megan on the other.

"Everything okay, Daddy?" Rosie asked when he opened his eyes.

"Yes, baby. Are you all right?"

She nodded.

"How about you, Ashley Meg?"

Ashley lay her head on her father's good arm. "You scared me. You went all ninja after those guys."

"I didn't mean to scare you, sweetie. Believe me, I did not ask for those bad men to hurt us."

"Dad, you kicked ass," Rosie said with a smile.

"Shhh. Do not let your mother hear you say that word."

"Sorry, dude. You rock," she said giggling.

"Dad, you kicked huge ass," Ashley said, mimicking her sister's giggle.

Mointz fell back asleep and the girls went back to listening to their iPods. Ronnie led Davis, Lauren and Danielle into the conference room. "Does Amina know anything?" Danielle asked about the seriousness of Amina's husband's activities.

Lauren shook her head 'no.' "Not from what we can see. She hates the daft prick. Amina would love nothing more than to have Ronnie or Cristopher take him out."

"She is in love with my husband, isn't she?" Danielle asked.

They all looked at each other wondering who was brave enough to answer that question. Lauren accepted the responsibility.

"Yes, Amina is in love with him deep down as is everyone who knows him. Who wouldn't be, Danielle? He saved her life, her father's and Kareem's. Cristopher saved me and Valmer right in front of her. Amina would not let anything happen to him," said Lauren.

Danielle frowned. "How can the Saudis go after him with all he has done for the kingdom?"

"Cristopher, while revered, is still a Christian and not a Muslim. The Royal Family obviously loves our boy, but most people in the kingdom are not as deeply vested in him," Davis said.

"Mom, it is not just the Chinese who were catering to the terrorists; the North Koreans and Russians have been too kind to our enemies too. Are you telling me you do not understand why people won't help?"

"Ronnie, I know people are jealous of Americans," Danielle snapped. "I am neither foolish nor naïve. Maybe I was a little slower than all of you to get in the game, but I have a lot to lose as well—probably a hell of a lot more."

Lauren hugged her. "We all lose if he goes off halfcocked, fighting without a plan. We must help him to develop a plan he can accept."

"Good luck with that," Ronnie said.

Chapter Thirty-Eight

Russia

"No vodka for you," Ashley told her father as they walked into their Club Level suite at the Ritz Carlton Moscow overlooking Red Square.

"I will take a bottle, though," Rosie Marie told her sister with a giggle. Her mother frowned.

Mointz chuckled. "The two of you need to sober up and get ready for soccer practice with the team."

Ashley Megan and Rosie Marie played on the USA's under-18 national soccer team. They were by far the best players already on the team at ages 15 and 14.

"Okay, Dad. I will take a rain check on the vodka," Rosie Marie said with a smile and left for her room to change.

"And what, pray tell, are you waiting for?" Mointz asked Ashley Megan.

"I love you, Mum and Dad," Ashley Megan said, taking the hand of her father's injured arm.

"What up, parents and sis?" Rosie said when she came to find out what was prolonging Ashley. She did not like seeing her sister cry.

"Come sit, ladies." Danielle told her angels how their father had been shot when he played his first Super Bowl taking out a terrorist. Danielle and Mointz had decided to tell the girls his true identity.

"Dad is a secret agent and also a Congressman?" Ashley Meg asked her mother.

Danielle nodded and hugged her daughter.

"Does the President know you moonlight?" a very flustered Rosie Marie asked.

"Rosie, your father works for the Defense Intelligence Agency just as your Uncle Ronnie runs the Navy's Criminal Investigation Service. The President knows what he does and who he is," said Danielle.

"I am trying to just be a politician now and travel as a diplomat here and there. What happened in China will never happen again, I promise."

Mointz promised because never again would he travel with the low-level security he had had. The President personally called Putin to keep the Mointz family, and anyone with them, safe and free from attack. He also told Putin if any government was linked to such an attack, the attack would be considered an act of war on America. Putin received the message loud and clear.

"Understand, ladies?" Danielle asked.

Rosie nodded, but Ashley clenched her teeth.

"I don't like not being able to help my father when he needs it," Ashley said "Sorry, Dad."

Mointz hugged her again and said, "I love you, baby. Please get dressed and we will speak later."

Ashley and Rosie left to dress for soccer and Mointz held Danielle for a long time. He needed a hug from Danielle like only she could give.

"Did you hear your daughter?" Danielle asked. "She is you; she is all you. Ugggh, I should be upset, but she is who she is because of her father and I love her for it."

"She is a special one," he said and winced.

"Mointzie, are you sure you're up for this?"

He chuckled, "No, but I am going anyway; Davis gave me real medicine to get me through. I feel decent enough; it isn't like I need to play in the Super Bowl."

"Did you see Ashley and Rosie perk up when you said you were accepting this mission? Your girls have your toughness embedded in them. Our little firecracker at home is probably tougher. I am sure Thomas and our little Patrick in my womb will have your intestinal fortitude, too."

"Well, you have more than all of us put together. Without you, I am nothing."

"Thank you, honey. Your words mean a lot to me. Now, if you will excuse me, I have to fix my makeup," Danielle cried on her husband's chest. She had told Ronnie she couldn't live without Mointz, but she had never really believed it until this moment. She was the most loved woman on earth.

Danielle slipped into the bedroom so the girls would not see her upset. Mointz followed her into the large bedroom adjacent to Rosie and Ashley's room.

"Sweetie, please stop worrying about everything and anything. We are all part of this. You are pregnant and about to be a mother again. Hormones are raging in you, but for the first time, I believe I can pull this off."

Danielle looked at him in the mirror. "Cristopher, do you believe the world will be saved?"

"Saved from extinction, yes. I now believe we can live in peace forever, if we continue to teach our children and grandchildren. We must first level the playing field by exterminating these rogue nations. Once we do it, we can have real dialogue with countries to fix this politically. Trust me, baby Angel."

Danielle turned around. "I trust you, love you, and I believe in you always. I just want you always in my life until I am old and gray."

"And until I cannot pee standing up," Mointz said, laughing.

Danielle giggled. "My husband, the funnyman. You do know the girls are now in their room wondering how they can help you."

"Our good friend, Derek Vaz, needs to train them in more than self-defense. He will have his hands full with all the Mointzes and Mahoneys," said Mointz and then quickly added, "for protection purposes only."

"Nice save, Mointzie."

Dinner with several Russian businessmen and dignitaries followed the girls' soccer practice. Ronnie and Gennifer had the girls all silly back at the hotel and all fired up with plenty of food and soda pop.

Lauren and Davis joined Mointz and Danielle at the dinner. Mointz was forced to take it slow and alcohol was not on the menu.

"The food is excellent, no?" Danielle asked Mointz as she savored a large plate of beef and cabbage.

"Very good. Actually, I am sorry you cannot eat any of the salmon," he replied. "The company stinks though?"

"Why do you say that, Babe?"

Lauren overheard their whispers. "Several of these people are not who they appear to be," Lauren muttered. "Most are ex-KGB and want Mointzie to bless their endeavors so they can seem legitimate in the West with Mointz's stamp of approval."

"Cristopher loves to burst their bubble, though, and show them whose boss," Davis stated.

"How?" Danielle asked.

"Yes, how?" Mointz joined.

"My friend loves to burst people's bubbles by acting interested and then stealing their dreams by losing interest quickly. No one is good enough for Mointz's standards," Davis replied.

Mointz chuckled. "Not true. I listen to everyone and I am always willing to help honest business people. Find one honest business person and I will not hinder their progress in the United States."

"Here might be one," Lauren said trying to suppress a laugh.

A gorgeous brunette with ice blue eyes and a dress to match made her way to their table. Her dress, sexy and yet not too revealing, had the hosts Sergei Pankratou and Oleg Sokolov dropping their respective tongues.

"Jesus," Trent said. "Is she who I think she is? Hubba hubba."

Danielle giggled and Mointz nodded to Davis, knowing exactly who she was.

"Mr. Mointz, my name is Natalya…"

"Salnikov," Mointz said, interrupting.

She smiled. "How do you know that?"

Mointz stood up and asked her to join them at the table and Natalya gladly sat down with a shy smile.

"I know your clothing company well," Mointz said.

She thanked him, wondering how her small Russian company could show up on his radar. "I am impressed you know my designs, Mr. Mointz."

"It is more popular than you can imagine in my state with its large Russian population. If I am not mistaken, you have a daughter Elena about nine," Mointz said.

Natalya did indeed have a daughter, Elena. She had attended several of his classes in 2016 at Providence College before the missiles started raining down on the world.

"What is your company's name?" Danielle asked.

"Salnikov Fashions," she replied.

Lauren smiled as Natalya wrote down Mointz's contact information. He promised to help her if she called him next week. Mointz immediately typed on his BlackBerry before she walked five steps from the table to keep eyes on her.

"Beautiful Russian woman," Oleg Sokolov said as Pankratou nodded in approval. If you looked up the word "wanker" on Wikipedia, their pictures would appear.

"She is lovely, Oleg." Danielle said. "How do you know her?" Danielle asked her husband, curious to know.

"Her daughter was one of my students at Providence College and I liked her very much," Mointz whispered. "Her company explodes but she is killed by a nasty Russian weapons dealer. She is either with him now or she knows him and he is backing her. Elena told me he supplied the Middle East with weapons to fight Israel. The woman does not stand a chance."

"Now she does. As soon as she mentioned her company name, I almost cried. Her designs are the best," said Lauren. "The poor, sweet girl could barely ask you if you would be interested in meeting with her when she came to the States. You have to help her get her boutiques off the ground."

"We had better get her to the States," Danielle said as their hosts got up to bring more people to the table.

"She plans to come to the US next month, she said," Davis stated.

"We are taking her with us. I want her packed and ready to go when we leave," Mointz said and stood up. "I have to use the restroom."

"Okay, what did I miss?" asked Danielle.

"Natalya was the first student he advised. He often told me how heartbroken Elena was being a multimillionaire and an orphan. Remember, Cristopher is always a teacher at heart."

"Another son-of-a-bitch will bite the dust," Lauren said. She started whistling the Queen song, 'Another One Bites the Dust.'"

"Well, the son-of-a-bitch is history. We might be able to save us a headache in the Middle East. There are arms dealers everywhere we go, but this is one big fish," Davis said.

"He really steps in it, doesn't he?" Danielle stated.

Mointz had not returned in over ten minutes and the party started to worry. Danielle called over one of the agents, Ralph, who happened to be a friend of Anthony's.

"Ralph, have you seen my husband?" Danielle asked when he arrived at the table.

"Ma'am, he left five minutes ago. He followed a woman out and asked one of the agents to give him a ride. Oh God, did I screw up?"

"No Ralph, but my husband did."

Natalya got in a Mercedes driven by a thug, Mointz noticed. He had the female agent driving an embassy BMW follow her.

Mointz's BlackBerry rang as soon as the silver BMW pulled out after Natalya.

"Mointz," he answered.

"F-Off, Mointzie. Where the hell are you?" Danielle asked.

"Hi, honey. I am seeing a man about a horse. Can you have my colleagues hook me up?"

Mointz gave Danielle a code to have Ronnie get to him ASAP. She knew it was no time to argue with her husband.

"Be careful. I promise to beat you up later," she said.

"Okay, love. Cheers," Mointz said. Still, he never just hung up on his wife like he did everyone else.

They hung up and the BMW stopped abruptly as Natalya entered a small club. Mointz decided to follow. His arm ached, but at this moment he did not care.

"Stay here, please and wait for Ronnie," he told the agent.

She reluctantly agreed as she watched Mointz get out of the BMW and walk into the club. The club was more like an American coffee shop and Natalya noticed him immediately as did half the people at the club.

"Congressman Mointz, are you following me?" Natalya asked nervously.

"Yes, Natalya. I am, in fact. Is there a place we can talk?"

She nodded and sat down at a table as she ordered two teas.

"Does your wife know you are here?"

Mointz explained how he knew she was involved with Tishchenko and how Tishchenko would be blackmailed into stealing her money. Natalya was amazed the Congressman knew every detail of her relationship with Tishchenko.

"He has threatened to kill me and my daughter. He seemed so nice when he came in to buy a dress for his wife. Tishchenko said he would help open more stores for me," she said in heavily accented English. "He is not a nice man."

"I want you to come to America with your daughter and be a success. You have an uncle in Rhode Island, yes?"

She nodded. "Why do you want to help me? I am a nothing."

"No you are not. You are one talented young lady and it is what I do."

Ronnie walked in with Lauren and Mointz laughed out loud.

"What is so funny, Congressman?"

"If you are a nothing, dear, how come you have caused the head of NCIS and the Majority Leader of the Senate to come to you? It seems like you are a big deal to me."

Ronnie walked over with Lauren and smiled, "Danielle is going to ring your neck. Do you ever wait?"

Lauren was about to say something and stopped. She only smiled and sat down.

"Natalya was telling me her mother was watching Elena and she was about to call a friend to join us," Mointz said.

"I was?" Natalya asked. Then she giggled.

She liked Mointz and she immediately trusted him. There was something in his eyes that told her he really cared.

Natalya did as directed. Mointz, as well as Ronnie, left the restaurant. Natalya and Lauren switched to vodka.

"The Congressman really cares, doesn't he?" Natalya asked Lauren.

"Cristopher Mointz does care. He is not only my best friend; he is the one person, besides my husband, I know will never let me down."

"I can't understand how he knows so much about me and my family."

Lauren smiled, "Cristopher knows a lot about everything."

Eugueni Tishchenko entered with two bodyguards. He recognized Lauren immediately; Tishchenko was no fool. He kissed Natalya's cheek. After an introduction, he kissed Lauren's hand.

Lauren explained she was waiting for two friends and Natalya had graciously asked Lauren to join her. Little did he know, Mointz and Ronnie waited in the BMW for a second appearance.

Tishchenko went on for an hour before he turned around suddenly as a commotion had started at the bar. His two bodyguards had hit the deck and, as he rushed over, Ronnie Mahoney stuck a 9 mm weapon into his stomach.

"Eugueni Tishchenko, pleased to meet you, maggot," Mointz said.

Tishchenko had no words left as he was taken out of the club and into a limousine Lauren and Ronnie had taken over to the club.

"Congressman Mointz, do you know who I am?" Tishchenko asked.

Mointz nodded to Ronnie who belted him in the throat. Mointz was still in pain from surgery only a few days ago.

"Yep. I know who you are and if you want to live, you will tell us all about your arms dealing in the Middle East."

Tishchenko bowed his head and knew he was busted.

"Tell me that is not your own blood," Danielle said when Mointz walked into the suite.

He shook his head "no" and sat down, exhausted, in a comfortable chair.

"What is wrong?" Danielle asked, kneeling in front of him.

"Tishchenko was one sick bastard. He was one of the worst people I have ever encountered."

"So you planned on meeting Natalya here?"

Mointz nodded. "I had planned on a side trip. I had Anthony research Natalya and I made sure the embassy folks invited her to the party. She is going to need your help adjusting and require legal help to get her business moving. I know you are busy, but can you help?"

"Of course, you know I will," she said, kissing his swollen hand. "Were you able to obtain any information?"

"Much more than I would have ever thought. Tishchenko made sure the Pakistanis and Iranians had nuclear technology."

Danielle covered her mouth, "What can you do about it?"

Mointz told his wife that he would use his meeting with Putin to push America and Russia into an energy-dependent zone with American technology to help the Russians tap their natural resources. Mointz was here to get the Russians to agree to an oil coop.

"What can you offer him to make him agree?"

Mointz smiled for the first time. "My friendship and the technology to get their oil."

Danielle frowned. "That isn't much, is it?"

"No, but bringing him into NATO and signing a free trade agreement will help big-time. I have the President's stamp of approval on this as well as several Senators and Representatives. I have promised to sit down with everyone when I get back. I have to do this, honey."

"What are you not telling me?"

Mointz hung his head. "Tishchenko told us he had given nuclear technology to Chavez in Venezuela, Castro in Cuba, Ahmadinejad in Iran, the Muslim brotherhood, the Pakistanis and Princess Amina's husband. Nice huh?"

"Didn't you know that already?"

"Not really. We definitely did not know he was passing nuclear technology. Everyone, and I mean everyone, missed this. Things could have changed, you know?"

"I now know why you do what you do."

"Sorry, honey. It never ends. Tishchenko does not act alone, unfortunately."

"Cristopher, who is he working with?" Danielle asked and held her breath.

"Chancellor Wilhelm Ikier."

Danielle gasped at hearing the German political leader was involved with terrorism. "All I can ask is 'why?'"

"Iker has always believed Germany was a world power. He wants to cause mayhem in the world to better Germany's economic position because Germany, by law, can't ever get involved. I guess he was another person we missed in the First Parallel; then again, Papa Phil was not CIA Director then. I spoke to Trent and Lauren on the way back. Sweetie, our lives have just become harder."

"Why, because you cannot go in and punch him in the nose?"

"I can do that, no problem. My problem is that Iker is democratically elected and universally loved. We do not know who supports him in Germany and NATO. We might be fighting ourselves. Hell, BMW could be making custom-fit tail pipe bombs."

Danielle giggled, "Stop. You love your 7 series BMW!"

"What can I say?" Mointz said and hugged his wife tightly. "I love you."

"I love you, too. We will get through this," Danielle said. Her smile could melt an iceberg and it always cheered him up.

"Well, I could use some sleep with my beautiful wife curled up next to me."

"Come on, Mointzie. I will give you all the love a woman can give a man."

###

Breakfast at the hotel had everyone eating well. The conversation focused on Wilhelm Iker and Natalya at first.

"I sent a full report to my father-in-law late last night. He was shocked, to say the least," Davis said.

Heidi, Rosie Marie, Ashley and Aleixa entertained Elena as they sat away from the adults. Natalya was at her mother's home while four agents collected their personal belongings.

Elena had stayed with her mother at the Ritz the night before. Lauren told Natalya, Elena could stay with the girls while Natalya packed. Mointz and Danielle accompanied Natalya home in the morning.

Mointz sat smiling at Elena and was not paying attention to Davis who was speaking.

"Do you agree, Congressman?" Davis asked. "Yo, Dr. Cris!"

Mointz snapped out of it. "Sorry, dude. She is so happy right now. I remember her sadness in school. There are so many things worth doing this time; we were able to get two wins."

"What's the plan going forward?" Ronnie said.

Danielle began, "Cristopher will become Vice President. Lauren and I believe every candidate will beg for his support in the primary. Cristopher can accomplish a lot more if he first serves as Vice President for eight years and then spends eight years as President. The Vice President has no travel restrictions and he can do backroom deals anywhere. He might still be able to accept a mission or two," Danielle said.

"McCain has a mind of his own. The old man might not listen to our boy here," Ronnie said to his mother.

"He will listen," Davis stated. "The man knows a good thing and is reasonable."

Mointz smiled at Danielle. She had become more involved in his mission than he ever imagined. Pride and love filled his body when she spoke.

"Never stand against a pregnant lady," Danielle said.

"Can McCain win with Cristopher on the ticket?" Ronnie said. "Didn't he get smoked last time?"

Mointz nodded.

"I would prefer Governor Huckabee," Mointz said.

"Why?" Lauren asked. "I love the Huckster and he was great on television, but you believe he would do better than McCain?"

"Patently," Mointz said. "I have to choose one way or the other."

"Technically, Romney is the man," Davis told everyone. "He would clash with Cristopher because the two are too close geographically and he will not be a fan of the Mointz way. Romney is a CEO type who likes structure and so does his staff. I agree with Cristopher, Governor Huckabee would be a perfect fit. Obviously, they fit well together religiously."

"I don't know Governor Huckabee well, but what I know of him is all positive," said Danielle.

"Valmer ran through a ton of different scenarios with Papa Phil and Danielle, you have nailed it all dead on. I need to go home and heal totally and, once I feel 100%, travel to Germany and Saudi Arabia."

"Cristopher, you can travel in a D'Artagnan costume," Ronnie stated, chuckling. "I will go as Ozzy Osbourne."

Danielle giggled. "Why D'Artagnan and Ozzy?"

"Mointz is a musketeer through and through: one for all and all for one. I am more of a bite-the–head-off-the-animal kind of guy."

"GROSS!" Gennifer said.

"I think you have the costumes backwards," his mother told Ronnie. "You are the conformist and my husband is the bat out of hell."

Ronnie laughed, "That is a MEATLOAF album."

"Not anymore," Danielle said sternly. "The terrorists went after my children; 'Bat out of Hell' is now your mantra to go get those sons-of-bitches."

436

Vladimir Putin watched every one of the girls' games and ate up Mointz's ideas. He was extremely impressed with Danielle Mointz and Lauren Gabriel as well. Mointz, on President Bush's authority, had given Putin an outline for cooperation between the two governments and a plan for membership in NATO for Russia. The Russian President had agreed to visit the United States and stay at the Mointzes's ranch in Virginia for Labor Day weekend.

Mointz and Danielle were taking the children from all three families to Ireland the following week for some family time with just the children.

The girls zoned out on the plane ride home; they had just played their last game earlier that day. Mointz started to feel better as Davis made sure he had enough medicine to keep an infection at bay.

Mointz sat next to his wife heading home and held her hand in his. They loved and appreciated their time traveling together with the children.

"Natalya's mother is talking Lauren's ear off now that she has learned Lauren's fluent in Russian," whispered Danielle.

Mointz smiled. "Why do you think I pretend to know only a little Russian? I had so much free time between the times I came back until the time we made love, I learned French, Spanish, Arabic, Russian and Chinese. How do you think I survived the period I couldn't seduce you?"

"Mointzie, are you serious?"

"Sweetie, I adored you. Not only were you the most beautiful woman on the planet, I had to suppress a lifetime of love until I kissed you. Remember how surprised you were after we made love and I fessed up?"

She giggled loudly.

"Shhh, up there," Ronnie said laughing.

"Maybe you are serious, Mointzie. Now, if you are such an amazing husband, figure out how you are going to seduce me tonight."

Mointz smiled. "I can always figure that one out."

The Mointzes collected Marissa and baby Thomas. They loved being back home. Mointz and Danielle crawled into bed at almost midnight and, as promised, Mointz figured out a way to make love to his wife. Danielle gently placed her head on her husband's chest and smiled brightly.

"There is a lot of security outside. We have to get used to it, I guess, but I feel safe just with you here."

"I wish it was just me. There will never be a time again we are alone. We have a few days here to relax because Congress is on break. Thank God, my sister took the attack better than I would have thought. I am sorry I put you in such a scary position."

Danielle kissed his cheek. "Thank you for trying to be sincere. Do what you have to do."

Chapter Thirty-Nine

August 28, 2008

"When Governor Huckabee asked me to be his Vice President, I had to ask the opinions of our five children and my wife. My three daughters loved the idea, my two sons wanted me to play ball and my beautiful and loving wife told me to follow my heart. Tonight, I proudly accept the Republican nomination for Vice President of the United States and I look forward to debating the issues with Democratic nominee John Edwards and his running mate, Joe Biden," Mointz said at the podium during the Republican national convention."

The 41-year-old Mointz had spent a busy two years since his shooting in China. The Rhode Island Senator, took care of Amina's louse of a husband, brought President Putin and Russia into NATO, and worked diligently with Fu Wong in China. Iker and his party received some public and private criticism regarding their soft terrorist policies.

Mointz's convention speech in Chicago had the largest audience in US television history and the Senator delivered a beauty. The world had continued to change and Mointz knew he had a lot of work to do. The wars in

Afghanistan and Iraq were over, thanks to the Senate committee work of Ellis, Lauren, and Mointz.

Mointz was 41 years old, the same age of Theodore Roosevelt at his Vice Presidential nomination. Governor Mike Huckabee joined Mointz on stage after the speech. The convention floor erupted in thunderous applause as Mointz's favorite Toby Keith's song 'American Soldier,' played loud and proud.

"A brilliant speech, my friend," Governor Huckabee said as the crowd screamed.

"Thank you, sir."

"C'mon, Cristopher. Why don't we go back to the hotel and enjoy the night with our families? We can talk on the way."

The Secret Service led Governor Huckabee and Senator Mointz into a limousine. The Governor smiled at Senator Mointz when they sat down. Mointz really admired and loved Governor Huckabee after spending so much time together during the primary campaign season.

"Remember during your vetting process I was briefed on all that you have done over the years and what you have done which is not in any file. When Director Gabriel briefed me, I almost fell out of my chair. What you and Senator Gabriel and soon-to-be-Admiral Mahoney have done with my friend, Senator Ellis, over the last 24 years is incredible. I can't even fathom how you have survived multiple shootings, assassination attempts and a helicopter crash while saving people from terrorists and criminal masterminds all over the globe. What you did in Hungary is legendary, but it is not even 1/100th of what you have accomplished. I know of the amazing relationships you have formed with foreign leaders and I believe every word of the report you shared with me on how to avoid the nuclear aggression you believe is coming. Please know this, Cristopher, you have my full support."

Mointz smiled. "Have you digested the economic proposals I sent to you? I want us to be in unison on the campaign trail."

"Compassionate Conservatism has always been my plan. The economy will grow and I definitely agree Americans need to build factories. General Perry to serve as Secretary of Defense is a splendid choice, if all goes our way. Do you have any thoughts on who to choose for Secretary of State?"

"Where do you see Senator Gabriel-Davis? Her husband is the CIA's Scientific Director and I know you two are best friends."

"Lauren loves being a leader in the Senate, but we need women and minorities in the Cabinet," said Mointz. Mointz felt badly that the nation's first African American President was not going to be elected in the Second Parallel, but Mointz did not have a choice, Obama's leading from behind in foreign affairs had caused many of the World's problems in the First Parallel.

"Cristopher, I would like Danielle to be Attorney General. I spoke with Lauren and Valmer and they agree with my choice. We need a strong, fair-minded person in that position. She has a brilliant legal mind and could serve in The Supreme Court someday when you are out of office."

Danielle as Attorney General and eventually a member of the Supreme Court had to come from Lauren and/or Ellis, Mointz thought.

"Governor, when we win, good luck trying to convince her. With regard to immigration, we need to reform immigration policies and really give hard-working people heroes to look up to," said Mointz.

"I could not agree more. Too many children are born here and their parents end up in limbo. Let's do the right thing for everyone and secure our borders by enacting comprehensive immigration reform."

Governor Huckabee and Senator Mointz arrived at the hotel. Danielle immediately hugged her husband. Then the children gave Mointz a group hug.

"Wonderful job, son. Your grandfather would be as proud of you as I am," Robert said to Mointz, pulling him aside.

"Thanks, Pop. Coming from you, it means a lot to me."

Governor Huckabee would present his speech the next day, but for Mointz, the campaign ended tonight as a landslide general election would follow and he needed to be ready to roll up his sleeves and get to work.

17-year-old Rosie and 16-year-old Ashley Megan sat next to their father after he sat down to catch his breath.

"We are proud of you, Dad," Rosie said.

"There is no doubt you will win, Pop. My history teacher says you will be the first Republican he will ever vote for," said Ashley. "Both of us will get to vote for you in your re-election bid."

"Thanks, kiddos. I love both of you so very much."

"Of course you do. You would be foolish not to," Rosie Marie said, giving her father a hug.

"No one will ever accuse you of being daft, Dad. You are amazing," Ashley said and gave him a hug as well.

Marissa made her normal beeline for her father and sat in his lap, while Danielle held Thomas and baby Patrick. The camera crew took a final shot of Mointz and his family.

Governor Huckabee and his wife sat across the room from the Mointzes giving them their moment in the sun. He admired how Mointz and Danielle interacted with their children.

"They are his life, Governor," Lauren said.

Governor Huckabee smiled and said, "And, so are you, my dear. I never realized how close the two of you were. He is one-of-a-kind."

"He is extremely proud to be your running mate, sir. Cristopher is extremely selective about who he brings into his heart and trusts."

Governor Huckabee smiled widely. "I know, Lauren. He could have picked anyone to support. I should be his running mate, but he has a big agenda and he gets 8 years to perfect his political skills. I will never forget the trust he put in me."

"The two of you should not be here," the vice presidential nominee said on the plane to Israel.

Danielle kissed her husband. "It is a campaign event and Lauren and I are here for only a few days with you before we all go home."

"Blondie, what can you possibly to do to help me?"

"Provide cover for you, moron. Be smarter will you? You are a Vice Presidential nominee, for Pete's sake."

"Maybe you to have a point," he said.

Hamas had continued to launch missiles at the fed-up Israelis and Mointz planned to meet both the Palestinians and the Israelis. The Israelis could not wait to receive Mointz with full fanfare and Palestinian leaders were also looking forward to meeting with Mointz, Prince Kareem and Princess Amina.

Danielle excused herself and headed to the restroom on the CIA jet.

"Amina is upset Danielle came, yes?" Lauren whispered.

"A little, but she has kept it to herself, as usual. She does hide her feelings pretty well."

"Patently. When we talked, she asked me if your travel schedule would change once you are sworn in. My father is over the moon that you are finally slowing down and taking precautions. I told Amina you probably would have to slow down. She was crushed."

"Papa Gabriel told me he is out soon and he wants Ellis to take it over. What say you?"

"Valmer would love it, he really would. I hope he gets the job. Trent will really get to explore the science with Drs. Hawkins and Knowles now that Valmer will give him even freer reign."

Mointz kissed her cheek, "You mean Valmer will let Trent run the show? Valmer always defers to Trent."

"Trent bullies everyone but you and Ronnie."

"And you."

Lauren noticed Danielle was not looking well.

Mointz saw it too.

"Honey, what is wrong?"

"Didn't I tell you it was a bad idea that night on the campaign bus?" Danielle asked.

"My Lord!" Lauren said. "Momma Bear is adding another cub."

Mointz kissed her. "We have six angels together. Yessss!"

"And then we are not having any more. I am done, Mointzie. Even though this is awesome," she said.

"Sweetie, you wanted another baby, no wonder why you didn't put up a big fight on the campaign bus."

"Guilty as charged. I know I said 'no' more after Patrick, but…"

Lauren playfully hit Mointz. "So you consented to this?"

Mointz grinned. "I love my angels, Lauren."

"I know it, buddy."

"The girls will be so happy," Danielle said.

Anthony came up front after his security meeting. "What is all the laughter about?"

"Cristopher knocked Danielle up again," Lauren replied.

Anthony smiled. "Maybe someday I will meet the one. Congrats, Danielle," he said and kissed her cheek. "How come you always cause trouble when she gets knocked up?"

"Don't blame me, I just found out."

"Yeah okay, boss," Anthony said and sat down across the aisle. "Ready to go to Israel and beg them to stop developing new settlements in the West Bank?"

"I do not beg anyone."

Anthony chuckled. "That is true."

"I am ready to tell Mahmoud Abbas he must deal kindly with the Israelis. Then I will make sure the Israelis back off. They both have some faults, but they need to develop an understanding. Palestine deserves a state with a good economy; however, Israel deserves peace.

"What about Iran?" Danielle asked.

"Next trip, sweetie. We need to make them feel isolated and then take them down. I will work with North Korea as Kim Jong-un and his mother Ko have maintained a good relationship with me. The young Korean President will need some guidance.

"Oh, I am *sure* they do," Lauren said.

"What is so amusing?" Danielle asked.

"Mointzie will have to wear his speedo again," said Lauren.

"You are a 'special lady,'" Mointz said, which Lauren knew was his code word for "bitch".

"Moi? No way, monsieur."

"Speak Hebrew; we're not landing in Paris."

"I don't know Hebrew and neither do you."

"Take me to Paris for a night on the way home please, Mointzie. It will be fun," Danielle asked.

"Yeah, Mointzie. Take us to Paris," Lauren added.

"I have been set up. Did you know about this?" Mointz asked Anthony.

"Who is my boss?" he replied.

Lauren, Danielle, and Mointz in unison said, "I am."

"Heaven help me. The three of you deserve each other," Anthony said.

Mointz's meeting with Shimon Peres, Israel's Prime Minister, was going better than expected, especially when Mointz, behind closed doors, told Shimon how strongly he supported Israel.

Mointz presented his entire plan for dealing with rogue nations and Peres smiled for the first time that Mointz could ever remember.

"Rumors have always told us you have a special relationship with the Saud family.

"Prince Kareem will take his father's place. He is a good friend and a good man."

"After you slapped him silly for selling arms to unfriendly Arab nations."

Mointz chuckled. "I would assume that Mossad was or is in the palace in Riyahd."

"They were in there when you saved King Fahd. We lost two of ours in the firefight."

Mointz slouched in his chair. "Sorry I was late, I was with…"

"We know," Peres said interrupting, "you do not have to go any further. Philip and I are friends."

Peres noticed the sadness in the eyes of the American, immediately he put his hand on Mointz's and called in a beautiful woman. Mointz knew her as Hannah Goldman, a powerful Mossad operative.

"Hello, Hannah," The 33-year-old was as surprised as the Prime Minister, Mointz knew her name.

"Mr. Mointz, how are you?" she asked, not missing a beat.

"Always glad to see a fellow Ivy Leaguer. Dartmouth, correct?"

Hannah nodded. "I can see you are in the know. As to myself, the Prime Minister has asked me to offer my services on your little mission to Palestine," she said.

Mointz responded in Arabic. "Can you still get what you need from Mahmoud Abbas? He is not overly popular in his home now."

Hannah was floored even further when she discovered Mointz knew where she worked. "It baffles me that you could possibly have found out."

Technically he hadn't; Davis had given Mointz all he needed to know about Israel's players over the years. Mointz was a quick study.

"I truly know everything, my dear," he said. "Do not worry. Your secret is safe with me, very safe, as only I, Senator Gabriel and one other person know about you. There is no way I would compromise your mission or put you in danger. However, after this is over I would recommend that you end your days as an undercover agent for Mossad."

Mointz knew she would be caught in 2010 and go through hell for a year before Mossad would rescue her from the West Bank.

"Is that an order?"

Mointz smiled at the Prime Minister and said, "Well, is it, Mr. Prime Minister?"

"It certainly is now."

The beautiful Hannah Goldman's face turned bright red. Mointz was getting used to all the faces from women when he aggravated them.

The Prime Minister and Mointz concluded their meeting and then Hannah brought Mointz to Mossad's office at the Israeli capitol building. Hannah was in complete disguise.

"Thank you for sandbagging me in there," she said.

Mointz grabbed her by the shoulders forcefully. "Get this straight, young lady. You are about to be caught. How long do you think you can survive doing what you're doing?"

She did not answer, but rolled her eyes.

"Do not fight me on this," he said and let her go.

"My country's safety and my career mean a lot to me."

"Good, because after this, your field days are over. Have a great career, just not in this field. If you get bored, come work for me."

Hannah stared at the impressive block of granite in her office. "Seriously?"

"I do not say what I do not mean," Mointz replied. "Now tell me what you know about a son-of-a-bitch by the name of Faisal Rahim."

Hannah Goldman was not sure if the American vice presidential candidate had lost his marbles or not. She knew he was only 41 and had enjoyed a more than distinguished career in the American intelligence community. However, this was something more than a politician asking questions. This was Mointz, the DIA agent, asking.

"He is the most ruthless terrorist in the world. We know little about him, but what we do know is that he kills for fun. I assume the Prime Minister knows about your activities?"

"Hell, no. The only people who know are in my inner circle. I want this man badly. My good friend, Fu Wong, believes Rahim is the man behind the attack on my family in China and he has been the force behind several attacks in Saudi Arabia. I am going to kill him myself."

"Then it is true that you took out his men when they breached the palace. Rumors run rampant in Mossad, but only my director and the Prime Minister know for sure. You are a legend and you impress me, but you cannot be serious in wanting to go after Rahim by yourself."

Mointz laughed out loud. There was no way he was not going after Faisal Rahim when he was this close to him. Mointz, with Danielle's blessing, was going to eradicate his biggest headache.

Amina gave Mointz all she could on Rahim from her contacts and Mointz formulated a plan to get the snake in the grass with Anthony's help. He hoped all it would cost him would be a night with Princess Amina to end Rahim's existence.

"I hope you know what you are doing. No one can find him and even if you do, you need an army to go after him. Mr. Mointz, you are the next Vice President of the United States and not in a 'Mission Impossible' movie with Tom Cruise."

"I am not five-foot-four, Hannah; I am going to arrive in Palestine in 24 hours. Find out what you can about Faisal Rahim and send out word through your contacts that I am meeting Nasir Hamid from Hamas' Intelligence Group. Tell them that I am trying to do a back room deal with him."

Hannah blinked. "Are you?"

"Meeting him? Absolutely. I plan to put a bullet through his head."

Mointz didn't put a bullet personally through Nasir Hamid's head, but a cousin of Amina and Kareem did, as a favor. The next day, Mointz arrived to meet Palestine leader Mahmoud Abbas at the Saudi Embassy.

"Mr. Mointz, it is absolutely splendid that you came here to see me and agreed to stay in my country," Abbas declared in a private meeting with Mointz.

"Sir, your people have not formed a country officially and I would like to see that happen, but I need a favor before we could even think about a shared vision for Palestine."

"What would that be?"

"I want Faisal Rahim's head; I want him to not pass go and not collect his 77 virgins."

Abbas looked like the cat that had just swallowed the canary. Mointz was one of the most uncouth politicians he had ever encountered. "That is not for me to give."

"Sure it is. You are Fatah; he is Hamas. Why would you protect that prick? They kicked you out of Gaza and no American president will step on the ball field with Hamas."

"Why this hatred by you? Is it personal?"

"He tried to kill me and my family. So not cool, Mr. Abbas."

He had already lost Gaza; he could not afford to lose the West Bank as well. Abbas was petrified Mointz was about to cause him pain one way or the other. He had no idea where Rahim was, but Mointz was making a point. Rahim was somewhere in the West Bank and Mointz was positive Abbas would ask his contacts and his many moles in the hierarchy of Fatah, who would leak the information to Rahim which Mointz wanted Abbas to do. The West Bank was not very big and Mointz was positive Rahim was close, very, very close to him indeed.

"Mr. Mointz, what if I do give you Rahim? The benefit would have to outweigh the possible consequences. I would have a hard time turning over a fellow Palestinian."

"Think of it this way, if you do not and I find out you knew where he was, I will come and kill you and everyone associated with you. Remember, I will be the second seat in the US government in a few months. I will have nice big guns to play with and I will be able to say 'hello' any time I want."

Mointz slammed his fist into his own hand, drilling the point home to the Palestinian leader. All was not lost, however, Mointz had promised to work for peace and if the terrorist cells started to dry up, he would push for aid from Saudi Arabia, Jordan and the U.S. Congress.

"I am a man of my word, sir. Peace is all I want to accomplish," Mointz said with a smile. "One last thing, sir."

"Yes, Mr. Mointz."

"Stay clear of Ahmadinejad in Iran. He is another one on the list of people I want to kick in the ass, comprende?"

Abbas simply nodded and knew right there and then he preferred to be a friend to Mointz rather than a foe because enemies would not stand a chance.

Faisal Rahim watched Mointz warmly shake hands with Mahmoud Abbas on the television in his small apartment in the West Bank. Word had indeed filtered down to him that Mointz had planned to meet with his Hamas rival, Nasir Hamid, who was also a popular figure in Palestine. Rahim was furious Hamid had the gall to make a deal with the American vice presidential candidate. For over a week from the time he first learned Mointz would be coming to Palestine, Faisal Rahim worked to develop a plan to take out Mointz. Though he didn't have a plan yet, he was at least crafty enough to leave no stone unturned in his attempt to find an opportunity. Moreover, Rahim would not put it past Mointz to use this trip to try and trap him and smoke him out. This past week, Rahim had a few of his surrogates working diligently to find an opportunity, one glorious opportunity to kill Mointz.

Al Jazeera television praised Mointz on its newscast. It made Rahim sick to his stomach how the Palestinians bowed down to the Americans. Rahim changed the channel. The local Palestinian news was as admiring, or maybe even more admiring than Al Jazeera of Mointz. Rahim could not believe the fools had allowed the Great Satan's true leader into Palestine. The only thing Rahim wanted to do was to leave the apartment and go kill every person who said anything nice about Mointz, but he knew he couldn't. His small apartment in The West Bank was the safest place on earth for Rahim for the next few days.

"Allah guide us," the caller said.

Faisal chuckled. "He always does. Jumah, how are we doing with our plan to kill Mointz?"

"Not well, I am afraid. The Saudis are part of his security detail. The king is a huge proponent of his. Right now, he is untouchable."

Rahim figured it was a shot in the dark, to say the least. "I see, Jumah. Keep trying."

"I will, my friend. I have some other news."

"Tell me, Jumah, is it good news at least?"

"Maybe. Depends what you make of it. Nasir Hamid was found with a bullet between his eyes."

"Could it have been Mointz himself?"

"Mointz generally shoots more than once, but who knows? He has not been accounted for in the last several hours."

Rahim, the terrorist, who reigned hate all over the world, slumped in his chair. Fear flowed into his veins. The prey might have become the hunter.

"Have four hours passed already?" Princess Amina asked as she rolled off Mointz. She was always the one on top as she liked to feel in control of Mointz in her fantasies. They were heavily guarded in the Saudi embassy compound.

Mointz smiled. "Yes, dear. It has been four hours. Haven't you worn me out enough?"

He needed Amina to hide him out today and the only way she would was to have him in her bed. The Saudi embassy in Palestine was the safest place for Mointz right now, especially when he planned on going after Faisal Rahim later tonight with Hannah and Anthony.

Amina was personally incensed Mointz was going to go after Rahim without much backup. "Please, rethink your plan for the evening, please," begged Amina. "I can think of other things to do."

"Princess, the United States government has given me full authority to…"

Princess Amina interrupted. "They gave you the authority to have it done, not for you to do it yourself. I was told there was no way you were to leave this building."

"When you needed me, I was there. Please do not tell me that I cannot protect my family when I have the son-of-a-bitch practically in my grasp."

Amina cuddled next to him. "Fine. I understand a little better, but can't you get people to do that work for you?"

"Who could I trust? Faisal Rahim has ties everywhere. People could miss and he could head right for my family. Your husband gave him the damn layout of the palace so he could kill everyone, including you, and take over the kingdom."

"And you let others take care of that prick, no?"

Mointz chuckled. "Prick—that is such an American word."

Amina kissed him. "I tried to go back to my Duke days. However, do not change the subject."

"I was the one who ended his life, personally. Does that make you feel better?" Mointz could not believe Amina wanted to open old wounds tonight of all nights. The man had wanted to exterminate her whole family and Mointz.

Amina showed her temper and pushed him away. "He was an awful man. Why do you have to get involved with everything? Who made you the executioner?"

Mointz quickly got out of bed. "Fine. He would've made your sweet little prince a murderer of men. And probably would have pissed on your grave as well as your family's. My means should not get me crucified."

Mointz got dressed and left.

"Cristopher," Amina cried out.

Mointz entered the room adjacent to Anthony's and slammed the door. The big man did not want to ask what had aggravated his friend, but Anthony was nosy by nature and knocked on Mointz's door.

"Come in."

"Heisman, you all right?"

"Problems with a princess, what can I say?"

Anthony felt relieved it was only that and said, "Speaking of women, Hannah sent a text on the special codex you gave her. No one knows Rahim's location; this is a wild goose chase."

"Mointz does! Did you doubt I would find out where he was?"

Davis and Mointz had bugged Jumah's phone. When he called Faisal, Jumah's cell gave the agency Rahim's position.

"Hot damn, we have the bastard. Where the hell is this tough guy?"

"Only a few blocks from here and after the gig later at the embassy, it will be time to take him out."

Princess Amina tried all her magical powers to get Mointz to be her Prince Charming again. He made her sweat it out a bit before squeezing her hand under the table. Amina got the point while Mointz mingled with the crowd.

Mahmoud Abbas and Mointz spoke with animation at dinner as Cristopher promised to go above and beyond to work with Abbas to improve the quality of life in Palestine and clear a realistic path for statehood, which would increase Abbas' popularity immensely. Lauren had set this event up perfectly to help Mointz move Abbas toward reform. Fatah would rid Palestine of Hamas terrorists and the United States would track the terrorists down. The path Abbas envisioned in front of him was the clearest path ever created for Palestine.

"Shall I have this dance, Princess?" Mointz asked Amina.

She could not help herself; the Princess glowed as they hit the dance floor.

"I am sorry I snapped at you."

"Princess, you are not sorry. I get the fact that you are stuck with Kareem in Riyadh, but you know who I am and what I do."

"My brother goes to America and parties like a rock star with you guys. I stay home most of the time and try to raise my son and run a kingdom. I know how you are and who you are. You have the most beautiful family and many friends to accompany your blessings. Yes, I am jealous and yes, I am over the top when you and I get together. You do not have to say anything because I know if I had met you first, you would be mine and mine alone. Danielle may be your bride and I know you love her, but you love me more."

Oh, Jesus, Mointz thought to himself. *The Princess is getting hormonal in her later years. Still sexy as hell and alluring as ever, she might be a little delusional about how I feel.*

"Please do not stress over it. Your secret is safe with me. I'll take what you can give me."

The music stopped and she curtsied to the Senator. Mointz politely kissed her hand in the room full of dignitaries.

"Thank you for the dance, Princess."

"Thanking me will come later," she replied and walked away.

Mahmoud Abbas introduced Hannah Goldman, a/k/a Dunya Al-Sayed, blessed with the complexion of her Palestinian mother, to Mointz. Mointz asked her to dance. The dirty look Amina gave to him was not lost on Mointz. Amina had said it earlier; she was a jealous princess.

Dunya Al-Sayed breathed sweet breath in Mointz's ear as the Lauren Gabriel Davis-sized woman was all of six feet tall. Dunya could smell Mointz's cologne. It did not take Mointz long to figure out she had fallen for him instantly. He tried not to laugh as he knew Director Gabriel and Davis loved to introduce women to him who quickly attached themselves emotionally to him.

"You are stunning in that dress, Ms. Al Sayed."

The Mossad agent blushed and said, "Why, thank you, sir. Coming from PEOPLE MAGAZINE'S sexiest man in 1998, that is quite the compliment."

"Is that in my file?"

"Yes, sir. It is."

"Have you thought about my offer?"

"What would you want me to do if I came to America to work for you?"

"I want you to protect the girls in my life like they were the most precious cargo on the planet and then become the head of the service when I get in office."

From all reports, Hannah was one of the brightest people in the intelligence business. Mointz was not going to let her walk out of his life. She was going to need to leave Palestine and Israel after this event; the sultry agent had a first-class ticket on the Mointz express.

"Surely, you speak in jest."

"What part of my personality suggests that I would be joking?" Mointz said as he spun her on the dance floor.

"Let me think about it after we get Rahim tonight," she said with a smile that confirmed she was definitely in.

"Okay, cupcake. Make sure you meet us at my suite at 11."

"Absolutely, sir."

###

"Cheese and Rice, did you have to drug her?" Anthony said. In that instant, Mointz hit him with a dart that dropped the big man to the floor.

"Be pissed at me later, you big ox," Mointz said as he dragged his friend to the couch and leaned him against it. "Your big ass can stay on the floor."

Mointz had laid Hannah on the bed. He calculated they would be out for at least six hours or until he hit them with Davis's adrenaline shot upon his return.

Amina opened the door dressed in a sexy little outfit with Natalya's boutiques stamped all over it. She kissed and hugged him immediately. "I notice you are alone. Where are Anthony and Dunya?"

"Knocked out in my room. Listen, I need a place to become an Arab," Mointz stated and lifted his knapsack.

"Why are they knocked out?" she asked.

"I drugged them," Mointz.

"Oh," Amina said with a giggle before realizing he was serious.

Mointz immediately applied Celeste Phillips' "camouflage" and within a half hour he looked more like an Arab than most of the men in Palestine.

"What say you?" Mointz asked Amina when he had finished.

"Incredible, absolutely 100% incredible."

"Princess, here is a list of all the things I need you to do when I call," Mointz said. He kissed her quickly before running out the door.

"Mointz! Are you insane?"

Mointz chuckled. He quickly scooted past two of the service agents he had sworn to secrecy about his meeting with Amina and Anthony. He sometimes wondered how the gullible agents, who were instructed to guard him, felt after their superiors crucified them once Danielle complained to them. Mointz, at six-feet–six-inches, tried to blend in on his ten-minute walk to Faisal Rahim's. Mointz called Davis back in the States on his way.

"Dr. Cris, you are free," Davis said when he answered the phone.

"Good morning, boss. What are you doing?"

"I dropped the boys off at school and now I am talking to you while I eat a bagel. Did you get Amina to do what I asked?"

"Patently, mi amigo. I ran out of there after I gave her the note. Man, is she livid!"

"Hannah and Anthony are going to be just as livid when they wake up. I would like to be your size for one day. It would allow me to do what you do and always get away with it. Did you receive my satellite photos of Rahim's?"

"Yes, sir. I am here now. Wish me luck."

"Try not to play games with him. Shoot him and get the hell out of there, please."

"Shoot and go. Got it."

Mointz could hear the television through the door of the fourth floor apartment. He put on his thermal goggles and saw that only his boy, Faisal Rahim, was in the apartment. Mointz's size 13 boots kicked in the flimsy door and had Mointz face-to-face with one of the world's most ruthless terrorists.

Rahim tried to reach for his weapon. Mointz shot him in the right shoulder.

"Who are you?" Faisal Rahim asked.

Mointz shot him in both legs. "Know who I am now, ass hole?"

"The voice is the same, but you don't look like Mointz."

Mointz wiped his face with a towel from his backpack and pointed his weapon in Rahim's face.

"Allah, be merciful!"

"You don't deserve to pray to your God; your people suffer because of your misdeeds. Die, you pig," Mointz shouted and put the final nail in Rahim's coffin. Mointz snapped a few pictures and sent them from his phone to Davis. The terrorist had met his maker, who sent him straight to hell.

Mointz called Amina, told her to do what he asked and quickly changed for the cameras.

"What the hell is your husband doing?" Lauren asked Danielle in her Tel Aviv suite.

"What, what?!" Danielle said refilling Lauren's wineglass.

Al Jazeera was showing video clips of the vice presidential nominee walking the streets of Palestine unescorted at one in the morning with camera crews following him.

"Did you know about this?" Lauren asked.

"No, I did not. I am going to kill him dead," Danielle replied.

Lauren cracked up. "You said a Yogism."

Danielle giggled. "I am still going to brain him when I see him. Where's my phone?"

Lauren handed Danielle her own phone and Danielle called her husband's cell phone.

"Hello, Blondie. What's up? My wife freaking out yet?"

"This is your wife. F-off, Mointzie."

Mointz waved into the camera and Danielle could not help but giggle. People from everywhere had now hit the street like he was their hero.

"I have to go, honey, I have people to meet."

"You are so busted when I see you tomorrow. Call me when you are safe and secure. I love you."

"Love you, too. I really do." He hung up, blowing her a kiss into the camera.

Al Jazeera interviewed Mointz, who brilliantly explained how he had wanted to prove to the American people how wonderful the people in Palestine were and how safe a place it was. The Secret Service drove him back to the embassy where he injected Hannah and Anthony with adrenaline, which went off like a fart in church.

"I would try to kill you, but I have no shot," said Anthony.

"Why did you drug us?" Hannah asked.

Mointz turned on the television and explained exactly what had happened as he watched himself on the big screen.

"Well, Hannah, are you joining us in the States?" Mointz asked.

"Hell, yes, sir! I am guaranteed there will not be any dull moments."

"That a girl."

Shimon Peres gave Mointz permission to take Hannah Goldman to the United States. He praised Mointz for the stunt he had pulled, much to the chagrin of his wife and friends. Mointz had given Israel his full support and promised that Iran would stop threatening to end Israel's existence very soon. Mointz "guaranteed it." Peres loved Mointz's humor and he respected him immensely, especially after Mointz had showed him the pictures of Faisal Rahim with a bullet in his forehead.

Hannah joined Danielle and Lauren for lunch. Shortly thereafter, Mointz made it to the restaurant under protection. Danielle ripped into the Secret Service for letting Mointz walk out of the embassy alone. When told about it, Governor Huckabee laughed; Mointz had told him Danielle always chastised the service when he left without protection.

Mointz had brought Princess Amina to join meetings between Prince Kareem and Shimon Peres. The princess always respected Mointz's marriage and tried to remain just a good friend in front of Danielle and Lauren. Mointz always maintained a fine line with her in public. If he had noticed an ounce of betrayal from the princess years ago, Lauren would have had to figure out a new way of extracting information. In reality, Mointz would have just told Danielle and wished for the best, hoping she would understand.

Mointz kissed his wife and sat down.

"He drugged me," Hannah pointed out to everyone.

"Mointzie drugged me in Los Angeles when he went after gang bangers," Lauren said with a smile.

"Someone needs to drug him soon to keep him from pulling his stupid stunts," Danielle said.

The Vice Presidential Nominee smiled, grabbed a roll from the basket, ripped a piece off and popped it in his mouth. "No offense, sweetie, I would not go down that path. Weren't you the one who told me emphatically to keep us safe?"

"I did not say to do all of it yourself. Ronnie is so mad at you."

"I know. He is blowing up my phone with text messages and phone calls. Ronnie will get over it."

"Ronnie, as in newly minted Admiral Ronald Mahoney, former head of NCIS and now rumored to be Secretary of the Navy or the new National Security Advisor?" Hannah asked.

"He is the one. He is like a brother to me and Danielle's nephew," Mointz replied.

"Have you ever drugged him?" Hannah asked.

Mointz chuckled, "Worse, I beat him twice when he was at the Naval Academy."

"Which helped you be the first Ivy Leaguer since Dick Kazmaier from Princeton in 1951to win the Heisman Trophy," said Hannah. "I am a football freak."

Hannah's smile and painless eyes made Mointz feel good about himself for saving her from Faisal Rahim. Hannah would never be held in Gaza and the Mossad agent was now free to prosper in life and her career. She had left word back in Palestine for Mahmoud Abbas she had run away with one of the Saudi's Royal family delegation and was in love. Amina verified the story with Abbas in a perfectly planned, unsubtle way during a meeting.

"My husband was a beast," Danielle said.

"Mr. Heisman could be the best I have ever seen," said Lauren. "I believe the only one who is in the same conversation is a man named Brady."

"Sir, didn't you play when you were shot in the hip by an Iraqi security member?"

"No idea what you are referring to, Hannah."

"This assignment will be a blast," Hannah said.

Lauren and Danielle rolled their eyes and smiled at each other. Hannah would fit in just fine.

"We really need to go to Paris," Danielle said. "The baby needs a croissant.

"Baby, what baby?" Hannah asked.

"Actually, I am pregnant again."

"Then how are you going to be Attorney General?" Hannah inquired innocently.

"Attorney General? Lauren what she's speaking of? I do not dare ask my husband."

"Cristopher suggested to the Governor you would make a great Attorney General," Lauren replied.

"Liar. It was your idea. I cause enough trouble on my own; don't make it worse for me."

Lauren giggled. "I know you do, Mointzie."

Mointz chuckled. "Hannah, how do you know that my wife is going to be asked to be Attorney General? Do we have a Mossad agent working for us?"

"Anthony told me this morning that Mrs. Mointz would be Attorney General when you and Governor Huckabee win. She would then be able to order FBI protection for you. He also told me that if I accepted the job, it would not be just a job; it would be an adventure."

"I am not qualified, am I?"

"Danielle, you get to control the FBI," Lauren told her in a voice above a whisper.

"Okay, I'll take it!"

Mointz slumped in his chair. His wife was now too bright for her own good. Danielle would be a great Attorney General, Mointz felt, and she would not back down from anything.

Chapter Forty

January 2009

The Vice President gets sworn in before the new President. Cristopher Mointz took the oath of office with his wife Danielle, his children, parents, and siblings standing next to him as Senate Minority Leader Lauren Gabriel administered the oath of office.

Chief Justice John Roberts administered the oath of office to President-Elect Huckabee minutes later. The new President and Vice President shared the stage together on the balmy January day. The global warming folks were out in full force, only to return to hiding as a cold freeze was heading DC's way over the next three weeks.

After the ceremony, Mointz and Huckabee stood in the Oval Office for the first time as President and Vice President. "Congratulations, Mr. President."

The Huckabee and the Mointz families waited for the two men to exit the President's office.

President Huckabee breathed in deeply. "What a moment. I never expected to be here with you and I know that you could have run against me and won a bigger victory than ours."

"Mr. President, I am in no rush. I have a lot to learn and do before I try for your job."

"You have a green light to steal second base at will, Mr. Vice President," the President told him. "Do not get hurt, please; I do not want to get impeached. No getting shot."

"No getting hurt or shot, I understand, sir."

"Please do," the President said as he sat at the desk Ronald Reagan had used. "Have you looked over the new list I sent you?"

"Yes, Mr. President."

"Cristopher, please call me Mike in here. This is our private time when we are alone. My inner circle is you, me and your gang of do-gooders," the President stated.

"I will do as you say, boss." Mointz smiled at him while he spoke. "Secretary of State will be Lauren as Ellis is taking over at the CIA for Director Gabriel, who deserves all the accolades in the world for the job he did. Ronnie has agreed to serve as National Security Advisor and General Perry is a great pick for Secretary of Defense

"And, your wife has agreed to serve as Attorney General," the President said. "Great news indeed. The two of you can watch each other's backside."

Lauren and Ellis held several knowledge transfer meetings with Lauren's father, who was tickled pink to spend more time with his grandchildren. The Director had beaten prostate cancer and was going to enjoy the rest of his years knowing it was his time to ride into the sunset. His last request was to make sure Danielle became Attorney General.

"Danielle is extremely pleased that you asked her to be Attorney General. I would never have believed it. She is a defender of the righteous and the underdog."

"I believe that is why she will make a great Attorney General. If nothing else, she gets to keep an eye on the legal community. How is the vice presidential residence at Number One Observatory Circle treating the family?"

"The girls love their ranch, but the Naval Observatory is pretty cool and the boys like running all over the place. Nice job selling the idea to her."

"I do what I can," said the President smiling.

"My parents are now in the guest house at the ranch and love babysitting for us. The whole family is now in the Virginia or the DC area. Lauren and Trent live only acres away and Ronnie and Gennifer are in Georgetown as Gennifer's professorship at Georgetown University is very special to her."

"Colleen has done a great job so far as your Chief of Staff."

"She has been with me since my days as a young Congressman. My sister and she live in our Georgetown home with my niece Aleixa."

"If we can get the Redskins to sign your future Hall of Fame brother from Seattle, everything will be perfect."

"We need the state of Washington in 2012. Let him stay there for now," Mointz said.

The President grinned at the Vice President, stood up and extended his hand. "Welcome to the administration, Mr. Vice President."

"Thank you, sir. It is truly an honor to serve with you."

"The honor is all mine, Cristopher."

Mointz left the Oval Office returning to the Naval Observatory to prepare for the evening's festivities, where he would attend several inaugural balls with the lovely Danielle. As he rode in his motorcade, he thought to himself how the mission from the First Parallel was far from over. He was eight years away from being sworn in as the 45th President of the United States, and with so much left to accomplish to save the world from itself, he needed to keep all options on the table to complete the mission. As the Vice President entered the Naval Observatory, he chuckled at the thought of his next mission. He would be able to continue to get his hands dirty as the Vice President of the United States. The only problem he could foresee was his growing way too fast daughters and goddaughter who were quickly coming into their own…

Made in the USA
Charleston, SC
11 March 2015